SESTIA

ALSO BY G. R. MACALLISTER

Scorpica

Arca

✦ THE FIVE QUEENDOMS ✦

SESTIA

G. R. MACALLISTER

SAGA PRESS

LONDON **NEW YORK** TORONTO
AMSTERDAM/ANTWERP NEW DELHI SYDNEY/MELBOURNE

AN IMPRINT OF SIMON & SCHUSTER, LLC

1230 AVENUE OF THE AMERICAS, NEW YORK, NEW YORK 10020

For more than 100 years, Simon & Schuster has championed authors and the stories they create. By respecting the copyright of an author's intellectual property, you enable Simon & Schuster and the author to continue publishing exceptional books for years to come. We thank you for supporting the author's copyright by purchasing an authorized edition of this book.

No amount of this book may be reproduced or stored in any format, nor may it be uploaded to any website, database, language-learning model, or other repository, retrieval, or artificial intelligence system without express permission. All rights reserved. Inquiries may be directed to Simon & Schuster, 1230 Avenue of the Americas, New York, NY 10020 or permissions@simonandschuster.com.

This book is a work of fiction. Any references to historical events, real people, or real places are used fictitiously. Other names, characters, places, and events are products of the author's imagination, and any resemblance to actual events or places or persons, living or dead, is entirely coincidental.

Copyright © 2025 by G. R. Macallister

All rights reserved, including the right to reproduce this book or portions thereof in any form whatsoever. For information, address Saga Press Subsidiary Rights Department, 1230 Avenue of the Americas, New York, NY 10020.

First Saga Press hardcover edition May 2025

SAGA PRESS and colophon are trademarks of Simon & Schuster, LLC

Simon & Schuster strongly believes in freedom of expression and stands against censorship in all its forms. For more information, visit BooksBelong.com.

For information about special discounts for bulk purchases, please contact Simon & Schuster Special Sales at 1-866-506-1949 or business@simonandschuster.com.

The Simon & Schuster Speakers Bureau can bring authors to your live event. For more information or to book an event, contact the Simon & Schuster Speakers Bureau at 1-866-248-3049 or visit our website at www.simonspeakers.com.

Interior design by Jaime Putorti
Map design by Laura Levatino

Manufactured in the United States of America

1 3 5 7 9 10 8 6 4 2

Library of Congress Cataloging-in-Publication Data

Names: Macallister, G. R. author
Title: Sestia / G. R. Macallister.
Description: First Saga Press hardcover edition. |
London; New York: Saga Press, 2025. | Series: the five queendoms; 3
Identifiers: LCCN 2025002028 (print) | LCCN 2025002029 (ebook) |
ISBN 9781982167950 (hardcover) | ISBN 9781982167967 (trade paperback) |
ISBN 9781982167974 (ebook)
Subjects: LCGFT: Fantasy fiction | Novels | Fiction
Classification: LCC PS3613.A235 S47 2025 (print) | LCC PS3613.A235 (ebook) |
DDC 813/.6—dc23/eng/20250211
LC record available at https://lccn.loc.gov/2025002028
LC record available at https://lccn.loc.gov/2025002029

ISBN 978-1-9821-6795-0
ISBN 978-1-9821-6797-4 (ebook)

FOR MY DAUGHTER
AND ALL OUR DAUGHTERS

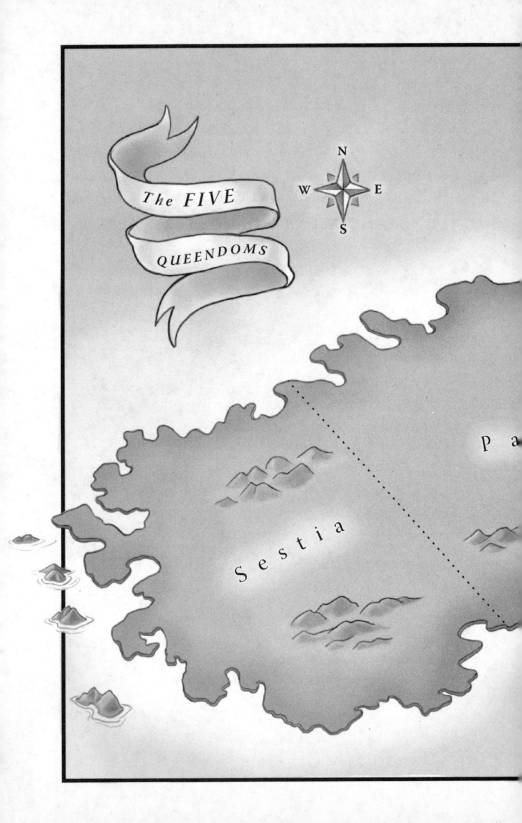

Major and Recurring Characters
Listed by Queendom

ARCA

Aster, child of Stellari and Rahul

Beyda, royal scribe assigned to Arca, a Bastionite

Eminel, queen of Arca, Well of All-Magic, Master of Sand, and Destroyer of Fear

Ingini, a member of Eminel's Queensguard

Rahul, former paramour of the Paximite politician Stellari

Sobek, a courtier and mind magician

Velja, god of Chaos

Yulia, a courtier

THE BASTION

Diti, daughter to Ravian

Hikmet of the Scholars, queen of the Bastion

Ravian of the Guards, a guard in training

PAXIM

Duente of Arsinoe, head of the Assembly

Evander, Stellari's husband

Fasiq, a giant

Garel, an innkeeper

Heliane, queen of Paxim (deceased)

Heliane the Second, born Asana, young queen of Paxim

Juni of Kamal, magistrate of the Senate

Marageda of Nordur, a senator

Panagiota, matriarch of the most powerful family in
  Calladocia

Phinesh of Nigelus, a senator

Roksana, secret daughter of Queen Amankha and
  Kingling Paulus

Stellari, regent of Paxim

Vish, also known as Vee or the Shade, Scorpican
  guardian of Roksana

Zofi, also known as Zo, daughter of Queen Heliane (deceased)

SCORPICA

Amankha, queen of Scorpica

Azur dha Tamura, an adopted Scorpican and mother to
  Madazur, known as First Mother

Dree, a warrior (deceased)

Galeigh, a warrior

Gretti dha Rhodarya, a warrior and councillor

Madazur dha Azur, first girl born after the Drought

Olan, a warrior (deceased)

Riva, a warrior

MAJOR AND RECURRING CHARACTERS ✦ XI

Tamura, a past queen of Scorpica (deceased)

Zalma dha Fionen, a smith

Wren, daughter to Zalma

SESTIA

Bateo, a servant in the Edifice

Concordia, High Xara of Sestia (born Olivi)

Darious, a boneburner

Emalio, a servant in the Edifice

Enifer, a daughter in Norah's household

Fortitude, a past High Xara of Sestia

Jeremiah, uncle to Olivi

Joiaca, a Dara in the Edifice

Justicia, a Dara in the Edifice

Necessitas, a High Xara long ago

Olivi, daughter of Norah

Rix, a servant in the Edifice

Sestia, god of Plenty, also known as the Holy One

Teresh, a farmer and mother in Norah's household

Timion, nephew to the boneburner Darious

Veritas, Xara of Sestia (born Norah)

Vetiver, a farmer and mother in Norah's household

Victrix, a past Xara of Sestia

Xelander, a high-ranking servant in the Edifice,
    favorite of Concordia

Yegen, a servant in the Edifice

XII ✦ MAJOR AND RECURRING CHARACTERS

THE UNDERLANDS

the Child, a guide for recently deceased spirits

Ellimi, deceased Scorpican queen, mother to Khara, grandmother to Amankha

Eresh, god of the Underlands, sister to gods Sestia and Velja

Oscuro, deceased consort of Queen Theodora of Paxim

Paulus, deceased kingling of Paxim

Puglalia, deceased former High Xara of Sestia

Semma, deceased Scorpican queen

Septin, deceased Paximite soldier

Sessadon, deceased sorcerer

PART I

DURING
THE
DROUGHT

The All-Mother's Years 501 to 516

✦ CHAPTER 1 ✦

PRIEST

Autumn, the All-Mother's Year 501
The Holy City, Sestia
Concordia

Every twenty years, the Xaras who ruled Sestia cast lots to find their successors, looking to the Holy One to show Her hand in the casting. Five girls were chosen: one to reign, three to serve in wisdom, and one, at the right moment, to die.

But like any ritual in any queendom, the system did not always proceed exactly as planned. Of the five girls chosen by lottery to serve the Holy One in the All-Mother's Year 480, only two remained twenty-one years later: the High Xara Concordia and the Xara Veritas.

Now, one held the life of the other in her hands.

The High Xara Concordia remembered well the first time she'd met the future Veritas. She'd been a slip of a girl, all elbows and knees. Concordia herself had been a sturdy child, thinning as she aged, while Veritas filled out and rounded. The rule was that when girls were brought to the capital to enter service, they left their childhood names behind. But on that first day, as they mounted the steps of the Edifice, the stern-faced old Xara Victrix turned her back on the girls. When she did, the one who would become Veritas whispered her name hastily into the other girl's ear, *Norah*, and too stunned to do anything else, the future Concordia traded her whispered name in return, *Olivi*.

For a long time after, the future Concordia broke no rules. She had been a devoted rule follower before she'd been taken from her family to join the class of future Xaras, a natural choice for the role. She threw herself into learning all that the Xaras had to teach her. But as one descended more deeply into centuries of sprawling Sestian edicts, statutes, and regulations, one couldn't help but stumble over the occasional paradox—exactly the situation in which the High Xara Concordia found herself now.

While the penalty for deserting the God's most sacred tenet was death, the law also stated clearly that killing any Xara was forbidden, no matter how grave her sins. When young Concordia irreverently pointed out to the Xara Victrix two rules in conflict and asked her which she would follow, the older woman first slapped her for speaking out of turn, then smiled.

"You will learn, child," said Victrix, "that most laws are like green saplings. They can be bent a great deal without breaking."

The Xara Victrix had been neither a good person nor a good servant to her god, thought Concordia, but she was also rarely wrong.

Today Concordia would decide how to bend. In a situation much like this, a few reigns ago, the High Xara Necessitas had ordered a disobedient Xara paraded to the tombs, handed a lamp and three apples, and sealed inside. The older stories were only rumor, but Concordia knew those, too. They said one sinning Xara was buried up to her neck in the dirt at a busy crossroads. A Xara who neglected the sacred flame was forced to lie down upon the hearth and sing hymns while the fire was rebuilt atop her body, then lit. They were the most powerful women in the nation, but precise laws constrained their behavior. Veritas had broken the most important law. Consequences must follow. The only choice was what shape those consequences would take.

"My queen," came a familiar tenor voice from behind her.

The High Xara turned from the window. "Xelander."

Her servant bowed his head, clasping his hands delicately in front of his narrow waist, which was cinched with a wide decorative belt denoting his station. He was the highest-ranking of all the servants in the Edifice, allowed in any room of the vast temple-palace except the holy *lacrum*. Xelander was capable of any duty, and he performed every one of them with grace.

"Where is she now?" Concordia asked.

"She was hungry," he replied, his slight shrug speaking volumes. "I took her to the kitchens."

"That is not a long-term solution."

"I am your most humble servant," he said. "I would no sooner tell you how to punish her than I would swan about in your vestments."

She smiled at that. "You'd look better in them than I do."

"Not so, my queen. No one else could wear the saffron to such advantage."

It was a polite lie, but a lie all the same, thought Concordia. Xelander would look splendid in her ceremonial saffron robes, had he been allowed to wear the color. The men who served in the palace of the God of Plenty were beautiful, and they took great care with their beauty. They wore their dark hair well past their shoulders, cinched their waists tight, and lined their eyes with precise rings of kohl. Some wore short robes and some long, but all their garments followed the curves of their shoulders and thighs, clinging everywhere the priests' robes were flowing and loose. Their forms were not intended to tempt the virtuous women of the priesthood to carnal delights; they were decorative, pleasant, like exquisitely carved urns or long-stemmed poppies. Only men who found their pleasures with other men were allowed to serve in the Edifice. *Priests should have men to tend them but not touch them*, or so went one of the thousands of platitudes the young Xaras-to-be had learned.

Still. High Xara Concordia had dozens of servants who dressed like Xelander, who might even be mistaken for him at a distance, but none other with his inborn elegance. He was also whip-smart, far and away her favorite. As soon as the rumor about Veritas had reached her ears, he was the one she'd dispatched to investigate. He'd brought her the truth, and the woman, within hours. Now she needed to handle both.

She said to him softly, "Is there no . . . natural solution to the problem?"

He caught her meaning. "You're thinking of the *pulegone* tea?"

"Yes."

"Much too late, I'm afraid."

The High Xara Concordia didn't curse, at least not out loud. She looked out the window again. The Edifice was a marvel, towering four stories above the city and gleaming like a new-laid egg. From the fourth story she could see leagues beyond the city's gates into the vast countryside. Most days, the view soothed her. Today, as she searched the rolling green hills where the sacred rams and their mouflon mates were pastured, she saw no answers there. The answer would have to come from her. Or from the Holy One Herself, should She see fit to speak to Concordia for the first time.

"What would you do?" the High Xara Concordia asked Xelander.

Startled, he lifted his head. His expression was one of concern.

"It's all right," she said. "I truly want to know."

"It's not my place, my queen."

"You have any place I choose to give you," she reminded him. "If I ask for your thoughts, you do me disrespect to refuse."

"I apologize," he said, though his voice was not apologetic. She suspected his protest was mere form. He was smart enough to have opinions. She should be smart enough to benefit from them. She wasn't aware of any past High Xaras who had been counseled by their servants, but then again, she differed from past High Xaras in ways no one alive knew.

"And so," she said. "Tell me. If it were your choice."

There was no pause before his answer. "I would make the choice hers."

"How so?"

"Her body was not hers to use as she did," he said, his dark gaze so steady it unsettled her a bit. She wasn't used to being looked in the eye, even by Xelander. "The body of a Xara belongs to the Holy One. Her chastity, her virtue, those are the Holy One's, and Xara Veritas did not have the right to give them away. You would be within your rights to remove what grows within her."

"I thought you said it was too late for the tea?"

"The dose it would take might well kill her," he said, with a shrug not so different from the one he'd made when he mentioned escorting her to the kitchens. "Removal can also be done with blades, or at least it's been tried. I've heard reports of experiments in the Bastion."

"So that could kill her too."

"Yes."

"You'd have her choose between herbs and blades?"

"I'd have her choose whether she wants it dead now or later. Killed inside her or killed in front of her. See what she chooses."

Both possibilities turned Concordia's stomach. Even if Veritas survived such butchery, even if her earthly body was returned to the Holy One's sacred service, could such a loss be borne? Would Veritas go mad from pain and sorrow? Farm women were known to do so, and as far as they'd come since, both Concordia and Veritas—

or Norah and Olivi, back then—had been farm-born once upon a time.

"But the choice isn't mine," Xelander said, finally looking away. "Nor hers, my queen. Only yours. And the Holy One's, of course."

"Of course," echoed Concordia with a lightness she didn't feel. As the holiest woman in the queendom, she alone could enter the sacred *lacrum* to speak with their god. Generations of High Xaras had done so and emerged, beaming, with an answer from the divine. But Concordia wondered every day if the High Xaras of the past had really spoken with their god when they went into the *lacrum* and locked the door. She herself had never found anything in that chamber but her own doubts, never heard anything but silence. Some days the lack didn't bother her; some days it wrung her out.

She heard the approaching footsteps just before a voice from the doorway boomed out, "Apologies, my queen."

Concordia didn't know the newly arrived servant's name, but she recognized him at once. He was a brute of a man, thick all over, ill-suited for the garb Xelander wore so fetchingly. Even the man's braid was crooked, done in a hurry and without proper care. But servants had many purposes, and this one excelled at his. The woman beside him had no chance of escaping the thick fingers with which he gripped her upper arm.

While her figure was unmistakably that of a woman, Veritas was barely taller than a child. Her hair was loose in a black storm cloud, the saffron-dyed streak above her right temple the twin of Concordia's own, marking them both as Xaras. Veritas wore no other sign of her station, no robe or sash, but she carried herself as the high-ranking holy woman she was, adjacent to royalty. Even in an ill-fitting rough-spun shift, too short in front and threatening to catch her heels in back, she radiated authority and intelligence.

The man with the crooked braid tilted his head in Xelander's direction. "He said to stop her if she ran. She tried to run."

Xelander said, "Thank you for your service, Bateo."

The hulking servant nodded in return and didn't budge.

"You may release her and go," Xelander added.

"Is that safe?" Bateo asked. He shook Veritas by the bare arm, frowning. His meaty grip must have hurt, Concordia noted, but the other woman's small, round face remained placid. Veritas's eyes were on the High Xara.

Concordia said, "You may leave us."

The big man turned to go with a dismissive grunt, braid swinging, and gave his erstwhile prisoner a half-hearted shove that sent her sprawling to the ground. She fell hard on her hands and knees, a soft rush of breath the only sound she made.

Concordia held herself back from running to her friend, consoling her. They had helped each other so many times in the early days. But things would never be as they had been, she reminded herself. Veritas had made the choice to sin, to give up that which belonged by right to the Holy One. A priest who broke her oath was no priest.

There was only one way to begin. "You lied," said Concordia.

"About what?" Veritas responded from the floor, a spirit in her that Concordia would not have expected.

"Many things, I take it." Concordia feigned patience. "I meant that you were granted permission to spend three months spreading the word of the Holy One along the western coast."

"And so I did."

"You traveled to honor Her."

"I did."

"Yet today you were found in the palace?"

"I returned." The woman wouldn't give an inch. She began to struggle to her feet, and though Xelander reached out a hand to help her up, she swatted it away and managed to get up on her own. She smoothed her borrowed shift—from whom had she borrowed it?—and stood firm.

Veritas's eyes were on Xelander, suspicious, something cold in her glare. Her words were directed to Concordia. "You would have seen me this afternoon in any case, without setting your hound after me."

"I heard a troubling rumor. One that, if true . . ." She couldn't complete the thought. "Tell me it isn't true, Xara Veritas."

Veritas said softly, "For your sake, I wish I could."

The truth hurt. "So you violated your vows."

"I still serve the Holy One," said Veritas. "We tell our people it's a great honor to serve Her through pleasures. During the rites, we tell the same thing to the entire world. The greater the pleasure, the greater the honor. Why should it be different for us, who love Her most?"

"You know why." Concordia's patience was quickly unraveling. "When the Holy One lost her beloved consort to the Underlands, she renounced pleasures ever after. We honor her sacrifice by joining in it. Our chastity is Her chastity. We are committed only to Her."

For her part, Veritas seemed unrattled. "That is the interpretation that previous Xaras have believed. But why would any just god deny us that which She created?"

"You claim She is not just?"

"I claim She does not ask us to deny ourselves Her greatest gift."

Every word the petite Xara said was pure blasphemy. Concordia couldn't see a way around it. Still, she wanted desperately to try. "Was it just the once? Were you carried away?"

Veritas shook her head.

"Don't try to tell me it was *love*," Concordia blurted.

"I doubt I can tell you anything at all. What does it matter why I did it or with whom? You know what I've done. You see the . . . evidence."

And that was the crux of it. Not just that Veritas had used her body for pleasure in violation of her sacred vows. That could've been hidden, denied. But under the borrowed shift her midsection had begun to thicken and round out, the curve of a baby just beginning to blossom between her generous hips. In the months the Xara Veritas had spent on the coast—if in fact that was where she'd been—her shape had transformed. The curve was small now, but it would grow.

Doing her best to keep her composure, Concordia told the only woman she'd known since childhood, "So you see the position you've placed me in."

"You were not foremost on my mind," said Veritas dryly.

Though of course it was true, it still hurt to hear. Nor did the Xara apologize, Concordia noted. The woman's lack of deference would've been unthinkable in any Sestian citizen, but of course Veritas was next in line to be queen. Had been, anyway, before this.

"There are no unchaste Xaras," Concordia told her. "You know the law."

"I do. The law says I cannot be killed."

"The law also says you cannot live."

Veritas looked up, her brown eyes wet with impending tears, but not tears of weakness. She reached out for Concordia's hand and held it between her own warm, dry palms. Concordia didn't remember the last time someone had held her hand. She wasn't sure she liked the sensation.

"Please, show mercy," Veritas said simply. "Please, Olivi."

And there it was. A name so old the High Xara Concordia had almost forgotten it herself, the name given her in the time before, when she was a sturdy, scampering girl in the farmlands. The harvests had been rich and the sun an outsize pearl in the blue sky above and her name had been Olivi, not an uncommon name, but purely and perfectly her own.

The queen couldn't put this woman to death, no matter what she'd done, no matter her blasphemies. She didn't have the strength. If the Holy One wouldn't speak to her, the High Xara Concordia reasoned, the choice was hers alone. Her voice was ragged with emotion but she forced the words out, passing the only sentence she could.

"Go," she said. "You are banished."

"Oli, I—"

"Leave my sight." Louder now. Commanding. "You are forever stripped of the rank of Xara. You will never again wear the saffron or taste sacred honey."

The Xara Veritas looked down, swallowed, seemed to gather her strength. But before she could speak, Concordia rushed to speak first.

"You are common," she said, nearly spitting the words. "The Holy One turns Her back to you. You're no longer welcome within the borders of Sestia."

"I only want to—"

"Wait," said the High Xara, bringing her palm sharply upward. "You can't take that with you."

"Take what?"

She ignored the question. "Xelander," she said instead, addressing the waiting servant. "A blade."

When she heard the word, the Xara Veritas made no effort to flee, nor did she ask again for mercy. She simply stared at the High Xara during the long pause while Xelander moved silently to do as he was bid. Concordia could not meet her gaze.

When the blade was in her hand, Concordia said, "Kneel."

Her rough-spun shift pulling tight as she moved, Veritas obeyed.

Xelander broke in. "My queen, do you think you should—"

"Hush," the High Xara said under her breath, not even turning, and then took the other woman's hair in her free hand.

Veritas showed no sign of fear. She waited, silent, on her knees.

With the tip of the blade, Concordia began to cut away the saffron-dyed streak of hair that marked Veritas as a Xara, starting at the hairline just above her wide-open right eye. In the beginning, as children, they had knelt next to each other as the High Xara Fortitude stripped the color from those sections of hair with a foul-smelling mixture of wood ash and vinegar, then painted on the precious saffron dye to mark them. They'd knelt as unremarkable girls from the country and risen as Xaras-to-be. Now, all these years later, only one of them was kneeling.

Concordia cut as gently as she could, but her hand was unsteady, and as the paler hair fell away from the darker, she nicked the tender scalp. She could feel the sharp tip of the knife drag where it caught on the skin.

Veritas flinched but didn't cry out.

It took all Concordia's strength to keep trimming until every trace of the saffron streak was gone, pretending to ignore the thick rivulet of blood that ran down Veritas's face like the dark ghost of a single tear. Discarded hair fell in clumps to Veritas's lap and slid soundlessly to the floor. Then it was done.

"Now. Take this woman away," Concordia told Xelander. "Provide her safe passage out of the Edifice. Put her on a public cart headed for Paxim. Do it by force if you have to. After that, if she's seen anywhere within the walls of the Holy City, make sure the archers have instructions to put an arrow in her heart."

She turned back to the window so she wouldn't see them go. At first there was only a long pause. She forced herself not to turn, not to bend.

Then there were shuffling footsteps, a heavy pair and a lighter, and after that, only silence.

In the distance, the white wool cloud-shapes of sacred rams moved over the broad green hillsides. Concordia watched them from on high until they blurred into pale smears, until she couldn't tell if they were moving or her tired eyes were only playing tricks. She watched them until the sun set and they were only faint shapes in darkness.

Concordia's doubts that she had chosen wisely started almost immediately, but of course, she kept them to herself. Who would she tell?

Two seasons later, she had almost managed to drown out the drumbeat in her mind that asked, *Where did she go, what will she do, what will happen to the child, what does the god want, should I have killed her, should I have let her stay?*

But then the Drought of Girls began.

The drumbeat got louder. The questions Concordia asked herself changed.

Is this my fault? Is this Her punishment?

What have I done?

✦ CHAPTER 2 ✦

MOTHER

Leaving the Holy City, Sestia
Norah

On the primitive public cart that rattled the former Xara Veritas's teeth and set her legs to aching, she drew a sand-colored scarf more closely about her head. Her scalp had stopped bleeding not long after they passed through the city gates. Still, she could swear she felt the distinct edges of that bare patch of skin under the thick cloth, hot like fire.

Xelander had harried her through the palace and out of it, practically nipping at her heels like a sheep hound, doing as the High Xara bid. She remembered almost none of what he said, with a single exception. As they were leaving the palace, he'd plucked the scarf from a basket of work and tossed it her way with a pointed look at her head.

"Cover yourself," he said, and no more.

Most of the cart's other passengers looked the way the former Xara Veritas felt: worn out, anxious, fraught. But when the exhausted-looking woman next to her caught her eye and offered a kind smile, the disgraced priest returned it.

"The Holy One's blessings be on you," the woman said.

"And you," she responded automatically.

"I'm Vetiver. What's your name?"

No longer a Xara, the new exile reached back into her childhood for the name she hadn't used since she'd counted her years on one hand.

"Norah," she replied.

They fell into conversation. Luckily, the other woman was talkative. Without giving away where she'd come from or where she was going—not that she knew—Norah learned that Vetiver farmed near a small village called Tika, in a good-sized household of three mothers with nine children and only one uncle to help out. The farm was a successful one—to plant and harvest, they hired seasonal women and men with the proceeds of the previous year's bounty—but the household itself was nearing crisis. The youngest child was sickly; the oldest ones did their part, but work piled up. Now one of the mothers, too, had fallen ill, and they all feared the worst. Vetiver had come to the capital to perform a generous offering and ask the Holy One, if it was Her will, to help them manage their burdens. Now they could only wait and see.

Norah asked Vetiver question after question as they traveled, all of which the farmer was happy to answer. Hours later, when the wagon began to slow for Tika, Vetiver turned to her with a look of keen interest.

"You didn't say where you were going."

"Looking for work," said Norah, and left it there, hopeful.

With a new light in her eye, Vetiver said, "Perhaps She sent you to us."

"Her will be done."

The woman reached for Norah's hand, warmed it between her own, her touch light. "Is there any chance you might come to our farm? Please? I hope you'll stay, but even if not, just for a meal and the evening? It'll be dark soon."

The smile that came to Norah's face was broad and genuine, even with her jaw aching from the relentlessly bumping cart. Perhaps the Holy One, in Her generous wisdom, was smiling on both of them. The High Xara might want Norah exiled from Sestia, but the country was not hers alone, nor could she see into its every corner. If Norah lived quietly, far from the capital, how would Concordia ever know?

Norah said to Vetiver, "Thank you."

When the cart stopped at the next crossroads, they climbed down together. The village did indeed seem small. Only the two of them disembarked. Norah looked back down the road they'd come along, marked with ruts and grooves; the crossing road was clearly less traveled. The driver, who looked as weary as the passengers, half-heartedly lifted the reins and signaled to the oxen to move.

As the rattling wagon drove off, Vetiver brushed the dust of travel from her clothes with brisk, short strokes. Norah mimicked her movements. She had a lot to learn in this world. It would make all the difference to have someone to learn from.

Norah knew nothing at all of life, she realized, frowning at her own foolish innocence. She'd been raised in the palace from the age of five. Everything she'd needed had been placed at her fingertips. Her only lessons focused on what a Xara must know. Now that she was no longer a Xara, she recognized how very much the priests of the Edifice, high-ranking Xaras and lower-ranking Daras alike, had left out of her education.

"Shall we?" said Vetiver, gesturing, and Norah followed her down the unfamiliar road.

As she settled into her new household, Norah cut her hair to her shoulders and bound it out of the way. She wore the sand-colored scarf for the first several months, until the missing hair grew to cover the bare spot. She spoke little, blending in. She had an easy spirit and a willing strength, and there were no complaints when Vetiver proposed she join the household as a fourth mother, that her child be welcomed as a sibling as soon as it arrived. No one knew Norah's history, as far as she could tell, and no one asked. She prayed in the morning and at night, calling upon the God of Plenty for Her love and blessings. Despite Concordia's judgment, Norah firmly believed she hadn't dishonored the god with her actions, merely found a new way to experience and honor Her love.

On the fourth day of the fourth month of the All-Mother's Year 502, Norah's daughter came into the world. It was an easy birth, labor beginning at midday and the child born by sundown, a clear sign of the god's favor. A hard birth didn't always mean disfavor from the god, but She chose who She would test, and She chose not to test Norah. Norah thanked Her in prayer.

Five days later, on her child's name day, the former Xara set foot in a temple for the first time since her banishment. The local temple was a fraction of the size of the Edifice, only magnificent compared to the town's humble wooden buildings. Still, Norah caught her breath when she walked inside.

Surrounded by white stone, cool air soothing her face and throat, she remembered what it had once been like. Growing up in the Edifice, living every day for her god's glory, breathing and eating and sleeping for Her alone. Just for one moment, the disgraced priest felt the smallest pang of regret.

Then her daughter sighed in her sleep, a sweet, faint music. The moment passed.

Following the name-day ritual, giving a small sacrifice for the spark of a new life, the new mother burned the delicate bones of a bee-eater on the altar and gave thanks. She had planned to name the girl Chlora, for the bright white cliffs of the western coast, but perhaps because her life as a Xara had surged back into memory, a new idea sparked in her mind as the flame burned. On impulse, she gave the child the name of the woman she'd considered her oldest, and for so many years only, friend. The one person who'd been a constant in her life in those years when the two of them could rely on no one and nothing else. The woman who, that fateful day, had held both the Xara Veritas's life and her unborn daughter's in her hands and given both of those lives back to Norah, setting her free.

As she stood in front of the altar, faint wisps of smoke rising from the shallow white dish that had blackened with ash, Norah made her decision. She cradled her daughter in one arm. She smudged a thumbprint of sacred oil in the center of the baby's small, wrinkled forehead. She told her, "You belong, as we all belong, to the Holy One. Your name, my child, is Olivi."

The infant promptly spit up her milk, cackled once, and fell to sleep with the suddenness of summer lightning.

Norah's giddy laughter filled the temple. Even the other worshippers' glares and grumbles didn't mar her delight. The ringing of laughter off the smooth white stone, in fact, delighted her even more. There'd been so little laughter in the Edifice. Here, Norah felt the presence of the god at the same time as she felt the community she belonged to, her expanded life, flowing like a river around her. She relished the echoes of her own merriment almost as much as she relished the soft breath of the warm bundle in her arms.

Surely, thought the former Xara, she was loved by the Holy One. A god who despised her would never bestow such blessings.

✦ CHAPTER 3 ✦

SILENCE

Four years later, the first Sun Rites of the Drought of Girls,
the All-Mother's Year 506
The Holy City, Sestia
Concordia

Four years into the Drought of Girls, no one who saw the High Xara Concordia striding the palace's long hallways would have known her feelings. Her head was high, her serene manner ideal for the approach to prayer. The wide neck of her ceremonial robe left an expanse of bare skin above the fine saffron-dyed wool, light as a whisper, and her shoulders had been anointed with rose oil and lily wine. Her lips, touched with honey from the palace's apiary, would make her words sweet for the Holy One.

As she approached the sacred *lacrum*, a beautiful servant opened the door for her, bowing, clearing the way. She did not even incline her head to him as she swept past into the chamber. Behind her retreating back he closed the door, sealing her from sight.

Alone at last, she stood at the altar for a long moment, complete silence around her, attar of roses hanging heavy in the air.

Then she fell to her knees, weeping.

At the first Moon Rites after she'd chosen to banish Veritas, there had already been whispers of the Drought. Attendees from other queendoms gossiped, hinted. They'd noticed in their own capital cities that not a single girl had been born in two months, maybe three. They weren't sure yet what it meant, if anything. They'd still had hope then.

Even after the Drought of Girls had finally been recognized and named, Concordia presided over the next three years of Moon Rites exactly as usual, making the lesser sacrifices with hallmark calm, even as news came that turned her guts to liquid and her heart to pulp.

Was it all her fault? wondered Concordia. Was the Holy One punishing her for exiling the Xara Veritas? Or was it the opposite—was she being punished for not being severe enough, for not killing the other woman where she stood for her unapologetic sin and blasphemy?

Now the All-Mother's Year 506 had begun. Soon, all five queens would converge on the Holy City to complete the Sun Rites. Four years since a single girl had been born anywhere, and they'd be looking to her for answers. She needed to decide if this Sun Rites would be the same as the others—the same sacrifices, the same gifts to the god—when the entire world around them had changed.

All around Concordia, the cool silence of the *lacrum* was deafening. The smooth walls, the gleaming altar, the seemingly bottomless well, all of it mocked her. This was where High Xaras since the beginning of history had come to listen for the voice of their god, guiding them toward the right path. Was she the first one to find nothing here? To suffer so? She'd been so naive when she took the robe, assuming that once she had the saffron streak, once she was addressed as High Xara, everything would fall into place. But this stony room and its indifferent God defied her.

She'd even begun to hope for help from another quarter. If the Holy One wouldn't speak to her, perhaps another god might. But none did. Not Sestia's chaos-loving sister Velja who the Arcans worshipped, not their sister, Eresh, who ruled the Underlands, not the All-Mother who had birthed three divine daughters, then yielded the world to their generation and vanished. None of the dozens, even hundreds, of minor gods, spirits that oversaw everything from olive pits to winter rain. Not a word from anywhere beyond.

Was it sacrilege merely to think of the gods in this way, as potential tools to pry a door open or seal it shut? Probably. If she were as holy as she should have been, her mind would work differently. Maybe then the god would speak. For her part, Concordia had wept, begged, commanded, howled, pleaded. She had worn her voice out to the point where she couldn't speak for days, but that only showed another harsh truth: once she banished Veritas, she had no one to speak to. When her voice returned, she found herself talking more and more often to Xelander, but she did not confide in him. A servant was not a friend.

She turned away from the altar toward God's Well, its circle of white marble opening into a narrow downward shaft full of clear water that left a whitish crust on everything it touched, like the salt left behind after tears.

Concordia reached back to the altar long enough to scoop up the ceremonial bowl that rested there, then lowered it into the well to fill it with water. The well was God's Well, and the water was God's Tears. She hunched back down on the cool marble of the floor, curling her body over the bowl so her own tears dropped into it, each with a tiny, near-silent splash. If she wept onto her fine saffron robe, woven from threads as thin as spider's silk, they would know. And no one could know. The silence of the *lacrum* was her bane and her terror, but it was also her sanctuary.

She contemplated the bowl in her hands, sacred and smooth. The water represented the tears the Holy One had cried twice: first, when she lost her beloved consort to the Underlands, and second, when she had journeyed beyond Death itself to rescue him and found him merrily disporting himself with ripe-figured shades in the fields of lust, his memory of her already fading. No wonder virtue was the greatest sacrifice she asked of her Xaras. There seemed to be no reason, no promise, in linking oneself to a man. Concordia still wondered what it would have been like, to indulge one's body in pleasures. When they were girls, she and Veritas had giggled over the very idea of it, dizzy with their secret audacity. Once they'd become women, they no longer discussed it. Not until Veritas's changing shape had forced the issue. Clearly Veritas thought the pursuit worthwhile, mused Concordia now. She'd sacrificed everything.

Concordia was virtuous and calm and utterly hollow. She could not believe the frivolous matters that had dominated her thoughts in the early, easy years of her reign. How she'd quibbled with the Edifice's many Daras over minor matters of religious observation, the precise length of hair and robes, the exact words to be spoken when crops were brought in from the fields. None of that mattered now, if it ever had. Now the questions were bigger. Too big. The entire future of the world as they knew it depended on the answers.

Why had girls stopped being born? That was the most important question, but it led to so many others. After all these years of blessings, had the god turned on them? Were their sacrifices no longer enough? Or was it the other way around—did the god no longer want a sacrifice, at least in the form it had been delivered for centuries?

Her tears were still dripping into the sacred bowl of God's Tears—irony, that—but more slowly now, a drip every now and again. As the next tear formed, she reached up to brush it away with the tips of two fingers. So much was out of her control. She had no idea how to secure the future of her nation, to win back the favor of their god. But this single tear, this she could wipe with her fingertips, rubbing the droplet across her skin until it was spread so thin it evaporated and disappeared, leaving no trace.

Enough tears for the day. She dabbed at her face with the altar cloth, then replaced both the cloth and the bowl on the altar, stepping back once she'd set the holy objects in place. Crying was indulgent. Yet it was hard to stop indulging once one had started; perhaps that was why Xaras were warned away from pleasures of all kinds.

But then her thoughts ran where they always ran: to the exiled former Xara Veritas. Where had she gone? Had she borne the child, named the child? She inspected her fingers and found a trace of wetness still on them, so she stepped forward again to wipe them on the altar cloth. Then, inspired, she used those fingers to count up months she'd never thought to count before. Veritas had left, when? Three months after that year's Moon Rites? Four? Autumn, it had been, wheat turning pale gold in the fields. And how ripe had Veritas been when she'd left, the very beginning of the swell rounding outward between her hips? Was it possible that Veritas had given birth to a daughter, and that her daughter had been among the last of the girls born from the blood of Sestia before the Drought began?

The wondering was fruitless, the High Xara told herself. She couldn't know. It was unwise to waste more time wondering. She had to focus on this year's Sun Rites, this year's sacrifice.

Whatever it was that Concordia decided in the privacy of this stony room, once she stepped outside and issued her decree, that decision was final. There was no going back.

So she let herself stay in the room a little longer. She even tried one last prayer, licking the sweet honey from her lips until nothing remained, breathing in so deeply that the oil of roses dizzied her. She asked the Holy One just once more to show Herself, to tell Her most devoted servant what it was She wanted—more sacrifice? No sacrifice? Something else entirely?

Concordia did her very best to listen, but as the silence stretched around and over her, her heart was in her throat again.

No one was coming to save her. No human. No god. She'd been foolish even to hope.

The decision was hers alone.

The altar cloth had dried by now, and the High Xara's cheeks felt cool and smooth, no longer inflamed from her angry tears. She smoothed back the stray hairs that had clustered nearer her face when she had been bent over and staring downward, paying special attention to laying the saffron streak flat. She ran her hands over her elegant robes, arranged the fabric to drape away from her shoulders, raised her chin just so.

All this done, satisfied she was ready, she rapped her knuckles briskly on the door to indicate she wished to exit the *lacrum*. She could open the door herself, of course, but that would lack the proper gravity.

While she waited for the servant to respond, she took one more expansive breath, and by the time he swung the door open, she had plastered on a dizzying, eager smile.

"Call the Daras," said the High Xara Concordia, breathless. "The Holy One has spoken. We will have the Sun Rites as before."

◆

The whole time she moved through the Sun Rites, Concordia felt as if she weren't even there. She followed the parade of queens—the stone-faced warrior, the kindly diplomat, the straight-backed scholar, even the lithe, dark-robed magician, who had to be well over a century old but looked as dewy-skinned and smooth-cheeked as a young woman of twenty. The other queens' faces had changed a great deal in the five years since they'd last met. In five years, new wrinkles had begun to appear, tiny cobwebbing patterns at the outer corners of Heliane's eyes, grooves alongside Khara's firm-set mouth. Creases emerged. Existing lines deepened. The Arcan queen alone remained exactly as she had been, like a carven figurine captured at the peak flush of youth. An elegant hawk of a woman, that beak-like nose, those all-seeing eyes.

As the procession brought them to the amphitheater and the dances began, Concordia let her attention wander, watching the old stories reenacted, trying to forget who she was, why she was here. She skimmed the dancers of myth, her eyes landing on one group, then distracted by the movements of another.

She watched a row of dancers, their faces streaked with ash, pass through a set of long scarves held high to represent a gate. Concordia suppressed a shiver as she watched them imitate the dead leaving the earth. In the early days of civilization, Eresh worried that so many humans dying so quickly would overwhelm the Underlands, her new domain. So she asked Velja to gift them with magic: a different gift for each human, something small. Their magic helped them sing the game closer for the hunt, made their arrows fly straighter, helped them build shelters, heal wounds, settle disputes. Magic helped the community survive another day, another year. But when the men misused their magic, selfishly keeping their spoils instead of sharing them, Velja took their gifts away. She left them only the magic of beauty to encourage women to share what their own gifts had wrought. Men with ram's horns on their heads danced first their shock and disappointment, then accepted their gift of beauty and became radiant, dancing toward the women with alluring gestures, a graceful leap skyward, a delicate outstretched hand.

Concordia wanted the dancing to go on forever, to give her joy and beauty in which to lose herself, but the time came all too soon. She wished she had taken a relaxing herb; she knew more about such things than most High Xaras. A decorative plant called *schimia* bordered the Edifice's kitchen garden on the north side, a succulent with thick pads of pale green, tips tinged purple. *Schimia* could easily be gathered for a tincture that eased the nerves. *Next time*, she thought.

But if there was to be a next time, she had to get through this time first.

The High Xara Concordia rose to the dais and spoke the words she had to speak. She lowered the blade she had to lower, slit the throats she had to slit.

Afterward, she handed the ceremonial blade back to the wiry, hardened Queen Khara without wiping it of blood. The blood always splashed, even if she was careful. On every finger, the bright red of yesterday's cherries mingled with the darker red of lifeblood freshly spilled.

Once the ceremonies were complete, she walked back to the palace and into her quarters. Without even removing her sandals or sash, she dropped to the stone floor to sit cross-legged. Hands in her lap, she watched as the lifeblood dried and darkened in color, crusting into a brickish red, nearly brown, as the day outside grew dim.

At length, after the room was dark, she heard a knock. She thought she should stand, but even while she was deciding, she heard a voice call, "High Xara, have you need of anything?"

She found her voice. "No."

Then the voice again, somehow both louder and more tentative, "High Xara, if it please you, may I enter?"

She made a noise that she supposed could be interpreted either way, and when she looked up, a lithe, wasp-waisted figure was coming through the door. He held his lamp high; it was Xelander.

Concordia didn't want anyone to see her like this, but if anyone had to, best that it should be him. Was it possible—should she tell him? How she felt useless, broken, a mere imitation of a Xara? Would he understand?

She looked up at him and saw that there was already understanding on his face, already a kind of sympathy. Perhaps she didn't need to say anything at all.

Closing the door behind him, Xelander took a moment to scan the room, then seemed to come to a decision. He set the lamp gently on a stand near the door. In three easy strides he reached the table where a bowl of cool water waited, left there earlier by another servant for the High Xara to use for washing. He lifted the bowl in both hands.

"If it please you, High Xara," he said, "permit me."

She said nothing, did nothing. It was such a relief to leave things to someone else.

Xelander set the bowl on the floor in front of her, the cloth next to it, kneeling and bending in a way that looked much like supplication.

"Your ritual robe," he said. "Shall we preserve it? I am certain you have already thought of this, but once the water loosens the stain, it could spread."

She nodded and did not move. She felt his hands on her shoulders, pushing the robe aside, letting its billowing softness slip off with a whisper. Carefully, he lifted and disengaged the sleeve while holding it clear, guiding the fabric with a sure hand. He repeated the motion on the other side, and bent at the waist to gently lift the garment away from her, leaving her in a plain saffron shift, her hair down around her shoulders in a mass of unbound waves.

She closed her eyes.

"If you'll allow me," he said, and she gave the barest nod. *Such a relief,* she thought again. Giving no commands, taking no action, feeling nothing inside. She didn't even have to look at her hands anymore. He would take care of it. The red would be gone.

The splash of water, the sound of the cloth being rinsed and lifted, then the cool wet towel was laid over her clasped hands. A heartbeat, a moment. Then she could feel him begin to scrub gently in the smallest of circles, starting with the first joint of the index finger of the right hand, circling, circling.

With her eyes closed, it was easier to say the words that echoed and murmured inside her head. She was going mad from keeping her fear inside. Here she could reveal it, share it, hope to let it go. "They doubt me."

Xelander worked her finger between two of his, circling with the wet cloth, working down to the base and then all the way up to the nailbed and then the very fingertip, meticulously, in a regular rhythm. Hypnotic. Reassuring.

"Who does?" he asked in a mild voice.

She let herself relax and speak. "Everyone. The Daras. The people. They think I should stop the Drought."

Silence while the cloth was rinsed in the bowl again. Then the next finger, the middle finger, was grasped gently. "I'm certain you would if you knew how. Wouldn't you?"

"Of course," she murmured.

"If you haven't found the answer yet," Xelander said, working hypnotically in that slow, careful rhythm, "it is because She isn't ready for the answer to be found."

Should she tell him that the god didn't speak to her? There was serious risk in that, the most serious. Her priesthood. Her life. Both could be forfeit if her secret made its way into the wrong hands. Could she trust him? Not yet, she told herself.

Instead she said, "I ask Her every day."

"And when She's ready, She'll guide you. In the meantime, you govern as best you can. After all, the Holy One trusted you with this office, did She not? It is yours, no one else's, until you choose to let it go." His voice had gained force; his grip on her hand stilled and tightened. Then he seemed to catch himself. "I apologize. I fear I speak too freely, my queen."

He dipped the cloth, worked on the next finger, squeezing, circling.

"Not at all," she said, "I want you to be free with me." In this moment, it didn't matter who Xelander was to the world, only who he was to her: a mind, a voice, a safe haven.

"To be free with you," he responded, his voice husky, low. "There is nothing more I could ever desire."

Her eyes opened then; he was so close, his eyes deep brown in the lamp's light, a hint of gold gleaming in their depths.

She addressed him with surprise. "What do you mean to say?"

"It's easier to show than to say," he answered, and his damp fingers—those slender, nimble fingers—reached up and traced the line of her cheek.

How long had it been, thought High Xara Concordia, since someone had touched her in any way that wasn't pure function? Not to bleach and dye her hair, to wash her feet, to cinch a belt at her waist, but to truly reach for her? Had it ever felt so powerful, this simple thing called touch? She was too stunned to speak.

This was wrong. This was forbidden. And yet.

In her silence, he continued moving. The thumb that had traced the line of her cheek now moved to her jaw, and gently, lightly, brushed her lower lip. Instantly there was an ache in her, a longing, where his touch had been and where she wanted it to go.

There was no mistaking Xelander's intent now. He was breaking every rule at once, holy and earthly laws alike, to touch her like this. To reach for her in the way women and men seeking pleasure reached for each other.

"But," she said, her mind reeling with uncertainty, canting away from her body, which remained stubbornly in place, aching with a want she didn't fully understand. "You can't—you don't—I am not a man."

"I am aware." His voice was a gentle, teasing purr.

She had never heard him speak this way. She had never heard

anyone speak this way. It lit a flame in her. "But all men who serve in the house of the Holy One—"

"I gave the pledge they asked of us," he breathed. "To find pleasure in men. What they ask us to swear is . . . too narrowly defined, let us say."

Everything felt out of control, thrilling and terrifying in equal measure. She was on the verge of letting the feeling sweep her away. Then, all at once, she remembered who she was. She was in control of everything. Life and death, sacrifice and abundance, plenty and want. And that included this man. Only she would decide how much he could truly know, how much he could truly have. She was the High Xara Concordia, Blessed of the Holy One, Queen of the Nation of Sestia. *She* chose.

She said, "Explain yourself."

"Gladly," he said. He didn't seem upset by the demand; he was still touching her. He would stop in a heartbeat if she said so. She did not say.

"Men are beautiful," he said. His fingers traced her jaw again. Then he ran them down the line of her neck to brush the outline of one breast, round under the drape of the light saffron-colored shift, the thin fabric no real barrier. "And so are women."

"But you can't want both," she said stubbornly. "Men and women are . . . different. Like night and day."

Lifting his hand up to cup her cheek, he asked in a whisper, "Is there not beauty in both the day and the night?"

And she gave no answer because he knew her answer already, had always known, and he leaned in to cover her mouth with his, and with that first soft, tender kiss, High Xara Concordia was lost.

✦ CHAPTER 4 ✦

ALL FIVE

Five years later, the All-Mother's Year 511
In the Holy City of Sestia
Concordia

Once she had tasted pleasures, the High Xara understood why Veritas had held so loosely to her status as a Xara. When one heard these things described, these actions sounded like nothing at all: a part of a body touching a part of a body, flesh on flesh, moving. If Concordia had not felt such pleasure for herself, she never would have believed it. There was a world of difference between hearing and knowing.

For years now, the High Xara Concordia and her servant Xelander had kept their shared, illicit passion secret. In public, Xelander was like an elegant statue: handsome, slender, nearly expressionless. Only in private did he transform into a hungry, lascivious tease, matching Concordia stroke for stroke and kiss for kiss until they both lay exhausted and spent. She loved everything about him in those moments: his sweat-dampened hair spread about both their shoulders, his garments lying in a hastily discarded heap, the musky scent of his body half atop hers, the woolly hair of his chest in contrast with her own smooth skin. Almost as soon as she'd had him, she found herself hungry for him again.

But whatever they did—and they did a great many inventive, intimate, exploratory things—she never let Xelander spend his rain inside her. Memories of Veritas were locked tight in Concordia's mind, not just because the disgraced former Xara's sins had swung open a door Concordia had once thought impossible to open, but because of what those pleasures had wrought: undeniable, unforgettable, unforgivable.

The stolen pleasures with Xelander were her own secret, a treasure she held close, but other matters took up the bulk of her days. There were still meetings with the Daras to attend, judgments to render, matters of state to dispense with. There were endless discussions about the Drought and what it might mean and what they'd need to do if it continued, discussions that never bore real fruit. But among all the other activities, she always found time to check in on the class of future Xaras.

Since their arrival in the All-Mother's Year 500, two years before the Drought, the High Xara Concordia had kept a weather eye on the five young Xaras-to-be. They were known, in the Edifice, by their key attributes: the curious one, the lovely one, the small one, the fearful one, and the radiant one. The time to decide between them was drawing nearer. At the Naming, Concordia would announce each girl's fate: which one would eventually succeed her as High Xara, which three would serve as Xaras alongside her, and which one the god had chosen for a different fate. This year the lottery would only choose a boy to sacrifice. At the next Sun Rites, Concordia would draw the sacred blade across that boy's throat and the throat of the girl the Holy One had chosen to die. At least that was how it had always been done.

She did not dislike the girls, not exactly. She was simply beginning to realize that she never wanted to hand off her title to a successor, never yield the role of High Xara at all. Ever since her pursuit of pleasures had begun, she had stopped feeling sorry for herself, stopped feeling guilty. She hadn't realized until she was discussing these feelings with Xelander, his long fingers lingering deliciously on the curve of her waist, that guilt itself was an indulgence.

So she hardened her heart when she looked at the young Xaras-to-be. If she were forced to pick a worthy one this very moment, one who could carry her mantle, it would be the radiant one. The girl was always cheerful, quick to learn, with a bright intelligence to her smile. Despite the constant praise from her teachers, she was not boastful or proud. She did not in the least remind Concordia of herself at that age; she was far, far better.

It was the curious one who reminded Concordia of her younger self, and not in a good way. Tired of her constant questions, the teachers had grown short-tempered with her. That was how the High Xara remembered the women who had raised her class of Xaras-to-be. Short-tempered. Chilly at best on the good days, and not so many days were good. She hadn't been the front-runner and she'd known it. She wondered if the other girls, the not-radiant ones, knew it now. She didn't let herself think about whether they worried they might be chosen for the great but fatal honor of sacrifice.

The Xaras who had raised her and Veritas had been distant and cold, but only one had been truly cruel. Victrix. That one had lectured her daily, forced her to pray on gravel until her knees bled, struck her in places where it wouldn't show. The young acolyte had lashed out at the older woman from time to time, as much as she'd dared, and that led to the discovery that changed everything.

It had been early summer of the All-Mother's Year 491, the day before the Naming. The next time the sun rose, the High Xara Fortitude would announce who was to succeed her as High Xara and who would go to the Sun Rites to lie down on the bone bed above the grain, never to rise. Concordia—who was not yet Concordia—intended to take advantage of everyone's distractions to play a prank on the Xara who had mistreated her so.

In those days the Xaras had decided that each girl would be represented by an object, so that everyone knew who was being talked about even though they were between names. Concordia's object had been a small onyx bear. Veritas's was a gnarled wooden snake, which Concordia had always thought an odd choice for such a sunny, pleasant girl. But the objects had been chosen when the girls arrived at the palace, long before they themselves were known.

The girl they all knew was the front-runner to rule as High Xara was a long-faced girl of frightful intelligence, slow to smile but not unkind. She was able to recall any fact she'd been told, even in passing, and could recite the many codes and guidelines of the priesthood at length. Once, a Xara had set her to begin a recitation just after they broke their fast, intending to test the limits of her knowledge. Come sundown, the girl was still reciting, her voice gone hoarse but the words still flowing. Her object, the one that represented her, was a smooth-edged disc of ram's horn sliced so thin it glowed when held up to the light. The other two Xaras-to-be, Concordia could never tell apart: Which was represented by the silver coin, and which the knucklebone of a goat? It hardly mattered now, she supposed.

She'd hidden under an altar in one of the prayer rooms, knowing it was where Victrix came to pray. All the Xaras, in fact, prayed there, one after another after another in the routine, starting with the High Xara, then followed by the other three. So Concordia thought she would hide there before the day's routine began, and while Victrix prayed, Concordia would speak from within the altar, pretending to be the voice of the god. Victrix was so smug and haughty, always saying she and the god knew best, and Concordia wanted to catch her out. She noticed a set of three hammered brass bowls on the altar, one dark, one medium, one pale, but thought little of it; the space under the altar, not atop it, was important to her plan.

But on this day, instead of one pair of footsteps entering the prayer room, Concordia heard many more. The High Xara had summoned all the Xaras and brought them here—why? And then, before she could show herself, the women were discussing the Xaras-to-be. The not-yet-named Concordia heard them begin to enumerate every vice and virtue of each girl of the five, and the god knew, her own vices far outweighed her virtues. She was surprised when the High Xara, her voice clear and imperious, cut the conversation short.

"There is no more need to discuss such things. I have already spoken with the god," said the High Xara Fortitude, "and tomorrow I will announce Her decision. To make sure there is no confusion, I have placed the symbols of the girls on this altar. When I unveil the god's decision tomorrow, with you and the Daras and the girls themselves present, Her wishes will be clear."

"The dark bowl for the sacrifice." There was the sound of something falling, a clunk. "The light for the new High Xara." Another clunk. "And here in the center, for our holy council, the three who remain." A clatter of pebbles, it sounded like, but she knew they were no pebbles. "As we pray here today, let us pray over the Holy One's wisdom. Let us thank her for the strength to follow through on what She has decided."

The sound of a cloth, perhaps. And then some muttering of prayers and a shuffling out, a door closing. Concordia listened for breath and heard none; then she stood and peeked over the altar just long enough to see that the High Xara had laid a cloth over the three bowls, each outlined clearly under its thin weave. Then she ducked back under the altar, heart pounding. Dare she look underneath that cloth? Instead she remained under the altar for a time, worried, pondering, trying to calm herself. She was glad she did; a quarter of an hour later, she heard the door open again.

Only one set of footsteps this time, and Concordia knew who had returned. Victrix had a breathing condition, a gentle, near-constant wheeze that accompanied her wherever she went, and in the dead silence otherwise, Concordia could hear that wheeze now. The young Xara-to-be heard the soft whisper of a cloth being moved, then a series of scrapes and strikes whose meaning was all too clear: hard objects removed from hammered brass bowls, then falling again, one, two, a clatter. The cloth, replaced. An extra-hard wheeze— satisfaction?—and then the footsteps, and the door, until Concordia knew she was alone again.

She was afraid to look and she looked anyway, and what she saw gave her grim satisfaction: her own figure, the bear, in the darkest bowl. Victrix had moved several objects—had hers been one of them? If the god had not intended Concordia to be the sacrifice, Victrix had put her there. When the High Xara pulled away the cloth the next morning, in front of all assembled, it would be too late to change what was revealed. To second-guess the symbols then would call into question the choices of the god. Concordia would be marked for death, and the chosen would be—who? The small, good-hearted girl who had once been named Norah, she now saw, the one whose symbol was the snake.

Concordia scooped up her own object immediately, warming it in her hand. Of course she would not willingly be the sacrifice. That couldn't be what the god wanted, only what Victrix wanted, that coal stone of a woman.

But where should she put it now, the object that would decide her future? Did she want to be High Xara? Or did she only want not to die?

Concordia only had time to make a snap decision. If the god

wanted something different, She would have to find a way to change things back again.

Fully aware she could be interrupted at any moment, she scooped the coiled snake out of the lightest bowl and dropped it into the center. She put her bear figurine in the lightest bowl, the bowl that would indicate the chosen. She closed her eyes and reached into the center bowl, telling herself she'd pick up whatever her finger first touched. It was the disc. She dropped it into the darkest bowl, replaced the cloth, and left the room as quickly as she could, before she could change her mind, before she could fully comprehend what she had just done.

The next day it all came to pass as she'd expected. The god did nothing to change what the women who served Her—and the girl who was about to—had laid in place.

All these years later, the High Xara Concordia watched the five young Xaras-to-be through the open classroom door and felt a pang for her own long-ago class of five. For the girls they had been. For the women only four of them had had a chance to become. For the fifth, that brilliant, long-faced girl whose disc in the dark bowl had sealed her fate, a fate she'd accepted without complaint or question. For Norah, who might so easily have been High Xara, but who had simply become Veritas and then, after a time, Norah again. And Concordia felt one more pang for herself, never enough like the High Xaras before her, never ruthless enough, never smart enough. Never blessed to hear the voice of the god.

As she observed the girls at their lessons, Concordia saw that each was focused on an open prayer book in front of her, each staring down into a private world. Two teachers stood at the side of the room, heads bent together.

One, a Dara whose name Concordia could never remember—did it start with a *B*?—was murmuring, "I just wonder if it was the right decision. If she had done more—who's to say whether the Drought would still be with us?"

They could have been talking about anything, anything at all. Any woman in the Five Queendoms. Or she could have even meant She with a capital *S*, She who ruled them all. But Concordia suspected she knew exactly what they were talking about. She stepped over the threshold to face the woman head-on.

"If you have something to say about my actions," the High Xara intoned imperiously, "here I am."

The Dara who had muttered under her breath raised her eyes to the Xara's, and there Concordia saw fear.

Good, she thought. *Be afraid.*

All five girls looked up from their prayer books, their bodies hunched and still but their eyes alert, moving. They all looked up, the radiant one and the small one, the fearful and the curious, and at last, a heartbeat after the rest, the lovely.

"I only said I wondered if the decision to conduct an unchanged sacrifice last Rites . . . ," began the Dara. But she trailed off, uncomfortable under so many bright, seeking gazes, and could not speak the words.

Concordia said, "I will finish your sentence for you. You think it was a mistake."

"I only wondered . . ."

"Cease your wondering," said the High Xara, her voice light, almost conversational. "But you might wonder instead what the books say the punishment for speaking against the High Xara might be. Do you know?"

The young Dara only stared, confidence draining.

"Perhaps you should have studied a bit more, instead of all this wondering," Concordia went on. "The laws are quite clear. I could have your tongue cut from your mouth, right here in this room."

"No, please, High Xara, I—please . . ." The young woman stepped toward her, her arms outstretched.

"No," Concordia said flatly, and stepped back, out of reach. "You have it all wrong. You think you question me, but that choice was not mine. I am no one. Think on the Holy One. It is Her choice you question."

"I am sorry!"

"Beg forgiveness from the Holy One. She alone will decide whether your doubt will ever be forgiven."

The Dara fell to weeping, prostrating herself, and Concordia felt an outsize swell of pride. She didn't look at the class of Xaras-to-be to gauge their reaction. Their reactions did not matter. She'd made her point. Now she could go.

As she went, she savored the feeling. In power there was joy. There was precious little joy to be found anywhere else, at least anywhere else she'd looked in years, other than in Xelander's seductive, unholy arms.

In truth she herself had questioned her decision to change nothing about the ceremonies at the last Sun Rites, and she'd done it far more harshly than this Dara. She'd laid more reproach at her own feet than anyone else could. Of course, there was no virtue in caution. What if, instead of going through the motions, she'd increased the sacrifice? Been bold?

She would have to, she realized, the next time.

If she didn't, and things continued as they had been, the endgame was inevitable. Eventually someone would start questioning whether she, the High Xara, was at fault. She had already asked that question a thousand times. She could hardly stand the *lacrum* anymore, the silence within its white walls a silent scream of accusation, but on the other hand, it was the only place she could hide from scrutiny, weep her quiet tears.

It was because she had no other outlet, she told herself. No one but Xelander to talk to, and she had to be careful with him. Too many private meetings, too many long periods shut away alone together, and even the stubbornly binary minds of Sestians might open far enough to admit suspicions. But he was very, very hard to resist. So she confined herself to indulging with him during her weekly bath, which he administered. Washing the High Xara's body was certainly the role of a trusted servant; no one needed to know what else went on once the door closed behind them.

And lately, after they'd had their pleasures, she had begun to allow herself one more kind of indulgence.

She talked to him.

All her uncertainty, her worry, the pressure she felt with the sole responsibility for a nation in the deepest throes of a drought of girls, she poured into their conversations. Xelander was an excellent listener. And he offered, from time to time, his own suggestions.

"I dread the choice," she said one day, after both the bath and its attendant pleasures, when they were spent. She sat in her bathing chair, resting her cheek on her crossed arms. He stood behind her, bending, combing out the dark waves of her hair.

"The choice?" he prompted.

"Between the five Xaras-to-be." She paused to let him ask a question if he wanted to; sometimes, his questions were what helped clarify her own thinking. Right now she was feeling the weight of the most important choice a High Xara could ever make. There were witnesses and assistants, but the responsibility was hers and hers alone.

What Xelander said was, "I am certain you will handle it with your usual skill and grace."

"I appreciate your confidence," she said, but put a mild rebuke in her tone.

"I'm sorry," he said. "Have I offended you?"

"I don't confess my fears to just anyone, you know."

"I know," he said, almost a purr. "And I have utter faith in you."

"I know," she echoed.

"Good," he said, setting his fingers to a particularly stubborn tangle, but gently, without tugging. "But you know I hate to see you upset. If there were anything I could do to help carry this burden, I would."

"Thank you. But this is my burden to bear. I will bear it."

"If you want to talk, I am here to listen," he said, his hands going still. "Or may I speak?"

It touched her that he still asked permission. He maintained his deference even though he had more access to her, in all ways, than anyone else in the queendom.

"Did you have something to suggest?" she asked him.

"Perhaps," he said, letting go of her hair. He came around to her right side and knelt beside her, their gazes meeting, his eyes alight.

She cocked her head. "Go on, then."

"We do not know—I do not, at least, nor does anyone else in the Edifice—why the god is angry."

"We don't even know She *is* angry," said Concordia in a burst of resentment, and then wondered at what she'd said.

"This is true. This might not be her doing at all. If that's the case, nothing you do will change the Drought, correct?"

"Which is bleak."

"It all depends on your perspective. Is this cause for despair? Or freedom?"

She looked down at him and waited for him to explain.

He went on, "Given that you shoulder a burden much greater than previous High Xaras—the challenging times we live in—you should have greater leeway to make your own rules, don't you think?"

"That makes sense. I'm not sure the people would agree."

"The people are ruled by you," he said, his voice firm. "It is your decisions that matter. And the god's. Since Her decisions and yours are one and the same."

"But I don't know what—" And then she stopped herself. Only she knew that the god did not speak to her. Not even Xelander knew, though from what he'd said, there was a chance he suspected. She sought the right words, then said at last, "I don't know exactly what to do. But you're correct. Perhaps I should view the lack of precedent as opportunity."

His nod was steady and sober, but there was also a light in his eyes. Mischief? Approval? Or just the shining gaze of a man in the presence of a woman he'd pleasured and been pleasured by, remembering both? She had no standard for comparison. She could only guess, unless she chose to trust, and guessing seemed the wiser course here.

"You need not make the sacrifices as they have always been made. If you don't want to choose between the girls, why not"—he gestured expansively—"just not choose?"

She rose from the chair, reaching her fingers out for her soft saffron robe, and he hastened to hand it to her. When he moved to help her put it on, she waved him off.

"Just not choose," she muttered. "Not do things as they've been done for centuries? You've been here nearly as long as I have, Xelander. I shouldn't have to tell you how this works."

"You shouldn't," he agreed. He looked down, his long lashes against his cheeks giving him a bashful air. "Only if you think things should be different, well, maybe make them different."

"And what would happen if I didn't decide between the girls? For what purpose?"

"You would be making a different kind of decision."

"To what end?"

"No particular end," he said, shrugging lightly, "unless you want it to be."

Concordia tied the belt of her robe and crossed her arms. "And what end did you have in mind?"

He responded, his voice stronger now, "I would never suggest not making a sacrifice at the Sun Rites. We can agree on that, yes? Sacrifices must be made."

"Of course."

"But what if this year's rites, this year's sacrifices, might take another form? One that might work to your earthly advantage as well as the god's heavenly one?"

She said, "You have something particular in mind?"

"Oh, my mind matters not here. It is only a functional, modest servant's mind. This is your choice and yours alone."

"And the god's."

"Yes, and the god's. And perhaps she is tired of a sacrifice of two. Perhaps that is not enough for her, after all these years."

"Why would She change Her mind?"

"That isn't for me to say. Only Her, and you. But, if I were to think on it, it occurs to me, perhaps she wants more. To break Her anger, if a sacrifice of two is no longer sufficient, perhaps a greater number? A holy number? Why not five?"

She paused, thunderstruck. Why *not* five?

Xelander went on, "But I have said too much, perhaps. Certainly I have lingered too long. I honor you, my queen, and now I must go."

Flirtatious words were on her lips—*must you?*—but she did not speak them. He knew when he needed to leave to keep the secret, and the secret must be kept.

Long after she had dismissed him, long after she had changed her bathing wrap for the saffron shift in which she slept, she was still thinking of this idea: Was he right? Could she make her own rules?

If no one knew the difference between her decisions and the god's—since she was the only one to translate the god's wishes here on earth—did that mean she could do anything, have everything, she wanted? Just by telling others the god wished it so?

As she stretched out along the cool sheets, settling her body into solitary comfort, she thought that yes, Xelander might have a point. And that bit about the sacrifice. Five, yes. It was worth considering.

The second Sun Rites of the Drought of Girls were like none before or since.

✦ CHAPTER 5 ✦

SACRIFICE

Five years later, the All-Mother's Year 516
Southern Sestia
Olivi, Norah

The rattling wagon underneath Olivi felt so familiar. The approach was always the same. She knew every hill and every hut, every turn in the road. She'd been no more than a child when she'd begun to accompany her uncle Jeremiah to the boneburner's once a season to deliver bones from the farm, bringing back ash that would help more crops grow. Now that she was ten-and-four, it might not be too long before she left her mother's home and made journeys like these as the head of her own household. Her sense of love was all the keener when she realized she might never make this trip in exactly this way again.

The summer trips were her favorites. They'd pass the small lake on the right just as the sun was rising, the light glinting off its smooth surface with a bright, sharp sparkle that was welcome but almost painful to her eyes. As the sun angled up, they'd see a cluster of small houses on the left, the farms of a particular family they only knew well enough to wave to. Then there was a sizable herd of freshly shorn sheep and rams, cropping the grass on a hill so steep she always wondered at how they could cling to the hillside without slipping off.

Her uncle on the seat next to her. Her own hands folded neatly in her lap while his hands held the reins. It had ever been thus.

Those three long hours in the cart, every one of those milestones, and then, that final cresting hill over which she could just barely glimpse the top of the shrine, so white and lovely. The temple seemed to grow larger as they came closer, its details resolving, sharp white against the backdrop of rolling green.

And every time they cleared this final hill, as soon as Olivi glimpsed the temple, her mouth watered for a glimpse of the boy.

No one had told her the boy's name, although she knew it, heard him called to by other children at play. There'd been no introductions, never even a direct conversation between the two of them. When Olivi had first come to the boneburner's as a girl of five, the boy had already been there. He was roughly her size and, she assumed, probably her age. On that first visit, his grin had been missing the two front teeth and he was everything she thought she wanted in the world.

At home, there were only the boys of her household. Their farm was large and splendid, but also isolated. Girls her age elsewhere in Sestia were dabbling in pleasures with neighbor boys, or girls if that was their preference, but Olivi's farm had no neighbors, and she could only wonder. Her imagination alone fed her wonderings.

And so the subject of those wonderings was the boy at the boneburner's, the line of his jaw so elegant and firm, the triangle of his nose so noble. There was something she loved so much about that nose. She didn't allow herself to think the word *love* at any other time when she considered him, but loving the shape of his nose seemed harmless enough.

Over the years, they'd both grown. His teeth grew in, though there was still a narrow gap between the front two, which she glimpsed in his occasional smile. For her part, Olivi's childish summer shifts and winter robes were replaced by close-fitting leggings that showed off newly curved hips, tunics slit and resewn with inserts at the front to create room for a budding chest. He, too, grew, his shoulders wider, his legs thicker. His feet appeared enormous. That nose, though, remained the same. She could barely keep from grinning ear to ear the first time she spotted it on each visit, her first sight of him in three months when he came into view as her wagon approached.

Her mother had always encouraged her to be bold, but Olivi had a cautious, watchful nature, and she kept her own counsel. Instead, she'd taken to playing a game with herself every time they visited: Could she get close enough to stand beside him and measure her own body against his? It was a delicious, delightful game, made all the sweeter by the fact that no one else knew she was playing. But perhaps the time for games had passed now. Perhaps this was finally the time she would address him.

After all, it might be her last chance. They were nearly grown, old enough that either of them might move to a new household in the next few seasons. Today would have to be the day.

So as soon as the cart slowed enough, Olivi jumped down from the cart and waved to Darious, the man who sometimes helped them with the bones. His sister, the boy's mother, had charge of the temple, but he took on her responsibilities when she was otherwise occupied. Darious greeted them today with the boy at his side, the triangle of the boy's nose reassuring Olivi with its constancy, the smile creeping across his face. Was the smile for her?

She would speak to him, she told herself. This time she would have the strength to do it.

It took an hour—once the sacks were delivered, the price haggled, the bones taken into the temple for burning—for her to find the right time. But as her uncle and his uncle stepped through the threshold of the temple and left the two young people together alone, Olivi put her hand on his arm. It felt warm and strong. She took a deep breath and leapt.

"My name is Olivi," she said.

"Timion," he responded.

Shocking, how easy it had been.

Then he added, "I'm glad to know you, Olivi."

How right her name sounded on his lips. She looked at him in wonder. Now that she'd begun speaking, she might as well continue. "I've meant to introduce myself for some time now."

"And today you decided?"

"Today I did."

That slow smile again, the front teeth with just that bit of space between them, his lips parting in a way that made her think there were many other things she would like to see and feel his lips do. The blood rushed to her cheeks just thinking of the possibilities.

"Olivi?" he asked, his voice a touch more nervous, seemingly working up his own confidence.

She turned her own smile upon him to let him know that whatever he wanted to say, to ask, she was ready to hear.

But instead of Timion's words, the next thing Olivi heard was the sound of oxen's heavy hoofbeats, the jangling of heavy traces, loud enough to drown out conversation. In all her years coming to the boneburner's, Olivi had never heard a sound quite like this before.

Someone else was arriving. And it wasn't just a small cart like the one Olivi's uncle drove. Too heavy, thought Olivi. Too loud. Even though she steeled herself, she was still unprepared when the oxen and the load they dragged came into view.

Drawn by a team of four wide-haunched, ink-black oxen, the immense white wagon was of an unusual kind: closed up all around, like a box or a house on wheels. It struck fear in Olivi's heart even before it pulled past her and she noticed the iron latch on the back. It was similar to the design of a pen she'd seen used for animals, though that one had not been wheeled. She guessed immediately from the size that this pen was for people, not animals, and she suppressed the urge to run as fast and as far as her legs could carry her.

Instead she looked at Timion, and he looked at her, and she saw her own fear reflected in his eyes. Though she wanted to reach out and grab Timion's hand for comfort, she stood motionless with her chin up instead. She would show them nothing. She would be strong.

When the white wagon halted, a man and a woman descended from the driver's seat, the man climbing down with obvious care, the woman leaping in a single smooth motion with a staff in one hand. She landed in the dirt and brushed invisible dust from her leggings with her free hand before the man had finished his descent.

Seeming to ignore everyone else, the woman—short-haired, her black leggings tight to her skin, her pale white tunic loose and billowing like a flag—beckoned Darious over and spoke quietly in his ear. Darious was a tall man, his curly dark hair swept up in a way that made him appear even taller, so it was striking when his posture changed. He seemed to lose several inches of height in no more than a heartbeat at the woman's words. Olivi was stunned to see him change so quickly, but the difference was obvious: the strength just seemed to slump out of him, all at once.

Then the woman looked over at Timion. "He's the one?"

Still looking down, still slumped, Darious nodded.

Brandishing her staff at Timion, the woman said, "Let's go."

Timion said, "Uncle? What is this?"

"I'm sorry," said the older man, his voice trembling, not meeting the boy's eyes. "The God of Plenty has need of you."

Olivi's blood ran cold. Younger girls might be called to form a new class of Xaras, but for boys of Timion's age, there was only one reason someone might be retrieved from their home and carted off in a closed wagon with an iron latch.

Olivi wanted to fling herself on the ground in front of Timion, or perhaps to fight the woman. She wanted to do something, anything. But she knew, though she had never seen anything like this, what would happen. The woman would strike her with the staff. Perhaps across the shoulders or back, just to warn her, or perhaps across the face, to split her cheek open and teach her a lesson for her interference. Either way, Timion would still end up in that wagon. The conflict was over before it had even started. Timion's uncle had recognized the inevitable. That was why he hadn't fought. Because fighting, tempting as it was, would not do a single lick of good.

Timion looked back at Olivi, a deep well of sadness and fear in his eyes.

"Don't tell me it's going to be okay," he said.

"I won't."

He said nothing else, not *Goodbye* or *Avenge me* or *Her will be done*. He simply took the seven or so steps that the woman with the staff indicated he should take. The woman in black and white placed a gag in Timion's mouth, which he accepted like a horse long accustomed to the bit. She tied it firmly—though it looked like she was being as gentle as she could—while he stood without moving. The man who had arrived on the wagon with the woman simply stood watching, but if he was needed, he appeared ready. He was dressed like the woman but in the opposite colors, a loose black tunic on top, fitted pale leggings on the bottom. But he stayed motionless as Timion followed his captor, waiting calmly while she unlocked the latch. Then Timion, who Olivi had adored from afar for so long, stepped up and into the darkness.

Olivi was still watching, standing as if roots had grown through her feet into the earth, though she desperately wanted to turn away. She would watch until there was nothing left to see. But what happened next surprised her. More precisely, she was surprised by what did not happen.

The woman didn't close the latch.

The guard from the Holy City—because that was who she obviously was, an emissary of the Xaras—had produced a paper from some hidden pocket and was looking down at it, brow creased. Olivi couldn't see what was written or drawn on the paper, but whatever the woman saw, it must be why she hadn't lowered the latch.

In that moment, Olivi half hoped Timion would leap down from the wagon and bolt across the open field to freedom, but that didn't happen. Instead, the woman turned back toward Darious.

No. Not Darious. More precisely, not just Darious. Because Olivi's uncle, Jeremiah, was standing next to the boneburner.

The guard thrust the paper in the direction of both men, asking, "Do you read?"

Darious nodded. Her uncle said nothing, but he didn't have to. When he saw what was on the paper, his eyes flicked up toward Olivi automatically. Then he looked away again, deliberately staring down at the ground.

"It's her?" the woman asked quietly, but not too quietly for Olivi to hear.

Her uncle made as if to shake his head, but the woman was watching him intently, having already caught his slip. She spun the staff in her hand and gestured to the man in white and black.

"The Holy One's looking out for us today, isn't She?" said the guard, her voice almost merry. "Shaved a few hours off our trip."

"She's here too?" The man's voice was incredulous.

The woman nodded. "Like I said, a kindness from the God Herself. Let's get to it, then."

Olivi didn't have time to fully grasp what they meant before the man walked over and grabbed her in a sharp, merciless motion. He slung her over his shoulder and began to carry her toward the wagon.

Olivi wasn't sure why the man was carrying her instead of giving her the dignity of walking, as he had with Timion. Then she heard the screaming. A moment after that, she realized it was coming from her own mouth.

She was in the wagon before she knew it. The man moved toward her mouth with a strip of rag, but as soon as his fingers got close, she gnashed her teeth. He shrugged and withdrew.

This time the door was slammed shut from the outside and latched immediately. It was a strong latch, too, Olivi realized after throwing herself against it more than a handful of times. She subsided only when her shoulder hurt too much to try again.

It was too late to run now that the full weight of what she'd be running from had crashed down on her. If she were being called as a Xara, it would have happened when she was younger. There would've been money, and praise, and negotiation. This was the other thing. The god wanted blood for the Sun Rites. A girl of ten-and-four and a boy of ten-and-four, chosen by a lottery in which the god expressed what She wished, would be hauled all the way to the capital to provide theirs.

With utter clarity, Olivi realized she was going to die.

A noise behind her brought her back to herself suddenly. Then she remembered who was here in the wagon with her, lying in the same prison on the same hay. Timion.

A part of her, a small part, was happy not to be facing this alone. She didn't really know the boy. Now she never would. But if she had to be hauled off to be sacrificed in the capital, she might as well go in his company.

Her mother would have other mothers to comfort her. And

though Olivi knew Norah would miss her, she also believed that Norah would accept the God's call without question. The farm, the family, would go on. Olivi had never really been necessary to either.

If the only purpose she ever served in life was to give this boy a companion at his death, for both of them to die nobly to ensure the God's favor for the land's next harvest, that seemed enough.

Olivi reached down and gently disengaged the gag from his mouth.

"I'm afraid," she said.

Timion answered in a hoarse whisper, "So am I."

"We can be afraid together."

"Everyone dies alone," he said.

"That may be true. But we're not dead yet."

"We may as well be."

They rode in silence for a bit, the jangling of the traces outside muffled by the wagon's thick walls. At last, she said in a conversational tone, "You know, I imagined this very differently."

"You imagined being carted off to the capital to be sacrificed to an angry god?"

"No," she said, "I was talking about you."

"Me? You thought of me?" There was still sadness in his voice, but something else too, now. Warmth. Welcome. And a kind of hope.

"I did. Often." She might as well tell Timion the truth now, the whole truth.

It turned out she had nothing to lose.

✦

Without exception, over the course of seasons and years, Olivi and Jeremiah had always returned from the boneburner's before sunset. Even in winter, they arrived while there was still a sliver of light in the sky. In summer, with the days starting earlier and ending later, after the hours of labor it took to keep the farm running, some days there was time enough to bask outside in the last golden glow while the family took their evening meal. Today had been one of those days. So Norah didn't start to worry until the last bit of the sun's golden disc had slipped below the horizon. But when she did, the worry was deep and relentless. She paced, her lips moving in a silent prayer to the Holy One, over and over. *Let my daughter return. Bring her back to me.*

Norah leapt up when she heard the cart approaching in the dark, rattling and nearly empty. She instantly recognized something wrong in the way Jeremiah slumped on the seat, his limp hands barely maintaining control of the reins. And of course, the most wrong thing: he was clearly, obviously, alone.

Norah set out to meet the cart at a brisk walk. She had a lifetime of calm to draw on, a belief that the Holy One would ensure that everything worked out for the best in the long run, no matter how dark things might look in the moment.

But a tremble of anger still welled up in her voice when she asked him, "Jeremiah, where is my daughter?"

Then she smelled the stink of liquor on him. He didn't respond to her question, if he'd heard it at all. His eyes barely focused on her for a heartbeat before his gaze slid away.

"Jeremiah," she said, and this time her voice was sharp. "You took Olivi to the boneburner's. Where is she now?"

In the dark, she couldn't make out his face. Perhaps it was better that way. When he finally spoke, his words cut deep.

"I didn't want to tell you," he slurred. "It's the worst good news."

"Good news?" she asked, then, not knowing what else to say, repeated, "Good news?"

He told Norah what he knew, what he'd seen. She understood.

In that moment of understanding, it felt like the earth had opened up beneath Norah and swallowed her whole.

Hours later, Norah wished she had made the journey to the Holy One's temple to pray. Perhaps she'd made a mistake kneeling in the circle of stones behind her own house. Maybe the Holy One felt that Norah wasn't trying hard enough, didn't suffer enough, if she wouldn't make the journey to the temple. But the loss of Olivi had felt too immediate. Norah threw herself into her prayers instantly, without pausing to think about whether she was in the right place. She only knew she had to beseech the Holy One. To beg for an explanation. Why, after all these years, had the god taken the one person in Norah's life she couldn't live without?

Four hours into her prayers, her knees aching, her stomach cramping, her ears aching with silence, Norah suffered. Five hours in, she felt a hand on her shoulder. At first, she thought it was the god's.

Norah reached up to pat the hand. It was real. She guessed from the familiar scent that it belonged to Vetiver. She looked up to see her longtime friend crouching over her, her brow creased with worry. Vetiver's hand held fast on Norah's shoulder, almost too heavy.

"Come inside," Vetiver said, her voice hushed, intent.

"Why? Is it a storm or a flood or . . ." But she heard nothing in the night, not a fierce wind, not the rumble of thunder. Only her own breathing, low and smooth, and Vetiver's, fast and shallow. When Norah fell asleep at night in the farmhouse, she could hear a dozen soft voices breathing, but out of all of them she could pick out Olivi's. Now she might never hear her sleeping daughter breathing in the dark again.

"Nothing is coming, and no one. Jeremiah told us what happened. Norah, she's not coming back."

"I know she's not. I'm asking the Holy One why."

"You know why."

"I don't."

Vetiver slid her hand to the center of Norah's back, pressing gently in the darkness. "The Holy One chose Olivi. She wants the girl for Her own. There is no changing that. You can fight it, yes. Wear yourself out praying. Or you can accept it as the honor that it is."

Norah stared down at her hands. For a moment she wondered if perhaps the Holy One Herself was speaking through the more familiar form of Vetiver, to help Norah learn, to help her see. But there was no reason to think her friend was anyone other than herself.

"You're correct. So was Jeremiah, in a way. He said this was good news." Norah forced herself to speak calmly. "It does not matter what I think, how I feel. The Holy One decides what She decides."

"Your voice just then," said Vetiver. "Your words. I can tell you must've been an excellent Xara."

Norah started. Such a strange night. Revelations in the darkness. Her whole world tipping on its axis, ready to crash. "You knew?"

"It was impossible not to know," Vetiver said, and Norah heard a smile in her voice. "When you came from the capital. So innocent despite your age. You knew nothing: not the word for a homestead, how to pay the fare, even the word for the vehicle we rode on."

She strained to remember. "It was a cart, wasn't it?"

"It was a *chudabidra*," said Vetiver.

Norah laughed. She had to laugh if she didn't want to cry. She said, "And you think Olivi being chosen has something to do with . . . my past?"

"I know she's gone. I know you're still here. I know that if it were my daughter taken to be sacrificed at the Sun Rites, it would break me. But we're different women, you and I. I don't think that you'll break."

Norah closed her eyes. It was more soothing to feel the dark around her than to see it.

Vetiver added, "If you want to go to the capital and beg for her life, you can."

Of all the things Vetiver had guessed correctly, Norah realized, her friend had no idea that Norah had been exiled. If Norah were ever to go to the capital, she'd be doing it with the understanding that it might mean her death.

Misunderstanding Norah's silence, Vetiver said, "We can manage in your absence. I have some money. It's yours if you want it."

In her friend's kind, supportive words, Norah heard what she'd left unspoken. "But you don't think I should go."

"The choice is yours, but no, I don't. What good would it do?"

"All these years, was She just treating me tenderly to break me?" asked Norah, her voice pinched, throat tight with unshed tears.

"As I said," Vetiver soothed her, the hand back on her shoulder, "I don't think that you'll break."

Norah whispered, "We are all Hers to do with as She wishes. Even Olivi." Even as she spoke them, the words felt hollow.

"You weren't wrong to think of your daughter as yours."

"Wasn't I?"

Exhausted, Norah turned and collapsed into her friend's arms. Vetiver held her tightly, stroked her back, as the former Xara's bitter, resigned tears came.

It would be a long time before Norah prayed to the Holy One again.

✦ CHAPTER 6 ✦

RITES

Midsummer, the All-Mother's Year 516,

the third Sun Rites of the Drought of Girls

The Holy City, Sestia

Olivi, Concordia

The night before the third Sun Rites of the Drought of Girls, Olivi, the intended sacrifice, didn't sleep. She was still awake when, before sunrise, the guards came for her.

They weren't the same guards who had washed her and guided her to the room in which she'd spent her restless night, and she'd liked the other ones better. The woman who had washed her had been gentle about it. She'd even spent time brushing the tangles from Olivi's wet hair, wrapping her fingers tight around each lock before setting the brush to it, making sure she didn't pull on Olivi's scalp. These guards were brusque and silent. Olivi told herself she was being absurd. A guard was a guard, and they were here to do their jobs. The attitude of whoever marched her off to her death might change the journey, but not the destination.

The slender man tied her wrists first, much more tightly than she would have liked, and then bent down to work at her ankles. He tested each knot, not gently. They were secure. Olivi supposed she had held out some kind of hope that this would be done carelessly, that she might have some prayer of escaping. She should have known better. The priests had been doing this for how long now? Hundreds of years, every five years, without exception. How many sacrifices had ever escaped their fate? Not a single one.

The gag went into her mouth before she thought to say anything, and once it was in, it was too late. What could she say, anyway? *Don't?* They would. *Stop?* They wouldn't. *I want to live?* They knew. They didn't care.

The fabric was tight against her teeth, her lips. Speaking was impossible, but she didn't need to speak words aloud for them to wing their way godward. The God of Plenty was a merciful god, a gentle one, at least the way Norah had described Her to Olivi all her childhood long. The god gave Her people green land and warm summers and the delight of pleasures for their bodies to revel in. Everyone seemed to think that the god's anger had caused the Drought of Girls. Olivi didn't believe it. The world would have to do far worse to offend the god that her mother had taught her to love.

And so Olivi prayed.

God of Plenty, Holy One, she said. *Let me die if it is Your will. I will go gladly if You want that of me. But I will love and serve You with my time on this earth, whatever amount is left to me. Hours, days, years. Only let me live.*

Once she was tied, incapable of movement, she wondered how she could possibly be expected to shuffle out of this room and into the amphitheater where the sacrifice would be performed. Then, once she found herself in the air, she realized she should've known. Hands and feet bound the way the feet of a ram would be bound, the man's arms under her back and the backs of her knees, her head against his shoulder, her bound feet dangling like a doll's.

In the hallway, she heard another door open, and a pair of figures emerged from the next door: a thick-necked woman in a guard's uniform carrying an all-too-familiar figure, bound at the wrists and ankles. Timion.

In the moment that the guard carrying her pulled abreast of the guard carrying him, Olivi made what she believed would be her last mistake. She looked straight into Timion's eyes.

She wished she hadn't.

His eyes were wild with fear, so base and pure it transformed his face into a haunted mask, almost unrecognizable as human. She felt his fear then like a physical thing, ripping her open. They had been so human to each other in those precious days when it was just the two of them in the wagon, coming ever closer to their doom, but sharing the comfort of each other's presence as they neared the capital. But since arriving, they had been kept separate. Olivi had been alone ever since. If she'd known, she might have proposed sharing more than conversation. Too late now.

Then the woman carrying him moved in front of the man carrying her. Olivi could no longer see Timion's face. The fear subsided somewhat but refused to go away, lodged in her heart like a hot coal. It stayed with her as they traveled. She hadn't been afraid before, but now she thought she would be afraid until the very moment she died.

The walk was longer than she expected—she had no idea how far they were from the amphitheater—and every step was interminable. They moved through the predawn down a hall and outdoors, along an enclosed walkway—some kind of tunnel?—then up a ramp into an open space where the smell of fresh air brought tears to her eyes. Every single thing that happened put exactly the same thought in her head, sometimes longer, sometimes shorter, but always the same. *This is the last time I will see this, smell this, do this. This is the last time. This is the last. The last. Last.*

Once they were in the amphitheater proper, she could hear the amplified sound of the curious crowd narrowing in on her, roaring, looming. They were eager. They were waiting.

Because of the angle of her head, Olivi didn't see her destination until she was laid down upon it. A narrow, hard bed with a wishbone-shaped curve, a kind of notch, at the top where her head was laid. She had never seen the ceremony and yet she had no doubt about what this shape was meant to do. This was where her blood would run. She could smell the grain below, its dry, crisp warmth rising up to meet her nose, waiting for her thick, liquid blood to bring it life to feed on.

They waited there for what felt like a long time. She couldn't see the guards anymore, couldn't see anything. She wondered why they weren't blindfolded. Or drugged. She'd been given food for fuel last night, but nothing to blunt the edges of her consciousness, nothing to cut her loose from herself. A mild drug to soften her mind, to open her to acceptance of her fate, that would've been a mercy. The god, she knew, was merciful. Why were Her agents, if agents they were, not merciful too?

Olivi was on the bone bed now, tied tight, her immobile limbs already starting to protest. Her heart and throat felt exposed, raw and open, though she wondered if that was only because she knew what was to come.

She thought she knew, in any case. But those Sun Rites were not like any other. When pandemonium broke loose, when the sorcerer took control and the rites fell apart, Olivi found herself the still, small center of a shattered world. She waited there, powerless, in the midst of death and destruction.

And she thought, *I wonder if this will turn out to be a miracle.*

✦

In the aftermath, after the sorcerer who had caused the Drought died at the hands of the Scorpican queen, chaos reigned. The crowd had fled. The sorcerer's body lay bloody in the center of the platform. The sacrifice, realized the High Xara Concordia, was not complete. On one bone bed lay a dead boy, and on the other, a still-living girl.

The High Xara surveyed the unthinkable.

There were no rules for what to do now, no precedent. The Sun Rites had never been disrupted like this, with horror and destruction, with a mad magician killing wantonly and then a queen committing murder with her bare hands. Chaos had always been invited to the Sun Rites, but it had never accepted the invitation with such abandon. It had never run rampant through everything the Five Queendoms held sacred. The savagery took the High Xara's breath away.

So as the amphitheater emptied out, leaving only the bodies of the dead behind, Concordia knew she had a decision to make.

These rites had started the same as any other—would she finish them that way? Without disruption, there would have been sacrifice. Death had been dealt, yes, but not in the proper form. What did it mean? Was this blood the kind of blood that would appease the god, or just make Her angrier?

The holy dagger lay in the dirt where the warrior queen had let it fall. This, at least, the High Xara knew was wrong. This was one thing she could fix.

Concordia bent to retrieve the blade, wrapping her fingers around the bone hilt, which was slick with blood. The boy's, the sorcerer's, perhaps more, she did not know. But she didn't wipe it. If she was to shed more blood today, she wouldn't shy away from what had already been shed. She'd force herself to go in with open eyes.

The High Xara Concordia asked herself what the god would want, and then, she asked the god directly.

What do you want of me?

Of course, there was no answer. There never had been. Why did she bother asking? Because even after all these years of silence, she still hoped. Perhaps this time would be different. Perhaps this time, she would hear the god speak. She had sinned with Xelander, yes, but she had given him up after the outrageous sacrifice of the Sun Rites of 511 had failed to bring the Drought of Girls to an end. The Holy One was merciful, wasn't She? So if a question was in Concordia's mind, she asked it. And the next time, and the next time, she would ask it again.

After everything, even the utter madness of what had just happened, she lived in hope. But she heard no voice.

What she did hear was the girl catching her breath, letting out a loud, wrenched sob.

There was one action, Concordia realized, she absolutely needed to take. She turned her back on the girl to face the boy. Blood still leaked from his wound, his sightless eyes fixed on the sky. There were no more sobs from the girl, but Concordia heard her ragged breathing as she moved.

The High Xara stood over the dead boy. She remembered the feeling of her hand ending his life, even though she hadn't been in control at the time, and muttered the briefest of prayers before continuing.

"Let the grain be fed," she said aloud, and turned all her attention to her task.

She put the blade hard against his skin without hesitation and opened his throat as she had opened so many others, a single slit, deep and long. Blood began to pour from the wound, through the notch, down onto the grain. It was still ruby. It streamed onto the waiting golden seed.

Against all odds, the Dara she had appointed as this season's mixer was still there. The Dara was staring into the distance, but a word from Concordia—"Dara"—spurred her to action. The High Xara gestured to the young woman to remind her of her duty.

The Dara lifted her mixing paddle, nodded, and began to stir the blood into the grain.

Then the High Xara turned back to the girl, the one who was marked for sacrifice. Her breathing had slowed. The girl stared up at her, but Concordia noted that her eyes were no longer wild. Even with her wrists and ankles bound, even with the air around them reeking of the sick sweet stench of death, the girl looked frighteningly calm. The girl watched the High Xara as she approached, and even as the High Xara palmed the bloody knife, she didn't moan or beg.

"Please," the girl said, her voice as calm as her face. "A word."

The High Xara had never heard the voice of the god, but this voice, she heard. She felt she had to listen. The girl's eyes were red and swollen with tears, but there was an intelligence in them, a clarity Concordia was not even sure she herself had after the unimaginable events they'd just endured.

"Please," the girl said again. "There has been enough blood today."

"Is it up to you?" Concordia found herself saying.

"It's up to the god. And you are Her hands on earth. So, I leave it to you."

"Indeed," she answered dryly. "It is, in fact, up to me."

The girl said, "What do you want me to tell Her?"

That startled Concordia. "What?"

"The Holy One," said the girl. "If I get to meet Her. What would you like me to say?"

Concordia's heart started beating faster, but she forced herself to appear calm, reaching up with one hand to brush back her saffron streak of hair. "Why should I send Her a message through you, when I speak with Her every day?"

"Of course," the girl said. "Of course, you're right. I didn't mean that. I just meant, if She asks me why I had to die, even though there were already two bodies' worth of blood, I should know your reason."

There was a long pause while the High Xara considered. She was well aware that the hilt of the bloody knife was beginning to stick to her hand as the blood there grew tacky. She thought she could even smell its coppery tang. Her palm began to itch.

"She chose you," said Concordia to the girl. She found herself almost hoping the girl would have a retort. The girl was clearly intelligent, more so than any of the Daras dared to behave in Concordia's presence, and she enjoyed this sort of debate. She'd once enjoyed this sort of verbal sparring with Xelander, though those days were gone, and with someone even before that, but she never let herself think that person's name.

The girl looked up. "She chose me," she murmured in agreement. "But what if what She chose me for was something different? After all, when Xaras are chosen, some are raised and some are sacrificed, right?"

The girl couldn't possibly know Concordia's secret, but her words came uncomfortably close to it. Concordia searched for the right words to counter the girl's. "She chose you for a sacrifice. That's why you're here."

"That's why I came here," said the girl. "But after what happened, all this—doesn't it seem She might have other plans for me?"

Concordia had to admit it made sense. The god worked in mysterious ways. One could not always look at how things had been and assume they would always be that way. If the Drought of Girls had taught them nothing else, it had taught them this.

The girl prompted, "What do you choose to believe?"

In answer, the High Xara turned her back on the girl once more. She lifted the dead boy from the bed of bone. His body was limp and awkward, just large enough to be difficult to move, though still soft in death. She set him aside tenderly and hauled what was left of the body of the sorcerer a few feet to replace him on the bone bed. This body was lighter than the other, almost too light, like a bird's. She then bent and slit the sorcerer's throat.

The blood was thick and dark. It almost gave Concordia second thoughts, but there was no going back now. The dark blood sank into the grain. The Dara with her paddle stirred it, coating the grain with blood until there was no trace of the golden color of the grain, only a dull red already crusting to brown. And the next season's seed was blessed.

From behind her, the girl whispered, "Thank you."

Concordia said, "I didn't do that for you. I did it for Her. I don't even know who you are."

Most years, she never knew the names of the sacrifices; she never even met them. It was easier that way. The god spoke through the drawing of lots and the appointed Daras in the Edifice handled the rest.

"Ah," said the girl, and her eyes were brimming with tears now, tears of relief. In a quiet voice, she said, "My name is Olivi."

Olivi.

Everything the priest had been keeping inside felt like it flowed through her in that moment, like a storm-swollen river, through her and out of her, finally too much to contain.

Hearing her own name on the lips of the girl she'd almost killed, the High Xara Concordia wept. She fell where she stood and cried for a long time, forehead pressed to her knees. She didn't even feel the hard stage under her knees as she wept for all that hadn't happened and all that had.

They wouldn't know for a long time what the next season would bring. But, from her kneeling position next to the bone beds, the High Xara squeezed her eyes closed tight and beseeched the god. *Please, let us live. Let us recover. We are Your loving children. This destructive force has been vanquished and we remain in service to You, awaiting Your generous harvest. May we have our girls back?*

And so faintly that she would never be sure whether her own fevered, hopeful mind had conjured the sound, the High Xara Concordia thought she heard a tender voice respond with a single word.

SOON.

✦

After she returned to the Edifice, after the unbelievable events of the Third Sun Rites of the Drought of Girls had come to a close, Concordia found her blood singing in her veins. Had she imagined the voice of the god? She couldn't rule it out. But in that moment she felt like a new woman entirely, one who might shed her skin like a snake and emerge from the darkness of the past years gleaming and new.

There was a hesitant knock on the door of her chamber, and she called, "Enter."

She'd expected her usual servant, but she should have known that on this day of all days, chaos would change her plans in every way.

Xelander said, "I apologize, High Xara. The one who usually serves this role for you is unavailable, and I was sent in his place. If you would prefer to bathe yourself or wait for tomorrow, I am happy to step back."

"No," said Concordia, something warm rising in her chest, a euphoria she wasn't sure she could control. On the outside, she remained calm. "You will perform your task."

He set up the bathing chair for her, prepared the sweet water, readied the small soft cloth with which he would touch her skin. Even during their entanglement, she had always followed protocol during the bath, readying herself to sit and be bathed under cover of a modest cloth. Tonight she threw that all aside.

She'd escaped with her life, and the villain who had been responsible for the Drought of Girls was dead. Soon there would be girls born again. From this moment, everything would get better.

Concordia let her bloodied clothes drop to the floor. Without a stitch of clothing to hide her nakedness, she took a confident step toward Xelander. She would have what she wanted and feel no guilt, not tonight.

If the Holy One disapproved of Concordia's actions, if She had something else in mind, She could say so.

PART II

THE
GATE OF
MEMORIES

The All-Mother's Years 516 to 518

✦ CHAPTER 7 ✦

THE UNDERLANDS

After the Rites of the Bloody-Handed

The Underlands

Sessadon

Death had not surprised Sessadon. Surprise had been drained from her by hundreds of years of life and half-life, by her experience with nearly limitless magic, by the endless variety of things she'd seen and done. She could not be surprised. But she could still, it seemed, be disappointed.

After dying, she awoke on the bone bridge into the Underlands and saw the approaching figure of the Child. This was the first disappointment. She'd heard the stories, and what she saw was only exactly what the stories had always said: standing on the bridge, the shade would be approached by a Child, and the Child would lead them into the Underlands. On the rare occasions she had imagined the Child, they looked exactly like the figure that welcomed her upon her death. She would have liked something more unanticipated.

The Child beckoned her.

"Do you talk?" Sessadon asked. "The stories never said whether you talk."

The Child simply beckoned again, as if Sessadon hadn't spoken. The sorcerer—was she still a sorcerer, now that she was a shade?—decided to get it over with. She simply followed.

Then they were off the bridge into some other space, impossible to describe or define.

Sessadon had thought herself completely beyond surprise. But she felt it flicker when a question poured from her lips before she realized she'd even formed it in her mind. She heard herself say, "Can you help me find my sister?"

Again the Child seemed not to hear. This was beyond disappointing. Insulting, even.

"Kruvesis," clarified Sessadon. She couldn't remember the last time she'd spoken the name.

Five hundred years ago, the sisters had been parted. Well, not been parted exactly, thought Sessadon. She was the one who had left. After she'd seen in Kruvesis's mind that the newly appointed queen would never trust her, she'd let the fire of anger in her burn bright enough to fuel violence, and she and some like-minded magicians had traveled up to the western coast of newly formed Scorpica to search for quartz. They'd all perished at the hands of the Scorpican warriors.

If every single shade who had ever walked the earth was here, Sessadon realized, those like-minded magicians, her onetime friends, were here too.

"Alish?" she asked the Child. "Can you take me to her? Or Derrica? Lux?"

No answer. The Child kept leading. Sessadon, despite herself, kept following. She was behind the Child now, watching its small back move through a landscape she couldn't quite perceive. She had an impression of shapes, and voices, but nothing quite coalesced.

They were all here somewhere. All her friends, five centuries dead. And, Sessadon realized quickly, not just her friends.

"Where are you leading me?" Sessadon asked.

No answer.

That was when she thought harder about who else occupied the Underlands. The shade of every person Sessadon had ever killed. How many were there? The hunter Hana, who had been her only companion for years on the lonely island, until Sessadon had pushed her too far and melted the pulp of her brain. The inhabitants of a Paximite town Sessadon had once emptied simply to practice her magic. The once-great Arcan queen Mirriam, the only sorcerer whose power could possibly rival Sessadon's besides her descendant Eminel. Sessadon had killed them all with weaponized magic, sent them flooding into this underground world. What would happen now that she was here among them? Could shades harm each other, bent on revenge?

The unexpected hunger to reunite with her long-dead sister—what would Kruvesis say or do, face-to-face again?—burned within Sessadon, a fierce light. But it seemed unlikely the Child was taking her to her long-dead sister. Much more likely that the shade of Sessadon was being led toward some other, less savory reckoning.

So Sessadon, still unsteady in her new form and unmoored in this strange waste, decided she would no longer follow.

She didn't flee, not exactly. First she stopped, watching the retreating back of the Child, testing for a connection between them. When the Child didn't turn or look back, Sessadon simply melted away, moving across the strange landscape, unsure of her destination, but determined the choice would be her own.

✦

In that early time underground, Sessadon realized, she was glad she had a mission. It was disorienting to be dead, to feel your place and to remember what it had been like to have a body, but to experience new dimensions of space and time. Space in the Underlands was infinite, or at least it felt that way, because no matter how far Sessadon journeyed, she never reached its end. There was something deeply unsettling about infinity.

Unsettling, too, when Sessadon first realized that here in the Underlands, she could no longer access the magic she'd had all her life.

She'd first noticed when she found herself on the edge of a gathering of shades, clustered in small groups in an area that looked almost like some sort of outdoor theater. Their voices, seemingly cheerful and unbothered, carried. If she hadn't known better, she would have thought this was a group of living people going about their business. But she had no idea who they were or what they might really be up to. So she gathered her body magic to cloak herself in power, vanishing from view.

Sessadon had done this a thousand times in life, taking it completely for granted. Until she noticed the shade of a woman in an intricately embroidered tunic staring directly at her, it never even occurred to her that the invisibility enchantment might not work.

The woman's mouth opened as if to speak. Sessadon turned away quickly. Could she just change her form? She wasn't really here, after all, in a body. She tried shifting her energy, but when she looked down, everything was the same. She looked as she had near the end of her life Above, black ringlets of hair interspersed with white, neither particularly short nor tall, dressed in a dark robe she hadn't known would be the last thing she'd ever wear. She continued to move away from the group of people, hurrying but not running, hoping they would simply let her go.

"You there!" called a man's voice. He didn't sound angry, but Sessadon didn't want to take the chance. She continued on.

The voice called out again. "You! Come on and join us! What pressing business could you possibly have?"

A chorus of laughter with an unpleasant edge. Sessadon tried again to enchant herself and disappear, but the result—or lack thereof—was the same.

It made sense, of course, that the god Eresh wouldn't welcome the use of magic given by her sister Velja. Or perhaps it had nothing to do with Eresh. To make magic, Arcans had always needed two things: sand and life force. There was no physical material here, sand or rock or water or otherwise. And life force was the one thing the dead would never have again.

Sessadon kept going and going until she could no longer hear the voices, but she'd stumbled into a more well-populated area of the Underlands, and she realized she would quickly need to orient herself. That could be the first part of her mission. And once she knew where things were and how to move around, maybe she'd have a better idea of where to find Kruvesis.

She wasn't sure what she'd say to her sister once she found her. It wasn't as if anything could change between them now. For hundreds of years she had nurtured that flame of resentment, her long-burning fury that Kruvesis had been chosen instead of her to lead their queendom—but did she expect the shade of her sister to apologize? What difference would that make? No, Sessadon had no particular vision for what would happen if she struck her aim.

So Sessadon was glad when a new mission, a more urgent one, revealed itself to her.

She had no idea how long she'd been searching when she realized that no matter where she went, the topic of discussion among the shades was the same.

The first gate is open, they said. *The first gate is open.*

The rumors were hard to separate from the truth, but Sessadon began to cobble together what had happened. She knew, like anyone knew from the stories, that there were five gates separating the

Underlands from what the shades called Aboveground or simply Above. The first gate between the Underlands and the living world, the Gate of Memories, had always been rumored to be located somewhere in Godsbones. The stories rarely agreed on any other detail. She vaguely remembered that the second gate was called the Gate of Warriors and the third the Gate of Heroes, but where they were and what one did to open them, she had no recollection. The gates were generally invoked when telling the story of Sestia, the god of plenty. When her consort died, she opened all five gates to plunge into the Underlands and rescue him, only to find him already enjoying pleasures with lustful shades Below, having almost instantly forgotten his lover Above. The only other time she'd heard the gates mentioned was when she'd been traveling in Sestia years before and heard a woman say, speaking of a lover she trusted to keep her most intimate secrets, *His lips are locked up tighter than the fifth gate.*

She couldn't keep searching for her sister with no certain reward; she needed another activity to keep the despair at bay. If she traveled the Underlands learning more about the gates, that would give shape to her search. If she happened to find Kruvesis along the way, so much the better.

She started by searching out Sestians, who should know the story of their god's journey underground better than others. She was also sure to speak with Bastionites where she could find them, with their excellent knowledge of the treasures tucked away in books. After these conversations and exchanges, whispers and shrugs, gradually a picture began to form.

Though the shape of the Underlands seemed to shift, and it wasn't possible to map it exactly, Sessadon's mind was more nimble than most after hundreds of years of magical life. So when she gave careful consideration to all she'd learned, she knew the place to look for the first gate. Because from her vantage point, it didn't matter where that gate came out Aboveground. She was not Aboveground. The most important thing to remember, she told herself, was that the gate went both ways.

The breakthrough came in a conversation with a long-dead High Xara called Puglalia, a woman who'd clearly gone mad before her death, because half her conversation was absolute nonsense. The other half, however, was gold.

"So a living person needs to pass all five gates in order to come down," Sessadon clarified, watching the other shade's face for answers.

"Yes. And they must defeat, bypass, or satisfy a Voa to open each gate."

"If a gate is opened, does it stay open?"

"Does any gate?" asked Puglalia, whose robe in the half-light of the Underlands was so pale, it almost gleamed.

Sessadon tried a different approach. "So the living need all five gates. But the shades are saying that the first gate is open. Why does it matter, if it's only one gate, and no one can pass with just one gate?"

"The living can't come down," said Puglalia, gesturing with a descending palm, *down*. "But with one gate open, under very specific conditions, a shade can go up." She flipped her hand, raised the flat palm toward the far-off, unreachable sky. *Up.*

Sessadon felt herself leaning forward. "Tell me about the conditions."

Puglalia leaned back. "Why do you want to know, anyway? You didn't say."

"Didn't I? I'm new here. I want to learn as much as I can learn."

"For what purpose?"

"Does everything need a purpose?" asked Sessadon, stalling.

"My purpose," said Puglalia, "was to serve the glory of the Holy One. Which I did, for decades. Even after I was no longer High Xara." Her voice had started out pompous, but as she went on, her words took on a tinge of deep melancholy. "Do you have any idea what that was like, dedicating myself to Her for years and years? Even once I could no longer hear Her voice?"

"Your service is legendary," said Sessadon, attempting to soothe. "Even here in the Underlands I've heard it spoken of far and wide. Which is why I knew you were the most important person to talk to. You might even be the only one who knows."

"I might, at that," Puglalia said. "Even though the Holy One did not create the gates, She approved their workings, just as Velja did. Though the god of Chaos was too fickle to bother Herself with the details. Only my god and her sister Eresh negotiated the rules that would govern passage between this world and the world Above."

"And those rules?"

"Too many to speak of." The Sestian shade shrugged.

Sessadon's mind raced, but she forced her voice to stay casual. "Let's talk of just the one gate, then. The one that's open now. How can a shade pass through?"

"First, they have to find it."

"Where is it located?" asked Sessadon, then immediately regretted her question. It was too brash, too direct.

And indeed Puglalia seemed to shrink away from answering what she'd asked. "Everyone knows from Above but won't go, and it turns out, almost no one knows from Below. If it were easy, everyone would do it. Like being Xara! Not easy. The furthest thing from easy. Ask my mother. My sister. Me."

Sessadon let the wave of nonsense wash over her, focused instead on how to get the long-dead High Xara back on track. "The first gate. What's it meant for? What did your god and Eresh agree on?"

"I'm told," said the shade, "it was meant as a way for shades to visit their loved ones Aboveground. Eresh wanted her citizens to be able to journey for this purpose at any time, but the Holy One insisted that they use bodies to do so. So they agreed that a shade could inhabit a body found in Godsbones, but that the shade wouldn't be able to use the body's voice or mouth to speak."

"Has this happened often?" asked Sessadon, vaguely horrified at the notion of a shade striving and longing and fighting, finally resorting to occupying a dead body that didn't belong to her in order to make her way back into sunlight, then having no voice, simply exchanging her prison Below for a prison Above. Sessadon herself had never loved anyone enough to make that kind of sacrifice, but if she thought about it, she allowed the possibility that someone might.

"It's rare," said Puglalia, "but perhaps not so rare now that the first gate stands open."

"How is that possible? Who defeated the Voa at that gate?"

"I'm told that Velja herself opened the gate, made some kind of deal with Eresh, though no one knows on what terms."

"Velja!" Sessadon couldn't help exclaiming. "But I thought She didn't involve Herself in the workings of the gates."

"Not at the outset. But She is Chaos. Involved one day, indifferent the next. In this and ever thus."

"Ever thus," agreed Sessadon. Then she stopped talking. Because sometimes only silence was the right invitation for the other person to sally forth. And the shade of the High Xara Puglalia did.

"The gates were meant as ways for the living and the dead to meet, if one or the other were dedicated enough to pass. In some stories, sometimes the Voa stand aside or disappear. In others, they require bloodshed. Who knows? Who needs to know? All I know, all I can tell you, and I will tell you, is that a Scorpican named Dree wanders Above this very minute in another Scorpican's body, and when she returns back across the bridge, Eresh will be eager to hear her report."

Sessadon reeled. So much information, almost too much. She

clung to what she could use. The shade who returned, when she returned, would come across the bridge. Sessadon could find the bridge. Of all the locations in the Underlands, it was the single one that absolutely everyone knew.

But there was something more important in what the High Xara had said, and she pounced on it.

"Eresh knows? That the Scorpican shade walks in another's body?"

"Yes, of course," said Puglalia dismissively. "She sent her."

Then Sessadon knew everything she needed to know. Not just where to find this shade when she inevitably returned, but what came next after that reunion. And why it mattered. And how this knowledge could set Sessadon free.

The god Eresh walked here in the Underlands with the rest of them. She could be found, she could be spoken to.

And if one gate could be opened, why not two?

Why not all of them?

✦ CHAPTER 8 ✦

BURNING BONES

Six months after the Rites of the Bloody-Handed,
the All-Mother's Year 516
Southern Sestia
Norah

In the fifteen years she had lived on the farm outside of Tika, Norah had never been the one to make the journey to the boneburner's. She had taken on nearly every task the farm had to offer—she was a hard worker, and after her idle years as a decorative, pampered Xara, she found the work satisfying—but not this one. Some farms brought their bones to be burned once a moon and some only once a season, depending on how far they lived from the nearest boneburner and the number of animal or nonanimal bones they had to burn.

Sadly, the first time the task fell to Norah, it was because there were human bones, not just animal bones, to be delivered for burning.

Over the years, the shape of her household had shifted, with two mothers leaving and one joining the farm. Now Norah was one of three mothers, alongside warmhearted Vetiver and fickle Teresh.

Vetiver had a walking marriage with a round-faced, reliable man who lived a few farms away. He often brought gifts to the household for the children he'd sired. The light that beamed from Vetiver's face when she saw her lover coming up the road made a pang in Norah's heart. Vetiver was her favorite person, always ready to share a task or a secret.

Teresh was less easy to get along with, blowing hot and cold. No one knew who the father or fathers of Teresh's children were, and she had never seemed to welcome her most recent child. When the baby turned sickly, she was quick to blame it on the unnamed father, who she said had been too thin.

"Weak man, weak blood," she said, shrugging and looking away.

After Teresh stopped nursing, her oldest daughter, Enifer, fed the child goat's milk and soaked, pulped grain. But as the season wore on, the baby's face grew pale, its cries both frequent and weak. When the child died, the mother pretended it had never been hers. The small body lay dead in her bed, and she rose and dressed anyway, not giving it a second look.

"I have seen many mothers take leave of their minds when they lose a child," Vetiver said worriedly under her breath to Norah. "But never quite this way."

"Nor I," said Norah. It unsettled something in her she couldn't quite define. When she'd been a Xara, the mad had sometimes been brought to the palace for healing, but fearing harm, the Queensguard never let petitioners into the presence of the priests. She rarely thought much these days about those years in the Edifice, and she tried not to think much about her daughter, either. Some days her years as a Xara felt like a dream. Some days, it was this life, the one on the farm outside Tika, that she wasn't quite sure was real.

Vetiver, her brow creased with concern, said, "Perhaps this is what she needs to do to survive. But we'll never convince her to perform the ceremonies. We will have to bless the child and put it to rest."

"I'll do it," said Norah, and she had, performing every step of the homegoing ritual with graceful, solemn hands. This was, unfortunately, not another first. When two other Xaras of their class had died, in those Edifice years, it had fallen to her as the Xara Veritas to bless them. Concordia had been by turns inconsolable and remote, one day as guilty as if she could have saved them somehow, the next acting as if she'd never known them at all. Even when they'd been nameless Xaras in training, Norah had always been the more levelheaded. She'd always had these able hands, small and steady. She'd always been willing to take on tasks from which others shied away.

Now Norah drove the cart with those same capable hands, accompanied by Teresh's daughter Enifer, now ten-and-five. It was hard going. Not the journey itself—the road was smooth enough, the day clouded and cool but dry—but how Norah kept catching sight of the young woman on the seat next to her out of the corner of her eye and thinking it was Olivi, when in fact she would probably never see Olivi again.

She had resigned herself to her daughter's death when Olivi had been taken for the Sun Rites sacrifice the year before, from the very place Norah was now visiting. If the god wanted her daughter, Norah knew better than to fight Her will. But more recently, when she heard tell of the wild events of those Sun Rites, no one could say for sure whether Olivi might have survived the day. Norah tried hard to fight down hope.

Having this young woman next to her, body pressing against Norah's arm and shoulder as they rode together, reminded her of everything she had wanted for Olivi. She wanted her daughter to have all the experiences she'd never had, for good or for ill. She'd wanted Olivi to live a larger life. To love, to work, to soar, even to leave Sestia if that was what she wanted. But these dreams were only dreams. Even if Olivi had somehow survived, which seemed deeply unlikely, her path was the god's choice now.

The boneburner's temple was just where Vetiver had told her to look for it, marked with the thick leg bones of a ram crossed in an X above the door. The walls were an off-white brick, and she guessed that ash had been mixed into the clay to make them. It looked less elegant than the palace-temple in which she'd grown up, but appearances could be deceiving. It was no less holy. As they approached, a figure emerged from the low, squared-off doorway.

"Hail," said the man, wiping his hands on a cloth, then tucking it into a band at his waist. He was dressed not in holy robes but in the simple woven garb of any farmer or shepherd, a tunic and leggings of undyed wool. "Do you bring bones?"

"Hail," she returned his greeting. "We do."

"May the Holy One bless you."

"And you as well."

He was handsome, this one, his arms and legs thick but with an uncanny dancer's grace. There was something elegant in the way he moved as he came to greet them. Norah felt a stirring. She rarely thought of Olivi's father, and this man didn't resemble him, but there was something that caused his image to flicker in her mind nonetheless. Lips curved in a smile brushing her skin. Familiar fingers, reaching.

"I regret that my sister is not here to welcome you," said the boneburner, touching his fingertips together. "She has charge of this temple, but when she travels, I step in."

"Is that allowed?"

He tilted his head at that, the beginning of a smile on his lips. Then he read her face again and answered seriously, "It's allowed. The Holy One doesn't tell us who can and who can't burn the bones, only how and when they should be burned. Don't worry. We follow all Her commandments here."

Norah leapt down from the cart, then raised her arms to grasp

Enifer by the waist and lower the young woman down after her. She tied the oxen's traces to a nearby post, obviously set there for that purpose, and turned her attention back to the man: not priest, not peasant, but apparently something in between.

Not seeming to mind Norah's scrutiny, he turned to her companion. "My name is Darious. What's yours?"

"I'm Enifer. She's Norah."

He looked to Norah and she nodded.

To the young woman, he said, "Pleased to meet you, Enifer. You're welcome to stay with us for the burning, if . . . ?"

He didn't have the chance to finish before Enifer began to shake her head in the negative. Norah reminded herself that Enifer had been the one to try to save the child and failed; no wonder she hadn't distanced herself yet from the results.

"I'm afraid we don't have much for entertainment here. The children are playing over by the pens. I often find it soothing to watch them. Or you might even join in."

Enifer nodded, this time in the affirmative, and headed in the direction Darious pointed. Now that Norah listened, she could hear the sound of children playing some kind of game. They were all boys, of course. It made sense that the homestead was close to the temple, since the flames would need to be tended for long hours. She wondered how much the children helped with the tasks of boneburning. Children would have their chores on any farm or homestead, but for the holy work of returning people and animals to the earth, it seemed those tasks should be trusted to larger, steadier hands. Then again, it would help them learn that death was a part of life. Perhaps the sooner that lesson was learned, the better.

As if he could hear her thoughts, Darious said, "This is a holy place, but it is also a home like any other. Have you never brought bones to be burned?"

"Never," Norah admitted. "But I understand how it works. You take the bones for burning and give us the amount of ash they would produce." The ash would be used for fertilizer on the farm, churned into the earth, tucked into vegetable beds, sprinkled along the grapevines' rows.

"Yes," he said, nodding.

A shout from the area where the children were playing surprised her, and she swiveled her head. It had sounded like a girl's shout—but there were no girls these days, only young women. She saw Enifer running, pursued by the children. It sounded like she was laughing, but the sight of her being chased by a crowd was still disturbing, and Norah's brow creased.

"Don't worry," said Darious, his voice soft and close. "They're just playing Xaras."

The unexpected word sent a cold chill straight to Norah's core. She stepped away from Darious, feeling the skin of her arms rising into gooseflesh, and echoed, "Playing Xaras?"

"They act out the Sun Rites. Draw lots to assign roles: sacrifices, High Xara, dancers, queens. Act out the whole ceremony, and then the player who's the High Xara has to decide. If she goes through with the sacrifice, they start all over again. If she doesn't—and it looks like Enifer didn't—they chase her down."

Norah listened to him, her stomach lurching, but kept her eyes on Enifer. The young woman was running and grinning, a child's easy grin, as if this were truly just a game. She was looping in great circles to avoid the running boys, staying ahead of them, taunting them with her quickness. Still, the whole idea of the game unsettled Norah deeply.

"Chase the High Xara down? What sense does—that's not how it works." Norah told herself she hadn't given too much away by protesting. Everyone in Sestia knew the basic rituals of both the Sun

Rites and Moon Rites: the sacrifices, the blade, blood running onto the grain.

There was a pause before Darious said, "Well, maybe it should."

"I'm not sure what you're saying," Norah replied carefully.

"Look," he said, breathing out a sigh. "I don't know how things are on your farm. But around here, people are worried."

"About the Drought, of course."

"Worried," he said again, "and angry. Looking for someone to blame. That sorcerer at the rites said she'd caused the Drought. And someone killed her. So why isn't the Drought over?"

He was probably looking at her, but she was still watching the children. Enifer ran and ran, laughing. She glanced over at the temple from time to time, and began to work her way toward it, but whenever she made a beeline in its direction, another child reversed direction and moved to block her.

Norah said, "What do they do if they catch her? In the game?"

"They won't," Darious said. "She just has to touch the temple and she'll be safe."

"But if they catch her before she touches it?"

Darious said, "I wouldn't worry. Your daughter seems to have this well in hand."

Norah bit back the words *She's not my daughter* before she could say them. Truly Enifer was, since they were mother and daughter in the same household, but Norah felt she would never really think of anyone but the lost Olivi as her daughter.

The man's voice was relaxed, remarkably so, as he said, "Now, let's see those bones."

Unsure what else to do, Norah turned and gestured into the cart.

"May the Holy One honor us with Her blessings," Darious said as he pressed three fingertips lightly to his forehead. The familiar words sounded so different in his mellow tenor voice. Norah realized she'd never heard a man say them. The servants in the palace, the ones who tended the Xaras, had never said *honor us*. They'd said *honor you*. The Xaras themselves, and the Daras in the ranks below them, had said *honor us*, but of course their voices had all been women's voices.

As Norah watched, Darious climbed up into the back of the open cart for a closer look. With careful attention he inspected the bones. She watched him to see if he reacted to the sight of a child's bones among the animals', but he showed no surprise. She imagined he must have seen anything and everything by now.

He looked at her, then down at the bones around his feet again, then back at her. "I can give you two and a half sacks of ash in trade. Will that do?"

"All right," she said, adding, "I did tell you I don't know how this is done. I hardly think you would take me seriously if I tried to negotiate."

"Very well," he said. "Three."

She returned his smile as he hopped down from the cart. Ever since she'd left the service of the god, she'd marveled at how the holy and the mundane were all tangled up in one another. As a Xara she'd had so many rules, so many limits, such precision. Everything she had to do and everything she couldn't do were dictated. But that wasn't the way in the world. For most people, worship was breath, with no separation between serving Her and just living. Just look at how this man praised the Holy One, took actions of service, firmly rooted in the everyday.

They made the motion of agreement, clasping arms. His skin was warm, the wiry black hair on his forearm rough under her fingertips. Then he brought a broad white rectangle of rough-spun cloth to carry the load, showing her how to work the fabric underneath the loose heap of small and large skeletons. Once that was done, they each took two corners of the cloth and worked together to carry the bones into the temple, edging through the narrow door into an equally narrow space beyond.

She'd expected the temple to be dark within, but it was brighter than the clouded day. Nearly the entire room was taken up with a blazing firepit, the leaping orange flames rising from a squared-off bed of black charcoal and white bone ash. The heat was searing, a white-hot intensity that reached not just everywhere on her skin but behind her very eyes. If she didn't take care where she set her feet, Norah realized, her own bones might end up with the others.

Darious gestured for her to seat herself on her heels and fold her hands in her lap. She did so, edging toward the door as much as she could, both to give him room to work and to attempt to avoid the worst of the heat. No matter how close she got to the door, there was no breeze. She tried to put it out of her mind, focusing on the boneburning. It might not be the kind of holy rite she'd once been used to, but the god was everywhere Her people gathered, and the two of them were here for Her. The least Norah could do was be fully present.

She watched Darious lower the bones carefully into the pit, making gestures of thanks to the Holy One, as well as some gestures she hadn't seen before. They were somewhat related to the gestures the Xaras used in blessing the animals sacrificed during the Moon Rites, but not entirely the same. A long sweep of the arm, a sudden clasp and drop of both hands. Closed eyes. Bowed head. He seemed fully at home in the fire.

Norah hadn't prayed since the day Olivi was taken. She had made a kind of peace with the loss of her daughter, but at the same time, she felt a distance from the god that she had never felt before, even when Concordia had cast her out. All these months she had held herself back. Here in the fire, that distance no longer seemed important. Their lives all passed in a blink. Life was a gift the god gave, and when She took it back, they should be grateful they had the gift at all.

Forgive me my petty whims, oh Holy One, she whispered into the fire as the bones burned. *Her life belongs to You. My life belongs to You. This man's life belongs to You. Your will be done.*

And as had happened from time to time in her years as a Xara, Norah heard the soft whisper of a warm voice responding. Today, here in the heat of the fire, the voice said, *Patience.*

The joy that rushed into Norah at the sound of her god's voice was nearly as intense as the heat of boneburning.

Yes, patience. She could be patient, Norah told herself. The god's ways and wishes would be revealed in time.

When they came out into the cooler air again, Norah checked automatically to look for Enifer. She could see the children at a distance beyond the curve of the temple's gray-white brick. They seemed to be solemnly recreating the Sun Rites, the young woman striding forward with stately, regal steps.

"She's all right," came Darious's voice, not loud, from behind her.

"Of course," she murmured, and turned her attention back to him.

After the heat of the burning temple, Darious was lightly coated with beads of sweat, his thick, wavy hair wet with it. She could smell a little of his musk under the current of smoke that touched them both. Her own cheeks were still warm. She had the urge to reach out and touch him, to run her fingers along the sweat-dampened skin.

She considered indulging. There was no shame in it. She could imagine these particular hands on her waist, these lips on the hollow of her throat. But when he spoke, his words drove all thoughts of pleasure from her mind.

"I was here the day they took your daughter," he said. "I'm sorry. I know it's both a great honor and a great loss."

People were like motes of dust, thought Norah. Swirling through the air, borne by currents they could not see or understand. This man had been nothing to her yesterday. Today he'd excavated her greatest pain.

"I don't know why I assumed it was your sister," Norah said. Then she hunted for words, steeled herself to speak them aloud. "Is there anything you can tell me about that day?"

He gestured for her to help him fold the ceremonial cloth they'd used to carry the bones. She took two corners as he took the other two, stepping back to flatten out the large fabric rectangle. When he spoke again, his voice was quieter.

"I don't think so. I imagine her uncle told you how it went," Darious said, bringing the two corners in his hands together to make a fold, then transferring one hand to the newly made corner, pulling the fabric flat again.

"Not much." Norah mimicked his movements, working as she spoke. She echoed the first fold, then completed a second, so the cloth that stretched between them flattened into a long, thin rectangle. She didn't want to have this conversation, which brought her faded pain roaring back to life. But this would be her only chance. She made herself think about that day, that girl. "There wasn't anything he, or you, could have done about it. If the god wanted her . . ."

He stepped toward her and her steps automatically echoed his, until they stood close, hands at the corners of the fabric touching. He said, "Well, if the god wanted her, but the Xara didn't kill her, maybe that's why we still only have boys."

Norah's mouth went dry. "The Xara didn't kill her?"

"That's what I heard. I can't promise it's the truth, but it's what someone told me." Their hands were still touching. He hadn't taken the corners of the fabric from her fingers.

"Someone you trust?"

"As much as I trust anyone." It wasn't an answer. Now his fingertips moved under hers, pushing the fabric into her hands.

Her body was steady but her mind tilted and swirled. She took the corners of the cloth and stepped back so Darious could pull the newly created fold taut.

Alongside her awakened pain, Norah felt something small come to life inside her: a tendril of hope.

The cool air felt soothing on her face. Darious was about to step back toward her, and then the folding of the ceremonial fabric would be complete. After that there would be no reason for Norah to linger. Her hope and pain would both have to be folded away with the cloth, for now.

The shouts of the children rose again, sharper this time, and the sound made Norah shiver.

Darious's voice was gruff as he said, "The High Xara failed, and the Holy One is still angry."

"But the High Xara listens to the Holy One's words," Norah told him, feeling a sudden anger prickling under her skin. "They speak directly. If the High Xara didn't complete the sacrifices of a typical Sun Rites, it's because the Holy One didn't want them."

"But how could that be? If the High Xara did what the Holy One wanted, why are there still no girls?"

Norah considered that for a minute, still angry on behalf of her friend. How dare this man question the High Xara's decisions—the Holy One's decisions? But then again, if the Holy One were contented, why did the Drought still plague both their queendom and the others? Only minutes before, in the fire, the voice of the god had counseled patience. She would do what her god asked of her.

"Only the Holy One knows," she said at last. "It isn't for us to decide. If the Drought continues for another year, even a generation, it will be because She has a reason."

With a mirthless smile, Darious said, "Well, I hope She changes Her mind soon."

Then Enifer ran past them in a blur, the children hot on her heels. Teresh's daughter leapt forward, splaying out the fingers of her hand, and slapped her palm against the brick of the temple.

"Safe!" she crowed.

Norah took one more look at Darious, his face no longer coy, his expression unreadable. Then she searched the faces of the children around them, panting, frustrated, denied their sport.

Safe? Norah, feeling more like Xara Veritas than she had in years, decided she wasn't so sure.

Patience, she reminded herself. That was what the Holy One had asked for. She would do her best to give it.

A few months later, when word reached their farm that the first Sestian girl in a generation had been born to a shepherd in the west, Norah thought of that game that the boys at the boneburner's had played. Would they stop playing now? Would they devise a new game that celebrated the High Xara instead of endangering her?

Thank you, Holy One, for the blessing of girls, Norah prayed.

And the god's voice, warm but firm, said, *One day I will ask more than thanks from you.*

✦ CHAPTER 9 ✦

AFTER THE AMBUSH

After the first Battle of Hayk, the All-Mother's Year 517
The Underlands
Paulus

Paulus, the former kingling of Paxim whose life had been cut short in a Scorpican ambush outside Hayk, would rather be alive. Of course he would. Even so, as a dead man, he began living something that felt very much like a new life.

Initially, after he crossed the bone bridge into the vast Underlands, he spent a long time moping. He missed Ama more than he'd ever thought possible. Every moment, every movement, reminded him what he'd lost. He obsessed over the profound mistake he'd made. What he would do differently if he were offered the chance to return to his last days and live them over again.

He'd been an overconfident fool. Riding out to face the Scorpicae in battle, even with the King's Elite at his back? He hadn't been ready. Ama had told him exactly that. And instead of trusting her, believing her, he'd snuck off in the night and flung himself into a fight he couldn't win. Any idiot could have seen the most likely result. So instead of living a full life alongside the woman he adored, Paulus was dead at the hands of the queen of Scorpica, and instead of a man, he was a shade.

But as long as he was a shade mired in the Underlands, surrounded by all the people who had ever lived, shouldn't he make the most of it?

He realized that he could wander the underworld's vastness, simply going and going and going with no limit. He didn't need to stop for food or drink. His body didn't tire because he had no body. And he'd always wondered what the real people behind the stories he'd loved were like. And what about the people who'd never made it into the history books? What were their stories?

He could ask them, now that he was here.

Paulus had the knowledge and the will to find every hero he'd ever wondered about. He had infinite time. And now he was putting that time to the best use he could think of.

The shade of Paulus found the shade of the man who had saved Queen Theodora with the plant that only he grew, the man all the stories had left unnamed. His name was Oscuro. Paulus passed innumerable hours in the company of Alev and Vela, whose tale he had read until the pages wore through. But he spent just as much time talking with people, especially men, who had lived full and interesting lives but left no clear mark on history. He recorded the stories of Sestian boneburners, Bastionite scholars, Paximite tradesmen. He traveled all over and he kept himself ready and open to learn new things. And even as he missed Ama down to his core, he had to admit, his real life had rarely felt so satisfying.

Then, during his explorations, he caught sight of something he recognized from the many stories he'd read: the First Gate to the Underlands. Here, he supposed, it was the first gate back to the living world. At first he thought he must be mistaken, that it wasn't actually the first gate, even though it perfectly fit the description. Because there was supposed to be a Voa standing guard, a woman as translucent as ice with hair and eyes that matched the midnight sky, and there was no such thing.

Instead, two shades waited in front of the gate, one seated and one appearing to float. Neither of them matched the stories' descriptions of the Voa, the guardians that kept shades and living bodies alike from passing through the locked gates. These appeared to be ordinary shades. Vague around the edges, so probably long dead. Thin enough to see through.

"What are you waiting for?" Paulus asked. He'd noticed that his voice sounded different in the Underlands than he remembered in life; there was a new depth to it, a more rounded timbre.

The floating shade looked at him and said, "Go away. We were here first."

"Actually," the seated shade said, "we weren't."

"We were here before he was," the floating shade responded, addressing his companion.

"Yes, but," and here the seated shade raised a finger. There was something about them that reminded Paulus of his teachers in the Bastion, a scholarly air. "To be precise, there were others here before us. But they left."

"Oh?" asked Paulus. He focused on the seated shade, since they seemed the more willing to talk. "Why did they leave?"

"Got tired of waiting."

Paulus ventured, "But you think it's worth waiting for?"

"Why wouldn't it be?" said the seated shade.

The floating shade interrupted, "If you don't agree, then don't wait. Who knows how long it'll be? And you're third. So you could wait three times as long."

"He can count," sniped the seated shade, the first time their voice had sounded anything other than friendly.

"How do you know?" the floating shade shot back. "We don't know him. He could be a murderer! A priest of the God of Death! Some Arcan queen's pleasure vessel! Anyone!"

"I'm the kingling of Paxim," said Paulus, then added, "Well, I was."

This seemed not to endear him to either shade. The floating one said, "Well, now you're just one of us, aren't you?"

Paulus had to agree. "Yes."

After a pause, the seated one said, gently, "If we get through this gate, it's not like living, anyway."

He perked up. "What is it, then?"

The floating one answered, still irritated, their words sharp. "Close as we're going to get! Now step back."

Automatically, Paulus complied, making sure he didn't seem to be any kind of threat. But now he was burning with curiosity. "You think you'll get through eventually, though."

"Someone did," said the seated one. "Just one."

"Two, actually," corrected the floating one, as if they couldn't help themselves. They both reminded him of his Bastionite instructors now. If he had to guess, he'd say that was where both of them were from. Down here it hardly seemed to matter. Whatever queendom they belonged to Above, they all ended up in the same underworld.

The seated one cocked their head. "Two?"

"The first one, remember?" The floating one had an exasperated tone. Paulus was glad to know he wasn't the only one to earn this shade's disdain; they seemed like they'd been a prickly person all along. "The one who went Above, they said she was a Scorpican, I think, and then she was dead again so quickly?"

"That's right," the seated one said. "She was sent up as a test. Eresh wasn't very happy."

Paulus said, with wonder, "You know Eresh?"

"Not personally," said the floating one, with such a condescending air that Paulus felt like a fool for asking.

More gently, the seated one said, "We just hear. Word gets around. You keep your ear to the ground around here, you can learn a lot."

"I'll keep that in mind."

The seated one went on, "They opened the first gate. That's why there's no Voa here."

"Who opened it?"

"That we don't know. But does it matter? It's open."

"Right," said Paulus, "but is it? If it's open, what are you waiting for? Why don't you go through?"

The floating one glared. "Someone has to die."

"People die all the—"

"In Godsbones," the floating one interrupted. "And now that the Scorpicae have gone home, how many people do you think are running around Godsbones?"

"Not many," he answered automatically, and then said, "I'm sorry, you said the Scorpicae went home?"

"Like we said," the seated one told him, not unkindly. "You need to start listening."

"I will. I promise. Only . . . I didn't know that. The war is over?"

"It is."

"Who won?"

The seated one seemed to consider this, and said, "Everyone who's not dead, I suppose."

A cruel joke, thought Paulus, but not untrue.

The floating one added, "As we heard it, there was never any declared war, so there was never any official surrender. There was a siege and a battle—lots of new arrivals that day—then after that, nothing. So then we heard that whatever it was, it was over."

"So it was all for nothing," Paulus couldn't help saying. He'd died along with hundreds of others, maybe thousands. "All that death and destruction, for nothing to change?"

"It changed things for the Scorpican queen," said the seated one. "She's dead."

"Tamura?" The death of the woman who'd killed Paulus brought him no satisfaction. He had placed himself in her path.

"I think so. Was she the second one or not?" the floating one asked his companion.

The seated one said, "The second one who went up? It was a Scorpican queen, that's what I heard, but I don't know if it was the same one."

"What happened to the second one who went up? She hasn't come back yet?"

"As far as we know."

Paulus considered this. Even the seated shade was running out of patience, he realized, so perhaps he should be on his way. But he first looked up at the gate, then down at the shades.

He asked them, "Someone needs to die for you to rise, is that right? That's what you said?"

"Yes," chorused both shades, one affirming, one annoyed.

"In Godsbones," he said.

"Yes."

"Why? Is there a fixed number of souls Above?" That sort of thing was sometimes in the stories. A need for balance.

"The soul can't travel up without a body," said the seated one. "The soul can pass through the gate only when a fresh body becomes available, right after its previous soul leaves. But a newly dead body isn't very useful, from what we know. You can't make it talk, even. You can see through its eyes, move its limbs—"

"But not perfectly," the floating one interrupted. "It only kind of obeys. That's what the Scorpican told Ercsh."

"Right. You're in the body, but it's not as easy as it was the first time you were alive."

"It sounds very limiting," agreed Paulus, but if he'd had a heart in his chest, he bet it would have started beating faster. "Not like living at all."

"Not much."

He would probably offend them with his question, but he couldn't help but ask it. "Then why are you waiting?"

The shades looked at each other. It was the floating one who answered. "It's the only chance we've got, isn't it?"

Paulus waved goodbye and left the two shades waiting there. He went back to his project, talking with both the ordinary people and heroes he met to hear their tales. But from time to time, he went out of his way to curve back past the first gate. The first three times, he found both shades still there. The fourth time, the floating one had gone.

"Did they rise?" he asked the seated one hopefully.

The seated one, sadder now, shook their head. Was it his imagination, or did their shade seem less substantial? "No. They got tired of waiting."

"And you didn't?"

"I'm tired," the seated one said, "but not tired enough yet."

✦

Time passed differently in the Underlands, but it seemed like at least a year had passed by the time Paulus started daring to hope for another chance at walking Above.

It happened while he was talking to the shade of a man called Septin.

Septin had died a few months before Paulus, in an accident at a Paximite military training camp. His name wasn't written down in any books—except the Bastion's records of births and deaths, Paulus supposed—nor was he remembered as a hero. One didn't need to be renowned to have a story worth telling.

"Tell me everything," Paulus said, carefully balancing the writing pad on his knee. The wonderful thing about the Underlands, unlike the world Above, was that his ink would never run dry. His hand didn't cramp, his eyes didn't burn with the effort of focusing on small print. Down here, he could write and read forever.

"I was so eager to join the force," Septin said, staring off into the distance. "My wife told me not to, that I was needed at home, but I thought she was just trying to keep me around to do the household work she didn't want to do. Maybe if the children had been younger, I would have listened. But the boy was nine and the girl was seven, and I thought, 'Oh, she can handle this herself, it's not like when I was up with them all night.' And I . . . I was resentful. I wanted to do something where it was just me. And I'd always thought the Scorpicae were so interesting. Before the Drought, you know, they ran the patrols in our neighborhood, and I just loved to watch them. So powerful. I thought joining the Paximite army, training with weapons, would give me some of that power."

Paulus looked up, and considered signaling his understanding with a nod, but Septin still wasn't looking in his direction.

"So I left. Took half the family coin—I felt like I deserved it—and whatever else I could fit into a pack."

Paulus wrote this down dutifully. He didn't approve of the man's choice to take money his family needed. He could only imagine how the head of the household felt when she found out. But the kingling also recognized he'd never really been in a position to need money, so he couldn't really judge, could he?

He looked up to see that Septin was looking at him now, his expression soft and questioning. "Not much of a story, really. Maybe I don't need to tell you the rest."

"Please do. Let's not stop now. What happened next?"

Septin shrugged, reluctance creeping into his voice. "Same old story, I'm sure you've heard this part from others."

"Try me," said Paulus. "It's different because it happened to you."

That seemed to help the man firm his resolve. "I reported to the nearest recruiting center. They welcomed me in, had me sign my mark to some papers, packed me into a wagon with the other recruits. Women and men, but a lot more men than women. All of us looking for something."

"Looking for something?"

"Who joins up otherwise? And I talked to those on the left and right of me. One whose sister had thrown him out, another tired of working day in and day out on someone else's farm, a youngster with six brothers who wanted to start contributing to the household. Common stories."

"Why were the women joining up? Did they say?" Paulus was curious.

Septin gave him a blank look, as if it hadn't occurred to him that the women might have reasons.

Paulus gestured. "Sorry. Go on."

"At first, it was everything I wanted. Sense of purpose. And I was good at it too." His voice was a little defensive, as if Paulus had accused him otherwise. "The staff was my weapon. Everyone wanted to learn the sword, but there weren't enough swords to go around by that point, and you could always count on having a staff around. So we all started with that, and I liked it so much I asked to keep with it."

Paulus nodded. He wrote everything down, and, when he'd finished, looked up to cue Septin.

But Septin was getting to the harder part of the story. His reluctance was written all over his face.

"We were just clowning, you understand. Blowing off steam. It wasn't his fault, you know."

"Of course it wasn't," said Paulus, then asked, "Who?"

"Our commander, we called him the Bull. He kept this stash of hammerwine in his bunk. And . . ." Septin trailed off. "You know what, I don't think I want to tell the rest."

Paulus tried his best to be patient. "Let's not leave the story unfinished."

Septin leapt to his feet. "But it is!" he blurted. "It always will be!"

"I don't understand."

The shade of the dead Paximite paced. "The story of the life I would have had. It was one stupid mistake. It was supposed to be a prank, the others dared me to do it. It was late at night, we'd been drinking, and I crawled through the window of the Bull's bunk to steal his hammerwine, but he woke up and he saw a shape he didn't know in the dark. . . ."

Septin was right. Paulus didn't need to hear the very end to know what had happened. And it wasn't right, it wasn't fair, but it had happened anyway. No more life.

Paulus said, "And the story of your life will always be unfinished. Because you didn't get to live it."

"Exactly," said Septin, his eyes shining with tears. The excitement had drained away, leaving the shade looking defeated. For the first time, Paulus regretted asking someone their story. He had meant this act as a kindness when it had turned out to be anything but.

"If I had to do it over again," asked Septin, "you know what I'd do?"

Live, thought Paulus. But he asked, "What?"

"I wouldn't have left. I would have stayed home. I would have lived happily with my family and never asked for anything more."

Paulus tried to find a soothing voice. He told the shade, "It's easy to see now what would have been wiser."

Septin said, his voice disgusted, "And because of my foolishness, my son's life was changed too. That's what I don't forgive myself for."

"We change everyone we meet." It was a platitude, but it wasn't untrue.

"Not just that," Septin said, waving his hand dismissively. "He was my son. He needed me and I deserted him. Left him alone in that house of women, without a man to guide him. No going back."

Paulus echoed, "No going back."

Then something changed in Septin's manner. He seemed to shake off his melancholy, then said, "At least, that's what I thought."

"I'm sorry." Paulus had lost the thread of the conversation. "You thought what?"

"That I couldn't go back. But there's a chance now," said Septin.

"A chance?"

"To live again. They say it's going to be possible. When she opens the second gate."

"Who?" asked Paulus, struggling to keep his voice level. "Who's opening the second gate? Eresh?"

"Of course not. I don't remember her name. Let me ask—oh, Novus might know." He hailed a shade with a long silver plait in the distance. "Novus! Here!"

The shade of Novus eyed Paulus suspiciously, but when Septin beckoned again, he came. "Septin."

"What was the name of that sorcerer who's going to open the second gate?"

The suspicion on Novus's face didn't go away. "Can the boy be trusted?"

"It's a *rumor*," laughed Septin. "It's not a troop movement. What's her name?"

Novus bristled. "Well, if it's not that important, you don't need me to tell him then, do you?"

"Sorry. Sorry, Novus. You've got the good intelligence. And yes, he can be trusted. He's a good one."

Paulus didn't know what constituted a "good one" in this man's world, but he did his best to look innocent and trustworthy. "I'm just intrigued," he said honestly. "I hadn't heard anything about this sorcerer, and I thought I knew a lot. So anything you know, I'd be grateful to hear."

This seemed to appease the older man. Novus said, "They say there's a sorcerer with a plan to open the second gate. I don't know her name."

"Did she open the first gate?"

"Some say she did, some say she didn't," Novus said. Then, seeming to consider first, he added, "I think she didn't. If she'd opened the first, why wait to open the second?"

"Makes sense," Paulus said, his mind turning the question over and over. "But are there any details on the plan?"

"Not that I heard," Novus said. "Just that she's plenty powerful."

"If I were a sorcerer who didn't have a great plan for doing something," Paulus said, "that's exactly the rumor I'd spread."

This put a grin on Novus's face, and he barked a laugh. "True enough. People only ever want to join a winning team; even dead people, yeah?"

"Exactly. But if I wanted to join this sorcerer's team," said Paulus, "do the rumors say where to find her?"

"No," said Novus, "but you look bright enough. I'm sure you can guess."

Paulus was, and he did.

He found the sorcerer where he expected, standing opposite the second gate at a fair distance, staring it down. The gate was a high stone arch, enormous. At this distance, from the side, it appeared empty; but when Paulus changed the angle of his approach to face directly toward the highest point of the arch, a massive creature shimmered into view.

It was so startling, Paulus leapt back and shook his head to clear the sight. He turned his back on the arch itself and hastened toward the clump of rocks near where the sorcerer was standing, regarding the gate, and now, regarding him.

He had never seen her in life, didn't know whether she had appeared Above as an older woman with snow-white hair, but he knew without a doubt who she was. What other sorcerer would be so furious and so confident that she would assume herself able to upend the entire structure of life and death? Only Sessadon.

For a moment, he paused. This sorcerer had caused the Drought of Girls, which had destroyed so many lives across the entirety of the five queendoms. Without the drought, no Scorpican invasion of Paxim; without the invasion, he wouldn't have met death at the Scorpican queen Tamura's hands. Then again, without the Drought, would he ever have met and loved Ama? He could never regret knowing the love of his life.

"Hello," Paulus said.

The shade of the sorcerer turned away and ignored him, looking up at the arch again, examining it.

He tried again, his voice more pointed. "Hello, Sessadon."

That got her attention. "Who are you?"

"You're intelligent enough. You can guess."

She looked him up and down then, and he tried to see himself as she would. He'd chosen to keep the form he'd had at the time of his death. He'd shed the armor and the black horsehair helmet, kept only the tunic and leggings beneath. But these were a deep purplish blue, the color of a sky after sunset. He saw the moment she realized she was speaking to Paximite royalty.

"Ah, I see," she said. "The famous kingling. What brings you here?"

He gestured toward the gate, its arch soaring high above them. "I hear you're trying to open that."

"Ah. You've got your ear to the ground, don't you?"

"Is it true?"

"What difference does it make to you?"

Paulus knew he had only one chance to get this right. He'd thought it through from every angle. He tried to imagine what his mother, a strategic and diplomatic genius, would do in his position. And he'd decided that offering Sessadon a deal would make her too suspicious. It was a deal, of course—he wasn't so selfless as he wanted to seem—but if she saw it as a transaction, she'd be quick to try to cheat him out of what he was trying to gain. If she didn't realize what he was getting out of it, she couldn't take it away.

So Paulus simply said, "I can be helpful."

"With the Gate of Warriors? You're not a warrior."

He pretended to consider this. "True."

The sorcerer said, "Then you're useless to me. Go away."

Paulus pressed, "But the next one."

"I'm not thinking about the next one."

"You should be. Always think ahead. After you open the Gate of Warriors, you'll have to open the Gate of Heroes. Right?"

"Right," she said, without conviction.

Paulus boasted, "I know all the heroes. Every story that was ever written about the brave women and men of the past. Semma and Ellimi and Khalimah of Scorpica, Paxim's soldier queen Theodora and the Dreaming Queen, Marisemi, the genius Devorah of the Bastion, every Arcan all-magic queen going all the way back to Kruvesis."

Was it his imagination, or did a flicker of annoyance cross the shade's face when he mentioned that last name? He noted it and pressed on.

"I see," she said, sounding bored. But he caught a false note in her voice when she added, "All the great heroes, of every nation. You think they might be the key to opening the Gate of Heroes?"

"Why wouldn't they be?" He realized he sounded eager now, but it was true, he was eager, and it wasn't a crime to let it show. "They're all dead. They're all shades. They're all here. I can help you find whoever you need to help you open that gate."

"And you don't want anything in return?"

"No."

She looked skeptical, but he could tell she was interested. He was offering something she needed.

"Please, sorcerer," said Paulus. "I just want to help."

"I don't need your help," she said.

He shrugged, but he knew she was more conflicted than she let on. He would never have associated with a person this terrible, not knowingly, during his living days.

But they weren't Above anymore, were they? And he might not be the only one willing to do things they'd never imagined themselves doing in their days Above.

He would wait. Certainly, down here, he had nothing but time.

✦ CHAPTER 10 ✦

A VISITOR

Autumn, The All-Mother's Year 517,
after the second battle of Hayk
Holy City, Sestia
Olivi, Concordia

As luxurious as Olivi's life in the Edifice was in the year after Concordia took her in, every day felt fragile. She wanted for nothing, and Concordia kept her close, but she had no official status and no certainty about her future. Once the Drought ended and news of girls being born all across the queendoms flowed freely again, Olivi was hopeful she might learn more about Concordia's intent.

Yet things only seemed to get worse. Concordia had become suspicious of the Daras, complaining under her breath to Olivi that they were plotting to replace her. Instead of celebrating the end of the Drought, Concordia seemed to resent it, her suspicion blossoming into a kind of paranoia. Olivi might have fled the Edifice altogether but for one thing: the voice of the Holy One in her head had told her, *Stay. Stay and be wise.*

So when a servant with flashing, kohl-lined eyes and a bounty of shoulder-length curls brought word that Eminel, queen of Arca, had presented herself alone at the door of the Edifice, in the same breath that Concordia muttered, "Send her away," Olivi asked, "What does she want?"

The interruption made Concordia turn her head toward her young companion. Her gaze could be penetrating, and right now it was almost unbearable. Still, Olivi met her eyes and held them. The voice of the god in her head was whispering, *Let the magician in.*

Concordia asked, in a falsely light tone, "What did you say, Olivi?"

"I was just wondering," said Olivi, matching her tone to the High Xara's. "She's come a long way. It might be worth seeing what she wants. You've heard the rumors of war. What if she's come to ask for help?"

"Help?" said Concordia. "Let her god help her."

"All right. That makes sense. Only . . . our god is sister to hers. If I had a sister, I might be more inclined to help her than to help a stranger, I suppose."

"Do you have a sister?"

"No," said Olivi, choosing her words with the utmost care. "You are my only family. I know I would help you without question. But you're right, I don't exactly know what sisters do, after all."

Her deference seemed to put Concordia in a generous mood. "I suppose family might consider helping family." She turned to address the servant. His name, Olivi believed, was Emalio, though she had noticed Concordia had stopped addressing any of the servants by name. "Do we know, then? What she requests?"

Emalio bobbed his head, setting his loose hair waving. "She said that she would only speak to you, and that only you will understand her request."

Concordia's expression was still tinted with disdain.

The god in Olivi's head said, *Make her see.*

"Queen to queen," Olivi said in a musing voice, as if it were only occurring to her in the moment. "One of your very few peers. She asks no more than equal recognition. I wonder if the Holy One would want us to hear what she has to say."

"You wonder?"

"I can only wonder, of course. You're the only one who knows. Should we go to the *lacrum* to ask her?"

"No harm in meeting the Arcan queen, I suppose," Concordia said, as if she'd thought of it herself, and perhaps she believed she had.

The servant bobbed his head again. "Shall I send her in?"

"A suggestion, High Xara?" Olivi said quietly.

The High Xara said nothing, but inclined her head slightly, which was enough.

So Olivi went ahead, speaking so only the High Xara could hear. "The prayer room. Might be more fitting."

"The prayer room," Concordia said to the servant.

"Right away."

By the time Emalio brought the visiting queen to them, the High Xara and Olivi waited in the prayer room, as penitent and humble to their god as anyone might hope to see. Olivi hesitated to speak directly to the young woman, but she observed her with hungry eyes, devouring every detail of her appearance and demeanor.

The young queen of Arca didn't, at first, look like a queen. Her clothes were plain and clearly coated with dirt from the road. And she smelled like horse, Olivi noted with surprise. Had she been riding? What an odd way to approach. And with no guards, no entourage, no indication whatsoever that she was royal.

Her demeanor, too, was not what Olivi expected; she was staring frankly at Emalio in a way that no one in the Edifice would have dared. Olivi had to admit, the man was worth staring at, his fine figure on display in his short tunic, but it wasn't proper to gawk so openly.

The time had come to speak. Concordia wasn't saying anything, so Olivi took the chance. As sharply as she dared, she addressed the foreign queen. "Their beauty is not for us."

Queen Eminel turned at that, looking suitably chagrined, and transferred her attention wholly to Concordia and Olivi herself. Olivi could see her evaluating the pair and coming to her own conclusions. Olivi often wondered how she looked to others, what they thought of her, but it was really only the High Xara's opinion that mattered. And, of course, their god's.

The silence was deafening to Olivi. It seemed that she would, again, have to be the one to speak. She had the feeling there should be some sort of formal acknowledgment that a queen had come to call, and though she didn't know the right words for it, she could at least use the Arcan queen's proper title. "You are Queen Eminel, Well of All-Magic, Master of Sand, and Destroyer of Fear."

"I am," confirmed the queen.

Olivi went on, sticking to the facts in an attempt not to wrong-foot international diplomacy with no preparation or experience. "You travel without a Queensguard."

"I do." The queen used one hand to reach inside the other cuff of her robe, rubbing at something, though Olivi couldn't see what.

Time for questions instead of statements. "And are you a priest as—"

Then, the High Xara's voice, irritated. "Enough interruption! We should be communing with the Holy One. I don't know why we would waste any time conversing with worshippers of Velja."

Olivi hated to disagree with Concordia publicly, and she knew Concordia hated it too, but she had no choice. The god had told her what to do.

She pressed on, subtly positioning herself between the High Xara and the exit. "But High Xara, the messenger said this queen has come all the way here to ask us a favor. Perhaps it is a favor the Holy One wishes us to grant."

"State your purpose, then," the High Xara said to Eminel. "I alone will decide." Reinforcing her position, her power.

The young queen's words were quick, unpolished. "I wish to know where the body of Sessadon is buried."

Olivi winced. Why would this queen want the sorcerer's body? And why in the world would the Holy One want her to have it? She rushed to object before Concordia could. "Impossible. The High Xara cannot and will not reveal sacred secrets."

Brushing the yellow streak of hair back from her forehead, the High Xara said, "If the Holy One wanted me to help you, She would have said so. The god speaks to me and only me, and I do as She commands."

"You do your god's work. I do mine," said Eminel. "The only difference is which sister we heed. We are alike."

More answers just led to more questions. Why did *Velja* want this? Were the sister-gods in pursuit of the same goal, some goal that was not yet clear to their earthly followers?

Concordia's voice was steady, her eyes narrow. She said to Queen Eminel, "We are nothing alike."

"We are both queens, are we not?" asked Eminel rhetorically. "We are both our God's chosen."

Olivi winced internally again. The Arcan queen could hardly have said anything worse, as far as the High Xara was concerned. The pain on Concordia's face was evident to Olivi, though she hoped it meant nothing to Eminel.

Then Concordia beckoned half-heartedly to Olivi, indicating that she should follow. "Come, Olivi. We have given the foreign queen enough of our time. The God appreciates our charity, but now She desires proof of our dedication. Let us go provide what matters."

Olivi lingered while Concordia closed her eyes and bobbed her head toward the Arcan queen, a minor sign of respect at best. Automatically Olivi repeated the motion.

The word leapt into her brain, sharp, almost painful. *Now.*

So Olivi reached out and grabbed the Arcan queen's wrist, demanding her attention in the only way she could think to try. The god was not in the habit of directing her this closely. This must be important. She dared not disobey, even if she risked Concordia's wrath. But luckily, Concordia seemed not to have noticed, her back already turned. Whatever Olivi did, she'd best do it quickly.

And the god told her exactly what to do.

Olivi mouthed words for Queen Eminel, first once, then a second time just in case she hadn't been clear. *Read. My. Mind.*

She felt the queen's presence inside her head almost immediately; it was difficult not to stagger under the intrusion. But an equally strong presence—the god's—was bolstering her, strengthening her. The god told her what to think, in words and pictures both.

The tombs in the northwest of the city. The entrance is hidden; there are no guards. Here is how you open the door.

An image of the trick door, its heavy bolt concealing a special catch known only to High Xaras, and now the two of them.

The rest is yours to do.

The path to the tombs, across the city and out of it. The way for Queen Eminel to find what she sought.

Then the god's presence was gone from Olivi's mind, and after a moment, the queen's mind subsided as well. There was nothing left to say. Exhausted, Olivi turned to follow Concordia, who shot her a look of annoyance but said nothing. In silence, she trailed the High Xara, careful to give nothing away.

Good, said the Holy One. *Well done.*

When Olivi later heard that the Arcan queen now sported a quartz hand, she would think back to that day, to that moment where, with her god's help, she'd shown the foreign queen what to do. She didn't fully understand what had happened, but she didn't need to.

She knew that she, not Concordia, had been chosen to help. It struck fear in her heart, because if Concordia would never yield the reins of power, did that mean the Holy One would one day require Olivi to take them from her by force?

Before she prayed, she carefully emptied her mind of that question. It was one she didn't want the Holy One to answer.

♦

In the days of the Drought, Concordia would have consulted Xelander, asking for his thoughts on the foreign queen's unannounced visit. But those days were over. The things she'd done in those dark years, the actions she'd taken to keep power, which he'd made sound so reasonable, now felt repulsive.

With the benefit of hindsight, she thought she understood her mistake. She'd treated him as an equal when he was no such thing. That would never happen again. She might dally with him from time to time—the feeling of flesh on flesh had lost none of its appeal, was still exquisite—but only when she chose, and she never let him speak a word. Their pleasures, on the rare occasions she decided to indulge, had taken on an air of punishment.

The only person whose company she could stand anymore was Olivi, who she kept close. Besides Xelander—and what a mistake trusting him had turned out to be—the only person Concordia had ever kept so close was the former Xara Veritas, small-statured and bighearted. But of course Concordia had exiled Veritas, shamed and rebuked her. Threatened her life—and her child's—and sent her away. During the dark years of the Drought, Concordia had even wondered if it had been that action, that banishment, that had earned the god's disfavor. When the sorcerer, with blazing eyes, had shouted her guilt at the Sun Rites of the Bloody-Handed, Concordia had been as aghast as anyone. But under her shock, she had to admit to herself that in that stew of emotions, she'd also felt relief. The God of Plenty had had nothing to do with the Drought, just as Concordia had said publicly all along, even if she'd had her doubts in private.

And now that the Drought had ended, its immediate threat gone, a new, unspoken question pulsed inside the High Xara's mind. Who would succeed her? The usual system, the class of five-year-old Xaras-to-be, had been disrupted. Concordia had thought through all the possibilities. She knew the Daras were eager to discuss them too, which was why she had stopped engaging with them.

She was beginning to realize that no successor to the priesthood could truly satisfy her, not when what she wanted was to remain High Xara without end.

She had no use for the guilt and confusion that had once crippled her. She would own her ambitions and she would discard anything that didn't serve her. Right now, what served her was to make her world small.

So she often prayed with Olivi, but she also spent hours praying on her own, going to the *lacrum* again and again, remaining there for an hour or more each time. Sometimes she went in the morning and again in the afternoon. She went once in the middle of the night, only a candle lighting her way to the silent altar, the shadows around her alive with imagined whispers from every quarter. She had held the candle over the God's Well and watched the reflection of its tiny, flickering flame wink up at her from the depths. Even then, even in that vast expanse of darkness, nothing came to her. She had never stopped praying in earnest, despite the lack of attention from the god.

It would be easier if she didn't believe, she told herself as she knelt in the *lacrum*, her poor knees aching. If she were just an impostor with no feeling for the god. But she was a High Xara who didn't deserve to be a High Xara, desperate for the approval and blessing of the god she served, and every day she felt hollowed-out that the god she loved did not seem, in any way, to love her back.

"I do everything I should," she whispered angrily, her hands cupping the bowl of God's Tears. "Why won't you speak to me?"

She lifted the bowl to throw it—but even as it rose a few inches in the air, sloshing the precious water in fat droplets against the marble, she knew she wouldn't follow through. She might have broken the god's most holy commandment, but she still believed, as she had believed all these years, in the divinity of the Holy One. Her objects were sacred and to break them would dishonor the god she loved.

Concordia replaced the bowl where it belonged, setting it down gently, and mopped up the spilled water with the altar cloth. She would have to stay in the room until it dried, or someone would ask about it. Just for a moment, as she looked up, the *lacrum* felt to her like a tomb, a marble vault into which she had been sealed while she waited to die.

Concordia shivered with the morbid thought.

She pulled her robe up around her shoulders. The spring had been a chilly one. The action stirred a breeze against her shoulders, and the scent of attar of roses drifted up to her.

She was not entombed. She was alive. She was High Xara. And as long as that was true, she would need to make decisions. They were hard but they were hers. If she didn't want to rule, all she had to do was choose a successor. She could do it today. Hand over the rule of the country and be High Xara no more.

Former High Xaras chose their own way. Some even raised families, if the god blessed them. After all, if they were no longer Xaras, their chastity was no longer at issue. They might establish their own households or join another, establish a walking marriage, set themselves up in business as boneburners, do whatever they liked.

Many of the former rulers, however, chose to keep the precepts in whatever part of Sestia they settled. Some remained in the palace for years after their rule was done, unwilling or unable to leave service once they'd begun. Every High Xara knew the tale of Puglalia, who refused to choose a successor from among the Xaras-to-be of her time until she was nearly fifty years of age, and who never left the palace after, wandering the halls as her mind went. It was said that she never understood why her robes were pale ivory instead of saffron, complaining that a servant had laundered the color out of her robes and must be punished for it. She lurked near the halls of power for so long that it was said the color leached from her body and hair, turning her pale as a spirit. And so, when she died, her ghost walked the halls for weeks before anyone realized it was her spirit and not her real body, which was discovered in a small, locked closet she'd apparently mistaken for the harbor of the *lacrum*.

But that was an old story. One never knew the truth of old stories, thought Concordia. What stories would be told about her once she was gone?

Should she leave the service and find out?

But even as she asked the question, she answered it. No, she would remain. There was nothing for her out in the world.

She rose with a heavy sigh and inspected the altar cloth. It was dry now. The bowl was no worse off for her fantasy of throwing it; its pale, smooth shape was unmarred. The flat surface of the clear water inside, calm as a cloudless sky, reflected back a vague but steady image of her face. She saw the oval shape of it framed by dark hair, the saffron streak the palest thing about her next to the whites of her eyes. But even her eyes and mouth were hard to make out in this light. She lowered her face until the tip of her nose almost touched the water.

"You're a fool," she said to herself. Pursing her lips, she blew across the water's surface. Ripples interrupted her reflection and broke it apart.

She poured the contents of the bowl back down into the well, leaving only a thin layer of water in the bowl's bottom, and set it in the center of the altar. The next day she would check it for patterns. That was what a High Xara was expected to do.

She was the High Xara Concordia. Who else was she ever fit to be?

✦ CHAPTER 11 ✦

THE REGENT AND THE INFANT

The All-Mother's Years 517 and 518

Ursu, Paxim

Stellari

In the autumn of the All-Mother's Year 517, Stellari of Calladocia, regent of Paxim and the most powerful woman in the queendom—perhaps in all five queendoms put together—began to find the mismatch between what she'd sown and what she'd reaped becoming unbearable.

She had always been good at imagining outcomes. Planning ahead. Setting wheels in motion to achieve a far-off goal. But now that she had all the power she'd been scheming for, there was nowhere to go but down.

It wasn't that she had no one to share her power with. That had never been important to her. She had allowed Rahul to matter to her, yes; but they'd been growing apart for years, ever since Aster's birth. Stellari hadn't known exactly how it would end, but she knew it would. So what happened didn't take her entirely by surprise.

When her day servant ushered an exhausted messenger—panting, legs coated with road dust up to the knee—from the house of Calladocia into the front room of Stellari's town house, she had a sick feeling she knew what had come to pass.

Still, she had to keep up appearances. To the day servant, she said, "Leave us."

To the messenger, she said, "What tidings from Calladocia? Is something not to Panagiota's liking?"

Barely able to get the words out, the messenger said, "She sent this missive," and handed Stellari a letter, sealed with a blot of wax as red as blood.

Stellari pointed toward a bench to indicate that the messenger could sit down, which he gratefully did. Had she truly cared for his well-being, she would have sent him to the kitchen for food and drink, but she wanted the messenger present for her reaction to Panagiota's note.

Breaking the seal with a careful thumb and unfolding the letter, Stellari put on a look of boredom as she scanned its contents. "Starts with the usual pleasantries, your mistress is always well aware of protocol, ah yes. Oh goodness! Here she says, 'We were led to expect that my grandchild Aster would remain in Calladocia for at least two weeks, to pay proper visits to the members of the family who have yet to meet him after you withheld his presence from us for so long. Yet after only three days, we found that Aster and his caregiver had departed without so much as a goodbye. I will remind you that even if Aster is not a daughter, he is a child of this house and this family.' That's the angry part."

She allowed her face to soften, then read aloud, "Please assure me that Aster is safe at home with you. His well-being is all that concerns me."

She folded the letter again. When Rahul had offered to take Aster on a visit to Calladocia, to see the family that had embraced Stellari and raised her to the senatorship that had set her on the path to where she now reigned, Stellari had approved of it. She'd sent them off in Panagiota's company with a smile and a wave.

But now stark realization set in.

To the messenger, she said, "Shall I pen a brief reply? That will be better for you than trying to remember my words."

Recovering, the messenger bobbed his head politely. "Yes, Senator. Thank you, Senator."

"Haven't you heard? I'm the regent now," she said, but ignored any answer he might attempt.

Showily, taking pen and paper from a nearby desk, Stellari wrote back a terse missive informing Panagiota that she'd clearly misunderstood the plans. She told her husband's mother that Stellari would be eager to accompany Aster to Calladocia on another occasion when she had the time, but of course with her new responsibilities as regent, time was hard to come by. She sent the letter off with the messenger as if she meant every word.

The truth was out of the question. Confessing that she didn't know the whereabouts of her own child, nor the man who'd cared for Aster since birth, would make Stellari look weak. She couldn't afford weakness.

She could hardly applaud Rahul for what he'd done—taken their child and disappeared without a word—but if she wanted to take a generous view, she supposed he had solved a problem for her. She'd feared the use of Rahul against her, and now that was no longer an option. Politically, his departure had made her less vulnerable.

Emotionally, though, she allowed herself a rare pang of something that felt like regret. Even in the days when Rahul had put her second, at least she'd been a runner-up. Now she was nothing to no one.

She'd had some hope for her husband, Evander, who lived here in the town house, as she split her time between the town house and the palace. They'd shared pleasures regularly, maintaining a weekly schedule to maximize her chances of bearing another child. She leapt into pleasures without hesitation and took no precautions, deciding this was indeed her duty, if she hoped to bear a daughter to solidify the next generation of the Calladocia dynasty. Still, she couldn't help but feel a wave of relief every time her monthly courses came. She was afraid to bear a son, even though she still imagined a girl in her arms, small and perfect, a daughter to whom she could pass on her power.

But once the novelty faded, as the All-Mother's Year 518 began, she realized there was something not quite right about her pleasures with Evander. It wasn't that she didn't want him, and his attentions had never been clumsy or awkward. Even from his first night in her bedchamber, he kissed her skillfully, found her secret places with nimble fingers, brought them both to the pinnacle of pleasure one after the other—first her, then a moment later, him. He always held her hips to his afterward, keeping them locked together, an old peasant trick for encouraging the man's rain to water the woman's seed. Evander did this regardless of whether he was under her, above her, or behind her when they achieved their pleasure; she almost grew to enjoy it, that long moment when they were more like one person than two, even if the fear that *this* might be the moment when a baby began to grow inside her never quite went away.

What she realized after several months of repetition was this: there was never more. He never stared into her eyes during their pleasures, never planted a kiss on her forehead after they parted, never laughed sweetly in her ear or teased her about her hunger. Never licked her sweat-slicked skin afterward, never purred or panted her name as if the pleasure had torn it right out of him. All things Rahul had once done and would never do again.

And she realized, too, that her conversations with Evander were never more than polite. She thought it because he was unfamiliar and therefore uncomfortable with her, but after weeks and then months spent in each other's company, that no longer worked as an excuse. There was every opportunity to learn more, but they stayed just as awkward. When she asked him questions, he answered them, but little more. And when she thought about it, he only ever asked her how she was feeling and what she planned to do with the day. Two questions, repeated with minor variations in the wording, but still, only two questions. It was as if she were a distant relation, not a wife, and though she knew there were as many ways to be married as there were marriages, she knew this was not all that marriage could be.

The most important person in Stellari's life, of course, was not her husband, but a shrill, fussy, nearly unmanageable infant who also happened to be queen of Paxim.

Perhaps it had been a mistake to side with the infant's relatives and support her for the queenship. Stellari could have supported the twenty-year-old. The two were equally close blood relatives of Queen Heliane, different branches of the same family tree. But Stellari had been concerned the young woman might have too many opinions, and she knew she would be able to exert more influence as regent than as consul. So she'd supported the infant Asana, who she insisted be called Heliane the Second. Stellari didn't realize how she would find herself pushed to the brink, with a mix of disgust and surprise, by the baby's high, piercing wails.

Another reason she'd favored the infant becoming queen was that the baby's mother had willingly accepted a generous payment to hand her over once and for all, promising not to return. That made one fewer person to tussle with. Women had clamored for the honor of nursing the infant queen, but Stellari had refused them, again not wanting anyone else to be in a strong position. She had a rotating cast of nursemaids, all trusted individuals from the best families, but Stellari was her only constant, by design. As a result, the wailing of Heliane the Second sometimes felt like a personal attack, deliberate revenge for the infant's isolation.

Of course, thought Stellari, babies cried. Everyone knew that. But the frequency of this one's cries seemed disproportionate, almost worrying. Stellari didn't remember Aster as a baby having these frequent fits of temper, this inconsolability. Then again, she hadn't been the one to care for Aster.

But to ensure that she managed access to the infant queen, she needed to be in the company of the infant queen, so she forced herself back to the palace again and again. It was in the child's nursery that Juni, now in the role of magistrate, came to find her one day in the spring.

"Welcome, Juni," said Stellari, raising her voice to be heard over the infant's complaints. She slipped a finger into the child's mouth to soothe her, but the infant turned her head away.

"Thank you," Juni said, but she didn't look grateful. "I have news from the Senate. Today's vote."

"Excellent. I knew you would make an excellent magistrate." Stellari sought to remind Juni at every turn that there was no way Juni could have risen to the role without Stellari's support; more senior senators should have had the chance, but Stellari spent a good deal of political capital to move Juni over from the Assembly, wanting someone in the role who owed her.

Juni didn't respond to her words, only looked down at the child, whose cries had gotten louder. "Is she well? Hungry, perhaps?"

"Just cranky," said Stellari. "What is the vote?"

"A resolution about the Sun Rites."

Stellari turned her back on Juni deliberately, keeping her waiting while she fetched a twist of fabric from a nearby table and dipped it in still-cool milk. The baby sucked on it eagerly, finally quiet for a moment. It wouldn't last, knew Stellari, but she'd use the time she'd bought.

"The Sun Rites are three years away," Stellari pointed out to Juni.

Juni remained cool. "Yes. Given the disruption to the peace in the past few years, it's more important than ever for us to take Paxim's role as peacemaker seriously."

"Really?" asked Stellari, shifting the baby, dipping the cloth in the milk again, replacing it in her tiny mouth. "We didn't start the war with Scorpica. We finished it."

"There was never a declared peace."

"There was never a declared war!" Stellari shot back, then realized her voice might be getting too loud. The baby's eyes went wide, but then she returned contentedly to her suckling.

Juni said, "Regardless, the Paximite queen must visit all four other queens as the Sun Rites approach, securing their agreement to attend."

"Is that tradition or law?"

"Both."

Stellari eyed the magistrate skeptically. She didn't like where this was going. She especially didn't like that she hadn't been able to attend the Senate session where this had been discussed, but she could only make it to about half the votes now, too busy in meetings about royal matters to spend as much time politicking as she once had.

Stellari said, "So this is a requirement for the queen of Paxim? And our foremothers didn't foresee that Paxim might not, at the moment, have a queen who can't speak? Or walk? Or eat solid food without choking?"

Juni's horrified look told Stellari it would've been better to keep her sarcasm to herself. That was the other problem with the child's fussy temperament. Stellari had fewer reserves of calm than ever before.

Stellari said, more gently, "I just mean that of course the queen is in no position to convince anyone of anything."

"And that's what the Senate voted on. They're willing to make allowances. One is that you, as regent, will speak on the queen's behalf."

"So they want me to travel to all four other queendoms?"

"Well," said Juni, "I wouldn't say 'want.' They require you to do so."

"But there is too much business to be done here."

"Which they understand. You need not visit all four queens immediately. Though they do want you to start soon, given the political situation. It may take a great deal of persuasion."

Stellari pondered the task she'd been assigned. Perhaps she could see this as a positive development. Traveling with the child would continue to keep others from getting close to her. Negotiations with other queens would increase Stellari's own power and visibility. It wasn't entirely good news, but it wasn't entirely bad.

"Very well," she told Juni. "It will be my honor to accompany the queen on these visits. We'll start planning right away."

"Splendid," said Juni. She reached out to pat the infant queen on the head, which startled Heliane the Second out of her milk-soaked reverie and set her to fussing again.

This time when Stellari dipped the cloth in milk and tried to give it back to the baby, she turned her face away. The infant began to complain, then cry.

Juni's eyes were already on the door. She said, "I think it's best that I go now."

"Please thank the Senate for their confidence and trust. I'm honored," Stellari said. She knew the woman wouldn't stay a moment longer than absolutely necessary, but it still hurt to see how eager she was to flee.

"Not at all," said Juni. "Regent. Queen." She gave a short nod to Stellari and a deeper bow to the squalling infant, whose face was now red.

"Magistrate," said Stellari, wanting to remind Juni one more time of how high she'd climbed and who had put her there, but the word was lost in the infant's wail. Juni didn't turn around on her way out the door.

There would be advantages to visiting the other queens, certainly, thought Stellari. When she had a quieter moment, she would figure out what they were.

In the meantime, she joggled the furious child in her arms, trying not to think about how unpleasant it would be to travel in the company of an infant queen who doubled as an unpredictable, unstoppable siren.

◆

Exhausted from days and nights in the company of the infant queen, Stellari retreated to her town house that night, hungry for a good night's sleep. She remembered belatedly that it was a night scheduled for sharing pleasures with Evander, but he wasn't there when she arrived. She wasn't sure whether she was disappointed or relieved. She climbed into bed alone and quickly fell asleep.

When she felt Evander slip into bed beside her in the dark of the night, he kissed her without preamble, sliding his fingers into the hair at the back of her neck to hold her head in place, and then proceeded through the same steps in the same order that he always did. Kissing down the side of her neck, then holding open the neck of her robe to cup her right breast in one palm, hefting its weight. Switching to kiss down the other side of her neck, moving the thumb of his right hand to brush her awakening nipple, and at the same time, nudging her knees apart with his own knee to place it between.

She observed the pattern of it with her mind, dispassionately, and realized with something like shame that even while her mind was completely disengaged, her body still responded. She already felt the hot need throbbing between her legs, and as if on cue, Evander raised his knee to press snugly against that exact spot. She ground against him as if her hips moved of their own accord; she found herself falling into the rhythm unbidden, small circles, swift and urgent. Then her robe came off, then his, every motion of his capable fingers swift and efficient, utterly predictable, that exact same order, which she'd never noticed before.

She moved through the whole exchange like a sleepwalker, analyzing it with her mind as if it were someone else whose limbs were tangled on the bed with Evander's. Hot breath without passion, gripping fingers without urgency. The head of his cock waited at her opening, a persistent, teasing pressure, until she canted her hips up to take him in. It wasn't a decision on her part, it was simply what needed to happen. One step and then the next, as if crossing a bridge over a river: there was nowhere to go but forward, until the water was crossed.

Even when Evander tucked his arm under her torso and rolled to switch positions, resettling her hips atop his, she felt a mildly curious distance. The tension still mounted within her as she rode him, and his circling thumb on her lover's knot still drove her into ecstasy. The pleasure cascaded through her body, irresistible. At that point she didn't think she could have stopped the wave from crashing even if she'd wanted to.

Stellari shuddered with a quiet cry, Evander shuddered in silence, and then they were both still. She'd never said his name and he'd never said hers, not in the throes of passion, if passion was in fact what this could even be called. For a heartbeat, two, three, she wondered if this time would be different. It wasn't. She felt his palms wrap around her hipbones and hold her in place, and for whatever reason, that was the final straw.

"What is it?" she finally exploded, naked above him, shoving his hands off her hips. His hands fell away like deadweight.

"What is what?" There was mild confusion in Evander's dark eyes, but he didn't seem shocked, she realized; her outburst didn't faze him. Had he been waiting for her to notice, all this time?

"You don't enjoy this," she accused.

He gave no response to that, only looked off to the side, then back at her. She could still feel his cock inside her *muoni*, their bodies interlocked, yet she felt she didn't understand a single thing about him. Anger flared within her. She forced herself to slide off his body and stand above him, hands on her hips, the sting of their mingled, salty sweat still in her nostrils. He lay on his back, looking up, only his eyes moving.

Finally letting her fury show, Stellari sneered, "Don't you like pleasure? Or is it that your interests lie elsewhere?"

His eyes remained on her face, not her naked body, as she stood over him. That gave her another idea. She seized on it.

"Oh, that's it, isn't it? The problem is that I'm a woman. Your mother could have told me about that before we married; we could have saved this whole charade. You've been doing your duty, but no, you're only interested in pleasures with other men. That's why you act like this. You don't like women at all."

With a leisurely stretch, Evander pillowed his hands behind his head before he gave his response. When it came, delivered in a voice colder than she'd ever heard, it was devastating.

"I like women," he said. "I just don't like *you.*"

Stellari punished him with silence for a week, then two. She didn't even look in his direction if she could help it, and whenever she accidentally caught sight of him, she forced her gaze away. She stayed longer at the palace and the Senate, tending to her other duties, spending fewer and fewer nights at the town house. Her monthly courses came and went. He sent her no notes, made no attempt to speak with her on the nights when she did climb into the bed they shared. They glided past each other like shades.

Finally, one night, she stood in the door of the bedroom with a lamp in her hand. She waited until he woke up. When he sat up and looked in her direction, she could see the resentment in his eyes.

She set the lamp beside the bed and did not turn it down. Stellari had so many things she wanted to say. She wanted to tell Evander how he'd hurt her, how unfair it was that he could say something so awful to her when she'd never done him any wrong. Part of her wanted to slap him just to see an expression on his face; part of her wanted to dismiss him, never mind that he had nowhere to go. Part of her wanted to shove him to his knees and tell him to beg for his life; she'd killed before and never lost any sleep over it, some people were more useful dead than alive, and if he wanted to stay in the latter category, he'd need to give her a good reason. More than anything else she wanted to look in his eyes and not see the dislike there—so obvious, now that she realized—but that was not in her control. She couldn't change how he felt. She could only change what she did about it.

She would not rail or threaten. She would not expose her emotions so he could see how he'd made her feel.

Instead, she looked her husband up and down, knelt on the bed, and said, "Start at the beginning."

Evander rose slowly to his knees, edged closer, and put his warm lips on hers. He raised his hand and slipped it into her hair, pressing her face close to his.

Then he kissed down her neck on one side, slipping his palm

inside the neckline of her robe, reaching for her right breast to cradle it in his cupped hand. She felt her body reacting, nipples hardening to points, warmth spreading to the join of her thighs. He kissed down the other side of her neck.

And they went on, step by predictable step, from there.

✦ CHAPTER 12 ✦

MOTHERLAND

Early autumn, the All-Mother's Year 518

Scorpica

Amankha, Azur

When the Scorpicae rode back into their homeland at last through the open gates of the Bastion, Amankha expected to feel something. Some pang of recognition, some wave of emotion. But she had been gone from Scorpica too long. Nothing looked familiar. This was where she belonged, thought Amankha, where she'd been born, where all her memories of her mother had taken root—Khara's sweet voice, her soft kiss, her warm but crisp commands to run *faster, faster* when they played running games among the sparse trees alongside the winter camp. Amankha ruled the entire queendom unfolding before her, every tree and coney and warrior, for Panic's sake. But she had not been here since she was a child. Even if the land had not changed much in her absence, she herself certainly had.

For a few more moments, her mount's feet made their sharp *clip-clop* sound against the stone of the Bastion, and Amankha wished and hoped for that feeling of homecoming. But she couldn't relax, and perhaps it was best that she didn't. Two dozen Bastionite guards, their helms and cloaks as gray as the stone under their feet, flanked the gate, their eyes tracking the Scorpicae's every move.

Amankha checked herself and deliberately looked away from the guards. She was afraid that whatever she saw on their faces would inflame her and she wouldn't be able to hide her reaction. But she could imagine what they might be feeling. In fact, she couldn't help imagining it.

Every one of these Bastionite guards knew that the Scorpicae had attacked other nations of the Five Queendoms. Had pillaged and even killed in an attempt to build their power following the Drought of Girls. Had suffered defeat. The diminished force returning was far smaller than the Scorpican army that had secretly marched southward through Godsbones more than a year earlier. While the previous queen, Tamura, had still ruled, hundreds of warriors had fallen at a place called Hayk, defeated by the joint efforts of the Paximite army and the Arcan queen. Scorpica had gambled everything and lost.

The gamut of emotions the guards must be feeling settled into Amankha's chest: suspicion, for certain, and burning anger, and no doubt some satisfaction that these warriors, riding home, had failed at what they set out to do. Were there guards who regretted this inglorious homecoming, though? Guards who sympathized with the cause of the Scorpicae, understanding that they'd felt they had no choice? The Drought of Girls had upended the world. The Scorpicae had been harder hit than any other nation because they couldn't rethink the role of men the way other queendoms had. Men had no role in Scorpica to rethink.

The fact that it had been Tamura, not Amankha, who'd made the key decisions of the Drought—to withdraw Scorpicae from their assignments in other queendoms, then to trek secretly down through Godsbones and attack first Arca, then Paxim—that made no difference. Amankha had slain Tamura and taken her place. She was queen of Scorpica now. For all intents and purposes, she *was* Scorpica, and with the pride she'd inherited from her mother and a long line of Scorpican queens before them, she would've died rather than fall back on excuses and apologies.

So Amankha dha Khara, head held high, led her warriors through the dark stone of the Bastion into the greenery of their wild homeland. She might not feel the powerful recognition she'd hoped for, but she still felt relief, even joy. She savored the delicious touch of wind on her scalp now that her hair was shorn down to a fuzz, in the style of a true Scorpican. In the years when she'd lived in the Bastion and then Paxim, she'd worn it in short, wild curls, but no more. Gretti had done her the favor of shearing her with sober gravity after Tamura's defeat. Gretti had helped Amankha in so many ways, just as she'd helped Khara years before, and Amankha had no idea how to show her gratitude. She never could have done this alone. And there was so much more to do. Everything that had come before, as hard as it had been, was barely the beginning.

So as the amassed warriors returned to their fertile land for the first time since they'd journeyed south under Tamura's rule, Amankha was quiet. But as the Scorpicae, who had been drawn into a narrow column to pass through the gates, now entered the unfettered landscape, they made joyful noises as they surveyed their much-missed homeland.

The loudest and most active among them, charging from behind Amankha to pass her without apology, was Azur, who surged forward with a cry of delight. Secure on her mount's back, Azur dha Tamura raised high her young daughter Madazur, whose birth had brought the Drought of Girls to an end for the Scorpicae. Azur was known as the First Mother because of her achievement; she was a fierce warrior, a strong and vocal member of the council, and a political player not to be underestimated. Amankha had seen firsthand the moment when Azur had decided not to second Tamura when Amankha Challenged her, despite the fact that Tamura was Azur's own adoptive mother, a woman who'd given Azur every advantage.

Even now, as she raised Madazur high with both hands, crying over and over again, "We are home, we are home, we are home," Amankha understood the action was not spontaneous. Azur did not stop celebrating loudly, bearing her daughter high, until every warrior in her vicinity was sure to have heard and seen.

The child had never seen Scorpica for herself, Amankha realized. Amankha had not yet returned to the Scorpican fold at the time, but Gretti had told her everything she needed to know. Madazur had been born deep in Godsbones, just before the invasion of Arca, far from here. When Madazur's mother set her down, hers would be the first baby girl's feet to touch Scorpican soil in more than fifteen years.

Relief and gratitude both filled her body like air, so strong she felt the rushing of blood in her head like she imagined the sea would sound. But still, even as they traveled deeper and deeper into Scorpica, no recognition. This land was as strange to her as whatever lay beyond the Salt Maw, beyond the Mockingwater, beyond the Scorpion's Pass. The slate was blank. So she had to savor the feelings she did feel, hold them close and let them fill her up.

Then, as Gretti pulled up alongside Amankha, another wave of gratitude flooded into her, because she knew what was next.

"My queen," said Gretti, her voice gentle. Amankha nodded in acknowledgment. They matched their mounts' strides until the two ponies moved as one.

Gretti would show her the way to the summer camp; they would have two months there before the winter set in. Amankha herself, queen of a land she hadn't seen since she was five years old, didn't even know which direction to go. It was north because everything was north, but beyond that, she had no idea. She would follow Gretti without looking like she was following, which sounded tricky, but Gretti would make it easy.

Amankha took a good look at Gretti in the afternoon light, the sun shadowing the older woman's eyes, the lines of wisdom at their corners. Gretti had known Amankha's mother, Khara dha Ellimi, had venerated her as the worthiest of women, when Gretti was a mere girl. Now Gretti was a seasoned member of the tribe with more than three decades on the earth, a councillor of great intelligence and perspective. These last years had been hard on Gretti, Amankha knew. Gretti had done her best to support Tamura during the Drought of Girls for the good of Scorpica, despite her personal dislike for the woman. There was only one Scorpican who Amankha knew and appreciated more than Gretti, and that was Vishala dha Lulit, who was halfway across the world in Paxim.

Before she could think too much about the mission she'd left in the hands of her *tishi* Vish, Amankha closed off that line of thinking. She couldn't be present here if she thought about where Vish was and who was with her. Amankha needed, above all else, to be present. She was the queen of this place, of these women. She had come too far and sacrificed too much to turn back now.

"Your mother would be proud," murmured Gretti in a voice too low for the other Scorpicae to hear.

The very idea brought the threat of tears prickling at the corners of Amankha's eyes. Fear and regret made her voice sharp. "She and I would have both preferred to know each other."

"We all would have rather seen those days," Gretti said softly. "We weren't given a choice."

"She had a choice," Amankha said.

"Did she?"

"She could have run." They'd never talked of this before, but now that they were in Scorpica itself, Amankha felt keenly the decision her mother had made. Khara had lingered in these hills and forests, remained in Scorpica in those first few years after Amankha was born, even knowing it meant certain death for her to stay. "She knew Tamura would Challenge her. She knew Tamura was the best warrior of her generation. She could have scooped me up and fled."

"Oh, Amankha," whispered Gretti, with sorrow that sounded bottomless. "Khara could never have run. Never."

Amankha thought of her own small daughter, so far from here, the child she'd kept secret even from Gretti. "Even for me?"

"Your mother did the best she could for you without abandoning her own nature," Gretti answered. "She honored you and she honored herself, and when a choice had to be made, she made it. That's what a mother does."

Silent, Amankha looked out over her unfamiliar native land, riding north, feeling more alone in the world than she ever had. Her lover, Paulus, was dead, her daughter, Roksana, was hidden away in secret, and she couldn't leave Scorpica in anyone else's hands, not even Gretti's, until the queendom's future was more secure. There was too much uncertainty for her to choose what she wanted to choose. In the meantime, she would have to make do.

"I suppose you're right," she said to Gretti, eyes on the unfamiliar green horizon. "Mothers make hard choices."

✦

As they rode across Scorpica toward the camp, Azur dha Tamura shifted on her pony's back, wrapping her arm more securely around her daughter. The girl was starting to drift off, exhausted by the excitement of the Scorpicae's return, comfortable in her mother's grasp.

There were, as always, other things on Azur's mind. Right now she was thinking of what it took to rule the warrior nation. She hoped that Amankha was capable of it, but she couldn't take such a thing for granted. Blood was no guarantee. And Amankha had no daughter to rule after her, as Azur did. Despite the Challenges that had brought upheaval to the queenship during the Drought, it was much more common for mother-queens to pass their charge peacefully to daughters. Azur might have been adopted and not born into this nation, but no one could say she didn't know the nation's very soul as well as any other warrior and better than most.

Besides pleasures of the body, which she enjoyed immensely, one thing had always brought Azur dha Tamura joy: ending a life. For years it had been hunting that satisfied her, using her expertise to bring down game large and small. Countless coneys had died at the tip of one of her arrows. The same was true of squirrels, of partridge and a dozen other birds. On the organized seasonal hunts, she had always been among the first and most deadly to strike the largest of their quarry, up to and including the wild, unpredictable aurochs.

When the undeclared wars in Arca and Paxim had broken out, it had been enemy soldiers who died by Azur's sword and spear, and the rush was even more heady. The power that surged through Azur's body when she met a soldier toe-to-toe and only she emerged alive? There was nothing like it. She killed and she killed, and each time, she felt a deep satisfaction that burned within her like a torch for days.

But then, she'd killed a fellow Scorpican, and what was more, she had to kill her twice.

On nights when she awoke in a panic, reliving the moment when she'd smashed Olan's head in and watched her bleed into the red sands of Godsbones, Azur told herself she'd been justified. Olan had been planning to attack her. Olan had first picked up the stone, swinging for Azur's head. It was only because of Azur's excellent reflexes and hunting-honed sixth sense that she intuited what was coming, tore the descending rock from Olan's hands, and slew the other woman before she could be slain.

She could still picture the moment right after. Blood, red. Jaw, slack. Eyes, sightless. Then, without even consciously thinking about it, Azur had used her toe to nudge the body off the red riverbank and into the river, watching as the current bore what had once been Olan dha Bakal away.

And that would have been the end of it. Azur returned to skinning the white wolf that they'd disagreed over, disposing of its horns in that same river, packing the fresh hide to carry back to camp. By the time she was in camp again, she was thinking more about the wolf than the woman. She didn't take particular joy in Olan's death, but neither did she regret it, not until the early morning she woke from a sound sleep to find a dark figure lying beside her, hot breath on Azur's neck.

Azur did what she had to do.

Even before she knew the person was Olan, Azur moved to defend herself. They were wearing a Paximite cloak, for one thing, and Azur thought she was fighting an enemy. It turned out she was, but not in the way Azur had first imagined. Someone was attacking her. She was within her rights to strike back. And when her dagger slid into the soft space between ribs, she hadn't felt like she was doing anything wrong.

Then she saw Olan's face. Wrenched in pain, but living, when Azur knew for certain she had killed the other woman days before. As she watched, the light went out of those eyes again.

There was no joy in that death, only confusion and pain.

Not long after, Amankha killed Tamura and gained the queenship of Scorpica. She ended the war and commanded the Scorpicae back to their homeland. Azur was shocked to find herself relieved. When fighting alongside Tamura, she had wanted nothing more than for war to go on forever. Now she couldn't believe her luck that it was over. All she had to do now was go back to Scorpica, be a mother, and find a new way forward.

There were other mothers now, with other daughters, and warriors at all stages of pregnancy. Riva and Galeigh's girls were the oldest after Madazur, conceived at the Moon Rites in Sestia they'd attended after the end of the Drought. Azur herself had not grown a child after the rites, but that was fine with her. It kept her from the disappointment of bearing a boy. She could always try again. For now, being First Mother would do. She clung to that superiority with both hands.

As they rode, and as these thoughts swarmed in her tired mind like bees, Azur wrapped her arm around her toddler daughter and squeezed tenderly. She'd despised Madazur as a baby, when she'd been just a hungry mouth who demanded and demanded and gave nothing in return. But now Azur could see glimmers of a future warrior in the girl, sharp intelligence in her eyes, a curiosity and stubbornness all her own. Madazur had drunk her first milk in the black-earthed caldera camp on the lip of Arca, had learned to crawl on the harsh red sands of Godsbones, but she would learn to walk and run and fight and glory in her own strength in the green valleys of Scorpica. Azur found she was looking forward to seeing her daughter become the person she was meant to be.

Azur knew that she would be the First Mother forever whether she liked it or not; with a glimmer of hope, she realized it was very possible she was growing to like it. She wanted to be around to watch Madazur grow, and if she took the queendom in the right way, she could then pass it on to Madazur. What a dynasty they would make.

Azur told no one any of this; she had no one but her daughter to tell. For a while she considered trying to befriend Riva, who'd been friendly to her back when they'd attacked a Paximite outpost together, but it appeared Riva had given up and moved on. Everyone was deferential to Azur—she was still the First Mother, after all—but no one appeared to seek out her company. Most of the journey back to Scorpica, when Azur looked up to see if anyone was looking at her, no one was.

Gretti dha Rhodarya, of course, was the exception.

Azur knew Gretti could tell the difference in her. Trying not to leave an impression on Gretti was like trying to walk on a plain of mud after the rain.

The very day they arrived back in Scorpica and settled into camp, Gretti took Azur aside.

"Walk with me?" asked Gretti, but it didn't sound like a request.

Azur took a moment to settle Madazur into a sling on her chest, the toddler facing inward with her legs hooked over her mother's hips, then followed Gretti down the path toward the nearby stream.

Once they were out of earshot, Gretti gestured at the child. "She's getting so big. Every time I see her."

"Yes," Azur agreed.

As they walked, Gretti reached over and tugged on the fabric of the sling that secured Madazur, frowning at the girl's dangling legs. "Is this strong enough to bear her weight now? You're sure she's safe?"

Azur kept her eyes on her daughter. "Are any of us ever truly safe?"

"I suppose not," said the older woman. "Some more than others."

Azur was losing patience already. She stopped walking; Gretti stopped too. "Do you want something from me, Gretti dha Rhodarya?"

"If you'll be blunt, I'll be blunt," Gretti responded, crossing her arms. "You can stay on the council or not."

Gretti had supported Azur's rise to councillor, back when Tamura reigned; a new queen could choose her own council, though the benefits of keeping the same advisers in place were obvious. "Are you saying I get to choose?"

"No."

Azur raised her chin, not wanting to seem intimidated. But the truth was that Gretti had the ear of the new queen, and Azur didn't. She would have to tread carefully if she wanted to keep her position.

Madazur shifted her weight in her wrappings, letting out a cranky sigh. Azur reached down and stroked her cheek to soothe her, then crooked a finger to tickle the girl's chubby neck. The toddler squirmed happily at the touch, her delighted giggle rising into the air.

"Is there any better sound?" asked Gretti mildly.

There was a time when Azur had resented her daughter. Now it seemed as if she'd been swimming in a dark sea in those days, about to drown. She didn't feel like drowning now. She said truthfully, "No."

Gretti began walking again. Azur followed. The motion pleased the toddler, who fell silent again.

As they moved on in silence, following the stream, Azur waited for Gretti to pose her question. Surely the older woman would ask for something in return for allowing Azur to keep her seat. She wasn't the type to leave negotiations open.

At length, Gretti said, "You have allies. You could use them to set up a Challenge."

"I do. I could."

Gretti said, "I won't even ask you to promise never to Challenge her. I know the foolishness of long-term promises. You understand, I imagine."

Azur had known, as had anyone with eyes in their head, that Gretti and Tamura had gone from being close allies to hating each other with a passion when the attacks on Arca had begun. She didn't understand exactly what had happened, but she gleaned that a promise had been broken and the damage couldn't be undone. "I do understand."

"So I ask a year. Give Queen Amankha a year to prove herself. In that time, serve wisely on the council and give her your best."

Azur was trying to be agreeable, but she certainly didn't intend to say yes to everything this new, unproven queen proposed. "You want me to be a puppet? I won't."

"No, I'd never ask that," said Gretti. "Simply advise her wisely. She might take your advice and she might not. I'm neither her mother nor her queen."

"But your advice is the most prized," pressed Azur.

"It is. And I earned that trust." Gretti's gaze met hers. "Perhaps in time, you will too."

Azur stopped walking, forcing Gretti to stop too. She wanted Gretti's full attention. "And if I don't?"

If Azur hadn't been watching closely, she would have missed it. But Gretti deflated just a little, her shoulders lowering.

Gretti said, "If in a year, you don't feel Queen Amankha is the right person to rule Scorpica, you are free to Challenge her. You know what happens if you do."

"Do I?"

Gretti looked away from Azur, down toward her daughter. She placed her hand on Madazur's back. "If you Challenge the queen, I will second her against you. You'll find a second to shore your support. You'll fight to the death. The loser will die and the winner will reign."

The baldness of it hung in the air like fog. Azur felt a chill run down her arms. She wasn't at all sure she could beat Amankha in fair combat, after what she'd seen the woman do to Tamura.

Her mind spun. She looked at Madazur, grateful to have her to focus on. To give herself time to think, she unwrapped the girl from her sling. She walked farther away from the edge of the stream and found a flat grassy area to set the toddler down. Once sitting, the girl reached out and gathered grass in her hands with both chubby fists.

Still looking down at the girl, Azur heard Gretti's voice say, "Well?"

Azur made her decision. This promise would cost her nothing. Let Gretti have what she asked for. Then, if anyone came to her, pushed her to risk her life for a queenship, she would have a reason to decline. Gretti likely didn't even realize what a good bargain this was for Azur.

"All right, then," said Azur, as if reluctantly. She turned toward Gretti. "One year."

"One year."

Briefly, they grasped each other's forearms in a warrior's seal. Neither held on a moment longer than needed.

Then, they heard the sound of approaching hoofbeats; a hunting party was returning. Azur reached down to lift Madazur, but the girl was distracted by something.

The something turned out to be the queen, whose pony had jingling bells woven into its mane. Amankha dismounted smoothly, her eyes taking in the scene. Azur wondered if the queen knew what Gretti had asked of her. If Azur had to bet, she'd venture that Gretti was doing this on her own; Amankha seemed like the type to do her own politicking, if she chose to.

The queen didn't hail either Gretti or Azur; instead she walked directly toward the grass where the toddler rested, looking only at her.

"Hello, dear," said Amankha, and lifted the child easily. She settled Madazur on her hip as easily as any lifelong *tishi*. "What's your name?"

She knew the child's name, of course, thought Azur. One could hardly fail to recognize the first Scorpican warrior born in a generation.

"Mazu," said the girl, her lips not quite up to the task of all the syllables of her own name.

"My name is Amankha," said the queen.

"Manka," echoed Madazur. "*Tishi* Manka."

"If you like," said the queen, apparently sincerely, a smile on her face.

"Mazu," said the girl, pointing to herself, then, "Manka," pointing to the woman who held her. Then she pointed to Azur. "Mama."

The queen turned her attention to the First Mother. "Welcome back to our motherland, Azur dha Tamura." She didn't even trip over the name of the queen she'd killed to take power, a woman who had served as adoptive mother to Azur as well as commander and queen. Ice water must run in this woman's veins. Of course, she wouldn't have made it this far if she were sentimental. "Do you prefer to be addressed as First Mother?"

Azur found herself shaking her head. "Just Azur."

The queen stroked Madazur's head, and Azur realized with a chill that if this woman meant her daughter harm, there was absolutely nothing Azur could do. She found herself taking half a step forward, not even meaning to.

Gretti said, "Azur has served well on the council. You'll keep her on, won't you?"

The queen's gaze slid to her most senior adviser, and Azur read an entire conversation in the single look that passed between the two.

"Of course," said the queen easily. "Madazur, would you like to go back to your mother now?"

The child nodded with enthusiasm, and the queen came toward Azur, who extended her arms toward her daughter.

But instead of handing the child over, the queen paused a moment, leaving Azur feeling foolish with her arms outstretched. Amankha leaned down and kissed Madazur on the forehead, a lingering kiss. Then, slowly, she transferred the girl's weight to her mother's embrace.

"A pleasure to see you both," said the queen.

That was the end of the conversation, and everyone busied themselves arranging things, settling into their new camp. Fatigue and excitement competed for the upper hand. A warm wind stirred the flaps of the Scorpican tents as the warriors settled in to sleep within the borders of their motherland for the first time since the Drought of Girls ended. Some celebrated with wine and songs, choosing to look ahead to a better future; some curled in on themselves, trying to shut out the memories, wishing they could erase what had happened, unable to forget the past.

For her part, Azur lay awake that night thinking of the kiss Amankha had placed on her daughter's head. She pictured it over and over. The bending queen, the tender press of her lips. The blinking, oblivious child. That pause, that long pause, before the most precious thing in the world to Azur was returned.

Had it been a benediction or a warning?

✦ CHAPTER 13 ✦

MAGIC

The All Mother's Year 518
Arca
Aster, Eminel

Aster both loved and hated the sound of Rahul's voice. When he was in a tender mood, his voice had a sweetness to it that comforted Aster like nothing else. It was softer, warmer. He'd say, *There, there*, and *Time to rest now*, and *I'm lucky to have you*. That voice took Aster back to earlier years, when Rahul's presence had been a warm, steady assurance that nothing could go wrong.

Those moods were rare. Far more often, like today, his voice had that hateful tone, too sharp. When he commanded Aster to try, try, try. Aster was sick to death of trying.

This morning, standing on the pale sand that dusted the roof of Rahul's cousin's small house in the Arcan desert village of Odimisk, they faced each other, as they did so many mornings. Just before sunrise was the best time for privacy. There were too many prying eyes in the village, Rahul said. This was a secret for only the two of them.

"Try again," he told Aster. His voice was steady, but it had a frayed edge, like the hem of a long robe dragged too often on the ground.

Blocking out the cool predawn air and everything else around them, Aster focused on the *psama* in their cupped palm. Six months before, when they'd first left Ursu under the pretext that they were traveling to Calladocia to visit Aster's mother's family, Rahul had pressed the pendant into Aster's hand. The look on his face was rapturous. He explained what it was, and what he expected Aster to do with it. *We're going to find your magic,* he said, and then lots of other words, all of which sounded like utter nonsense to Aster. But Rahul clearly believed. He looked like he might not believe in anything in the world so much as this. And he was the only person who'd ever seemed to care a whit about Aster, so Aster listened, and Aster tried. Now that they were surrounded by sand, Aster didn't need the *psama*, but Rahul felt it might help to have something to focus on. As if anything might make a difference.

"Now," said Rahul, pointing at the tiny pyramid he always produced to test Aster's magic. Aster hated that little pyramid.

Aster focused, stared. They tried to gather their strength for an incantation, but it was like trying to coil one's own rib bone, or make a sound with your knee. Was magic even *in* the body? If so, where? Rahul used more words each time he attempted to explain to Aster how he did his magic. Each time it got less clear.

"What are you trying?" he asked. "Air? Fire?"

"I tried fire first," Aster said, voice tight. "Wait. I'll try air."

Since they'd arrived in Odimisk, he'd insisted on tests like this every single day. If circumstances and privacy permitted, up to three times a day wasn't unusual. Yet the results were the same. It didn't matter whether Aster tried to float the little pyramid upward with air magic, set it ablaze with fire magic, bury it with earth magic. Nothing worked.

"Other Arcan girls can do this," Rahul hissed. "You can too."

Aster kept their eyes down as they spoke the truth Rahul refused to hear. "But I'm not an Arcan girl."

"You're half-Arcan," Rahul answered quickly. "And all girl. No one knew that back in Paxim, during the Drought, because my illusion magic protected your secret. They thought you were a boy. But you never were."

Aster hated it when he said this. As if Rahul knew who Aster was, then or now. As if he cared. All he wanted to know these days was what kind of magic Aster had. And if Aster did have magic, what use would Rahul put it to? That was one of the many reasons that every time Aster failed to produce magic, they breathed a small sigh of relief. They almost never bothered to correct Rahul about their gender, either. He would just tell them they were wrong about themselves. About the magic. About everything.

Rahul yanked the pyramid out of Aster's hand and let it fall to the ground. "Try earth," he said. "Bury it."

Aster focused downward. One hand gripped the *psama*; with the other hand, they tried extending a finger, pointing directly at the pyramid. When nothing happened, Aster wasn't surprised, but they kept their brow creased in concentration. How things looked were just as important as what they were. Having a father obsessed with illusion magic taught a person that early on; having the power-hungry senator Stellari for a mother, obsessed with her own place in the world and uninterested in her child to the point of neglect, only reinforced the lesson.

"Think of how special you are." Rahul was almost purring now, egging Aster on. "Think of all that lives inside you. No one knew. None even suspected. My greatest enchantment . . . so far."

Aster didn't feel like anyone's greatest anything. The others in the village clearly viewed both Rahul and Aster with suspicion. The cousin had opened his home only grudgingly, and asked them both to keep to themselves. Aster had no friends their age. As far as Aster could tell, the only time Rahul saw anyone but his cousin was during secretive all-male gatherings around the time of the new moon, when a dozen men came to the house one by one, and Rahul sent Aster up to sleep on the roof so they couldn't hear the conversation.

It was one night after such a meeting that the roof door banged open and a man stormed out, shouting. No one chased after him, but Aster was close enough to hear angry whispers from the bottom of the ladder. Not long after, the other men came out one at a time, silent, peering around for observers before they slunk away.

Once the last stranger was gone, Aster wiggled closer to the top of the ladder and peeked down. Rahul and his cousin were the only ones left, as Aster had suspected. They stood facing each other, their anger and annoyance plain.

"You can't stay here anymore," the cousin was saying flatly.

"Where are we supposed to go?" Rahul's tone was pleading. Aster had never heard him plead. It was unsettling.

His cousin refused to meet Rahul's gaze, looking away. "Not my concern."

"But our plans . . ."

"I can't risk it. My sister catches wind of this and I'm done. I support the cause, you know I do. But you can't rile them up like that."

"It's Aybal's fault for storming off, not my fault for getting him upset!"

"Either way! Your plan is madness. I can give you five days to figure something out. Once things have calmed down, I'll be in touch about a new meeting place. All right?"

"It's not all right," growled Rahul.

"Whether it is or not," the cousin returned, a weary tone in his voice, "that's how it's going to be."

Rahul waited a long time to respond. When he did, he said quietly, "Do you have any suggestions? Where we can go?"

"Actually, I do," said the cousin.

The nearly deserted village of Adaj was not far. It was, Aster saw, exactly as the cousin had described: perfectly lovely, a bit far from water, but full of houses for the taking. Houses that were occupied were marked with a broad-leaved fig tree on the roof; the roofs of unoccupied houses had been planted with succulus vines, which needed little water and could be trusted to grow on their own. So Rahul spent a day choosing a house for them, placed his household image of Velja on a high shelf, and it was as if they'd lived there all along.

Every once in a while, Aster thought they saw a woman with wings soaring through the sky, but decided they were probably imagining it. The heat made them dizzy if they weren't careful. What had wheeled overhead was probably just a bird, stretched by imagination and a touch of heatstroke.

With no worries about prying eyes, they could resume testing either on the roof of the house or within it. Aster vastly preferred indoors, but their preference was not what mattered.

Time and again they climbed the ladder to the roof. Time and again Rahul produced the small pyramid.

Time and again, Aster failed.

"Have you decided to try today?" Rahul snapped.

"I am. I swear."

He practically snarled, "Don't swear."

"I'm just telling you that—"

"Don't tell me anything. If you can't say what I want to hear, I wish you'd just keep your mouth shut."

That hateful edge was in his voice again. Aster wished for magic, magic they could use to silence him in an instant. See how much he snarled at Aster if they could just snap their fingers and take his voice away.

It was an awful wish, an unkind one, and Aster didn't really mean it. It was just that they were so, so tired of these days. These efforts. It felt like walking into a wall, gently, over and over. The wall would never move.

"Aster!" said Rahul, his voice even harsher.

Saying nothing, Aster turned their face to him, trying to look open and welcoming. Responsive. Like a dutiful Arcan child.

"Have you been saying your prayers?" He fixed Aster with an intense stare, as if his eyes could bore all the way to their soul. "Velja won't smile on you if you don't pray."

"I know."

"So you've prayed to Her? Every day?"

Aster thought about what to say. In the end, the truth would do. "Yes."

"Good girl," said Rahul.

Aster thought, *He's not right, but he's not wrong.*

Rahul looked away then, up to the sky, as if someone up there might have a better idea about how to make this child behave. He sighed in a way Aster felt was showy, a sigh that was meant to signal something. When he looked back, his voice was falsely cheerful. "Shall we pray together?"

Aster answered, "I prefer . . . can I pray alone?"

"Of course. That's fitting. Perhaps Velja will smile on you yet." As best Aster could tell, he seemed to mean it. He liked Aster best when they were obedient.

Rahul patted Aster awkwardly on the shoulder before he departed, scooping up a jug to carry water, heading off in the direction of the stream.

If Rahul had known what type of prayer passed Aster's lips, he wouldn't have approved at all. But it was, in the strictest sense, a prayer.

Then Aster descended the ladder. The dwelling Rahul had chosen was small, just one room at the base of the ladder and two alcoves off it large enough for pallets. In the main room sat their household image of Velja, the traditional one, with one arm ice and the other arm fire. It was made of stone, carved by unknown hands.

Aster had examined it in every detail when they were praying, trying to find the secret of Velja, trying to figure out whether they believed in Her at all. Surely an entire nation couldn't be mistaken about their god. Surely their magic came from somewhere. But not everyone could be right about Velja, if some claimed She only favored women, and some, like Rahul, believed she also gave powers to men. And what about people like Aster, who the Paximites would have called two-fold, but Arca had no words for?

Well. Aster had told Rahul they would pray. So they prayed. Aster didn't kneel, nor bow with pressed hands. They stood on their own two feet. In a conversational voice, not a whisper, Aster spoke to Velja as if She were in the room. And Aster had only one thing to ask.

"Please don't give me magic," prayed Aster to Velja, reverently, intensely. "Please. Please, please, please."

✦

When Queen Eminel, Well of All-Magic, Master of Sand, and Destroyer of Fear was impatient, everyone knew. She had a habit of drumming the fingers of her left hand against the arm of her throne. Because the hand was quartz, a magical hand she had built out of Sessadon's quartz heart, the tap of every finger made a chilling noise somewhere between a click and a thud.

Eminel made the noise when she was bored, too, but rarely was anyone around to hear. Four taps, pinky finger to index, over and over again. Something about the pattern soothed her. She rarely even realized what she was doing. If she were in her quarters, tapping the quartz fingers against the wood of a study table instead of her throne, Beyda would stop her. Sometimes the scribe would quietly murmur under her breath, "Fingers," and Eminel would know to stop. Sometimes Beyda simply reached out and put her own hand on Eminel's wrist. Beyda was the only person Eminel would allow to touch her without asking permission first. They'd known each other for long enough now, and in many ways, Beyda was the only person alive Eminel considered a friend. Eminel had allies, not friends. She was, after all, a queen.

There was a third kind of situation in which Eminel made the noise, different from the others. Deliberate. When the queen of Arca ducked through the secret tunnel between the scribe Beyda's study room and her own chambers, before she walked through the propped-open door into Beyda's territory, Eminel tapped her fingers against the edge of the doorframe. That way, she alerted Beyda to her presence without startling her. Once and only once, Eminel had walked into the room without announcing herself. Beyda didn't notice. When Beyda finally looked up and caught sight of a dark, breathing shape just over her shoulder, she'd let out a bloodcurdling scream that rendered Eminel's left ear ineffective for days. Neither of them wanted to repeat the experience.

So Eminel always announced herself with a light tapping of her quartz fingers, but today, it seemed, Beyda didn't hear. Carefully, Eminel eased her head around the doorframe and watched her friend studying. Beyda was truly absorbed in today's work, clearly. She hunched over a slate, shoulders rounded high and head dangling low, her cheek almost pressed to her hand, which scribbled madly.

Eminel took one step into the room and tried tapping her fingers on the doorframe again, with the same result. Beyda didn't look up. Curious, Eminel reached out with her magic almost without meaning to, borrowing Beyda's eyes without touching her mind to get a closer look at the slate itself.

Eminel caught a few words in the swirl of chalk markings, countless letters written and then smeared away, new markings incompletely covering old ones, layers and layers of incomprehensible words. Whatever it was Beyda was so intent on, it was far from simple. Eminel could have gone into Beyda's mind and understood everything her friend knew instantly, but she held herself back. Instead she searched for recognizable scraps of language on the slate, spotting just a few.

Lake of glass
Girl helps a girl—more than?
Arrow that rends the heart
When the

Eminel felt an almost irresistible pull, wanting to lean closer to the slate with her own eyes. Instead she began to repeat her friend's name, quietly at first, then more loudly. "Beyda. Beyda."

Beyda made a grunt in her throat. She blinked a few times, slowly, then placed one fingertip squarely on the slate. Only then did she look up. "What?"

"Good morning to you too," said Eminel pleasantly.

Beyda blinked twice, three times. "It's morning?"

"How long have you been working?"

The scribe shrugged with one shoulder, her fingertip still not moving from the slate. "Not long enough to solve this. Did you need something?"

"To invite you upstairs for date buns and warm milk. Honeyed, of course."

"No," said Beyda, characteristically blunt. "Is that all? I want to get back to this."

"What is it?" asked Eminel. "Can I see it? I want to know what could possibly interest you more than date buns."

But Beyda turned one shoulder away, curving her body over the slate. "Nothing you need to worry about. Something I've been working on."

"Something new?"

"Something very old," Beyda said, and then looked like she regretted saying even that much.

Eminel hid her irritation, knowing it would do no good. She kept her tone warm and friendly. "All right, then. I wish you luck. Come visit me when you want a break."

No response.

Walking slowly, leaving the door open in case Beyda changed her mind, Queen Eminel returned to her chambers through the long, winding tunnel. But there was no call from behind her, no sound of words, even when she paused to listen, no sound at all.

Once back in the careless luxury of her rooms, all rich carpets and plentiful cushions, Eminel rang for a servant to bring date buns and honeyed goat's milk anyway. She waited without patience. When the food arrived, she ate it all herself. Hours later she had both a guilty conscience and a stomachache.

The next day, Eminel adapted. She rang for the buns and milk first. When the tray arrived, she bore it with careful hands and slow steps all the way down the tunnel to Beyda's threshold. Eminel rapped her quartz fingertips on the door, calling Beyda's name, then peering around the doorframe without waiting for a response.

The scribe's position was unchanged from the day before. She wore what appeared to be the same garments, her cheek lying on what looked like the same pile of documents. Eminel considered peering at the scribe's work again, but she was no more likely to understand it today. She told herself to wait. If this were anything like Beyda's previous projects, when the scribe had some kind of breakthrough, she would bubble over with the need to tell someone about it. Invariably, that someone was Eminel.

Eminel tapped her quartz fingers on the doorway harder and harder, calling Beyda's name softly at first, then more and more loudly. Finally her friend stirred. Beyda lifted her head and wiped at the corner of her mouth as she took stock of her surroundings. Then she quickly looked down at the scroll she'd been lying on and wiped her fingertips across it to make sure it was dry. Only once that was done did she look up at Eminel.

"I brought buns," said the queen.

Beyda began to shuffle the papers in front of her, rolling and stacking with brisk fingers, until half the table was covered with her research—none of it showing, Eminel noted immediately—and the other half was cleared. She gestured to the empty space and Eminel set down the tray.

"Thank you," said the scribe. Those were her last words for a while. When she stuffed a sweet bun into her mouth, she chewed with the obvious hunger of one who has forgotten to eat for at least a day.

Eminel waited as patiently as she could, until the second bun had been devoured. Then she asked, all politeness, "After you've finished chewing, would you mind telling me, do you think you're close to a breakthrough?"

Once the scribe had swallowed the last of the second bun and laid her sticky fingers on a third, Beyda said, "Not close. Already had it."

"Oh! Anything you want to tell me?"

In the time it took Eminel to frame and deliver her question, Beyda had already torn the third bun in half and popped the first half into her mouth. It didn't take long for her to chew and swallow, then answer, "No."

Eminel knew she was failing to hide her disappointment when she quickly echoed, "No?"

"The breakthrough is that I need more information. Things I can't get here." The scribe gestured sharply. It was unclear whether she meant to indicate the room, Daybreak Palace, or the entirety of Arca.

"Oh! Is that all? I can get you anything you need, of course. Just tell me. I'll send messengers to borrow or buy whatever it is you're lacking."

Beyda simply shook her head and mumbled through the second half of the third bun, "No."

"What?"

"Wait. *Milk*," Beyda said, her voice accusatory. "These need milk."

"Milk? It's right there."

Without apology, Beyda moved her focus a handspan to the left and found the first cup of honeyed milk, still warm. She drained it in a single gulp, groaned with pleasure, then wrapped her fingers around the second.

Eminel didn't point out that she'd intended the second cup of milk for herself. She could always get more. "Sorry—what do you mean by 'No'?"

"The things I need, we can't bring here." Beyda brought the cup of milk to her mouth, sighing again, not looking up. "I have to go to them. And even then . . . anyway, can't be brought."

"Where?"

"I have to . . . travel."

"Oh," said Eminel, still surprised. She could feel how much Beyda was choosing not to say. She resisted the urge to leap into her friend's mind. It would be so, so easy. She searched for the right response. "I suppose I can come with you, but it will take some doing."

Beyda shook her head. "No. I need to go alone."

"Where?"

"I can't tell you."

"Beyda," said Eminel, rapidly approaching the limits of her patience, "you're not making sense. You work day and night until you forget the world exists, and now you're saying you have to go on some kind of secret mission, and you won't even tell me where?"

Beyda tilted her head and considered her friend's words. Then she said, "Yes."

Eminel threw up her hands, one quartz and one flesh, both equally involved in showing her exasperation.

Beyda said, "I only need to pack a few things. I may leave later today. Maybe tomorrow. I can't say how long I'll be gone."

"You sound awfully sure."

Brows creased, Beyda replied, "I am sure. This is something I have to do."

"You sound awfully sure I'll let you go."

"*Let* me?"

"It's not up to you. It's up to me. And I don't think it sounds like a good idea."

Beyda simply repeated, "Let me?"

She'd been so good, thought Eminel. So kind. Brought her friend sustenance like a servant, held back from using her powers, been so polite, and yet, she was getting no consideration, not even courtesy. She, a queen of nearly unlimited power, had been so patient! Did Beyda have any idea how hard that was? And nothing. No respect at all.

Her annoyance climbing, Eminel found herself saying, "Let me be clear then, Beyda of the Scribes. If you won't say where you're going or how long you're going to be gone, I forbid you to go."

Beyda finally looked up. When she spoke, her tone was incredulous. "You forbid me?"

"I am your queen."

"You are *a* queen," emphasized Beyda. "You are not *my* queen."

"You are my assigned scribe. The Board of Scholars sent you to serve the queen of Arca, and that assignment hasn't changed. So yes, you're mine, even if you're not my subject. I don't approve this journey. So you won't go."

Something shut off in Beyda then, Eminel could see it. The scribe didn't rail or beg, didn't react in anger. Another woman might have snapped, *Oh, I won't?* or let her face harden into a sneer, but not Beyda. She simply looked away from Eminel and stopped speaking, as if whatever power that made her function had been cut off. For a moment, she looked lifeless as a statue.

Then Beyda set to her task again. The scratch of chalk on slate was the only sound in the room.

Eminel could have offered to send for another cup or two of honeyed milk to accompany the last two date buns that remained untouched on the platter. She could have apologized for her peremptory tone. She could have been the one to reach out, make peace.

But she was annoyed at Beyda's unapologetic disobedience. Queen Eminel, Well of All-Magic, Master of Sand, and Destroyer of Fear, had ruled Arca for nearly two years now. She was no longer used to being disobeyed. She had taken apart and rebuilt a court, helped win a battle that prevented a war, grown into her powers and mastered them. She was the chosen of her god; the god had said so Herself. A queen like Eminel simply got her way. A queen said, *You won't go,* and the person stayed.

So it was a shock to Queen Eminel when she returned later that afternoon to the same room and found it empty. She'd decided that even though she didn't need to apologize because she wasn't in the wrong, Beyda was unlikely to make the first overture, so Eminel came to fetch Beyda for a rousing game of *whishnuk.* The queen tapped her fingers on the doorframe, but there was no one there to answer.

The scribe, along with every last trace of her—robes and pens, slates and scrolls—was already gone.

✦ CHAPTER 14 ✦

DIPLOMACY

The tenth month of the All-Mother's Year 518
Arca: Daybreak Palace and beyond
Stellari

Stellari controlled as many aspects as she could of her first diplomatic journey beyond the borders of Paxim, but far too many proved to be outside her control. She had to travel with the young queen, that was unavoidable. But once Panagiota found out that Stellari would be traveling, she wrote a very strongly worded letter insisting that Evander come along, and Stellari decided it would be easier to give in than fight back. So Evander would join the journey as well. Stellari decided that at least her husband should travel in a separate carriage. Another one was needed for the servants and one for the Queensguard. Before she knew it, there were five carriages in all, turning the whole affair into a caravan.

Now that the toddler-queen was almost a year old—small for her age, but already walking, albeit unsteadily—she was much easier for Stellari to manage during the day than she'd been as an infant. It helped that Stellari had come to see that toddlers and senators were not so different as all that. One only needed to know what someone most wanted in order to gain power over them. What Heliane the Second wanted was a constant supply of peeled clementines. Stellari provided them. In the daylight, that meant Stellari could finally have some peace.

The nights were another matter entirely. During the day, Heliane the Second might nap, but she seemed to have left off sleeping during the night at all. As the caravan traveled, every time Stellari thought she could safely drift off to sleep, a hiccup from the queen's cradle turned into a soft cry and then a moan and then a shrill alarm. Sleep remained stubbornly, impossibly, out of reach.

So Stellari was a bit dizzy from exhaustion as they approached Daybreak Palace, though she held herself upright with sheer will. The palace itself was stunning: an immense front door, a forbidding facade pressed into the mountainside, nothing like any edifice she'd ever seen. Once received, she was ushered inside without fanfare, into a throne room where Queen Eminel waited. The room was larger than Stellari would have guessed was possible from the outside, cavernous and high-ceilinged. There wasn't much ornamentation, but the room didn't need much. There was nothing to look at but the queen. She was sight enough.

Stellari knew Queen Eminel was young, not yet twenty years, but she looked ageless and eternal, sitting motionless on her throne. She wore a remarkable greenish-black robe that cascaded down to pool at her feet. Even if the room had been filled with ornaments, she would have drawn every eye. Her chin was high, her feet bare. Her left hand matched her right in every conceivable way—long blunt-tipped fingers, curled slightly over the throne's solid arms on either side—except that the right hand was perfectly normal flesh and the left made of bluish-white stone. Stellari had heard rumors that the Arcan queen wore a quartz hand, but she thought they'd been exaggerations. The reality was striking, even distracting.

The queen of Arca, looking down from her perch, spoke first. "Welcome . . . what should I call you? Since you are not the queen."

"You may call me regent," said Stellari, keeping her voice level, though she bristled at the insinuation.

"Regent Stellari," said Eminel. "Thank you for your visit. May I know the reason you have journeyed all the way here?"

"Well, it is the responsibility of the queen of Paxim to secure the other queens' participation in the Sun Rites. That is the purpose of my visit."

Eminel eyed her coolly. "Even though you are not the queen."

"Queen Heliane the Second of Paxim is, as it happens, too young to act as diplomat. Therefore it is fitting that I convey the message for her."

"And she is back in Paxim, I suppose?"

"She arrived in our caravan," said Stellari breezily. "She is . . . napping." She had considered bringing the girl inside with her, but, having analyzed all the possibilities, decided against it. She needed the legitimacy of the child's presence without the inconvenience of actually having a toddler in the room. She would not give this queen a chance to ignore her. Stellari would hold on to the power she'd grabbed with both hands.

The Arcan queen stroked her snake necklace with her quartz hand, her fingertips making faint tapping sounds against the glass. "I see," she replied. "And why are you here so far in advance of the rites?"

"It was our Senate's wish. Rather than waiting until the rites are nearly upon us, they asked that I visit each queen well in advance, to remind each of their duty."

"I know my duty," said Queen Eminel. "I'm amused that your Senate thinks they need to tell people things they already know. I assume that if I told you I wasn't planning to go to the rites when the time comes, you'd be authorized to try to persuade me?"

Her mood appeared no sunnier than it had when Stellari had walked in, and the regent had no intention of begging. She was happy to say her piece briefly and be gone. "It is important to all nations that the Sun Rites be conducted. We don't know what would happen if we failed to complete them."

"Could it be something worse than the Drought of Girls? Because we continued having Sun Rites during the entire Drought, and all those sacrifices changed nothing."

"Because the gods weren't responsible for the Drought. The sorcerer was."

"Believe me," said the queen dryly, "I'm aware."

Stellari didn't understand Queen Eminel's terse response, but she wasn't about to expose her ignorance. She knew that Eminel had been named queen there in the Holy City, so she must have been involved in the rites in some way, but what exactly the young magician had witnessed, Stellari didn't know. After all, Stellari herself hadn't been present. But she couldn't regret that. Several members of Heliane's entourage hadn't survived the experience. If she'd gone, the same might have happened to her.

Stellari stuck to the script she'd planned. She said, "The role of the queen of Arca at the Sun Rites is to represent Chaos. So there is nothing in particular you need to do. You only need to journey to the Holy City, eat cherries in the sacred grove the day before the rites, and watch the rites themselves. If your god moves you to do something else during that time, you may do whatever it is She asks of you."

"You forgot testing the ropes. I believe that's something else every queen does during the rites." Eminel's face was unreadable as stone.

"Yes, of course. That's part of witnessing."

"But you didn't include it in your description."

Was she being baited? She was tempted to respond with the same derision she heard in the Arcan queen's voice, but for now, she kept her voice civil, if frosty. "The High Xara will give you full instructions when the time comes. After all, they are her rites, are they not?"

"She has no choice," said Eminel. "The Holy One is her god. Sestia is not my god. Nor, for that matter, yours."

"My role is to encourage you," said Stellari in a voice empty of emotion. "I can't force you to attend."

Eminel's laugh was nearly a snort, making it clear what she thought of Stellari's chances of forcing her to do anything at all.

Stellari tried not to be insulted. "I can only remind you that five centuries of tradition have laid the groundwork for our world to exist. If you choose to spit on that tradition, that is your right."

"Well, thank you for your message."

"And thank you for such a warm welcome."

"I'm sorry not to get the chance to meet the young queen, but I doubt she would have much to add to the conversation. I do hope you enjoy your travels back to Paxim, which should begin as soon as possible. Shall I have the Queensguard show you out?" Eminel snapped her fingers and her Queensguard appeared.

Stellari said nothing else, merely bobbed her head and turned on her heel, feeling the guards hasten to flank her as she exited through the same door where she'd come in. As she strode through the long, dug-out halls of Daybreak Palace into the bright sunlight of the daytime desert, she thought about how rudely the queen of Arca had dismissed her, and how she might see that as an opportunity.

The Paximite Queensguard stood at attention as Stellari stepped up into the carriage she shared with the tiny queen. A glance told her the girl was still napping. She'd likely pay the price that night, but for now, she couldn't help but enjoy the silence.

An attendant next to the carriage's open door said, "And from here, Regent Stellari?"

Stellari said, simply, "Home."

SESTIA ✦ 169

The caravan turned northward once more.

The recalcitrance of the Arcan queen had given Stellari an idea. She was required to visit these queens, to speak with them, but was she really accountable for whether they decided to attend the Sun Rites when the time came? No. It was effort that the Senate demanded of her, not results.

Stellari had to make the visits. But she didn't have to make them easy.

Given Queen Eminel's clear derision, it seemed like there was a good chance she wouldn't come to the Sun Rites at all, thought Stellari as the carriage rode smoothly northward, leaving Daybreak Palace behind. That would be an excellent turn of events. If the Arcan queen stayed home from the rites and something bad happened afterward—and didn't something bad always happen?—she would make a perfect scapegoat.

And there was no reason to stop with Queen Eminel. Any queen who failed to attend the Sun Rites could be blamed for any bad result in the years afterward. Stellari didn't really need to practice diplomacy at all. In fact, the more she irritated the other queens, as long as she didn't go too far, the more likely they were to play right into her hands.

The very idea gave Stellari a surge of her old confidence. If Arca boycotted the rites, that would open up a number of possibilities back in Paxim for whipping up particular sentiments. Even better, what if the Scorpicae declined to participate? Their relationship to the other queendoms was already so fragile. Before she'd become regent, Stellari had been able to pluck strings like this and make perfect music. If she put her mind to it, she could do so again.

Yes, thought Stellari. This had been a very satisfactory visit indeed.

✦

Stellari understood, on the deepest level, that sometimes good luck looked like bad and vice versa. She'd seen enough reversals of fortune to know. This meant that she could never truly exhale in relief, but on the other hand, neither would she ever lose hope entirely.

So when the carriage she rode in with the young queen lurched sideways and slammed to a halt in the middle of nowhere, she didn't perceive it as an ill omen. She simply took it in stride.

The stop was sudden and jarring, yes, and she instinctively threw her arms around the toddler-queen instead of bracing herself, although that might only have been because others were looking.

"Are you all right?" said the nursemaid.

"Who cares how I am?" Stellari snapped, heart hammering. "How is the child?"

The toddler, having been awoken from a sound sleep, began to howl in a voice even more shrill and skull-piercing than usual. A cursory look showed no injuries, so Stellari decided it was shock, not pain, that had set the child off. Though she'd heard the child wail nearly as loudly for no reason at all.

"Here." Stellari thrust the child in the direction of the nursemaid and climbed out of the carriage.

The road looked unremarkable, the area around them mostly countryside, with only one small building in sight. Ahead of her, the lead carriage, which contained the Queensguard, had stopped. She guessed that it had only stopped because the queen's carriage had. The driver of the queen's carriage and the lead carriage driver exchanged a wave.

She was just about to turn to look at the carriages behind when a man's voice, annoyed, came from behind her. "What's going on?" A heavy hand came down on her shoulder.

Evander, of course.

"Why did we stop?" he demanded.

He had no right to demand, and her response needed to show that. She turned to face him, grimly. "Because I said so. Go back to your carriage." She didn't know what the real reason was; her mind was working through a list of dozens of potential explanations. Foremost in her mind was the idea that the queen's carriage had been sabotaged, but she wasn't about to plant the seed of conspiracy in anyone else's mind if it wasn't already there.

Evander eyed her with a critical gaze. When he spoke, his voice still had that confrontational edge. "Can we be on our way, please?"

"When I say we can."

"When will that be?"

Sharper, firmer, with a glare. "When I say we can. Go back to your carriage."

He rolled his eyes and walked away. He stood next to his carriage but didn't climb back inside.

By now all five carriages had stopped, drivers talking and pointing, oxen standing patiently in trace. Two of the drivers were inspecting the queen's wagon closely while the queen howled in her nursemaid's arms.

The nursemaid said to Stellari, "She wants a clementine."

Of course she does, thought Stellari. She reached into the pouch at her waist, only to find that in the lurching of the carriage, the clementines she carried had been crushed into a sticky pulp, leaking juice everywhere.

Stellari handed the pouch to the nursemaid anyway. When the woman extracted a crushed fruit and extended it in the queen's direction, the child only howled louder.

Then Evander was back at Stellari's side, huffing out a breath. "I'll ask nicely. Please, Regent, I'm eager to get back to Ursu. Can you please order the caravan to start up again?"

"And again, I will tell you, Evander, we'll go when I'm good and ready. Why are you so eager?"

"Don't make me say it."

She could barely hear his words over the queen's unhappy cries, but she kept her composure. "If you're eager enough to plead like a child, you're eager enough to share."

"Fine, then. I'm ready to be out of your company. Good enough?"

She'd egged him on to say it, but it still hurt to hear. She didn't show the pain. Frostily, she said, "Don't bother waiting until we get to Ursu to leave me. You can leave me right now."

He looked around. "I . . . can't. There's nowhere to go."

She waved her arm in a grand, furious gesture. "There's the whole world, for the love of Panic. You're welcome to all of it. Anywhere I'm not."

"What?" He seemed genuinely confused.

The queen's shrill cries had only increased, and Stellari could no longer focus on anything else.

"Give her to me," she demanded of the nursemaid, and the woman handed the child over instantly. Stellari took in the scene as she marched in the only possible direction.

As she did, she could hear and feel movement behind her. A member of the Queensguard, of course. Without looking back, she said, "Follow at a distance, thank you," and heard the woman's answering, affirmative grunt.

The only building along this stretch of road was a small cottage, time-worn but in good repair. It wasn't a farm, but there was a vegetable patch of some size alongside the house, thick with healthy green growth. A well in the front yard. Nothing at all remarkable about the place, except perhaps the pair of dogwood trees between the house and the road, one young, one mature.

There in the doorway of the house stood a thin woman. Stellari couldn't immediately tell her age, but there was a stiffness to her stance that suggested she wasn't particularly young. Stellari raised a hand to gesture to her, a simple wave, and the woman lifted her own hand to give a minimal wave back.

As she neared, she said, "I'm so sorry to intrude. Didn't mean to disturb your peace. But would you happen to have any clementines? Or an orange, anything like that?"

The thin woman didn't respond. Did she not understand? Was she hard of hearing? Her gaze was focused over Stellari's shoulder. Toward the member of the Queensguard, Stellari realized. She'd been thinking of explaining who she was, but given the carriages marked with the royal seal and a uniformed member of the Queensguard standing right there, she realized no explanation was needed.

Then a high giggle sounded from inside the house and a girl toddled out from behind the legs of the thin woman, holding, of all things, sections of a peeled clementine.

"Look!" Stellari exclaimed to the tiny queen, crouching down so they were close to the little girl.

From above them she heard the thin woman's voice, raspy and low. "Her favorite."

The queen's cries subsided into hiccups. As they watched, the girl with the clementine held out a section toward the tiny queen. The queen quickly took it and jammed it in her mouth, chewing with gusto.

The little girl who lived in the cottage laughed, a sparkling, merry sound.

The two toddlers looked a little alike, Stellari realized. Not close enough to be sisters, perhaps, although their faces weren't dissimilar. That chin was the same, she decided. The shape of the eyes.

Stellari set the queen down and the two toddlers stood together, eating and cooing and licking their sticky fingers.

Stellari looked at the thin woman, who still stood in the house's doorway. Her mouth was twisted in an emotion Stellari couldn't quite read. She was out of practice, she realized. She used to be able to tell what anyone was thinking at any particular time. She concentrated harder.

The woman was worried about something. Possibly her daughter's—granddaughter's?—safety. Maybe, realizing who the toddler-queen was, she feared some sort of punishment for being in the wrong place at the wrong time. Stellari had to respect a woman who was ready for any possibility.

"Everything's fine," she said quietly to the woman, making sure her voice sounded cheerful, unthreatening. "They'll just play a bit, and we'll be on our way."

The woman nodded.

Stellari moved back toward the carriages, picking her driver out of the group and moving toward him with purpose.

"Tell me," she said when she reached him. "Is there a problem with the carriage?"

"We can't find anything, Regent," he said in a low voice. "Maybe one of the oxen was spooked. And one of the wheels was a little loose, so we tightened it."

"But you can't be sure what caused it to stop?"

He looked a little sick to his stomach as he said, "No."

Then she saw Evander striding toward her, his face still stormy with discontent, and she realized she had the answer.

"We'll switch carriages," she said. "Move this one to the back of the caravan; no one will ride inside, just in case."

"What carriage will you and the queen ride in?" the driver asked.

She pointed to Evander. "His."

Evander said, "I don't want you in my carriage."

"Good news," she replied. "You won't be in it. I told you, you're on your own now."

"That's ridiculous!" he fumed.

"For the All-Mother's sake," she said, rolling her eyes. "I'm hardly dropping you into Godsbones with nothing but a broken bow. You can find your way from here. Either you come to Ursu or go straight home to Calladocia. I don't really care."

"You can't treat me this way."

"I can and I am."

"You'll hear from my mother."

"I'm sure I will," Stellari said dryly, and turned her back on him.

She finished giving instructions to the drivers, who nodded their understanding. She walked past the carriage that Evander was vacating, heard him grumbling and slamming things around as he gathered his belongings. She neither slowed nor stopped for him.

As she neared the cottage, she looked at the girls, who were now sitting together, their little heads bent together in concentration.

She wanted Evander to be gone when she turned around, but she also didn't. Could she still call him back? Could they still try again? No. He could have been another beginning for her but he had turned out to be another dead end. She watched the girls and wished she were watching her own daughters play, but she would never have any, and for some reason now that seemed like the most unfair thing that had ever happened in all the world.

Sentiment, useless sentiment. She shook it off. Listened to the sounds of irritation behind her. Felt the bustle of those riding in the caravan climbing back into their positions. Focused on the feeling of the air on her skin, the smells of oxen and road dust, the beat of her own strong heart.

When she returned to Ursu there would be countless distractions. A nearly infinite number of things to do, track, manage. So for now, in this moment, she let herself savor two simple things: the laughter of happy children and just the faintest scent of sweet clementines on the breeze.

✦ CHAPTER 15 ✦

THE SECOND GATE

The Underlands

Sessadon

S essadon liked to think that death had taught her something.

Even when she'd had Eminel as her constant companion, she'd kept too many secrets from the girl. When Eminel discovered on her own who and what Sessadon really was, she'd lashed out in fear, calling on all her considerable magic to destroy Sessadon. Perhaps if the older sorcerer had shared more with the younger one, things would have ended differently.

Sessadon had feared being alone in life, but now she understood that even when she'd had someone else with her, she'd still been alone. She'd made the choice to hold herself apart, and she'd chosen wrong. If she were going to succeed in her mission to help Eresh reclaim the world of the living, she would need help. Maybe even a team. She couldn't do it alone, and this time, she'd be smart enough not to try.

So when Eresh said, "Let us see whether you are worthy to help me gain power," Sessadon was already thinking about who she might need to ask to help her.

But first, the shade of the sorcerer would need to know what it was Eresh wanted. So she said, in her humblest voice, "Just give me the task and I will complete it."

"It should be simple for you," Eresh said, the sneer on Her face redoubled in Her voice. "All you have to do is open the second gate."

Then the god was gone, swirling off to who-knew-where, somewhere in the vast Underlands where Sessadon might or might not be able to follow. But She had been clear in Her charter; there were no real questions to ask, no clarifications needed. Sessadon needed to find the gate and open it. She had journeyed widely enough through the Underlands and spoken to enough shades to have a sense of how to proceed, but she knew it would not be as easy as all that.

The second gate was the Gate of Warriors, located on a far island well away from the Bridge where spirits entered the Underlands, next to what the Scorpicae called the battlefield beyond. Sessadon had never really quite understood all the nuances of how one could move from place to place within the Underlands, but it was indisputable fact; the battlefield was here and she could find it. That, she reflected, was likely the easy part.

She stared up at the gate countless times, making a study of it. The arch was made of thick stone, soaring high overhead, and the Voa guarding it was visible only from a certain angle. Sessadon knew the name of the creature, Ocnet, and its makeup from the stories, but she still wasn't prepared for the actual sight of it: an absurdly large creature that filled almost the entire archway, sporting eight heads and eight hands, each wielding a vicious weapon.

She would need magic to beat it. But she didn't have magic. So she would need an army. But would the Scorpicae, once her enemies, provide it?

Perhaps she should work with Paulus after all. He had come to her—of his own volition!—and offered help, and she'd been too suspicious to accept. But only warriors could help her attack the Gate of Warriors. She would worry about the next gate after this one was open. One step at a time. It was the only way.

When finally she squared her shoulders, turned her back on the gate, and prepared to cross the border into the battlefield beyond, a familiar, long-fingered figure blocked her path.

"Sorcerer," said Eresh in a warning voice.

"Yes," Sessadon responded, trying to sound humble and receptive, when in fact she was deeply annoyed by the god's sudden appearance. How was she supposed to get anything accomplished with interruptions like this?

"Did I say you could take an army to help you open the gate?" Eresh phrased it as a question, but Her tone made it more an admonishment.

"I'm not here for an army," said Sessadon, though in fact she had been thinking exactly that.

"I said *you* must open the gate."

"And I will. I only ask"—and she made a snap decision—"that I be allowed five warriors."

"Five?"

Sessadon felt it all slipping away. If she didn't succeed, she'd be just another shade down here, no future, no goal. Alone again, this time forever. She couldn't accept that. "If you won't approve five, I can do it with one."

Eresh's gaunt face had a sneer on it, but she seemed to consider the suggestion. After a long wait, she said, "Very well. One warrior. Who I choose."

"I must choose her," blurted Sessadon, and then, more measured, she adjusted her tone. "I mean to say, Eresh-*lah*, I ask that I be allowed to choose her. After all, it is my skills you test with this task, correct? Let my power of persuasion be part of what I prove to you."

Smiling without warmth, Eresh seemed to approve of the addition to Sessadon's task. "One warrior, yes, very well. Choose her and persuade her. Luck be with you both."

Then the god was gone again, the path in front of Sessadon empty once more. The sorcerer felt mostly relief, but it was fleeting. Only one warrior? Against an eight-handed, eight-headed Voa built expressly to withstand defeat? But Sessadon reminded herself that the warrior wouldn't be the only one fighting. Sessadon would be there also, and even without magic, she could serve some purpose. Couldn't she?

She would simply have to find the most powerful, competent, bloodthirsty warrior possible. And convince her to go on a mission that wasn't hers, one that might damage or even destroy her in the end. Sessadon wasn't really sure what happened to shades who were destroyed in the Underlands, but she imagined any of the five Voa must be able to do some kind of damage to shades, or there would be no consequences for challenging them.

Sessadon was still considering all this as she stepped over the border into the battlefield beyond. The moment she did, she heard the unmistakable sound of swords clashing. It jarred her, almost sent her back across the line. She didn't belong here. But of course, she'd already known that.

So she continued, and as she crested the top of a small hill, she knew she was in the right place. Warriors were arrayed as far as the eye, or what passed for an eye in the Underlands, could see. There was no horizon. Tens of thousands of warrior shades fought and laughed, ducked and parried, lounged and leapt. It was easy to see at a glance their contentment, even if what was happening here made Sessadon feel vulnerable, endangered.

"*Mokh* your eyes," said an angry voice near her right ear, and the fierceness of it felt as sharp as a blade. In fact, Sessadon knew before she turned that the woman would have a blade—look at where they were—but at least it was still in its sheath.

Sessadon looked to the shade's face. She knew her. Tamura, the Scorpican queen who had murdered Sessadon with her own two hands.

As calmly as she could, Sessadon said, "My condolences on your passing." It was a fairly standard greeting down here, she had learned in the time—years?—since her arrival in the Underlands, and she hadn't meant to put a sting in it. But it resonated more than she'd meant it to, at least with her. Look at the two of them, both so fierce and ambitious in life, and where had it gotten them? They were both here, both dead, just like thousands and tens of thousands before them. Whatever they'd clung to in life, it was all gone now.

Tamura said, "What in the name of the Scorpion are you doing here, sorcerer? This is not your land."

The dead queen's angry voice caused a stir, the sound of swords nearby slowing and halting, and a host of Scorpican shades moved in their direction. The sight of so many warriors set off a wave of panic in Sessadon; in life, a crowd like this could have smothered the breath out of her. Even as a shade those instinctual physical feelings lingered.

She held up her hands quickly, though trying not to look frightened, and said, "I am on a mission for the god."

This halted the advancing Scorpicae, but Tamura folded her arms, her glare challenging.

"Whose god?" sneered Tamura. "That Velja of yours, the one who loves chaos? We don't need more chaos here."

"The god who owns all of us now," said Sessadon, gesturing widely to encompass Tamura, the nearby warriors, all of the Underlands. This seemed to reach some of the nearest shades, their ghostly expressions softening, but again Tamura was not moved.

"She doesn't *own* me," Tamura said. "No one ever did."

"You know what she means, Tamura," chided a voice somehow both sharp and gentle, and a shade from the crowd stepped forward.

The new shade's features were a little more delicate than those of the warriors around her, her manner slightly tentative, with a sadness in her eyes. She and Tamura stared each other down for a moment before the new shade turned her attention to Sessadon appraisingly.

"I didn't know you, sorcerer," she said, "though I've heard plenty here. My name is Khara dha Ellimi."

The name didn't ring a bell with Sessadon, but she didn't have time to react, in any case. Another shade was stepping forward to stand at Khara's side.

"And I am Ellimi dha Lanwys," said the short woman, whose face was creased with sun-lines, her close-cropped hair gone almost entirely white. Shades seemed to resemble themselves around the age of their deaths unless they made an effort to change their appearance, so it seemed likely this woman had died between her fiftieth and sixtieth year, a ripe old age for a warrior. She had a compact strength and a wary look. Sessadon guessed she'd been a highly respected woman in her time.

Sessadon looked back and forth between the two new shades, then made another guess. "You were both Scorpican queens? Mother and daughter?"

They nodded in unison, and Sessadon could see the resemblance, though Khara's height must have come from whoever her mother had coupled with to water her seed.

Khara pointed to her mother, saying, "I followed her as queen." Then, with a slightly more clouded tone, she pointed to Tamura and said, "Then, after, this one followed me."

"She inherited your title?" guessed Sessadon. She had not followed how Scorpican queendom worked; the only Scorpican she had ever cared a whit for was Hana, the hunter with whom she'd shared the lonely island, and whose mind her magic had accidentally reduced to a puddle of mush. It was not helpful to think of Hana.

Tamura broke in again, with a sharp voice. "I took the queendom from Khara when I slew her in a fair Challenge."

"And were then slain yourself in a Challenge just as fair, don't forget," said the white-haired Ellimi, her tone not gentled in the way her daughter's had been. Sessadon wondered if shades' personalities were more concentrated than they had been in life; they seemed to quickly show who they were and who they'd been. Perhaps it was all just simpler down here. Not better, but simpler.

Chin high, Tamura ignored the jibe from Ellimi and kept her attention on Sessadon. "Enough of history. Tell us clearly, sorcerer, why do you stand here?"

"I'm assisting the god," Sessadon replied, making sure she could be heard by all the shades who were now listening. "And I in turn need assistance. I offer a great opportunity. I see you all here sparring with delight, enjoying your sword-matches in the afterlife, but who wants to be challenged to true battle?"

"By *you*?" came a derisive shout from the crowd, and a ripple of unpleasant laughter made its way through hundreds of Scorpican shades.

"No, no, not me!" Sessadon called, forcing a laugh, struggling to keep her tone inviting. "A real enemy, with real weapons. One of the strongest creatures in the Underlands, if not the very strongest."

"In the Underlands?" asked Ellimi. "You mean a Voa, then?"

"Yes, a Voa. Nearly unbeatable, armed to the teeth. Even as shades, you can have new triumph. Whoever beats the eight-handed Voa Ocnet will earn everlasting glory."

"If only it were so simple," Tamura responded loudly, a glint in her eyes. Her response seemed intended for the crowd, not Sessadon. "Nothing I love like a good battle. But if it's going to help you, sorcerer, I refuse."

There were unmistakable sounds of assent in the shade-crowd, probably from those whose lives had overlapped with Sessadon's. She'd made few friends in her long life. She certainly hadn't thought she'd ever need them.

But nor would she give up easily. Raising her voice just as loud as Tamura's, and turning herself to address the same spectators the Scorpican queen had addressed, Sessadon said, "If anyone here should have a grudge, it should be me."

Fewer noises of assent, but at least she was not answered with silence. Tamura gazed at her impassively.

To press her point, Sessadon added loudly, "You killed me with your own two hands, Scorpican! Do you not remember fitting those fingers around my throat? Cutting my heart from my chest?"

She paused for effect, letting her words sink in. Then she continued. "Yet I, in the name of the greater good, am willing to forget what you did to me, if not forgive. I can set that aside. We all die. But some of us might have the chance to live again. Let us now, as shades together, achieve something remarkable."

This time the sound of the crowd was muddled. Some seemed swayed by the idea that Tamura was in the wrong, but others hissed, probably approving of Tamura's effective, brutal use of violence. Sessadon hadn't pitched her complaint quite right for an audience of born warriors, she realized. Hopefully it wouldn't be the last mistake she'd ever have the chance to make.

But Tamura seized on Sessadon's misstep, her manner growing more agitated. Clearly, dying hadn't quenched the fire she'd had in life. "You'll set aside what I did? Tell them what *you* did! You caused the Drought of Girls."

Sessadon's mind swam, trying to think of a defense, but the Scorpican queen didn't give her the chance.

Tamura gestured at the crowd, an almost desperate, graceless motion. "She deprived us of daughters, our whole generation! None of us bore a daughter for fifteen years, unable to water our seeds, to do our duty. We did everything we could to keep our nation alive. And that might not be enough."

This time there was no ambiguity in the sounds the shades made. Tamura's anger was spreading.

Now a few shades pressed closer to Sessadon, and if they overwhelmed her, there would be no defense. What would they do to her?

In desperation, Sessadon found herself shouting. "But wait! I'll tell you why the god needs our help! There are threats Above!"

Tamura's only response was a grim, wordless shrug.

Sessadon pleaded, "Do none of you still have loved ones Aboveground? Would you not relish the chance to go there? To be with them? Keep them safe?" She hadn't planned on telling them what would happen once the second gate was open, hoping the allure of beating the Voa would be enough, but she'd been wrong. Clearly she needed to hold nothing back. There might not be a later.

The white-haired queen Ellimi stepped forward. Her voice was strong as she said, "I certainly do. And I would."

There it was.

Sessadon addressed her next comment directly to Ellimi. Her last chance. "Then you understand the urgency. If we can open the gates, we can send up shades to help. We'll be able to better our loved ones' lives."

Tamura sputtered, "Ellimi dha Lanwys, you can't believe that she—"

The small queen's shade moved in a blur, and when she was visible again, her hand was on the throat of Tamura's shade. The intended threat was unmistakable. "Tamura dha Mada, you will not tell me what I can or can't believe. Is that clear?"

Tamura took one step to distance herself from Ellimi, and Ellimi let her. Expressionless, Tamura said to the crowd, "I won't listen to another minute of this farce."

With balled fists she stalked off, disappearing from view. If Sessadon had still been a breathing human being, she would have breathed a sigh of relief.

When Tamura turned away, so did many of the other Scorpican shades. Perhaps they were losing interest or choosing to show their derision, Sessadon didn't care which. Only a handful remained, watching.

The sorcerer turned her attention back to the remaining shades, feeling the first seedlings of hope take root.

Not mincing words, Ellimi asked, "Is my daughter's daughter still living?"

Khara said, "Mother, I don't think it's wise to—"

"Hush," Ellimi interrupted in a cold tone. "Wise or unwise, I never got to meet my granddaughter. And she is up there in that world now, where this woman is telling us threats abound. If I can help Amankha, I will."

Sessadon was thrilled but couldn't show it; she'd almost snatched victory from the jaws of defeat, but the knot was not yet tied.

"I regret that I may only take one warrior to fight the Voa," said Sessadon, who really did regret it. She would still have preferred an army. Instead she could only make sure her single champion was the strongest available. "To determine who should have the honor, I propose a battle of queens."

"I have no intention of competing in any such battle," Khara said. "My battling days are done."

Another shade that Sessadon didn't recognize edged forward. "I will battle."

"Thank you for your interest," said Sessadon politely. "And who are you?"

"My name is Mada," said the woman. She had the long legs of a born runner, a sharp nose, and angry, resentful eyes.

"You were never a queen," Tamura said to Mada. Her voice was firm, but there was a slight undercurrent of regret in the way she looked at the other woman.

"I'm sorry," Sessadon said. "I only want the strongest and best. Only queens."

"Crawl back in your mother's *muoni* and choke there," Mada said grimly, and then she was no longer present.

Sessadon turned to the white-haired shade of Ellimi. "What about the older queens? Before you, Ellimi dha Lanwys?"

Ellimi shrugged, something derisive in the gesture. "The longer you spend in the Underlands, the weaker your connection to the Aboveground becomes. Many shades begin to forget, or choose to. They lose their connection to the land of the living."

"A land almost destroyed by this sorcerer, lest we forget," Khara broke in, her voice sharper than it had been. "Mother, I hope you know what you're doing."

"Khara," her mother said, the emotion in her tone impossible for Sessadon to identify.

And whatever Khara heard in Ellimi's voice, it caused Khara to pause and turn around. Her manner softened. Her form flickered a touch but then grew more solid, and she took one step closer to Ellimi.

"If you do see Amankha, when and if you return Above," Khara said to her mother, her voice tight and just beginning to break, "tell her I wish I could have seen her grow."

Ellimi reached out her arm to her daughter for the clasp of warriors. The two gripped each other's forearms with utter solemnity. Ellimi said, "I will."

Then Khara's shade, like the others, was gone.

Ellimi turned to Sessadon again. "Well, sorcerer, you didn't get your battle, but you've got your fighter."

Sessadon felt a surge of pride. Against all odds, she'd convinced someone to join her. Despair had turned to excitement. Now she had every reason to think victory was at hand. The shade of the warrior in front of her might be small, but she was fierce, and Sessadon had every confidence in her as champion.

Ellimi tossed her head, her pale, close-cropped hair catching the light like a swan's wing. "Now tell me more about this eight-handed Voa. I can't wait to cut off every single one of its arms. And its heads. The only hard part will be deciding which goes first."

"Excellent," said Sessadon. "I think this is going to go quite well."

◆

Once Sessadon truly saw the full glory of the eight-headed, eight-handed Voa called Ocnet, her confidence went up like mist. Her repeated glimpses of the edges of the Voa had not given her true perspective.

The moment Sessadon and Ellimi stepped in range of the gate, around them whipped a loud wind, even though whatever the wind was stirring to make howls and hisses remained unsettlingly invisible. Sessadon felt a change inside her, a shimmer, her shade form becoming more solid somehow. Then, a heartbeat later: as the impassable stone of the gate seemed to wrap around them in every direction, the creature stepped into view.

In her glimpses, Sessadon had seen that the heads of the creature were ugly, snarling, monstrous. But she had, for whatever reason, thought they were all monstrous in the same way.

She saw now there were so many ways to be monstrous, and none of the eight heads resembled the others. One like a lion, another like a bird, another wolflike, unearthly gray saliva dripping from its visible fangs. But the two worst, the most frightening, looked all too human. One even reminded her of her friend Alish, slain by the Scorpicae ever so long ago, with sharp brown eyes under thick brows, a dainty nose oddly counterbalanced with a strong jaw. She met that head's eyes and wished she hadn't. At least she wasn't the one who had to lop it off to get what she wanted.

Sessadon herself was speechless. But from next to her, as if she'd heard what was inside the sorcerer's mind, Ellimi said, "As I said, I just have to decide where to start."

Ellimi drew her sword and then, pressing her lips into a tight line, transformed the sword into a long-handled, double-headed axe.

"Can you do that?" asked Sessadon. She had seen shades change their own forms, but not items they wielded. In fact, the Scorpicae's swords in the battlefield beyond were the only objects she could remember ever seeing a shade touch or move. Perhaps there was something special about the relationship between Scorpicae and their weapons, as if the weapons were part of the women themselves, both before and after death.

Then the Voa's lion head roared an ugly, loud roar underpinned with a gurgle that sounded like swallowed blood, and Sessadon's conscious thoughts drained away.

Ellimi raised her voice to be heard over the singing wind, answering Sessadon's question with her accustomed arrogance. "I just did."

Sessadon said, "But can a shade-axe truly injure a Voa?"

The long-dead Scorpican queen didn't reply with words. Instead she leapt forward, aiming for a birdlike head on a long neck that protruded from the far left of the creature, the easiest one for her to reach with a right-handed draw.

Sessadon got the unambiguous message. *Here's how we find out.*

The axe bit into the flesh of the creature's neck, just below the birdlike head, and blood—red, but a strange brick red with a decidedly orange tinge—gushed forth, cascading down.

Ellimi grinned.

But even as the blood poured, it quickly became clear that the axe hadn't cut deep enough to sever the head from its neck. The warrior's grin faded. Soon the weapon brandished by the creature's nearest arm—a long-handled war mace studded with what looked like enormous wolves' teeth sticking out in all directions—was swinging straight for Ellimi's own head.

Sessadon shouted a warning, but her voice was lost in the shriek of the birdlike head with the bleeding neck, which was still thrashing in agony.

Even without hearing the sorcerer's warning, Ellimi saw the approaching blow. She braced her feet and turned the axe's haft to block the Voa's weapon with her own. The mace thumped into the haft with an enormous impact, and Ellimi staggered back one long step, then another. Then she continued to withdraw, retreating far enough that the Voa's longest arms couldn't reach her, obviously reconsidering her plan of attack.

Ellimi shot Sessadon a look over her shoulder, the enormous creature looming over them both. The queen's shade called out, "If you have any ideas, sorcerer, I'm all ears."

Sessadon stared uneasily up at the creature. The birdlike head was starting to sag, its cries growing softer, the blood still running unimpeded down the thick, fleshy bulk from which all the heads and hands protruded.

Unsure how to help, Sessadon protested, "I'm not a warrior."

"Then what good are you?" answered Ellimi.

Whether or not the warrior queen had meant it that way, Sessadon instantly thought of her answer. "I'm a magician."

"Then hurry up and magic that thing, please," Ellimi said, gesturing toward the snarling creature.

Sessadon felt that now was not the time to explain that her magic didn't work in the Underlands. They were in too deep for that.

The awful screeching of the birdlike head had finally fallen silent, and they both turned to watch as it sagged all the way to the ground, its eyes closing, and died. As the last life left it, the hand clutching the war mace sagged too, the weapon falling harmlessly to the ground.

Ellimi said, "So. If we kill the head, the hand dies. That makes things easier."

"Good," Sessadon said. Thinking, she added, "Good work."

The lion head roared again, angrier, sharper. Even at this distance, Sessadon thought she could feel the warmth of its hot breath. They had barely made a start. The creature was bound by the gate. That was their only advantage.

"So," Ellimi said, her voice grim but, somehow, also excited. "About that magic."

Sessadon braced herself, looked back and forth between the creature and Ellimi, and got ready.

Her magic didn't work here, she knew it didn't. But she thought about what she would do if it did. What enchantment would she cast? She discarded most of the possibilities, and then remembered how Eminel had transfixed her, drawn her attention, at the crucial moment for Tamura to strike. That was the spell she would use if she could. But she could draw attention without magic, couldn't she? It wouldn't hold as long, but maybe it didn't need to.

Raising her hands and holding them both out in the Voa's direction, palms forward, the sorcerer drew close to the creature.

She would have to try. And if the Voa ate her, she'd still be all right, wouldn't she? It wasn't as if she could be more dead than she already was. Then again, maybe she could. She didn't want to find out.

Sessadon reached out toward one of the creature's snouts and watched its seven remaining arms whip through the air, Ellimi's small form darting and weaving between the war hammer and the longsword, between the dagger and the axe.

Sessadon murmured a mind-magic spell she remembered, a transfixing one, that would grab and hold the creature's attention. There was no power behind it, nothing but her own belief that something was needed, and that would have to be enough.

Look at me, she murmured to the Voa, and the mock incantation was complete.

The golden eyes on one of the heads stared straight at Sessadon. The head itself was like a bear's, thick with golden fur and high round ears and a mouthful of broad, sharp teeth. The sorcerer fixed her gaze to ignore everything but the eyes, those golden eyes, full of anger and something that looked like it might be sadness, and she was still staring into those golden eyes when the head dropped from its neck and rolled, severed by Ellimi with her double-headed axe—in a single blow, this time—sending a spray of blood arcing through the air.

The team of two shades fell into a rhythm, a pattern. They kept moving forward. Each head fell, one by one. Sessadon transfixed an enormous wolf's head with blue eyes, a scaled head with greenish-yellow eyes and a sharp, forked tongue, and the head of an aurochs with eyes that blazed as red as a sunset over Godsbones, almost too bright to look at. And as each of the heads lowered itself to near Sessadon's height, Ellimi's axe sliced the head off and sent it rolling. By the fourth head, Sessadon had been sprayed with so much reddish-orange blood she could no longer see, but she only paused to wipe the blood from her eyes and let the rest of it stay. She wasn't sure how long she'd have a physical form like this; it seemed to be some manifestation from the Voa, that the creature had to make her and Ellimi real in order to fight them. But if all went according to plan, whatever this form was would be left behind as she defeated the creature, proceeded through the gate, and woke up in someone else's body on the other side.

All went according to plan—almost.

Head after head fell, arm after arm weakened and dropped its weapon. The weapons must have had some physical form too, because after each one, Sessadon was convinced she could hear some kind of a clang or thud, the sound of the lost weapon landing on whatever, in the Underlands, passed for earth.

Finally, only one head remained. Sessadon looked at Ellimi, hoping she could see this through. Even more blood-soaked than Sessadon herself, the Scorpican queen seemed to be tiring. The warrior didn't grin after each victory anymore. But when she saw Sessadon looking at her, Ellimi shifted her hands lower on the weapon's handle and gave the sorcerer one grim nod.

Sessadon wiped the blood from her eyes once more and transfixed the last head—*Look at me,* she murmured, and tasted the creature's red-orange blood on her lips as she did so—and held it, held it, held it for Ellimi to strike.

The axe swung down once more. The creature howled. The black-eyed head fell, rolled with a thud, and came to rest at Sessadon's feet.

Sessadon could both hear it and feel it when the gate opened. First came a sucking sound like an enormous creature taking an enormous breath, then nothingness, then a soft feeling of something like a cool breeze wafting outward, centered in the frame of the gate that had sheltered the Voa during its fight.

The gate sprang open, a vast circle like a dark mouth appearing, stretching wider and wider until it reached the frame of the gate, until there was nothing inside the frame but blackness. Darker than night, darker than ink. Its blackness felt vast beyond measure.

The gate was open.

The gate was open, and before Sessadon could even speak to acknowledge it, before she had even been completely sure it was happening, Ellimi had stepped through and was gone.

With the feeling of a pounding heart, Sessadon strode toward the gate, stepped over the fallen, mutilated body of the Voa and all eight of its discarded heads, and closed the distance to the gate, ready to go through with one more long stride.

And passed right through the gate to the other side—without leaving the Underlands.

She looked up at the stone arch, still too huge to see past to the left or right or upward. She was on the other side of it, but it looked no different from here, just as massive, just as heavy.

Shocked and furious, Sessadon held in a scream. What had happened? The second gate was open, clearly. They'd defeated the Voa. Ellimi had stepped through and vanished. Was she already inhabiting a body Aboveground? Or had there been some trick to it—had Ellimi gone on to a more permanent death, not Aboveground at all?

"No," said the voice of Eresh, suddenly present, though She hadn't been only moments before. "The gate is working exactly as intended. Now that the second gate is open, risen shades can inhabit the body of anyone who dies in Godsbones, and speak with their borrowed tongue."

It took almost no time to understand. The second part was less important than the first. With a sinking feeling, Sessadon said, "And hardly anyone dies in Godsbones."

"There was one," Eresh said. "An old hermit. He was driven out of his favorite caves by the Scorpicae two years ago. He resettled and was living in a new, quieter cave far to the west. He died of old age."

"And because his is the only dead body in Godsbones," said Sessadon, taking no pleasure in understanding, "the first shade through the gate occupied it. And that was Ellimi."

Eresh nodded. "You're not unintelligent, it seems, sorcerer. You simply lack foresight. You didn't plan, and now you can only react."

"So this was just an empty test?" asked Sessadon, gesturing at the gruesome remains of the Voa, unable to contain her irritation. "I'd open the second gate for you, just like you told me to, and you'd laugh at me because you knew it would make virtually no difference?"

"I wanted to see what might happen."

"You sound like your sister."

Eresh shrugged. "Ellimi could have let you go through the gate first. She didn't. Now you're sad about it."

"Not exactly sad."

Eresh still seemed unmoved. "That's how it looks to me. In any case, if you don't like where you are, you can certainly change it."

"And how can I do that?"

"Perhaps you *are* unintelligent," Eresh mused, contempt plain in Her voice. "Opening the second gate didn't get you what you wanted. What comes next?"

Sessadon caught on. "Opening the third gate."

"Yes."

The sorcerer was too tired to be truly eager, but she also knew how important it was to use the god's attention while she had it. "And I have your permission to do so?"

"You have my permission to try. Only, just a moment, this." Eresh raised one hand, made a quick motion with Her long fingers, something like pinching and plucking.

Sessadon *felt* the pinch, even though that wasn't remotely possible, and it unnerved her. "What was that?"

"You're elsewhere now," Eresh said loftily.

And when Sessadon looked, she saw it was true. No gate, no dead Voa, nothing else remotely familiar. She appeared to be in a stony area, black like volcanic rock, all jagged and bare. "Where am I?"

"Oh, at the edges of the Underlands. You'll make your way back to the more familiar parts, and eventually to the third gate, I'm sure. It may take you some time, I suppose. But the journey will prove your commitment."

"But that's not fair!"

"Oh, sorcerer," said Eresh, Her tone both sad and mocking, "there is nothing fair Above. What made you think things would be any different down here?"

PART III

THE
GATE OF
WARRIORS

The All-Mother's Year 519

✦ CHAPTER 16 ✦

ANSWERED PRAYER

Spring, the All-Mother's Year 519

Adaj, Arca

Aster

Rahul and Aster were not completely alone in the desert village of Adaj, but as far as Aster was concerned, they might as well have been. Aster never saw anyone up close. Rahul didn't want Aster to be seen. He'd selected this house well away from the other inhabited houses, and as purely and fiercely as he believed Aster was a girl sent to help him reclaim power, he had insisted Aster continue to wear boy's clothes to maintain the fiction of boyhood.

"They'll ask too many questions if they know you're a girl," he'd say, tapping a finger against Aster's nose before heading out to fetch water.

Aster wondered how many questions they'd ask if they knew that Aster was both boy and girl in one body, but it was impossible to talk to Rahul about such things. In the early days, Aster had tiptoed up to the edge of the subject, trying to feel out the best way to address the truth. But Aster had long since realized that truth did not interest Rahul. It could only upset him. So Aster let things pass and did their best to get along, hoping that eventually Rahul would simply realize that his plan was going nowhere.

But Rahul still insisted, every day, that Aster try to do magic. It was becoming farcical, really. The worst thing was that even as Aster thought it was obvious that all this effort was wasted, Rahul only seemed more certain that a breakthrough lay just around the corner.

Was it faith, thought Aster, or madness?

Certainly Rahul had become angrier whenever he watched Aster fail. He had begun to storm off in frustration more often than not. Aster was never sure how long it would take him to return.

Then, one day, after Rahul stormed off, Aster flung the *psama* to the ground in frustration. They immediately regretted it. If Rahul came back, he'd be furious that Aster had treated the magical object so callously.

So Aster reached out with one hand in the *psama*'s direction. Quicker than a blink, the pendant came flying back to land in their outstretched hand.

Aster was so shocked, they dropped the pendant again. It landed softly on the sand. And this time, deliberately, Aster called the *psama* up with beckoning fingers.

And, as if drawn by a string, it came.

Aster stood trembling. Magic. The exact thing they'd never wanted. And here it was, inescapable.

Eventually, Rahul would find out. That was Aster's first thought. They hadn't wanted magic for their own reasons, but especially because it would prove Rahul right, and he was hard enough to live with even without knowing his vision was within reach.

What options did Aster have? Running was one, of course. But they knew nothing of Arcan geography. Had no money, nowhere to go. All they could do was hide the magic as long as possible.

And over time, Aster decided to try new things. Never when

Rahul was around, and always careful to leave no trace. Moving other objects without touching them, from the lightest feather to the heavy door at the top of the ladder. And movement was just the beginning. Aster could warm a small cup of water, or chill that water until it was cold enough to numb Aster's tongue. They could, if they focused carefully, even hear the thoughts inside Rahul's head. Usually his thoughts just echoed the words Rahul spoke out loud—*ridiculous child, ungrateful child, when will she finally show promise*—so Aster rarely bothered, but it was enough to know. The power was both frightening and heady, a source of secret pride.

As careful as Aster was, keeping the secret for more than a season, it could not last. One night, sharing a meager meal of porridge in the light of a single candle next to their hearth, Aster made their mistake. Rahul sat in the better chair nearer the fire, where the pot of porridge sat on the coals.

"May I have another scoop?" asked Aster, breaking the silence.

Rahul didn't look up, intent on his own bowl. "Sure. Help yourself."

"You're closer," said Aster.

Rahul grunted, indicating that he wasn't going to put himself out to help. Annoyed, Aster reached out and took most of the remaining porridge, scooping it into their bowl with a satisfying splat. Except— instead of their hands, they'd used their mind to take action.

The next thing they knew, Rahul had leapt up from his chair, sending it tumbling, and dropped to his knees.

Aster, shocked at his sudden movement, let their entire bowl of porridge drop.

Rahul didn't seem to notice. He reached out and grabbed Aster's hands tightly, painfully tight. His voice was rich with wonder as he said, "Magnificent. Do you understand what this means?"

Aster gave a negative shake of their head.

Rahul didn't acknowledge the response; he was in some other place, Aster could see, his mind already working at lightning speed. This frightened them more than all the energy he had poured year after year into finding Aster's magic.

Aster had never allowed themselves to think very deeply about what Rahul so badly wanted that magic for.

In a halting voice, they said, "Well, can you tell me? What happens now?"

Rahul's grin was wide, terrifying. "I figured you had some magic. I mean, my daughter, right? I don't know if you realize how strong I am, how unusual it is to be able to accomplish such a wide range of illusions, for a man."

Aster had heard him say this many times back in Odimisk, to other men whom he spoke with in shadow, but he was afraid to speak. Rahul seemed not to need an answer, anyway.

He said, "So it follows that my daughter would be talented. I just didn't know how talented."

Aster shrugged. "I just do little things. Move things around here and there."

"Just moving things?"

At this point, there was no reason to hold back. He'd gotten a taste now. Rahul wouldn't stop until he'd swallowed Aster's world whole.

"Move them around," Aster mumbled, staring down at the floor next to the hearth, where thick porridge puddled around their overturned bowl. Every word felt like a stone. "Heat things up, cool things down."

"Like water?" Even without seeing his face, Aster could hear his joy.

"Yes, like water. Milk. Oil. Any liquid."

"Can you make fire?"

"A little."

"We'll work on that," he said, partly to Aster, partly to himself. "What else? Can you affect bodies? Other people's, your own?"

Suddenly, Aster's annoyance flared. They couldn't stand to be bled dry by a thousand cuts. So Aster held up one hand, spread their fingers wide, and made Rahul's fingers do the same.

Now, Aster watched his face. Anger and amazement flickered there as he tried to force his hand to close. It would not. Not until Aster said, "Here," and let their control drop. Rahul's anger became joy again. Then, one expression that Aster had never seen on their father's face: pride.

"At last. All our hard work paid off. Velja is truly great."

Aster didn't explain the role Velja had played, which was to answer Aster's prayer with the opposite of what they had asked for. Aster had prayed to have no magic at all. Velja's apparent answer was to give them all-magic, the most powerful magic there could possibly be.

Rahul said, "Now we can do what we came here to do."

Aster felt like everything was crumbling. Yet they couldn't help saying the three words they knew Rahul wanted them to say. "What is that?"

Rahul's grin was like a wolf's, sharp and threatening in the hearth fire's flickering light. He said, "You're going to help me kill the queen."

✦ CHAPTER 17 ✦

MOON RITES

Midsummer, the All-Mother's Year 519

Holy City, Sestia

Olivi, Concordia

As the Holy City prepared for the Moon Rites, on an errand for one of the Daras, Olivi took a shortcut through an alleyway. Her hasty steps carried her almost straight into a tangle of limbs and faces it took her several long, stunned moments to interpret. When Olivi finally figured out that she was looking at three people and not two, her blood rushed to her cheeks, hot like scarlet fire.

Back home on the farm, pleasures were quiet, overheard sighs from neighboring bedchambers in the dark, not intertwined bodies in daylight, and certainly not in a public place where anyone might see. Not a long-necked woman with a bearded man behind her, his hips rocking against hers in a slow, regular rhythm, and a lush-figured woman in front of her, one hand bringing the first woman's mouth to hers, the other hand dipping low to disappear between their entwined legs. Reeling from the shock and some other feeling she couldn't identify, Olivi's mind was too busy to suggest to her body that she might simply move and be gone. The long-necked woman writhed as if in pain but moaned in a way that clearly indicated pleasure. The only motion Olivi made while she watched, mind working madly, heart hammering, was when her mouth fell open in a soft squeak.

At the sound of Olivi's shock, the woman with generous hips and breasts, whose back was pressed against the alleyway wall, turned her head. Bare as the day she was born, she cocked her head with a smile and released the other woman's neck to reach out toward Olivi, beckoning with her long fingers, a clear invitation to join them.

Olivi remained frozen.

After the length of several heartbeats—Olivi's heart was as fast as a bird's now—the long-necked woman growled to her distracted lover, "No, don't stop." A plea, a command.

Turning at last to go back the way she'd come, Olivi heard the laughter of all three of them, two women whose laughter pealed like bells and one man's laugh as deep and brassy as a gong. Just before she emerged from the alleyway back into the street, she heard one woman's laughter cut off with a sharp, warm groan. Innocent as she was, Olivi could still guess what she was hearing. The urgency of that groan, the way it seemed to tear itself free of the woman's throat against her will, lingered with Olivi as she hastened back to the Edifice.

When the Dara she'd run the errand for asked why it had taken her so long to return, Olivi told an abridged version of the story, saying a pair engaged in pleasures had been blocking her shortcut, so she'd gone the long way around. She couldn't say what had kept her from mentioning that there'd been three people and not two—was there a difference, to the Holy One? Did the god smile on two more than three, or the other way around?—but the Dara had chuckled at Olivi's obvious naivete.

"You should find someone to pursue pleasures with," the Dara suggested, raising an eyebrow. "You're old enough. The city is flooded with willing participants. But only for another day or two. Take your chance while you can."

Olivi had bobbed her head quickly, handed over the package she'd retrieved, and stepped away. Yet she was curious enough that it lingered in her mind, and finally, she gathered the courage to mention it to Concordia.

Pretending nonchalance, she said, "Is it one or two more days of the Moon Rites? I thought perhaps I might . . . join in."

"Join in?"

She felt the blood rushing to her cheeks again, but she'd come this far. She'd see it through. "Pleasures. That's what the Holy One wants during the rites, isn't it?"

The look on Concordia's face was inscrutable. Olivi regretted her question instantly, but there was no taking it back.

After a long moment of hesitation, the High Xara said, "Xaras refrain from pleasures because the god demands it of us. We can have no earthly attachments. We reject pleasures of the body because after Her consort betrayed Her, the Holy One never sought pleasures of the body again."

There was something mechanical about the way the High Xara said these words, as if she were reading from a text. Olivi just wanted the moment to be over, so she did not point out the obvious, which was that she herself, Olivi, was not a Xara of any kind. Nor even a Dara. There was no word for what she was.

What role did the High Xara expect her to play in the long term, if any? That was exactly the kind of thing Olivi couldn't bring herself to ask. Just as she never asked whether she could send a message to her mother. Olivi felt better pretending that she'd never had a family at all, that her existence was only this circumscribed dance in the walls of the Edifice.

Concordia sometimes seemed to be training Olivi for the role of High Xara, teaching her the thousands of rules and strictures and responsibilities that governed life at the Edifice. But at other times she seemed to treat the young woman as a servant or a shadow, telling her what to do, dismissing her with an offhand wave or a sharp word. Sometimes Olivi even worried that Concordia intended that at the next Sun Rites, Olivi would be the sacrifice.

Of course Olivi knew the sacrifices were always ten-and-four years of age, and Olivi would be ten-and-nine by the time of the next Sun Rites, a woman and not a girl. But she remembered well the story of what had happened two Sun Rites ago, when she herself had not even been ten years old. The sacrifices were always one boy and one girl, until they weren't. It had been the time of the Drought and desperate action had been called for, and the High Xara had done the most desperate—some said bravest—thing, giving the greatest sacrifice the Five Queendoms had ever seen. But it hadn't ended the Drought, and so over the years the story of that sacrifice had changed, from something brave to something foolish or even malevolent. Some people complained that the High Xara had not done enough, and others complained that she had done too much. The complaints didn't end when the Drought did. The gossips wondered whether the High Xara had made her choice for the god's sake or her own.

Because here she was, years after most High Xaras had passed their power on to their successors, and she had no successor at all. She still hadn't gathered another class of Xaras-to-be. Perhaps when there were five-year-old girls again, said some, she would. But if that particularly bloody Sun Rites during the Drought had proven anything, it was that no one could predict exactly what High Xara Concordia would do.

So while Olivi thought it was highly unlikely she would be designated the sacrifice to the Holy One, neither did she think it impossible.

In the meantime, there were Moon Rites to complete, and she

didn't think she would be substituted for any of the traditional sacrifices at those rites: mouflon, ram, goat, dove, sparrow. The day before the Rites, in the *lacrum*, Concordia turned to Olivi and said, as if it were a perfectly regular thing to say, "You'll help me with tomorrow's sacrifices."

Stunned, Olivi said, "Will I?"

Concordia seemed unbothered by the young woman's shock. "Yes. The Holy One wills it."

Olivi couldn't help venturing, half-question, half-prayer, *Do You? Is that what You wish?*

But she heard no answer from the Holy One. She felt only a warm, smothering silence, like a blanket or a fog that would not lift. And the next morning, as the rites began, she joined the procession as always, following the High Xara in her saffron through the torchlit dark.

Seeing the shadowed outlines of the amphitheater again, hearing the breathing audience in the predawn quiet, was somehow both joyous and terrifying. Olivi could shake neither feeling, both twisted up in a knot that sat squarely in her chest between her throat and her heart, as if she had swallowed a stone.

Olivi breathed shallowly, expectantly, through the ritual dances. At the Moon Rites there were no bone beds, only a broad altar with grooves cut for blood-draining. The High Xara was the only queen in attendance. And as the sun rose, Olivi could see that this year's audience was typical for a Moon Rites, nowhere near as large as the Sun Rites' crowd had been. When she heard the long, mournful note of the ceremonial horn, she heard the answering calls of the dove and the sparrow, the bleating of the goat, the muttering of the mouflon and ram, and then she finally began to relax. The Moon Rites were different enough from the Sun Rites that even though the place was the same, the expressionless High Xara in the same ceremonial saffron, Olivi's body allowed her to let go of the threatened feeling.

Once the ritual dances were complete, the High Xara stepped forward and looked out over the gathered audience. When she spoke, it was in the voice of command. "Let the god be fed."

The mouflon was first, wrestled onto the altar by burly attendants, Olivi hovering uselessly nearby. Unhesitatingly, the High Xara drew her blade across the animal's throat. Olivi's breath caught, knowing what came next.

Blood ran down, down into the notches, down, down onto the grain, staining the gold red, blessing the future as a Dara stirred the blood in.

The other four animals died the same way, not without struggle but without undue suffering, and Olivi stood by the entire time. Had the god really wanted her nearby just for this?

And then Olivi heard Concordia call her name, not loudly but clearly. "Olivi. Here."

Olivi's skin prickled as if she'd been doused in a cold pool, the world rushing at her too fast to feel.

But she went to the High Xara's side immediately. She couldn't help coming when she was called, no matter what. In a sense, she'd been training for this every day with Concordia. Olivi took the few steps between them with due haste, as if she had been summoned to bring a bowl of water or offer a rag, and she stood at the priest's side, heart hammering. All she could do was keep her eyes unfocused, not looking at the High Xara's face or eyes, and particularly not anywhere near that sharp, bloody knife.

"Closer," said Concordia.

Olivi took one more step. Her shoulder was almost touching the High Xara's now, her pale yellow robe about to brush the priest's royal saffron. She swallowed.

When the High Xara spoke again, it was in an urgent, plaintive whisper, too soft for anyone but Olivi to hear. "Take the knife from me. Lay it on the cushion the Dara Joiaca bears. With reverence. Show nothing on your face, absolutely nothing. Do it quickly now."

Finally Olivi let herself look down at the High Xara's hands, and when she did, she saw they were shaking. The tremor looked uncontrollable, even painful. Concordia's right hand had tightened into a kind of claw around the blade's hilt, like a panicked crake clutching a branch for fear of falling.

As she'd been bid, face impassive, Olivi reached over and eased the blade out of Concordia's hands. Olivi got blood on her own hands in the process when she had to uncurl the High Xara's frozen fingers one by one. It was like taking the blade from a statue, or a corpse. She forced one finger to straighten just enough to pull it free, then did the same with the next, hoping she wasn't hurting Concordia, but knowing she couldn't stop regardless. The High Xara had commanded her. She would follow through.

Olivi's eyes met Concordia's, and the fear she saw there stopped her cold; but Concordia hissed wordlessly, reminding Olivi that she was to show no emotion. So Olivi rearranged her facial features into a calm, emotionless mask. Then she got back to the task before her, shoving hard on the base of the High Xara's thumb with the pad of her own thumb until the priest's cramped, spasming hand finally released the bloody, sacred dagger.

Turning deliberately, as if she had all the time in the world, Olivi then lay the sharp blade on the pale cushion borne by the Dara Joiaca, a slight woman who usually wore a bored, incurious expression. The Dara Joiaca did not look bored now.

Once the sacred blade was squared away, it was time for the procession to begin, but the High Xara didn't move. Olivi panicked, but didn't let herself react. All eyes were on the High Xara at this point in the rites; everyone knew what was supposed to happen next. There was a huge chance that whatever Olivi chose to do would be the wrong thing. So she did nothing, only waited with the rest of the crowd, an entire amphitheater of held breath.

Then the High Xara turned at last, gesturing to Olivi to take a place at her side—but for the first time, Olivi noted with surprise, Concordia gestured to her right instead of her left, as was tradition.

When Olivi took her new place on Concordia's right, she realized why Concordia had placed her there. The High Xara's right hand had curled up into a claw again and was trembling, the tremor so strong it might be visible from a distance. Having Olivi next to her, between her and the audience in the amphitheater, blocked the crowd's view of the trembling right hand. But would that be enough? Olivi wondered whether the closer women, including the Dara Joiaca, could see.

Just to be sure they wouldn't, Olivi reached out and tucked the High Xara's trembling hand beneath her own arm, making it look as if she were simply escorting the priest out of respect. They matched their steps to the same rhythm as they proceeded down the steps and back toward the temple-palace, the rest of the attendants trailing behind.

As she sometimes did in these situations, Olivi sent up a quick prayer to the Holy One. *Let the High Xara be healed, if it is Your will.*

And in that same moment, the answering voice came back. *Yes, help her. Take her to the* lacrum *and tell her to dip her hands in the well. If she is truly penitent, I will take her affliction away.*

When the Holy One spoke to Olivi in the High Xara's presence, Olivi wondered why the High Xara didn't seem to react. Why didn't the god just speak to her directly, instead of using Olivi as a go-between? She supposed that perhaps the god spoke this way when She said something Concordia didn't want to hear. Olivi assumed Concordia's physical weakness was shameful to her; if it weren't, she wouldn't try to hide it.

Then, for the first time, the question came into Olivi's head: Did the god actually speak to Concordia? Surely it was heresy even to wonder. She quashed the thought. How outrageous that she should even think it.

Now was not the time for questions. Now was the time to move forward, to bring the Moon Rites to a close. The sacrifice had been given and accepted. Pleasures would fill the city tonight, angled hips and slick fingers and caught breaths, everywhere except the Edifice.

Three years ago, thought Olivi as they walked in a somber, slow procession, she had almost died at the rites. She had almost been slain and bled as a sacrifice, but against all odds, she'd been saved. Today she had played a small, important role in the nation's rites once more, even if no one knew it but the High Xara and the Holy One.

But as often as she told herself that her questions were groundless, those questions kept cropping up again in her head. The High Xara couldn't live forever. If Olivi wasn't named a Xara, then who would be High Xara after? And what would happen to Olivi then?

✦

In the moments after the end of the Moon Rites, Concordia couldn't remember what she was supposed to do. How was it possible she was still making and remaking herself, after all these years as High Xara? Uncertainty didn't become her. Yet here she was, feeling lost and strange, her hand curled into a claw as if she were becoming some sort of animal.

Perhaps, she thought, she was. Perhaps that was why she could no longer move and think and talk like a woman. Why she was reduced to this shivering, bent thing, dragging herself along behind the former sacrifice she'd chosen as a companion, following the young woman as if she, not Concordia, were the leader.

Luckily, what Olivi said next snapped her out of her reverie and reminded her who she was, who she'd always been.

"Perhaps we should go to the *lacrum*?" suggested Olivi.

Concordia stopped in her tracks. Outrage brought her clarity. Hand still trembling, the High Xara said in an imperious tone, "We? That is not your decision to make."

"I'm sorry." The younger woman's apology was quick, seemingly reflexive. "I don't mean to step out of my place. Of course it is your decision alone."

"The god's, really," said Concordia, letting her voice soften slightly. In truth she desperately wanted to go straight to the *lacrum*. It was Olivi's suggestion that she, too, be allowed in the sacred place that was outrageous.

And yet. Concordia didn't know what she would have done without the young woman there to assist her during the rites, to hide her infirmity from the crowd. The need made her feel weak; the weakness made her feel angry and resentful. She couldn't keep anyone else as close as she kept Olivi. The young woman had been there to bear the brunt of her anger so many times. Might she be allowed to share something better?

Olivi waited quietly, patiently, and Concordia made up her mind.

Concordia said, "Very well. Let us go to the *lacrum*. The god will allow it just this once, in recognition of your extraordinary service today. She is pleased by today's sacrifice. Let us unveil ourselves before the god and ask Her wisdom on how we should live."

"Yes, good," murmured Olivi.

If the servant outside the *lacrum* thought it strange that Olivi trailed Concordia into the sacred room, he knew better than to show it. He opened the door, stepped aside, and, once they'd crossed the threshold, closed it behind them.

As she set foot onto the white marble, Concordia was hit with two opposing feelings, equally strong: the comfort of the familiar and the forbidding sense of cold that crept up out of the stone to surround her. This was where she most and least belonged. And all the while that she thought this, that she considered what the god might want of her, she still felt the tremor in her bent hand, the insistent reminder that she had not escaped punishment for what she'd done, no matter how belated it might be.

What do you want of me? she asked the god. *Shall I cut off my hand and give it to you? Cut my own throat? Do you want me to suffer for you? I will. Only ask it of me.*

She said none of this aloud. She was too aware of the young woman next to her, and though Olivi's opinion was really of no importance, Concordia still feared her censure. The young woman was one of the only people in the world who looked at her with pure respect untinged by any doubt. She would not take that from the girl. She would not take it from herself. She needed it like air.

"Let us pray, then," said Concordia.

"An honor," Olivi said. In her voice there was wonder.

So, for hours after the sacrifice, the two of them knelt in silence on the cold white marble. Concordia kept pressing her knees harder and harder into the floor, magnifying the pain, hoping it would distract her from the tremors that had still not left her. No change. By turns she put one hand inside the other, pressed the back of the palm hard against the stone, even knelt on it, all to try to quell the shivering.

"The well," Olivi said quietly. They were the only words she'd spoken aloud since their prayers had begun.

Concordia wasn't used to hearing the young woman's voice in the privacy of the *lacrum*, a place intended for listening to the Holy One's voice alone.

"Hush," she snapped. She was so angry about Olivi's sacrilege, unintended or no, she gave no thought whatsoever to what her companion had actually said.

But after another while—the pain in her knees creeping upward through her legs, making her hips ache, as if they were being grasped by icy, relentless fingers—she thought back to that moment. And for the first time she heard the words that had been spoken. *The well*, Olivi had said.

As if Olivi had spoken only seconds and not minutes or hours before, Concordia said crossly, "And what about it, then?"

"What?" The young woman blinked.

"The well," said Concordia with obvious irritation. "What about it?"

"She . . . you should put your hands in," said Olivi, not meeting the High Xara's eyes.

"Why?"

There was a long pause from Olivi, who was obviously turning something over in her mind, but whatever it was, she didn't say. Her gaze didn't lift from the white marble upon which she, like the High Xara, knelt. Instead she held a hand out in the direction of the well, with a gesture that looked like equal parts emphasis and hopelessness.

"Tell me," said Concordia, through gritted teeth. "Why should I put my hands in the well? The god has never allowed such a thing before. Her guidance on the topic has been very clear. Why would I do this—this potential sacrilege, today of all days?"

When Olivi's small voice came, her words all flooded out in a rush, hard even to distinguish one from the next. "If you're penitent, you'll be healed."

Concordia almost roared. *"Penitent?!"*

Shocked, Olivi shrank away, her eyes wide. She rocked back hard on her own heels, and obviously the weight caused her pain, but she made no sound. Those eyes, though. They were full of fear.

Concordia knew she'd frightened the girl, but perhaps the girl needed frightening. How insolent she'd been. What in the name of the Holy One was Olivi thinking, suggesting she knew better than the High Xara herself? Up was down and down was up. It had been a mistake to allow the girl into this sacred space. There was no one she could trust. No one.

"I have no cause for penitence," growled Concordia, leaning closer to Olivi, letting her presence express the implied threat, hovering over where the young woman had drawn herself into a crouch. It was enough. "I have done *nothing* wrong. Do you understand?"

"Yes," said the young woman in a whisper. The fright on her face made her look much younger than her years, a helpless, hopeless girl once again.

Concordia thought of other frightened girls she'd known and then brushed the feeling quickly away. She did not let her intensity relax. The point must be made. "You, child, will not presume to tell me what to do. I take orders only from the god."

The young woman's shoulders shook in a tremor not unlike what Concordia was already seeing in her hand. Was Olivi crying? Concordia did not want to see that.

"Perhaps you are the one who needs to take penitent actions to atone for your sins," said the High Xara, her tone lofty. "Unless you are hearing the voice of the god yourself, like I do, you do not speak for Her."

An idea sprang to mind. "Stay here on your knees, child. I will return for you when I feel you have done enough. It may be hours. It may be days. But I alone will choose when to set eyes on your face again. No other opinion but the god's matters. Certainly, and especially, not yours."

Concordia spun and left the *lacrum* before Olivi had a chance to respond. She didn't bother calling the servant, just opened the door herself and closed it behind her. She didn't want to hear a single word more.

Something about the young woman's certainty had shaken her.

What reason could she, the High Xara, possibly have to be penitent? And how could Olivi think she was the one to tell her so? Concordia's anger flared again, like an oil-soaked rag flung into a fire. Let the girl kneel there and wonder if Concordia was ever coming back. Fear was useful, the High Xara thought. More useful than compassion or mercy, it seemed.

With satisfaction the High Xara noted that her hand was no longer trembling; she didn't allow herself to think that the tremor might eventually come back. She simply dusted her palms together and headed back toward her chamber, satisfied. She would give Olivi a long few hours to consider her sins, and when the young woman was released from the *lacrum* at last, she would shine with gratitude. That was the only possible outcome.

But on the way to her chambers, the High Xara was intercepted by Rix, whose beautiful face made her gut roil. She always thought of him in conjunction with Xelander; she had sent Xelander away for a time, not liking how he looked at Olivi, but the association between the two servants remained. She had pulled herself out of her funk by pure will, but upon his approach, her bad mood returned again instantly. Inside, she burned, though she kept her face placid, impenetrable.

"You have a visitor," Rix said, his voice respectful.

She fixed him with a glare, let him stew. At length, she responded, "It has been a long day, Rix, as you might imagine if you gave it some thought. So, consider this and you will understand. I am not in the mood for visitors."

"Of course, High Xara. That is your prerogative," he said humbly, bending his head.

He was already walking away, narrow hips swinging under the fitted skirt of his tunic, before she changed her mind and called him back. "Wait."

Rix halted instantly. One might even wonder if he had been expecting her to interrupt his exit.

"Who is the visitor? Not some queen again?" she asked, making sure it seemed she couldn't possibly care about the answer.

"No," Rix said, turning, intertwining his delicate fingers at his waist, all politeness and deference.

"Emissary from another queendom? Or one of our own?"

"She didn't explain herself," he said, a note of apology in his voice, as she felt there should be. "She has simply repeated that she has a very important message for you, one only she can deliver."

"And what does she look like?"

"Like a Sestian farmer, I suppose, if I had to guess. But no dirt on her tunic. She just looks like . . . anyone."

Concordia arched an eyebrow. "Well, I suppose I might as well go see. Though you don't make her sound very interesting."

"I apologize," he said, sounding like he meant it. "Next time I will look more closely."

"I doubt there will be a next time," she said. He wasn't saying anything particularly wrong, but his failing to pay closer attention irritated her, and she felt a strong urge to put him in his place. "Your talents are probably better put to use in the kitchens, as they previously were. You will return there as soon as our staff is at full strength again."

"Whatever you deem best, High Xara," he said. "Wherever you want me, I will be more than happy to serve."

Something in his voice made her think he was offering what Xelander had offered, but she brushed that thought aside. Not every servant in the Edifice was hungry to lick and nip at women's flesh, to hear a woman smother her own cries of pleasure with whatever fabric came to hand, to violate the most important tenet of what set Xaras apart. It was only her own weaknesses that made her see weakness everywhere, Concordia decided. The day had been too long, too eventful, for her to think straight anymore. She needed to dismiss this visitor and then she could retire for the night, pull the curtain on this day. She took a moment to think, to center herself, closing her eyes and opening them again.

"Very well. Lead me to where she waits," she told Rix, and he headed down the hallway with squared shoulders and his head held high, as a servant should.

The visitor was probably no one of importance, she decided as they walked. No woman of Sestia could really expect to present herself at the Edifice, ask to see the High Xara, and be ushered into the priest's presence—what kind of world would that be?

So her expectations were low as she entered the receiving room. She was thinking only of her much-needed rest, with a faint, tickling awareness that she should probably release young Olivi from where she still knelt on the white marble of the *lacrum* floor. She had allowed the young woman in, which was her prerogative as High Xara, but leaving her there alone might not have been a wise choice. Certainly Olivi had not manipulated her into it—it had been Concordia's own idea—but now it jarred her as so wrong, the idea of Olivi in that sacred room by herself, she almost turned and ran back down the hallway, audience be damned.

As it was, she calmly said to Rix, "Please tell Olivi to leave the *lacrum* and go to her own quarters."

"I'll do that right away," he said.

As she entered the audience room, she thought perhaps she should have asked him to stay. If the visitor turned out to be someone important, she might want to entertain them in style. The day and the prayers had exhausted her. She needed to get this over with.

But then she caught sight of the visitor who waited for her, and every other thought flew right out of her head.

The woman's clothes were rough-spun, undyed, with no ornament or even color. They would not have set her apart from the crowd anywhere in Sestia; she was not in any way remarkable. But her clothing was not what caught the High Xara's eye.

It was the shape of the visitor's figure that was heartbreakingly familiar, her compact curves, her stature unchanged by the years. The woman looked up and Concordia saw the twinkle of her wide-set eyes.

At first Concordia thought it must be only coincidence, the resemblance of the visitor to her oldest friend, but then something between hope and fear caught in her chest, rising up into her throat and silencing her. She simply *knew* this woman. After all this time, with everything that had happened to them both, everything Concordia had seen and done, a chord of recognition struck between them and would not be denied.

As the High Xara finished entering the room, the woman knelt, showing respect to both Concordia and the Holy One she served. It was exactly what a visitor from the countryside would do, thought Concordia, with one exception: this one rose from her crouch without being bid, unfolding her limbs with confidence, and when she was standing again, she looked directly into Concordia's eyes.

It was Norah, once known as the Xara Veritas. Two decades older, weathered from the sun and wind, the marks of the outside world everywhere on her small body, but underneath all that, she was the same. The only one Concordia could talk to, the only one who shared her history and her whispers, her fears, her hopes. The one she'd been sure she'd never see again.

The last time Concordia had seen Veritas, she'd just been beginning to show her pregnancy, on the day when Concordia had exiled her and forced her to her knees, cut the saffron streak from her hair. The woman's hair was dark now, of course, with no sign of the special standing she'd once had. Of course, Concordia told herself, of course. It had been so long. Hair grew much faster than that. Lives had been given and taken away, futures spun and cut off, since the last time this woman had set foot in the Edifice. The very Drought of Girls had begun and ended since they'd seen each other. Since Concordia had stood on bright white floors like these and sent her only friend in the world away.

Concordia's head spun. What she wanted most was to run to the other woman and scoop her up in an embrace. She had wondered for two decades whether she'd caused her friend's death by sending her from the Edifice in disgrace and banishing her from Sestia entirely. With great relief she saw it wasn't so.

But what she should do now that the woman herself stood in front of her? She had no idea.

"High Xara Concordia," said the visitor, her manner not as tentative as it would have been if they were strangers, but with plenty of uncertainty in her voice. It had been so long for both of them. Concordia didn't know what had brought Norah here, but it must have been something very serious, knowing that when the High Xara had banished her, she'd forbidden her return to the city under pain of death. And yet. Here she was, in the very flesh. Risking death. Concordia needed to know why.

"And shall I call you Norah?" Concordia responded.

Quietly, the woman who had once been the Xara Veritas said, "It is all anyone has called me for years."

"I hope you are not here to reclaim your previous title. I was very clear."

Norah's body tensed; Concordia saw it. She was wondering whether she'd made a huge mistake, coming here.

Norah said, "It isn't my title I wish to reclaim."

Concordia suddenly found herself afraid. She didn't entirely want to know what her oldest friend had to ask of her; if the High Xara had any sense, she'd send the woman away without even hearing her out. She had said she would have the woman killed if she set foot in the city. Here she was, in the city.

Yet Concordia could not enforce the consequences she had threatened. The sight of Norah's familiar face, even with the passage of time stamped on every feature, was far too dear.

"Before you make your request, some tea?" asked Concordia.

Norah looked slightly startled, but then she nodded. "Kind of you to offer."

Concordia almost made a joke that she was nothing if not kind, but it would be so hollow, when everyone knew she wasn't. What she really wanted was some lily wine, but tea was more appropriate for a visitor, and she felt a sudden need to do everything as correctly as she could with Norah here.

She called for a servant to bring tea, and let the silence sit heavily on them both as they waited. She was too afraid to say something wrong, so said nothing. When the door opened, she assumed it would be the servant, and called, "Enter."

But the figure that came through the door was no servant, bearing no tea. Even in the briefest glimpse, it was obvious who had come. No one else was allowed to wear a pale yellow robe dyed with saffron, only Concordia's special attendant, and only for today's rites.

For a moment, all was still. Then Concordia heard Olivi's voice speak first, sharp and wondering, from where she stood in the doorway.

Olivi said, "Mother?"

✦

Having Norah back in the Edifice was wonderful and beautiful, and Concordia wondered if it might be the happiest she'd ever been.

Her precious joy lasted five days.

No one knew that Norah was the former Xara Veritas, and neither Concordia nor Norah was going to tell them; Concordia kept her close, had a pallet placed in her own bedroom for her friend to use, and insisted that only Rix wait on them, no other servants. Rix had come to serve in the Edifice after the Drought had already begun.

While Concordia had been glad to hear it confirmed that what she had always suspected was true—Olivi was her old friend's daughter, born only the day before the start of the Drought—she feared what might happen if Olivi and Norah were able to spend time together alone. So she spoke to them both separately, laying things out in no uncertain terms. Olivi, she threatened to send from the Edifice if she was caught speaking with her mother; Norah, she reminded of the death sentence that accompanied her exile, and nothing more needed to be said.

After that, Concordia and Norah never talked about the bad things, only the good things. Delightful stories of their youth together here, how Concordia was always tricking the old Xara Victrix, who'd had it in for her, and stories of Norah learning her way on the farm, her utter confusion the first time she was asked to milk a goat, to strangle a rooster for the pot, to change the straw in the pallets.

On the fifth day, Norah and Concordia were enjoying tea in their shared chamber. Concordia was enjoying lily wine alongside her tea; she had relaxed enough that she wasn't afraid of offending Norah. Norah had accepted a cup of wine, but drank from it only occasionally, while Concordia had refilled her own cup several times. She was teasing Norah about her habit of setting aside her favorite bites of a meal to savor at the end. "You always did that."

Norah laughed. "I always saved the best for last. And you always ate it first."

"You never know what might happen! Why wait?" said Concordia.

"You should try it for once," Norah chided gently. "The anticipation makes it better."

Concordia eyed her with feigned suspicion, but did as her friend asked. While they chatted, instead of enjoying the tenderest bits from the center of the cake, she set them toward the far edge of her plate.

Then, when Rix came to pour more tea for them, he spilled it on the table, soaking the last bites of cake the High Xara had been saving. So relaxed from Norah's company and the lily wine, Concordia didn't even chastise him, but she saw him tense up as if she had, almost shaking with worry that he'd be punished. She considered reassuring him, but that didn't seem right either. She would simply let the moment pass.

Voice trembling as he cleared away the ruined remains of the meal, Rix said to her, "I am so sorry, High Xara. There are no words. But you'll be pleased to know, I will be back in the kitchens soon enough."

"Oh?" she asked idly, but she wasn't even looking at him. She was looking back and forth between her tea and wine, trying to decide which to sip next. He had at least spoiled only the food and not the drinks.

It was Norah who asked, "Back in the kitchens? Why?"

Rix said to Norah, "I am not the ranking servant here. The most senior has been on pilgrimage, but he has sent word that he returns tomorrow. So the next time you take tea, I will only be preparing it. The one who serves will be a man called Xelander."

The next thing Concordia heard was another crash, another teacup falling. *How clumsy Rix is today,* she thought at first. But when she looked up, Rix only looked confused, not chagrined.

Norah looked down at the broken cup. Her fingers, realized Concordia, had been the ones to let the cup fall to the floor.

"You said he was gone," she said to Concordia.

"I did?"

"Xelander," said Norah, her voice oddly tight. "You said he was gone."

"He was. On pilgrimage, like Rix said. And now he's returning."

But then, even through her haze, Concordia noticed how Norah's back had gone rigid, her fingers nerveless.

Concordia said, "Norah? Are you all right?"

Norah blinked and reached down for the shards of the cup.

Rix said, "Let me—" and reached out, but it was too late. Concordia heard the sudden intake of breath as Norah cut her finger on a sharp edge.

"Rix, fetch me a clean bandage," Norah said, even though it wasn't her place to command a palace servant. She'd given up that right years before. But her voice rang with a Xara's authority, and without even glancing at Concordia to confirm the order, he nodded and left.

Once the two women were alone again, Norah turned to Concordia, her eyes wide. She reached out for Concordia's hands, which Concordia gave her, even though Norah's blood still flowed red from the cut on her finger.

"He can't know," said Norah, her voice low and urgent. "Promise me. No one can know."

"Know what?" asked Concordia, looking where Rix had gone.

"Olivi," said Norah.

"You aren't making any sense," Concordia said gently, almost laughing. "Perhaps you'd have too much wine. I mean, you've had too much wine."

"Xelander," Norah said, with that tightness in her voice again. "Has he—does he know who Olivi is?"

"He knows she was chosen as the sacrifice for the last Sun Rites, and that ever since then, she has been my companion." She didn't mention that she'd sent Xelander on pilgrimage once he started showing too much interest in Olivi, terrified he might try to seduce the girl the way he'd seduced Concordia herself. She couldn't bear to watch anyone else make that mistake, but especially the younger Olivi. It would be too much like seeing her own weakness played out like a pantomime before her own eyes.

Norah said, "But he doesn't know whose daughter she is?"

Concordia shook her head. "Yours, you mean? No."

Norah gripped Concordia's hands harder, so hard it began to hurt, each knuckle a little burst of pain. Above their joined hands, Norah met Concordia's gaze, held it intently. "Not just mine."

And then, even through the haze of the wine, Concordia saw everything clearly.

✦ CHAPTER 18 ✦

NEGOTIATIONS

The Bastion

Amankha, Hikmet

The queen of Scorpica didn't know what the regent of Paxim was playing at, but she didn't like it one bit. The visit had been scheduled for more than a season, and now the plan had changed? She was suspicious.

But though her instinct was to reject the offer, she realized almost instantly that she couldn't. She was the queen of a nation that had violently attacked two fellow queendoms. Stellari could set whatever conditions she wanted. If Amankha had to crawl, she would crawl. Whatever it took to start building trust again.

It had crossed her mind, of course, that this was a trap of some kind. She wasn't a fool. But she was just as unable to refuse the invitation as she was to accept it without reservations.

On the appointed day, Amankha approached the gates of the Bastion with a small entourage, only Gretti and Azur, to accompany her. No guards, no ponies. The warriors didn't even wear swords on their hips. Amankha would have bet a fair bit of coin that Azur had at least one weapon secreted on her person, probably a dagger in her boot, but weapons weren't forbidden in the Bastion. No one would search them. It was only that they needed to project an image without threat. The three of them had agreed how best to do so.

While she had been through the gates of the Bastion several times since her return to Scorpica, Amankha had never gone this deep into the fortress itself as an adult. Unlike Paxim, Sestia, and Arca, the Bastion had no palace, per se; the building was the city and the city was the building, all fused stone, all one enormous, sprawling thing. Stone went upward into towers and turrets. Stone went outward into walls and barbicans. Stone went downward into cellars and caves. But within that maze there were distinctions. The areas where she'd lived as a child were familiar, but her vantage was different now and so was the section of the Bastion through which she moved.

Even if the meeting with Paxim's regent was as useless as she expected, she would at least gather useful intelligence. She would look for weaknesses, though the Bastion was not known for them. She would know where in the massive fortress queens did business, though the way they led her through the twisting halls seemed engineered to keep her from understanding exactly either where she was or where she'd been. But she paid close attention. She had, after all, been raised by scholars. There were ways in which she belonged to them as much as she belonged to the queendom she now ruled.

Her past with the scholars might now provide a much-needed path to reconciliation between the Bastion and Scorpica. She'd heard that the new queen of the Bastion was named Hikmet, and she was curious to know if she was the same Hikmet that Amankha had grown up with, after she was left at the Orphan Tree and called Ama for years to hide her identity.

If Hikmet of the Guards now ruled the Bastion, she and Amankha could build a bridge. Amankha had already been planning the conversation in her head. She'd remind Hikmet of their similarities, of the possibilities of working together, of the ways their nations had historically benefited each other. Today's meeting could provide the perfect situation, without having to make it a diplomatic occasion where Scorpica requested an audience.

She was just trying to decide whether to ask their escort if Hikmet would be present when the guard said, "Here is where the rest will wait. Only the regent and the queen will attend."

Gretti said quietly, "Amankha?"

Amankha nodded in her direction. "It's all right."

Azur said, "But that's not—"

"Azur," Amankha said firmly, then repeated, "It's all right."

The woman's grumble faded behind her as she followed the escort to another door and, at their invitation, stepped inside.

There in the room stood the regent of Paxim, regarding her with barely concealed contempt. Amankha hadn't expected that the person whose message had asked her to come would be staring at her with an expression that clearly indicated a preference that she leave.

While she waited for the regent to speak, Amankha looked her up and down; they had been in the same rooms in Paxim many times, but she wasn't sure Stellari even recognized her. Did the regent know that Ama the former bodyguard to the kingling and Amankha the queen of Scorpica were one and the same? If so, she was doing an excellent job giving nothing away. Then again, that was what she was known for: complete savvy, complete control.

"I have nothing to say to you," said the regent, removing Amankha's last shred of doubt that she had read the woman wrong.

"You arranged this meeting, Regent," said Amankha, feeling stupid. She hated the feeling. "And this is how you receive me?"

"I issued the invitation that my nation requires me by custom to issue. I was surprised when you accepted." She didn't sound surprised; she didn't sound like she knew what emotions were, much less what they felt like.

"One should always be ready for surprise," Amankha said.

"Oh? Should we have been ready when your people attacked us? Besieged and held a city, killing its inhabitants, not letting go until we handed you a defeat so ringing it finally ended your unjust invasion?"

Amankha resisted being baited, but a flame of temper flicked up into her throat. It was hard to talk around it. "The past is behind us. The queendom of Scorpica is ready to speak diplomatically with your queendom, which has a reputation for dealing fairly. Is Paxim's willingness to speak with civility and intelligence also in the past?"

That got a little more emotion out of the regent. "Your insults do not endear you to me, Queen Amankha."

"Endearing myself to you isn't my main goal."

"Thank the All-Mother. It would be foolish, unless failure brings you joy."

It was tiresome to be hated so fiercely, thought Amankha. Fighting to keep calm, she said, "My main goal is to rule my nation wisely and support my people. I imagine your queen would say the same, if she were grown enough to handle this conversation herself."

The regent seemed not to hear her at all. After a lengthy pause, the Paximite spoke indifferently. "In two years there will be Sun Rites."

"I am aware."

"Your role is to bring the knife."

"I am aware of that as well." Amankha let her voice frost over. She didn't want the woman to think she was a pushover; the less she revealed, the better. "And the queen of Paxim is supposed to make sure I bring the knife, correct? Only you're not the queen."

"The queen is too young for this conversation. She doesn't know how many of her subjects you killed," said the regent. "Let's wait a few years before she has to hear about that."

Amankha struggled to find a level response. "If she were your daughter, that would be your decision. She isn't."

"Says a woman with no daughter." The regent's eyes flashed. "So I'll thank you to keep your mouth shut."

"Insult me all you want. I am doing my best to keep this conversation civil."

"Why?" asked the regent. "You're clearly angry. I'm not to blame. It's exactly what I'd expect of you."

Amankha said nothing. She couldn't trust herself to answer without anger, so she chose not to answer at all.

"Look," said the regent. "I'm going to do you the favor of being honest. Most people would probably prefer that you not bother coming to the Sun Rites at all, after your nation's actions."

Amankha said, "And what would happen then?"

The regent, shockingly, shrugged. "No one knows. It's never been done."

"So if we don't gather to give the God of Plenty her due, perhaps nothing bad will happen at all?" Amankha studied the regent. "Have you considered that possibility?"

"I have considered every possibility," the regent said with utter confidence. Amankha believed her.

Amankha went on, "Then perhaps I can stay home."

"You can, of course. You can do whatever you like. My role is to make the request."

Tradition dictated a different owner of the role, of course, but with the queen barely out of babyhood, Amankha knew why only the regent could have these conversations. What she didn't understand was why the woman was so lackadaisical about it. If she were the one in charge of this task, Amankha told herself, she'd use every arrow in her quiver to persuade her fellow queens, and she wouldn't leave without a firm commitment. That was what Heliane would have done. What Roksana, if she were ever allowed to take the crown that her father's blood entitled her to, would learn to do.

But this woman was no Heliane, to say the least. And there was absolutely no way Amankha could let this woman find out about Roksana. So Amankha could only respond to what Stellari actually had said, not what others would have said in her place. "Very well. Let us acknowledge the request has been made."

"Then with that, queen of the Scorpicae, I bid you farewell."

For her own farewell, Amankha knew what she would do, even if the regent didn't understand it.

The queen of the Scorpicae formed a fist and raised it to her lips, nodding her head downward as she rested the closed fist against her mouth. *I salute you*, it meant. *I salute your strength.* A sign of respect, of acknowledging a peer of equal merit, but not the same as a deal done.

"I will consider your request," said Amankha, though she already knew what she was going to do when the time for the next Sun Rites came. She'd made her decision long before she entered this room, before she'd received Stellari's second communication, before even the first. Nothing that happened here would change her mind.

◆

Hikmet of the Scholars, queen of the Bastion, listened with puzzlement to the entire conversation between Paxim's regent and Scorpica's queen. When the regent of Paxim had informed her—not asked—that this meeting would take place in the walls of the Bastion, Hikmet had felt no qualms about siting it in a meeting room that the builders of the Bastion, whoever they'd been, had fitted with small tubes in the walls that carried sound to another room nearby. Hikmet told herself she needed to know the trustworthiness of both the Scorpican queen and the regent who would rule Paxim until the young queen came of age. Knowledge was beyond important—it was essential.

And even as she listened to their awkward, simmering conversation, Hikmet was straining to focus on the Scorpican queen's voice. It was her, wasn't it? Her friend Ama? She'd always wondered about the other girl's background. It was forbidden to ask an orphan what they remembered, but even if a child's curiosity couldn't be expressed, that didn't mean it wasn't there.

They'd both grown up in the same dormitory, though Hikmet was a year older, so there had been a year after she tested into the Guards that Ama had still been a nursery student. Then Ama had tested into the Guards—of course she had, with her remarkable dexterity and strength—and they'd enjoyed each other's company. Ama might or might not have considered them friends, and they'd never shared any secrets, but they'd chosen each other as sparring partners repeatedly. That counted for something.

Once the regent flounced off, Hikmet sent one of her Guards to bring Amankha to meet her in another, more comfortable room.

As soon as the Scorpican queen entered, a grin appeared on her face. Relief flooded through Hikmet.

"Hikmet of the Guards!" exclaimed Amankha. She was older, of course, having grown into the gravity that had rested on her like a mantle even in childhood. She had a scar on her cheekbone and sharp intelligence in her watchful eyes. "I hoped it was you!"

"As I hoped it was you. But I left the Guards behind long ago. I became Hikmet of the Scholars once I took a position on the board."

"Scholars." Amankha shook her head in mock disapproval.

"Now, now. It's only a title."

"Ha, 'only,'" Amankha echoed. "Queen Hikmet. You're 'only' in charge of the entire Bastion. How does it feel?"

"How does it feel to be in charge of Scorpica?" Hikmet asked rhetorically. "Queenship is messy. Some days it feels like too much. And some days it feels just right."

Amankha nodded.

"But let's get to business," said the Bastionite queen. "I thought I'd use the occasion for us to have a conversation, if you don't mind."

"I don't mind at all. A conversation about what?"

Hikmet said, "About working together. Because there used to be a relationship between our two nations, and now there isn't. And I think you and I are the best-suited women in the entire world to forge some sort of relationship again."

"I fully agree." The queen of the Bastion hadn't realized how much tension her old friend had been carrying in her shoulders until they dropped.

"Wonderful. Have you thought about the specifics?"

"I certainly have." Amankha leaned forward. "We start small. Once upon a time all Scorpican warriors were assigned to serve in other queendoms. Perhaps one day we will reach those levels, but that would be too much all at once. We need a small step to begin. Agreed?"

"Agreed."

"Let me assign a few warriors—five?—to teach military skills in the Bastion."

Hikmet found herself nodding. It was a good plan.

Amankha went on, "And perhaps you send us a few of your women to educate ours in other things? A midwife, or—"

Hikmet held up a hand. "I want to. I do. But the Board of Scholars will never approve sending a woman of childbearing age outside our walls, even for a short time. Our previous queen . . ."

She trailed off, unsure whether she should tell the head of a foreign government what had led to the dismissal of the previous queen midway through her two-year term. It had been an argument about childbearing. Each member of the Board of Scholars had been asked to devise a proposal to encourage the women of the Bastion to bear children. During the Drought, they'd hidden their women away to keep them safe, and now that women could bear girls again, the Bastion needed as many as possible. Hikmet, for her part, had proposed encouraging women of childbearing age by promising financial payments; others had argued that the Bastion should offer better placements, or better accommodations, or other rewards. They differed on whether women should be rewarded for having any child at all or only girls. The queen, Orla, had argued that mere encouragement wasn't enough. More was required. She outlined a program of required pleasures, compelling all women of childbearing age to attempt impregnation a certain number of times per month, with these requirements waived only while a woman was actively pregnant or for two months after a child was born. Even women who preferred to take their pleasures with women would be required to attempt to have their seed watered by men; with passion, Orla argued that a woman's duty to the Bastion outweighed any personal preferences in a time this crucial. The board had been so horrified at Orla's proposal that a vote had been held to force her resignation on the spot. Right afterward the same group voted to raise Hikmet to the queenship. That had been half a year ago and her head was still spinning.

Amankha, a calm look on her face, interrupted Hikmet's thoughts. "I understand. I can imagine they don't want to risk anyone who could bear a child, especially not on the soil of, well, a recently warlike nation. But what if all the risk is on our side? We send our instructors to you, all excellent warriors, for a longer assignment, perhaps a year. But we also send women to you as students for shorter periods. Our midwives, for example."

Nodding again, Hikmet said, "I like this idea."

"Obviously nothing too sensitive. I wouldn't send our smith to learn how to make weapons." The queen grinned, a bit suddenly. "Also, she doesn't think she has anything to learn."

Hikmet returned her smile. "That sounds familiar. I have a number of tradeswomen who feel the same way."

Eagerly, Amankha continued. "And I know the first fighter we'll send. The best warrior we have. Her name is Azur. She's here with me today. She also happens to be the First Mother, so she holds a special position of honor in our queendom. So it's obvious that I trust you and wish to be trusted by you."

"She'll agree to come?"

Amankha considered this. "I think she'll be glad to."

"Even if she can't bring her child?"

"She understands that no child's future is bright if Scorpica cannot regain the trust of the other queendoms. So, do we have an agreement?"

Hikmet nodded. "I hope so. If it were up to me, yes. I will make the most persuasive case I can to the Board of Scholars."

"How long will it take them, do you think?"

"I'll convene a special session. A week, perhaps, or two?"

"Use your best judgment," said Amankha. "If the board will be more likely to listen if you wait, then wait."

Hikmet said, "You're a wise woman."

Amankha smiled wryly. "Some of my countrywomen might not agree with you."

It was such a relief to speak to an old friend. "I'm certain there are countrywomen who don't agree with me, either. Agreement isn't the standard for everyone."

"It is for the board," pointed out the Scorpican queen.

"And there are those who don't even agree that we need to have agreement. So, we do the best we can."

They reached out and sealed the deal not with a warrior's grasp or a Paximite handshake, but the Bastionite pledge they'd both been taught as children: right hand to each other's left shoulder, left hand to their own hearts.

When the queen departed, Hikmet thought, *I hope they like this plan. Or I will be the shortest-reigning queen the Bastion has ever had.*

✦ CHAPTER 19 ✦

The Mentor, the Message

Summer, the All-Mother's Year 519

The Bastion and Scorpica

Azur, Amankha, Ellimi

Azur had been happy to agree to a temporary assignment in the Bastion, and the early weeks had gone well, all things considered. But even several months in, she still felt a cold shock every morning when she opened her eyes and looked up to see nothing but gray stone above her.

The first few nights in the Bastion, Azur had refused to sleep on the bunk they'd issued her. Scorpicae had bedrolls, not bunks. So she stretched out with a single blanket on the cold stone instead. Three days in, she was bruised and aching. Azur was not a fool. The fourth night she slept on her bunk—grudgingly, but at least she slept. Still, time had not accustomed her to the sight of stone every morning instead of tent or sky.

The sleeping conditions were one of only two things she didn't like about her assignment in the Bastion. The other, obviously, was being separated from her daughter. But each week, another warrior would bring Madazur for a visit just on the other side of the gates, and they'd spend a few hours together. Those memories were enough to keep Azur going. In the old days, assignments had been two years long, but Amankha knew better than to make any such promises in the new world order. Azur would likely be here for as long as the two queens involved in dealmaking thought she should be here, and she was not unhappy with that.

As for her actual assignment, teaching the Bastionite Guards how to fight, Azur excelled at it. No one would have guessed she'd have the temperament for teaching—she'd kept to herself after the death of Ysilef years before—but it turned out she could be patient and inspiring for the right students. Even for those without much natural skill, she was encouraging. For the truly talented, she was tireless in helping them reach their full potential.

Her most diligent student was named Ravian, a quiet woman of around twenty years, not much younger than Azur herself. Ravian was unusually quiet among the students, though probably not less so than the average woman or man of the Bastion; not surprisingly, the students who'd been chosen to train as Guards tended to be among the queendoms' most aggressive and direct.

One day, Ravian had stayed late after training to continue to work on a specific dagger technique. It was the day Azur had decided to show her students five ways to cut an opponent's throat. Generously, one might say she'd done it to show that she was genuinely interested in helping the Bastion defend itself, but honestly, she'd done it for fun. Four of the examples she'd shown were relatively simple: a quick crossways stroke from behind, a feint-and-reverse during a face-to-face battle, and standing over a kneeling opponent or kneeling over a facedown opponent, pulling either one up by the hair to expose the throat. The students were able to copy all of these, if not master them, without issue.

The fifth was a much more complicated skill, to be used when an opponent had the fighter in a choke hold. The dagger had to be lifted up behind the fighter's head in order to slit the throat right behind the back of their neck. Azur didn't really intend for the students to be able to succeed at this. She just enjoyed watching them try.

At the end of the session, most of the students packed their weapons away in the usual repository, then murmured to each other as they departed. But not Ravian. She practiced over and over again, going through the motions. Azur always remained until the last student was gone, so she settled in to watch, waiting for Ravian to tire. And waited. And waited. But Ravian didn't seem aware that Azur was waiting for her, or even, it seemed, that someone else was present.

Finally, just after Ravian slashed the air behind her yet again, Azur spoke up. "You need to practice on someone?"

She'd meant to give it as direction, but it came out, instead, as a question. Almost an invitation.

"Yes." Ravian lifted her eyes to Azur's, and Azur was struck by the roiling she saw there: determination, exhaustion, a dash of anger, but resolution, too, and more than a little pride.

Azur moved to stand behind Ravian wordlessly, getting into the proper position. She hooked her arm around Ravian's shoulders and held the other woman's back to her chest. It had been a long time since she'd been this close to another person, and it certainly hadn't been for the same purpose. She could feel warmth creeping into her cheeks and fought it down. This was demonstration, not engagement. She was here only to help her student become better. And if there was warmth elsewhere in her body as the two stood so close, well, that was even more crucial to ignore.

For the better part of a quarter hour, Ravian continued to practice, this time with Azur to aim at. The Bastionite moved her arm over and over in the precise arc that Azur had suggested in order to get her blade into the right place. In the end she struck home so soundly that Azur said aloud, "Well, good thing it's a practice blade," and Ravian's responding laugh was so boisterous that Azur was shocked it had come from this shy woman's body.

"Good work," said Azur as they parted.

"Thank you. Good teaching."

Azur shrugged. "I do my best."

Ravian cocked her head. "You don't strike me as the type of woman to indulge in false humility."

Even a year earlier, Azur would have taken the invitation to flirt. She would've stepped closer, asked Ravian, *What kind of woman do I strike you as, then?* But those days were gone. Azur felt the urge to flirt, yes—among other urges—but kept it to herself. Feeling it didn't mean she needed to do it. She had plenty of reasons to hold back.

Instead of lowering her voice to a seductive purr, she simply responded, saying, "Not false. I just teach. You are the ones who have to learn. A farmer's skill is useless if their seeds don't fall on fertile ground."

"Well," said Ravian, packing away her practice blade, "I hope you see how quickly we're growing."

"I do."

Ravian looked around them and said, "Where do you go, anyway?"

"Excuse me?"

"When you're done teaching for the day. I'm curious."

"Are you allowed to be curious?" teased Azur. She didn't intend to flirt with Ravian, but she could be human. Let the woman see that not everyone was a bone-dry scholar with no sense of humor. "I didn't know that was permissible here."

Ravian beckoned for Azur to fall into step with her, and the Scorpican did, even if she had no idea where the other woman was headed. "Curiosity isn't a problem in the Bastion, not at all. It's just not as desired as conformity."

"I see. And speaking of conformity, how did you end up training as a Guard?"

"You're curious too, it seems."

Azur again had to keep the flirtation out of her tone as she said matter-of-factly, "I am."

"I scored a certain way on a certain test, years ago," said Ravian. "That's how it works here."

"And you can't change?"

Ravian thought about this, and eventually said, "Changing is . . . discouraged."

"How? Are you punished if you try?"

"Depends. In most cases it's just not allowed. Like if I want to be an Engineer? I can't. I didn't pass the Engineers exam."

"Seems awfully constricting."

"In a lot of ways, it's reassuring. Everyone does what they're best at, makes their strongest contribution. We're all doing what we're meant to do."

Azur had never thought that much about Bastion society. She found every word Ravian was saying fascinating. Though the further they got into the conversation, the more she wondered whether it was Ravian's words or Ravian herself that kept Azur's attention. The woman was such an intriguing conundrum: shy but skilled, withholding but forthright. Even physically, her narrow face was at odds with plush lips, thick brows with small eyes. Her face shouldn't have been attractive, but it was. Or at least Azur was finding it more so by the minute.

Ravian led her through twists and turns that Azur would never be able to replicate, and then ducked under a small doorway. However deep they were within the fortress's walls, Azur could feel fresh air.

Then, suddenly, they stood in front of a small bench facing an even smaller window, and a tiny square of deep blue showed them the sky.

Ravian sat down on the bench. Azur followed. The Bastionite

nodded with satisfaction and, reaching underneath the bench into the darkness, pulled out a small wineskin. She uncorked it and, without drinking, extended it in Azur's direction.

"What's in this?" asked Azur conversationally.

"Does it matter?"

Azur considered. "I mean, some people would ask questions."

"Are you asking?"

"I just did."

Ravian said, "But do you care, really? That's what I mean. Sometimes we ask questions just to ask. Because we think we should. But either you trust me or you don't. Either you drink something I hand you or you don't. Because maybe you're the kind of person who doesn't let herself drink fermented beverages, and whatever I hand you might be fermented, so you won't partake if it is, and that's fine. I wouldn't judge you for that. But if you're not that kind of person, and if you don't think I'm trying to poison you—which I'm obviously not—than you don't really care what exactly is in that wineskin, and you're asking just to ask, and my answer doesn't matter in the least."

"Wow," said Azur. "You've really thought about this."

Ravian shrugged. "Not particularly. It's how we're taught. As scholars. We think through the logical applications and ramifications of just about everything."

Azur said, "Sounds boring." But she softened her judgment by lifting the wineskin that Ravian had handed her and taking a good, long drink.

She stared out the window at the darkening blue sky. Night was almost upon them. She should be on her way to sleep, but there was something about this moment, this place. Right here and right now, this felt like the only place in the world.

Azur handed the wineskin back to Ravian and said, "So tell me more."

Ravian drank. Then she asked, conversationally, "About what?"

"About your life in the Bastion. You really get your specialty when you're eight years old, and it never changes?"

"It usually doesn't, right."

"But what if you get tested and you're not particularly good at anything? Is there anyone like that, or are they, I don't know, thrown off the highest parapet or something?"

Ravian's sidelong glare made it clear that she didn't appreciate the implication, but at the same time, she didn't move away. "It's not like that. If you don't have a specialty, you serve in the nursery."

"So that's who raises the children? The people who don't fit in anywhere else?"

"That's not how we think of it." Ravian pondered, then asked, "How do you raise your children? It's not like the mother can do it alone."

"Scorpican mothers don't," said Azur. "When I'm home, I spend lots of time with my daughter, sure, but the other warriors are her *tishis*. It means something like mother's sister. Since we're all sisters, in a way."

"You have a daughter? I didn't realize."

Azur was astounded. "You didn't know? At home they call me the First Mother."

Ravian cocked her head. "First Mother? After the Drought? So your daughter's two years old."

"Yes."

"Mine too," said Ravian, her voice instantly soft and fond. "Almost. She'll be two next week."

"What's her name?"

Ravian took another drink. "Diti."

"I'd love to meet her sometime," said Azur, and meant it.

A cloud crossed Ravian's face. "The nursery strongly discourages visitors from outside. They let me come sometimes, though not as much as I want to."

"Oh," Azur said. "I hadn't thought about that. It isn't up to you, how often you see her?"

Ravian shook her head. "It's definitely not up to me."

Azur thought about how tempted she would've been, in those dark days after Madazur's birth, to hand the newborn over to someone else to raise. Then she thought about how much she missed her daughter every single day now, how much she looked forward to seeing her grow. She couldn't imagine what it would be like to know her child was so nearby and still out of reach.

"What's your daughter's name?" asked Ravian.

"Madazur."

Ravian said, "I'd love to meet her, too."

"Wonderful," said Azur. There was silence between them. Then she added, "Don't think I'm going to take it easy on you next lesson just because of this, by the way."

"I certainly hope not," said Ravian, and they both stared out the window until the light was gone from the sky.

✦

Every time Amankha rode through the stone gate from the Bastion into Scorpica, she wondered what reception she'd receive. She left only once or twice a season, escorting some of the exchanged warriors to or from the Bastion to show the importance of their mission, but each time felt momentous. Still, every time she returned, she couldn't help wondering if a Challenge might be in the offing.

Today was no different. The summer camp was bustling. Among the tents, the warriors busied themselves with the life of the camp. Those who looked up and saw the returned queen greeted her with smiles, then went back to their business. There was no parade to welcome her, but neither was there a mob with torches calling for her removal. She would take what she could get.

But when she saw Zalma the smith walking toward her, face creased in a frown, Amankha knew that this was what she'd feared. Bad news. It was only a matter of what news, and exactly how bad.

Zalma said, in a voice that did not entirely disguise a kind of morbid glee, "A visitor has come for you."

"Oh?"

"We did not want to deal with him without your say-so. Gretti said we could not kill him. I think you will probably want that honor."

Amankha's head spun. She didn't want to kill anyone, but she might not have a choice. This sounded serious, whatever it—whoever he—was.

But she wasn't prepared for the sight, among her warriors, of a tattered old man. He didn't look like any kind of a threat. As a matter of fact, he looked barely alive. Suntanned until his skin was leather, he almost looked like a life-size doll someone had stitched together of hide and old rags. Part of his arm was blackened, and the hood he wore over his head obscured everything but his whiskery chin. He was a worn relic, a scrap of a human, left over.

"Why are you here?" she asked. Had he been a woman, she would have used the polite Paximite word of address, *thena*, even though they were not in Paxim. But there was no such term for a venerable man, not that she knew of, certainly not here. So she had nothing to cushion the blow of the question.

Then the man stayed silent so long, she started wondering what she might need to do next. What if he couldn't hear her? She didn't want to repeat herself. This situation was obviously fraught. Scorpicae rarely reacted well to a stranger in their midst.

"What reason could he possibly have?" came an angry voice, and Amankha didn't have to look up to see who it was. Zalma, now with an audience for her discontent. She was swinging her heavy hammer and wearing her broad grin, and there was something chilling in that smile.

"Let him speak," said Amankha.

The smith, obviously disgruntled, turned expectantly toward the raggedly dressed old man.

"I will give my message only to the queen," he said.

"Scorpica is the queen and the queen is Scorpica," the smith responded. She wasn't wrong, thought Amankha, even if the superiority in her tone made Amankha's fingers itch to deal her a slap. "Tamura would have killed him just for daring to enter the queendom."

"I am not Tamura," Amankha said, too fast, realizing too late that this was probably exactly what the smith wanted her to say. To certain ears, it likely sounded more like an admission than an edict. She would have to be more careful.

"We know who you aren't," the smith responded dryly, speaking to her but playing to the assembled warriors around them. "Show us who you are."

The old man spoke again, repeating, "I will give my message only to the queen."

Amankha looked hard at the old man. There couldn't be much strength in him; she stood by her original assessment that he didn't pose a physical threat. His only weapon appeared to be a sort of cudgel worn at his waist, and she wasn't sure how much strength could be left in his aged, leathery arms.

But she warned herself not to assume him harmless. Assassins could come in many forms, and appearances could be deceiving. Her enemies might have made a plan to take her out by playing on her sympathies with a harmless-seeming stranger. Unfortunately, she had more than one enemy that she could imagine resorting to underhanded measures. Maybe the smith herself had put this man in the queen's path.

"Let us walk by the river," she said to the old man, and gestured. She struck a compromise with herself. She wouldn't take him into her tent, where she would be more vulnerable. But she did want to hear his message alone, in case it really was something only the queen of Scorpica should hear.

They walked downriver, the rush of the water on the rocks making a kind of music to accompany their footsteps. She noticed that the old man shuffled, his toes dragging in the dirt, and this made her worry even less that he might attack. She kept her hand on the pommel of her sword just in case, but she found herself growing genuinely curious: What would drive a man like this to come seeking a woman like her?

When at last she felt they'd traveled enough distance from the others, Amankha said, "Very well, then. You say you have a message for me that you have brought all this way. I am ready to hear it. Tell me what it is you want to tell me, and be gone."

The old man's chin came up. He still looked weak, but there was a sparkle in his eye, a satisfaction. In that moment there was something about him that didn't seem old at all.

"I am not the old hermit whose body I wear. My name is Ellimi," said the old man, his voice notably stronger than it had been at the camp. "I am your mother's mother. I am so proud and happy to meet you at last, Amankha dha Khara. And I come with a warning from the Underlands."

✦

Her borrowed body was uncomfortable, but Ellimi dha Lanwys was nearly ecstatic. She had not only succeeded in coming back from the Underlands and walking the earth once more, but she had taken charge of this strange body, and then, with pure determination and not a little luck, had made her way to Scorpica. She had managed to convince those who received her not to kill her—no small task, that—and to wait for the return of Queen Amankha. It must have aligned with their own goals somehow, because they eventually agreed. Now, disguised, Ellimi stood in front of the granddaughter she'd dreamed of, a reigning queen of Scorpica obviously worthy of the name.

Ellimi herself had been quite short in life, so she'd chosen the tallest man she could find at the Sun Rites to sire her daughter, climbing astride him in a semi-private bathing pool so she could wrap her arms around his neck and line up their hips with ease. Khara had been quite tall as a result. It was hard to say whether Amankha was taller than her mother had been, especially since Ellimi was looking from a different vantage point in the hermit's body. The hermit had probably once been of medium height, but was hunched by age and starvation. She peered up at her granddaughter through the milky, hazy eyes she'd borrowed. Amankha was clearly solid and strong, and she bore herself like the queen she was.

When Ellimi said, *I come with a warning from the Underlands*, Amankha had no visible reaction. But Ellimi guessed what she must be feeling: skepticism, annoyance, perhaps a dash of regret that she had not gone ahead and slain the old man when her subjects had suggested it.

In the hermit's croaking voice, Ellimi said, "How can I prove to you that I am who I say I am?"

"Explanation first, then proof," said Amankha thoughtfully. "Explain to me how you could be my grandmother, returned from the dead, when I can see with my eyes that you are an old man in rags, who looks to be on the cusp of death himself."

So Ellimi explained about the gates to the Underlands, how she had helped open the second gate and had rushed through to be the first to come back Aboveground. "I wanted to see you," she said. "I wanted to rise again."

Amankha was frowning. It was a lot to digest; Ellimi wasn't surprised that her granddaughter couldn't instantly accept the impossible.

So Ellimi said, "I understand if you need more time."

"No," Amankha said immediately. "No time. I don't know how long we'll have you, so I need all the answers you have as quickly as you can give them. Tell me. You were in league with others to open this gate? So you're not the only one who came back?"

"I might be, but I'm not sure," Ellimi said truthfully. "When the second gate is open, a shade passing through it can occupy the body of someone recently dead in Godsbones. That's what the stories say, and I'm here to tell you, the stories are true."

The frown did not change. Amankha's mind seemed to be working quickly. "Isn't that the first gate? Occupying the bodies of the recently dead?"

"You know more about the gates than the average Scorpican," observed Ellimi.

"I'm not the average Scorpican," Amankha responded. "I spent time in Paxim with . . . someone who loved the telling of stories. But in case our time is short, please, explain the difference between the first gate and the second."

"Opening the first gate allows the transfer of the shade into the body, but the shade can't speak."

Amankha nodded. "And with the second gate open, shades can—you can—speak with the mouth of the stolen body."

A bit more sharply than she intended, Ellimi clarified, "Not stolen."

"A matter of perspective," said Amankha, and Ellimi didn't know her daughter's daughter well enough to know whether this was sincerity or sarcasm.

"True," Ellimi admitted. "But according to the stories, the first two gates were established so that shades could visit Aboveground if they missed their loved ones. The first gate, to watch; the second gate, to speak."

"And both of those gates are open now, you're telling me. Is that the warning you spoke of?"

Ellimi felt her granddaughter's patience slipping away. Patience had rarely been a hallmark of Scorpicae in general, much less Scorpican queens. "Yes and no. The warning is that the shade who asked me to open the second gate is no doubt already working on the third. I don't think she'll stop. I think she wants to open all five, and bring the dead back to walk the earth."

Those words landed with Amankha, clearly. The shift in her expression was clear. Though she still had a skeptical air, she also looked troubled by what she'd heard.

Ellimi hastened to say, "I don't know if she will succeed, but I do know she's trying."

"And you came back to warn me that the dead might be coming to swarm the world of the living."

"Yes."

Amankha stared out over the turbulent waters of the river. Her tone was notably cooler when she said, "And you realize that you, an old man claiming to be a dead hermit from Godsbones, could be saying all these things for other reasons. They could all be lies, front to back. You could be a spy from another queendom. An Arcan magician trying to do me in. Anything, anyone. So why should I believe you?"

"Khara asked me to convey her greetings," Ellimi said.

Amankha's laugh was sharp and dark. "Anyone in the world could know who my mother was, and know she's dead. That's a lazy way to try to prove something. What do you know that only my grandmother could?"

"I know your mother entered the world in silence in the dark of night, slipping from my womb so quietly I wasn't sure she had come. I know she was uncertain about becoming queen, even when I was ready to hand the crown to her. And when I knew her, she'd birthed nine boys, not a single warrior among them, and she was called the Barren Queen."

Amankha said, her eyes accusing, "Every Scorpican knows that, what she was called, who she'd birthed."

"Was everyone there when she was born? Could everyone speak to that?"

"She never told me about her birth," said Amankha, and there was a tinge of sadness to her voice.

"Is there nothing only your mother knew, and passed to you before she died? Some secret we share?"

Amankha looked away, down the river once more. "You have secrets, and I have secrets. But I don't think we share any."

"I won't beg," said Ellimi in the body of the hermit, trying not to show her desperation. "I came to meet my granddaughter. I had a chance and I took it. Ask yourself, what possible benefit would there be in making this claim if I were not who I say?"

Amankha said, her voice smaller, "To be honest, I don't know."

Ellimi said, "You see the body I inhabit; I have little to offer. I ask nothing of you. I do not ask for a place in Scorpica."

"That's not what you want?"

"*Mokh* what I want," said Ellimi. "I understand how this queendom works. I can't stay here. I'm not welcome in this body, nor should I be."

Ellimi could see Amankha considering this, wanting to contradict it, but knowing her grandmother was correct. Any man, even a clearly harmless old man like this one, couldn't stay in Scorpica. Nor had he asked to. That alone had done more to convince Amankha than anything else her grandmother, in this unrecognizable body, had said.

Amankha said, "Then where will you go?"

"I have no destination," said Ellimi, realizing it was true. She had struggled even to make it this far, and she hadn't thought beyond this moment. "I wanted to warn you. And meet you. I've done those things."

A nod from Amankha, understanding.

Ellimi went on. "But—I don't want to just die again and return to the Underlands as a shade. I'd rather stay Above. But if I can't be near you, I don't know where I want to be."

A different light came into Amankha's eyes. "I have an idea."

"Of where I might go?"

"Of where I might send you."

"Oh?" Ellimi's voice was soft, but she was curious.

Amankha said, "It's a long journey."

Ellimi shrugged, then wiggled the toes of her borrowed body against the firm ground of the riverbank. "If this body can make it, I'm willing to go. Anywhere and for any length of time, until the moment the magic that got me here gives out. Where would you have me go? The Pass? The Bastion?"

Amankha seemed to decide on a course of action. Her eyes cleared.

In a firm voice, she answered Ellimi's question with a question. "Ellimi dha Lanwys, former queen of Scorpica, having journeyed from beyond death to find me, would you like to meet another member of the family?"

✦ CHAPTER 20 ✦

SEEKING

Daybreak Palace, Arca

Eminel

Queen Eminel, Well of All-Magic, Master of Sand, and Destroyer of Fear, was lonely.

It wasn't uncommon for powerful women, she knew, to have few friends. And although she'd become more comfortable in her court after showing her strength at the end of the Drought of Girls, she was still suspicious of her courtiers. There wasn't a single one she trusted.

Of course she associated with them, sometimes even let them into her bedchamber for pleasures, but that was the only way she let them in. Even now, a slender and enthusiastic member of the Jale matriclan kneeling at her feet and applying an eager tongue to Eminel's lover's knot, Eminel might as well have been alone in the room.

After the end of the Drought of Girls and her own transformation, she'd found herself awakening to a desire for pleasure, but how best to achieve it? With Beyda gone, she'd had no one to counsel her. She figured it out herself. She remembered well all those *whishnuk* pegs, all those games played; it was her own hand that moved the pegs, not the pegs themselves choosing to move.

So it was her right to choose, and she chose. After she'd put it about that she might consider any Arcan for marriage, not only men, it had caused a bit of a stir. She'd let herself dip into a few minds here and there to hear what they thought. An indulgence, she knew, but not a risk. As with most of her pronouncements, some Arcan courtiers grumbled secretly, but power-hungry as they were, no matriclan would pass up the chance for advantage.

So they sent their women and their men and those who were neither or both to meet her one by one, often bearing gifts of small luxury. Eminel never knew what to do with these offerings. She didn't need anyone to give her an openwork bracelet or a raw emerald or a flowering branch from a rare tree.

The breakthrough had come quite by accident, the previous summer. An earth magician from Merve, her hooded eyes flashing, insisted on looping a delicate string of silver bells around Eminel's ankle. Eminel had been wearing a summer robe, its hem high above her knees. When the courtier turned her head to kiss the inner curve of her queen's knee and worked her way up from there, Eminel realized this kind of gift was worth accepting.

The bells jingled as the queen's first lover guided Eminel to the floor to receive her pleasure, long fingers tracing patterns on her hips and legs. The music of the bells seemed to grow louder as the courtier lifted Eminel's belled ankle onto her shoulder, then faded as blood pounded in Eminel's ears, rushing like rapids, until all sound was wiped from the world by remarkable, blessed release.

As dizzied as she'd been, as overwhelmed, Eminel never lost her presence of mind. She sat up, thanked the earth magician, then unclasped the anklet and handed it back.

Since then, Eminel had on many occasions enjoyed the touch of hands and mouths and whatever else her courtiers chose to lay against her skin. To avoid the appearance of favoring any member of the court, she treated them all the same: the queen would receive pleasure without giving it. Eminel's hands, flesh and quartz alike, touched no one's skin but her own.

So now, as the pleasure built within her, Queen Eminel leaned back in her chair, hips pushed forward and head thrown back, eyes closed. Her nightrobe had been opened but not removed. As she luxuriated, it had slipped from her shoulders to drape over the chair behind her, hem pooling on the floor. The Jale courtier's hands were splayed on the queen's inner thighs, palms pressing her legs wide. Eminel's own hands closed on the arms of the chair, tightening, tightening.

When Eminel let herself ride over the edge into a cascade of pleasure, a trembling so fierce her whole body seemed on the verge of flying apart, the queen's gasp echoed off the walls. Letting the court hear that she was pleased was, as with every other choice, deliberate. One might even call it a strategy. The more one matriclan was known to please her, the more others competed to do the same. They offered their oldest, their youngest, the lush-bodied and the slim, alone or in groups, at any hour of the day or night. The queen rejected most. She was sure to avoid any discernible pattern, obeying only her thirst and her whim. She kept the matriclans guessing. On days or nights when she was in the mood to be visited, there was no shortage of offers. No one bothered to bring other gifts anymore.

As her climax subsided, her body draining of tension, the queen opened her eyes.

"You may go," Eminel said to the courtier, not unkindly. But she had nothing to add, nothing to soften the order; she'd forgotten to ask this one's name. The courtier complied. Within moments, the queen was alone again.

All alone. So alone.

In a way, she even missed the odd, haunting dreams that the god had sent her in her earlier years of queenship. But she hadn't spoken to the god since Velja had instructed her to build her quartz hand, two autumns ago. Usually she thought that was for the best. But on days like this, it added to her loneliness. Another voice, once so essential, that Eminel no longer heard.

The warmth of her pleasure dissipated quickly. She reclined in the same chair, the same open robe trailing behind her, but it was as if no one else had been there at all. That was the problem with this approach, Eminel realized. Had she welcomed a true lover, perhaps afterward they would have lain together on tangled sheets, running leisurely fingers across each other's damp skin, one nuzzling the other's cheek or nestling their chin into the crook of a warm and waiting neck. But no. These things were not for her, at least not until she chose a spouse or two. Even then, would she be able to relax? To trust?

The only person in Daybreak Palace she'd ever trusted was Beyda, and Beyda had been gone a year.

Perhaps it was time. She could send a Seeker—that was an obvious option—or she could try something more immediate.

Sitting up in the chair, Eminel closed the robe to cover her body and tied the knot at her waist. She stretched out her fingers and looked at them. The last time she had reached across borders, Beyda had been here, and they'd seen the decrepit magician Nuray, imprisoned in the Fingernail. Eminel hadn't wanted to repeat that experience. But she was more powerful now, more experienced. How far could she reach if she tried? Even with the idea barely half-formed, she began to adapt the incantation slightly, accounting for the quartz hand. The hand was so much a part of her now that she sometimes forgot it was no longer flesh, but the difference did affect her spell-casting, and her body told her what it needed.

Before she could second-guess herself, Eminel reached up and drew a circle in the air. She gathered her power. Summoning and reaching, clearing the way, bringing together each component effortlessly. She blew breath gently into the circle, filling it with her magic. The wall of her chamber began to thin and fade, dissolving into nothingness, as a new vista appeared: the deep gray of Bastion stone.

Then, more quickly than Eminel expected, Beyda's face came into view. Even though she'd done it on purpose, Eminel still found it shocking, so she took a moment to calm herself and look at the image of her friend.

It was definitely her, Eminel knew. Shadowed somehow, not quite looking exactly as she had when she'd departed Arca, but still, it was unmistakably Beyda. She looked deeply concerned about something. She hadn't yet noticed the portal that had appeared near her. Instead she appeared to be looking down at her hands.

Eminel blurted her name. "Beyda!"

The scribe turned immediately at the sound. Her face, so drawn with worry, spread in a bountiful smile. She didn't look surprised at all, only pleased. "Queen Eminel! It's so good to see you."

Instantly, the past year fell away. It was as if she'd just seen Beyda the day before, shared date-filled buns with her, bickered over who would get the last swallow of honeyed milk. Eminel was almost convinced she could just reach out and touch Beyda's face. She even felt her quartz hand lifting. But she stilled it, returned it to her lap. They were separated by time and distance and the memory of what had led to their parting.

"I wasn't sure you would want to see me," admitted Eminel. She hated how small her voice sounded. Despite all her magic, despite her power, talking to her old friend changed something in her. Took her back to an earlier time. When she'd first come to Arca, so uncertain. Beyda had been her salvation.

Softly, the scribe said, "I've missed you."

"Come back," Eminel said. She was boiled down to her essence now. She could only tell Beyda the absolute truth, say what she most longed to say.

Beyda's answer was quick. "I can't."

"I'm not angry," said Eminel hastily. "I promise. I just—"

"You don't understand," Beyda responded, her voice tightening. "I can't. They won't let me leave." She looked over her shoulder, then back at Eminel again.

"They . . . who?"

"The Board of Scholars," Beyda answered, her voice dropping low. Was she afraid of being overheard? Eminel was alone in her chamber with absolute privacy. She hadn't even thought about whether the same was true for Beyda.

Eminel leaned forward, trying to see more of the space around Beyda, but she saw only stone. "How is that possible? Are you—imprisoned?"

"No, the Bastion doesn't have a prison," said Beyda. "But I'm not allowed to leave. I'm in a dormitory."

"With the scribes?"

"No, I'm not a scribe anymore."

"Beyda!" Eminel said with some exasperation. "What in the name of the Underlands is going on?"

Beyda looked around and seemed to be satisfied that no one else could hear her. But she leaned closer toward Eminel, with an intimacy that almost brought tears to the queen's eyes.

"It's a prophecy," the scribe—former scribe?—whispered.

Eminel felt like a fool, but she had to ask. "What is?"

"The song."

"Beyda," she said, reaching for patience. She had forgotten how differently her friend's mind worked. "What song?"

The Bastionite hummed low in her throat, a faint melody. Her notes were imprecise, but Eminel understood. There wasn't a child in the Five Queendoms who didn't know the tune. As Beyda hummed, Eminel's mind filled in the words she knew best to match it.

When an Arcan calls on all her magic
And the answer's a thousand leagues deep
When a lake of glass swallows the desert
Peace be upon the land, and sleep.

"The lullaby?" Eminel said with disbelief.

"The *prophecy*. I finally figured it out. Years I've tried, you know. There are so many different versions. I had to trace them back. The oldest scrolls, the deepest knowledge. But I found it. Most of it, I think. The important bits. Finally."

"Beyda!" Eminel called her friend's name with joy this time, with understanding. "That's amazing! A prophecy—what does it foretell?"

Beyda smiled, but it was a wry smile, not a joyous one. There was a long pause before she spoke again. "Well, that's what I was trying to find out in the Archives, but they caught me."

"I can get you out," said Eminel hastily. "Send a diplomatic mission demanding your return."

"You shouldn't—"

The queen's mind spun with ideas, desperate ones, to save her friend. "Or if I can get close enough, I can dissolve a wall. I'm sure it can't be that challenging—"

"Eminel," her friend interrupted, still quiet, but firm. "No."

"I could—"

"No," she repeated. Almost loud, this time. "I'm not in danger. And I'm so close to the answer. Leave me where I am."

The queen was dubious. Why shouldn't she just bring Beyda back, magically or otherwise? She'd missed her so much. But she wouldn't do it against her friend's will. They'd just found each other again. "Well, if that's what you want."

"It's what I want," Beyda confirmed, her voice confident. "Of course, that might change. And if I do decide to break out, it would need to be done secretly. I won't let you risk your queendom. Believe me, I've thought this through."

Her friend had, Eminel remembered, always been thorough. "I believe you."

"So if you know any talented outlaws, someone who might enjoy helping with a complicated escape plan, you might want to have them in readiness."

The idea roared up into Eminel's mind like a flame.

It must have shown on her face, because Beyda responded immediately, though Eminel hadn't said a word. Her friend's voice was a little surprised, a little proud. "You know someone like that, don't you?"

Eminel answered, "Several someones."

They agreed to speak again at the start of the new year, though if Beyda needed help before that, she'd find a way to get a message to Eminel. Eminel wanted to check in sooner, but Beyda insisted she needed time to work.

"They're keeping me here," she said. "But here is where I need to be to find what I'm looking for. So the joke's on them."

Worried for her friend but willing to accept her reassurances for now, Eminel bid Beyda a fond farewell and let the portal between them close. Soon enough she was staring at her unremarkable, featureless wall again.

After a long breath, she shook herself, tied the knot of her robe more tightly, and got ready to take the one action Beyda had asked of her.

This time, scrying wouldn't be enough. She didn't have a strong enough connection; she hadn't seen them in years, had no idea where they would be located. But she knew what to do.

Eminel flung open the door of her chamber. Two of her Queensguard, one stationed on each side of the door, turned.

"Queen?" they asked in unison.

"Find me the nearest Seeker immediately," Eminel told them both, and shut the door. Even as she closed it, they conferred in hurried voices, and then she heard through the door the sound of fast footsteps receding.

She was the queen, and she would have what she wanted.

She didn't even need a particularly talented Seeker, she thought, which was why she'd asked for the nearest. Looking for the Rovers wasn't likely to present a challenge. Minds retained the extraordinary, which the Rovers certainly were, and Seeking magic should easily pick up the trail. Hermei might escape someone's notice, and depending on how they carried themselves these days, so might the twins. But a charismatic giant with a silvered scar who laughed like a wolf and dressed like a beacon?

No, no one who'd met Fasiq would ever forget her.

✦ CHAPTER 21 ✦

THE TOMB

Late summer, the All Mother's Year 519
The Holy City, Sestia
Concordia

The sky was a clouded-over gray and a gentle rain had begun to fall as Concordia walked outside the palace walls toward the cemetery. Few people were out. No one took notice of her or stopped her, and she'd readied a story in case they did. An offering. She would pop the honeyed apricots one by one into her own mouth before she emerged back into the rainy afternoon, returning to the palace empty-handed.

The *lacrum* had been her sanctuary, but it was not foolproof. Ears were still listening. Only the Tomb of the High Xaras, isolated and with stone walls as thick as the Bastion's, would do for what she had in mind.

She'd barely made it through the inner passage and pulled the interior door behind her when she could wait no longer: she opened her mouth and screamed, her throat afire with anger, screamed as loud and long as she wanted to. She was in the only place in the Holy City where no one, anywhere, could hear her.

As soon as Norah said the words that made clear who had sired her daughter, Olivi, it all came clear to Concordia: awful, simple, undeniable. That was why she screamed. For years, Xelander had tried to manipulate her. More than once, he'd succeeded. He craved power, and pleasure was the weapon he used to achieve it. She hadn't even been the first resident of the Edifice he'd tried it with, and if she didn't stop him, she doubted she would be the last.

She barely remembered nodding to Norah, freeing her hands from the woman's painful grasp, as Rix reentered the room with the bandage he'd been sent to fetch. He knelt at Norah's feet and wrapped her bloody finger, not seeming to notice as he did that Norah's blood was on Concordia's hands too.

The next morning, when Concordia rose, head throbbing, she wondered if Norah had fled the Edifice rather than chance seeing Xelander again, and if she had, whether she'd taken her daughter with her. Part of Concordia wished Norah had whisked Olivi far away. Concordia couldn't reconcile how she felt about the younger Olivi, her only clear successor, now that she knew Olivi was Xelander's daughter.

If she decided to make Olivi the next High Xara, what would it mean to give all her power to someone who might have inherited such a venal, calculating personality? If she did, it felt like Xelander would win. Concordia could not let him win. In a way, she'd rather die, leaving Sestia in crisis, if it meant denying him the satisfaction.

It was all so maddening. So, in the cool, stagnant air of the tomb, Concordia screamed out her rage with no one but the bones of long-dead High Xaras to hear her.

She had felt for him—what? She had never put a name to it. But she'd trusted him with everything short of her greatest secret. She'd nestled against him, taken him inside her, felt the thorny pangs of jealousy when she heard rumors about his other lovers. She could admit it now. It was easier to say what she had once felt when, after Norah's revelation, she knew she would not feel it anymore.

She could just stay here in the tomb and die, she realized. No one even had to know. She could lie down, throw the apricots in the dirt instead of eating them, and eventually, starvation would carry her off. No, what would be even better: she could go back and die in the *lacrum*, that room where she'd been taunted by silence for all those years. She could dive headfirst into God's Well, drown herself in that holy water, saffron robe drawing her downward. Would that make the god happy, at last?

Would the Holy One speak to her if she were on the verge of dying, that longed-for voice wending its way to her ears only when she readied herself to set foot on the bridge to the Underlands? Was that what it would take? But she feared that even then, she would not hear the Holy One speak. Anyway, she was not yet ready to die, she decided. She was racked with grief and anger, but still, she would live. For now.

She still had work to do. Xelander had returned from his pilgrimage, swaggering and suave and intoxicatingly beautiful, unaware of what had transpired in his absence. He was vulnerable, not knowing what she now knew. Which meant Concordia still had choices to make.

She wasn't angry enough to lower herself into God's Well, nor to starve herself here in the tomb. She would eat the honeyed apricots on the way out, taking the food intended as a sacrifice to the god, since the god had no use for them. No. She would not die now.

It was not her own life she wanted to end.

✦

The High Xara, who did nothing in haste, bided her time. No need to rush. Xelander had been false from the first—for years! how had she never seen?—and the only difference was that now she knew it. She knew now that he had laid his lustful hands on Norah when she was the Xara Veritas, that he had been responsible for her downfall, and once she no longer had power he could exploit, he'd turned his attentions to Concordia herself. A man so deceitful could not be trusted to come clean, no matter how obvious his guilt. So she would not demand his confession. Instead she made a plan. It was a simple plan, relying entirely on her and no one else. She had decided that was the only kind of plan she would ever make again.

One night, as he and another servant stood guard outside the door of her chambers, she turned to the other man first.

"Thank you for your service," she said, her tone matter-of-fact. "I wish a cup of yellow-flower tea this evening from the kitchen. Made with fresh water drawn from the well, understand? I will know if you use water from a jug. Steeped ten minutes. No more, no less. That is all."

The servant bobbed his head and headed off in the direction of the kitchen, long plait swinging behind him.

She turned her head to Xelander as if she had forgotten he was even there, and said in her most level voice, "Some fool failed to clear the afternoon washing from my chamber. Assist me."

He nodded, opening the door and gesturing for her to precede him, then shutting it behind the two of them. Once he did, they were alone. The lamplight was warm on her skin—or was the warmth of her anticipation, the knowledge of what was to come?

"It's been too long," she said simply. "I will have you tonight."

He reacted without apparent surprise, only pleasure. "My queen," came his voice, a low, deep purr, and she knew he was congratulating himself on being so irresistible. He had been out of her graces with no sure sense of how to get back in; was it as easy as accepting a proffered invitation? Now that she knew what he was, it was so simple to guess his thoughts, to understand how he was angling, even in the face of uncertainty, even when he wasn't in control.

He closed the distance between them with three long strides, and then his fingers were already sliding up the curve of her waist, brushing the swell of her breast, but she said, "No. Not here."

A small crease between his eyes deepened, showing his concern. When he'd first seduced her, there had been no such crease. His face had been unlined, his waist as slender as a reed. He was thicker through the body now, a touch slower to move, though still undeniably beautiful. He was not as young as he'd been. Of course, neither was she. "Not here?" he asked.

"Here, we only have a few minutes alone."

He thought. "Ah. The tea."

"Yes. I needed him gone long enough to tell you."

"Tell me what you want," he said, the purr already back. He had not taken his hand off her breast. Now his thumb brushed upward, grazing the firm nipple under the thin cloth of her shift. It was a strategy, she knew now, and a promise.

"I want privacy when I have you," she said. "To be alone, truly alone. I want somewhere we can shout our pleasure and no one will know."

"I never knew you wanted that," he said.

She felt a giddy response bubbling up to her lips but bit it back. In time, yes, in time. Instead she told him where to meet her, the one place she could be certain of absolute privacy. They couldn't be seen together, of course, she said. They would have to go by different routes. But could he go now? Yes, he nodded, he could.

She cupped him between the legs then, gently pressing with her fingertips, moving her wrist in careful circles until she felt the evidence of his lust. How quickly he still grew firm under her touch. When she leaned in toward him, he turned his face for a kiss, but that was not her intent. She pressed harder with the heel of her hand, encouraging his need. He let out a faint groan—was that real? she wondered. At least his arousal could not be faked, but she could count on nothing else. With her free hand she lifted his hair off his neck, brushing it away, then leaned in just until her lips hovered above the curve of his waiting ear.

She paused to tease out the moment. She knew he could feel her hot breath on the side of his neck, stirring the fine dark hairs above, tantalizingly close.

The High Xara whispered, "Hurry."

✦

The sliding bolt was an enormous beam hewn from blackwood, slick and heavy as stone. There was no key; none was needed. No one had permission to touch the bolt of the Tomb of the High Xaras besides a High Xara, and the penalty for forgoing permission was exile. The tomb was only opened when a High Xara died. Holy One willing, there would be no others fitting that description for a long time to come.

As she'd bid him, Xelander waited for her in the darkness; she could see his outline as she drew near, the only figure she'd seen since passing through the cemetery gates. No one walked these grounds, on the far side of the cemetery past the vaults of lesser Xaras, especially not at night. Rumors were that the shade of Puglalia sometimes walked here, ranging out from her usual palace haunts, searching for the tomb where her body rightfully belonged. They were so alone they could have been the last people in the whole world.

"Here?" he asked, his voice startlingly loud in the night silence.

She replied in barely more than a whisper, her voice as soft as fog. "Inside."

He nodded, and turned his attention toward the door, waiting.

Concordia gripped the underside of the massive beam and put her shoulder to it, shoving with all her weight until it creaked in protest and slowly, as if regretfully, gave way.

There was a trick to it, of course. On the day of succession, the previous High Xara had shown Concordia how to slip her index finger into a notch behind the thick wooden holder and pull the pin, which freed the bolt to glide on an internal rail despite its weight. From the outside, she supposed, it looked very impressive.

Xelander certainly seemed impressed. His eyes were wide in the night, glimmering with reflected starlight, as she reached for his hand to pull him through the doorway. Only the chirp of crickets and the hoot of a far-off masked owl flickered in the night. She shut the door behind them and fit the metal hook through its eye. Then they were not just in complete darkness, but complete silence as well. She could almost hear him smile.

The first portion of the passage was narrow, not much wider than a body. They both had to bend low to squeeze through. She knew Xelander could not see more than a handspan in front of his face. She left the torches all along the passage unlit. She knew her destination, and there was no need for him to know where they were going until they'd arrived. He was fully reliant on her. Let him be.

It was not the first time he had been helpless in her hands, but it reminded her of the other times. The memories flooded her body, stirred her blood, as if it had only been days and not far longer since she'd last touched him like that. She felt that delicious ache between her legs, driving her on.

She slid aside the interior door and they emerged into the larger room. There was a sconce just there, so she fumbled for the flint in the dark and lit it. She watched Xelander's familiar face take in the room around him in the flickering shadows, seeing it for the first time. The tomb was dry and cool, its air stagnant but not unpleasant, the musky smell of incense that might have been burned generations ago trapped in the unmoving air.

Concordia lay her palms flat on the wall. "Five handspans thick," she said. "We can be as loud as we like. No one will ever hear us. We can scream each other's names until we're hoarse."

His face in the candlelight was all taunting lust, unapologetic and delicious. "Ah, then. Would you have me scream your name, Concordia?"

"Scream whatever you like," she said, her hand immediately working at the wide buckle of his decorative belt. Her name was not Concordia, not really, and she felt an intense bolt of pleasure that he didn't know her true name, would never know it. "But yes. I would have you scream."

She lay Xelander down on a blanket she'd brought for the purpose, its creamy, thick wool under his back, her knees. She pushed aside his clothing and stripped it off; when he tried to slip her robe and shift from her body, she wagged a finger at him and set back to her own work. She wanted to stay in the saffron, this time. Their limbs caught the faint light in the darkness, no different in quick glimpses than the statues that lined one wall, the faces of generations of High Xaras watching their bodies move in rhythm, tremble, exult. It was a holy place, but that was part of the point, for her. She wanted to show the god what she knew. How this man was like the Holy One's own long-ago consort in his way, precious in the way all life was precious, but not as holy as a Xara. Not making the decisions of import, not in control. Never in control.

And for the first time Concordia made Xelander spend his rain inside her, his eyes wide as she pushed down at the vital moment. Out of habit, it seemed, his jaw locked hard against a moan of swelling pleasure.

"Scream," she commanded, her voice hoarse, and as his pleasure crested, he obeyed her command.

A moment later, she whispered, "There. Let us see how the Holy One chooses to bless us now."

The flickering candlelight showed the uncertainty on his features, but as she leaned down to kiss him, he still welcomed her lips with his own open mouth, warm and hungry.

She felt so much like laughing. She felt alive. Alight. Afire.

After they were both spent, they lay on the soft wool, entangled, his fingers darting under the folds of her robe, her palm resting on his bare hip.

"How would you feel about fathering a child?" she asked.

"Goodness!" His voice was teasing but she heard the unsettled tone underneath. "I know you have no experience with such things, but I assure you, it would be too soon for you to know."

She had made him afraid. That was good.

"But how would you feel?" Concordia said. "Knowing you gave your rain to make the child of a Xara."

"You are not just any Xara," he said, lowering his lips to her neck. She recognized the attempt to deflect for what it was.

She said, "Indeed, I make my own rules. You told me that once, years ago. Before the Sun Rites where I put five innocent girls to death with my own hands. Do you still believe it?"

"After this?" He gestured at the tomb around them, at the statues of the dead High Xaras standing witness, then at his own nakedness. "Yes, certainly. You certainly do make your own rules."

"So perhaps I could bear a child," she answered, her tone even, measured. "Perhaps I could be the first unchaste High Xara, and no one would blink an eye."

"Come now," he said. "You are not so naive. They would blink."

"They might. But if I said it was a sign that the god had blessed me? And if I had a daughter, a perfect little girl, dark eyes, thick curls? Perhaps she could be the first daughter of a Xara to become a Xara herself. Do you not think they would honor me then?"

"If that's what you wish," he said, but his words rang hollow.

Xelander had always been an excellent actor, but his facade was slipping badly tonight. Perhaps it was the cool of the tomb around him, so unlike the palace, such a powerful reminder that none of them—no servant, no person, not even a Xara—could live forever.

"I don't know," she said, pretending to muse. "A child. From a Xara. It does seem risky. Why would someone do that, do you think?"

"I apologize. I am certain it is because I lack your cleverness, but your meaning eludes me. Again, I am sorry." His hands idled, then went still.

"I mean to ask, why would someone want to water a Xara's seed?"

"Goodness," he said again. "I don't know that anyone would *want* to. It wouldn't be his choice, anyway, would it? It would be hers. The god's, really."

"So if someone lay with a Xara it would be for pleasure, you think. Not part of some grander plan."

"No man in his right mind would lay with a Xara. There would be too much at stake. For him to overcome his reason, well, she would have to be truly irresistible." He kissed her then, his suave facade firmly back in place.

She left off testing him. She knew as much as she needed to know. She enjoyed watching him squirm, true, but it was not as satisfying as she thought it might be. That was not really why she had brought him here. Loose-limbed and trusting now, after their pleasures, she had him where she wanted him for one more, final action.

"I hunger," she said.

He cocked a brow. "Are you not satisfied?"

"You slaked one hunger," she said, "now help me with the other. The apples I brought are over there. Fetch me one."

He followed her pointing finger and saw a table in the shadows, holding a lamp and three apples. The lamp was unlit, the apples red-cheeked and ripe. He stretched an arm off the lambswool toward his nearby clothes, which she'd left in a heap.

"No, no," she purred. "Go as you are."

He did as she bade him. She watched his retreating form, not the same as he'd been in their earliest stolen moments together, but still pleasing, as he stepped farther and farther into the shadows.

Then Concordia silently rose, ducked back into the narrow passageway to the outer door, and left the tomb.

She did not slow, did not look back, and she was sliding the interior door to the narrow passage closed before he noticed she was gone. That door had no lock, but neither was the latch easy to find from the inside, especially for someone who'd never tried it before. Someone who was lost and disoriented. Someone who wasn't sure what was happening to him or why. And by the time he understood, by the time he made it through the tunnel to the outer door, if he ever did, it would be too late.

She emerged into the night and slid the bolt home behind her. She replaced the pin and that solid, heavy beam lay across the door to the tomb, not to be opened again until another High Xara died. If Concordia stayed in power, it would be her own death that next opened the door. *Let it be many, many years from now,* she thought, adding with grim relish, *Her will be done.*

Once outdoors again, Concordia listened for the crickets, the owl, the sweet call of the nighttime world. There was nothing to see out here in the dark, but so much to hear. She stood with ready, patient ears.

Then she remembered how certain she'd become that she would never hear the voice of the god. How her hand had trembled at the previous rites. How more and more often she'd felt out of control. How now that she'd done this one important thing, rid the world of a predator once and for all, there seemed nothing else worth waiting for back in the Edifice.

Why should she stay?

The god had not chosen her. She'd tried to force herself into that honored position, clung to it for years, taking the role of High Xara that had never been meant for her. However many mistakes she'd made along the way, she'd done the best she could. Now, perhaps, it was time to see what else she could do. She remembered thinking, back in the early days with Xelander, that they could leave the Edifice together. In a way, if she walked and just kept walking now, they would. She might go anywhere, do anything, become anyone, and neither of them would ever return.

Yes. The freedom of it was intoxicating. No rules. No listening ears.

She took one step, then another. She had a fleeting thought that it was not fair of her to leave without deciding succession, without laying the groundwork for another High Xara to follow her. But that had always been the god's business, not hers. Let the god decide what came next.

She—Concordia, Olivi, whatever she decided to call herself from here on out—would leave Her to it.

The night breeze felt warm on Concordia's face after the chill of the stone tomb. If Xelander called out, which he certainly must have, once he realized what she had done—pleading for his life, cursing her name, both together—she wouldn't hear. His voice, even terrified, even screaming, did not penetrate stone.

The walls of the tomb were thick, just as she had told him. They were built to last.

✦ CHAPTER 22 ✦

A BANQUET

Late Autumn, The All-Mother's Year 519

Ursu, Paxim

Stellari

Stellari wasn't a queen, but she was the closest thing to it, and she chose to take her cue from the strongest queen she'd ever known. Stellari had never liked Heliane, but she'd absolutely respected her. Except for that foolishness with her son, Paulus—may he rest in peace—Heliane had ruled well. Through all the losses of her family, she hadn't lost focus. If Heliane had a presence in the Underlands, Stellari thought grimly, the dead queen was probably laughing at her now. Stellari had taken great pains not to amass a family and friends around her, and yet, what had happened? She'd lost the few she did have.

She didn't need friends, she thought. But she did need allies. And if she couldn't rule with love, what remained? Strategy. Promises. Threats.

For the hundredth time, Stellari looked down and noticed a discarded walnut shell on the floor near her foot. She was on the verge of calling a servant to clean it when she remembered, again, that it wasn't real.

The banquet room in the palace hadn't been used in years. Perhaps she shouldn't have used it tonight, especially since the realistic mosaic on the floor was proving so distracting. But after returning from her visit to meet with the Scorpican queen, it was the right time to shore up her power back at home. Why not make sure the right people were paying attention?

"Over there," she directed the willowy servant with the sharp nose, and quietly fumed while the young man seemed to take forever to set down the tray of sweets on the side table. He disappeared back through the archway in the direction of the kitchen before she could tell him he hadn't put it down in the right place. If she were queen, she would fire all the servants and hire new ones. She was even considering it now. But she had a very difficult line to walk—powerful but not the most powerful, independent but watched—and she couldn't put a single foot wrong if she wanted to stay on the right side.

Even as she was thinking of it, another servant stumbled into the room, a woman whose facial skin had been bubbled and stretched, some kind of burn scar. One arm hung limp at her side. In the other, she held a platter.

"Regent, where shall I put this?"

"With the others," Stellari snapped, barely looking at her. They'd hire anyone these days.

The woman moved slowly to set the tray down, and once it was set, she remained.

"What are you waiting for?" asked Stellari. "Go back down to the kitchen."

"Will you need additional help with service tonight?"

"What kind of question is that? I've already asked for what I want."

The woman looked down, abashed. But she persisted. "I'm so sorry. I was told the orders were unclear. I'm sure they were clear and the person receiving the orders was at fault."

Stellari said, "Who told you they were unclear?"

The servant said, "I don't mean to get her in trouble . . . I'm so sorry, Regent . . ."

"It was the cook, wasn't it?" How frustrating. But she didn't need to get into it with this person. "Never you mind. Yes, I've requested one person for service, and that's enough."

"Will the young queen be at dinner?"

Now Stellari looked at the servant's face more intently. Something familiar about it. Though she was sure she'd be able to place someone with a scar like that, and that part felt unfamiliar.

The servant seemed to realize she'd made a misstep. "I mean . . . it's just . . . it would be a dream come true to meet her. I've never met anyone royal."

"You haven't worked here long, have you?"

"No."

"Let me give you some advice. The servants who last the longest in the palace are the ones who seem to belong here. They don't gawp at the queen or ask too many questions. Like you're doing."

"I'm so sorry, Regent, I . . ."

Stellari held up a hand. "And they certainly don't fall all over themselves apologizing." A charitable impulse struck her. "You might do quite well here. I don't know one way or the other. But keep your head down, do what you're told, and you have every chance of succeeding."

The servant seemed to take this kind advice in the spirit Stellari meant it. She gave a quick bow, eyes downcast, and left the room.

Turning her attention back to the table, Stellari focused on the tray the servant had set down. She wrinkled her nose and moved the tray herself, shifting it one way and then the other. Then she stood back to take a look and make sure it achieved the right impression.

Stellari generally preferred plain food, simple things, but she'd asked the cook to put on a show. Unfortunately, this wasn't the cook she had once paid handsomely to spy for her. She'd retired that woman to the countryside with another handsome payment, ensuring her silence. She couldn't have too many people knowing her secrets. She'd gotten where she was by doling out her trust only when absolutely necessary, in increments as small and tight as the child-queen's closed fist.

The food had to be perfect, though not showy. She would start with something plain and get fancier. The first few courses would remain in the kitchen until the guests arrived. A simple soup of pumpkin mashed with milk and garlic. Fried artichokes, one per guest, crisp and hot and fragile. The meat course would include turkey minced with spices and cooked in a cabbage leaf, sauced with ground walnuts and cream and topped with bright red pomegranate seeds. Her mouth watered just thinking of it. The meal would culminate in the sweets from the side table, which would be displayed from the beginning: more sweets than the small group at dinner could possibly eat, but something for nearly every taste, from the simplest milk pudding to a sumptuous twist of pastry filled with wine-poached apricots and topped with flecks of gold.

Unfortunately, as she gazed at the display of sweets, she noticed that several desserts were sprinkled with pistachio nuts, which she despised. Terrible choice, those little green flecks like bug guts. Ruined, the pudding and the honey cakes and the pastry pockets filled with sweet cheese. Her tension turned to anger.

She reached for the bellpull to summon the cook, but as soon as her hand curled around the rope, she stilled it. No. As much as she wanted to, no. She couldn't punish the cook now, when the guests were already on their way. Later would have to do. Still, it galled her.

She attempted to calm herself by looking around the gorgeous banquet room, but it wasn't soothing. The last time she'd been in this room, as the magistrate, she'd been summoned here by Queen Heliane, along with Juni, the head of the Assembly at the time, and Decima, who'd been consul. Stellari's path to power of course required the removal of Decima from that position. The following year she'd personally overseen the arrest of Decima for treason, cut her braids from her head with a sharp blade, and thrown them onto the floor of the Senate to show that the woman had been stripped of her power. No member of the Senate had seen or heard from Decima since. They absorbed her power as quickly as they'd scooped up her braids from the Senate floor and tucked them into their own hairstyles. It was in their best interest not to ask questions, so no one did.

But that was later, Stellari reminded herself. At the banquet, Decima had been at the height of her power, laughing and smiling with her friend the queen, as comfortable as she would have been in her own home. Heliane's purpose in calling the banquet had been to flex her power—the summons had been abrupt, even for her friend Decima—and to force them to sit at table with her son, Paulus, who'd recently entered adulthood, as the Drought of Girls rolled on. With no girl to inherit her queendom, Heliane had made other plans. Paulus had seemed like an intelligent young man, handsome, with his curly hair pulled back, his white clothes spotless. Stellari hadn't planned his death, but it dovetailed into her plans at the right time, and everything had turned out nicely. Still, that banquet had been humiliating. If this one went well, perhaps it could wipe the memory of that one away.

It took an hour to get everything exactly as she wanted it, though the sprinkled pistachios still bothered her, and she changed her mind three times about who would sit at her right hand and who at her left. Besides herself, Juni of Kamal would be the most powerful of the women to attend, as the magistrate of the Senate. Should Stellari acknowledge that by giving her the seat of honor, or run counter to it in order to put Juni in her place? It was a tough decision, and, once the guests arrived, irrevocable.

As it happened, Juni was the first to arrive, so Stellari could test her without giving her hand away to anyone else.

The servant announced her—"Juni of Kamal, magistrate of the Senate!"—but Stellari didn't even have the chance to tell him to send her in before she was already there. The look on her face was one of impatience. Stellari would try to be gracious, but she could already tell it would be hard.

"Juni, welcome!" said Stellari, indicating the room with a warm gesture. "Such a pleasure."

Instead of answering her, Juni turned to the servant, the only other person in the room with them. "Could you leave us a moment, please?"

The servant should have checked with Stellari, but didn't; he left immediately through the open door.

Stellari tried not to let her irritation show. Keeping her tone warm, she said to Juni, "I'm so delighted you came at my invitation."

"I'm not here to answer your invitation," said Juni. She plucked at the sleeve of her pale blue robe, but her eyes stayed on the regent's. "I'm here to tell you that you don't have the right to invite me."

"But I did," said Stellari stubbornly. "And you came."

"I can come to the palace anytime I like, actually," Juni responded, her voice maddeningly even. It was one of the things Stellari hated about her most. Even when Juni had reason to be upset, she never sounded upset. She was either impossible to rattle or just awfully good at pretending to be calm when she wasn't. Stellari thought of herself as highly capable at hiding her emotions, but Juni was so level, did she even have emotions? It was infuriating. Juni smoothed her hair with her palm, letting her hand linger on the side of her neck, far too casual an attitude for the occasion. "The palace belongs to the people."

"The palace belongs to the queen."

Still with no apparent emotion, Juni answered, "And you are not she. I shouldn't have to remind you."

"And you don't." Stellari made no effort to keep the snide edge from her voice.

A pettier person would have responded with spite. Juni simply said, "Excellent. You're so capable, Stellari. The nation is lucky to have you looking after our interests."

Then there was silence, which Stellari felt she had to fill with a "Thank you."

"You're welcome," murmured Juni.

The servant—what was his name again?—had returned, and his voice sounded from the door. "*Thena*, your next guest has arrived. The head of the Assembly, Duente of Arsinoe."

"Welcome!" cried Stellari, with a good approximation of cheer, before Juni could get her hooks in.

Duente was exactly the kind of woman Stellari needed in charge of the Assembly, which made sense, since she'd handpicked her to rise. She'd been able to pull enough strings for that, at least. Duente was hungry for power but hamstrung by conscience, straightforward enough to tell the truth but smart enough to keep secrets. And above all else, she was awed by Stellari, who had confided enough of the truth about her rise from powerless child to powerful woman to make Duente think that she, too, could have everything if she just took the right steps and avoided the wrong ones. She lacked polish, which Stellari didn't mind—it made her easy for others to underestimate.

Slack-jawed, gaping at the ornate floor, Duente said to her host, "This room! It's glorious!"

"Thank you," Stellari responded quickly. "Here is your seat, to my right." She was careful not to look at Juni. It would offend her, not being given the seat of honor. Let the message sink in.

The dinner itself was an unpleasant, uneasy blur.

Duente had a good appetite, and she was the only one who ate everything. Stellari had not called attention to it, but she had certainly noticed that Juni had taken not a single bite of the feast nor a single sip of the drink placed in front of her. The luxuriant side table of fruits and pastries sat there, glossy and untouched, and Stellari felt personally attacked whenever she looked at it. She was tempted to leave the food there until it rotted.

Pointedly, Juni said, "I believe you are overdue to report to the Senate on your travels to the other queendoms, to secure the queens' attendance at the next Sun Rites."

"Is that what you believe?" Stellari asked breezily.

"You do owe us those reports."

"I made reports."

"There are murmurings that the reports were not satisfactory," said Juni, and even though there was no emotion in her voice, Stellari felt a twist in her gut.

Then the willowy servant was back again, saying, "Regent, we need your presence for a moment."

"Can't it wait? I'm in the middle of an important dinner with important women." Usually she wouldn't mind the interruption; it was a reminder to her guests that she was essential to the running of the country. But with Juni needling her, she needed to show strength in front of Duente, lest one woman's skepticism prove contagious to the other.

The servant wavered a bit, but then said, "My understanding is that it cannot wait."

"Very well. Please excuse me, *thenas*. I'll return as soon as I can."

They murmured pleasantries, but she didn't look at them to evaluate their true feelings, since those didn't matter. They could grumble or approve, but she would spend a few minutes dealing with this interruption and return afterward. They would have to accept that. She merely needed to keep the interruption short.

Once they were out of her guests' hearing, Stellari asked her most pressing question outright. "Is it the child?"

"It is," said the servant, his voice a little unsteady.

"Tell me nothing's happened to her. Tell me she's all right."

"Nothing's happened to her," he said, with obvious relief that he was able to tell the truth.

"So what is it? Can't sleep? Children." No one else in this queendom held as much power as she did. So why did she feel so powerless?

When they stood at the door of the toddler-queen's chambers, Stellari noticed right away that there were fewer guards than usual, and the ones who were there were clearly on edge.

"An intruder?" she guessed. The look on the nearest guard's face said everything. In an accusing tone, Stellari said, "How did they get this far? How did you let them?"

A voice called from deeper in the rooms. "Please don't blame them. It was me."

The sight that greeted Stellari was, in a way, not that unusual. The child-queen was curled on her royal bed, hair fanned over the pillow, face red from heat and a light sheen of sweat on her brow.

But standing over her was a woman who was both unfamiliar and too familiar, and finally Stellari realized her earlier mistake.

The woman who stood over the bed—unarmed, thank the All-Mother, Stellari realized—was the badly burned servant who she'd chastised earlier. But now, Stellari recognized why she'd looked familiar: she was also the child-queen's mother, who had taken a substantial payment in recompense for promising she would never do the exact thing she was doing now.

Stellari wanted to tell the guards to slay the woman where she stood, but given how close she was to the toddler, it seemed unwise. Perhaps words would do.

In a frosty tone, she addressed the intruding mother. "You were not invited here."

Tears shone on the woman's scarred face. She said, "A mother needs no invitation."

Stellari kept her tone cold. "Anyone needs an invitation to the presence of a queen. Even a mother. Or someone who claims to be."

"Claims!" wailed the woman.

"You gave her to us. Took a payment."

"That wasn't me! That was my sister! She stole her to give to you. I've been waiting for my chance to see her again ever since."

Stellari doubted that was true, but she couldn't be absolutely certain, and there was no sense in quibbling. This enterprise was too delicate. The woman was too close to the child-queen, closer than she ever should have been able to get. "You should have known she was better off without you."

"Never!" the woman shrieked.

The child stirred, probably disrupted by the loudness of the voice. Stellari considered her options. Leap forward and grab the child before the mother could? Soothe her? Intimidate her?

While she was deciding, the child awoke. The first person she saw was Stellari, and she put her arms out to be lifted.

Stellari surged forward and grabbed the child, and even as the mother made her own bid, Stellari wrenched the child away.

"Hey!" yelled the child sleepily.

"Asana, dear child, do you know me?" the mother said, her voice syrupy.

The regent shifted the child on her hip, put her own body between the girl's and the mother's. "You were told how to behave. You agreed."

"I didn't know," the woman said softly, her eyes on the child's red, scrunched face.

Stellari asked, "Didn't know what?"

"How much I would miss her."

Stellari told herself not to roll her eyes. This was why emotions were so useless. They made people act counter to reason.

She had to handle this carefully. She'd be within her rights to set the guards on this woman, but she hesitated to do so in front of the child.

"Please," the woman said. "Just let me spend a little time with her. Wherever you want. In the palace, if that's easiest. Just let me be near my daughter."

"She doesn't belong to you. She belongs to the queendom."

"It's *her* queendom," said the mother. "Shouldn't she get a say?"

"She is a child, barely out of babyhood," Stellari explained, not so patiently. "If she were allowed to make decisions, she'd live in a palace of cloud-candy and fly a winged horse up a rainbow."

"Rainbow!" echoed the child with a fierce burst of joy.

Stellari fixed her mother with a glare. She was sure the woman caught her meaning: the child had a child's mind, with a child's wants, not a queen's.

"But what could it hurt?" asked the mother. "A little while. All through the Drought of Girls, I never thought I would have a daughter, and then I did—she's the most precious thing imaginable."

"She's precious to all of us."

"Including me! Please! She should know her mother."

Stellari did not spit that she'd never known her own mother, that thousands of women in the queendoms never did, and what difference did mothers make anyway? Then she remembered how much she'd wanted a daughter. Back in those early days of the Drought, when she hadn't drunk *pulegone* tea to wash Aster from her womb, worried that saying no to a son meant saying no to the possibility of a daughter. She had wanted one so much. Serving as regent to the child-queen was likely the closest she'd ever come. And though there was little she enjoyed about the reality of it, it had been such a pretty dream. Perhaps this woman's dream and reality were not as far apart as her own.

"I'm sorry, there's nothing I can do," Stellari said wearily.

"But she's my *daughter*," said the mother, a tired refrain.

A servant cleared their throat from the doorway. "Regent? Your guests are asking whether they should remain."

That was when Stellari made her second mistake.

"All right," the regent answered the child-queen's mother, almost spitting the final word. "You may stay with her until I return from my banquet. Then you go on your way."

"Yes. Absolutely."

Giving in to the woman once was, Stellari decided, an allowable compromise. A bit of appeasement was not weakness if it was supplemented with threats. She lowered her voice and put one hand over the child's nearest ear. She spoke to the mother only.

"Understand, this is one time. I will never allow you to take her home. She is no longer yours, not in any way. Do you understand?"

The mother's voice was quiet. "I understand."

"This will never happen again."

No hesitation whatsoever. "I understand."

Stellari handed the child to her mother. The girl squeaked and squealed, but let the mother deal with that for once. If she was so eager to parent a child, let her see what parenting this particular one felt like.

Stellari reassured herself that there was no way out. She would leave one guard in the room to watch them, and guards were everywhere in the hallways beyond. If the mother wanted to attempt to leave, let her. The second she tried to remove the child from this room, she'd be stopped. She had no chance at all to take her out of the palace. And now that Stellari could give all the palace guards a description, the queen's mother would never be able to sneak in again. It was only this once.

Back with the head of the Assembly and the magistrate, all went well. She was able to soothe Juni's concerns, offer the women the fine sweets she'd laid out, and send them on their way with warm assurances.

It was only when she went upstairs to throw out the intruder that her high spirits came crashing down.

When she swung open the door to the child-queen's rooms, the stillness that greeted her was the most awful she could imagine.

She had not thought through all the possibilities. And now there would be hell to pay.

When Stellari had rushed back to her guests, because it was easiest, she'd let the mother stay. She thought there was nowhere the two of them could go. But the woman's most desperate path to escape, one Stellari had failed to foresee, was the one she—and her daughter—had taken.

✦ CHAPTER 23 ✦

JOURNEY

From Scorpica to Paxim

Gretti

Not even for a good reason could Gretti dha Rhodarya force herself to attend the Moon Rites. She couldn't see herself ever setting foot in the Holy City again. Strange, what a hold those days had over her, even though so many years had passed since.

Her first time in the Holy City she had been young, a bladebearer of ten-and-five. She had followed Khara, her queen, who seemed almost a magical figure to her. On the road back to Scorpica, when they were set upon by bandits, Khara had saved her life. Three seasons later, Gretti had birthed a son, who was taken from her and sent off to some nation that made use of its boys and men. She had rarely thought of him in the years since.

But now, ever since she'd returned to Scorpica following Queen Amankha, Khara's daughter, that son was on Gretti's mind. He would be older now than she'd been when she gave birth to him. About the same age as Amankha, as a matter of fact, since Gretti had become pregnant only days before Khara. As it happened, she gave birth two days after Khara had, and she barely remembered what it had been like. The camp had been in an uproar, Khara having been forced by a Challenge from Mada to kill or be killed, and very little attention was left for a young warrior giving birth, especially once it became clear her child wasn't a warrior. Gretti didn't even know who had taken him away. She only knew she'd never seen him again.

In the waning months of the war, when Queen Tamura was still in charge, Gretti had started to wonder what her purpose was. She still wondered now. She wasn't too old to have a child, and now that the Drought of Girls was over, no one knew whether or not that child would be a warrior. She would try, she decided. But she would not go to the rites to do it.

As warriors traveled to and from the Bastion on their short-term assignments, helping strengthen the bonds between their two countries, goodwill wasn't all they'd brought back. So many warriors had returned to Scorpica with bellies set to swell that Gretti privately doubted there was a man left in the Bastion who hadn't watered a warrior's seed with his rain. She had no desire to hunt in such well-trod ground.

So when her queen asked her to deliver a message deep in Paxim, near the capital, even though it would take her away from Scorpica for more than a month, Gretti leapt at the chance.

"Here's the message," said Amankha, handing her a packet. Then, almost as an afterthought, she said, "The old man will accompany you."

Gretti looked askance at the old man called Elm, but he seemed clean enough, and if the queen said to take him along, she would.

They traveled together for hours and then days, putting down their bedrolls whenever Gretti suggested, but they didn't converse. When Gretti asked Elm direct questions, he might answer with "Yes, please," or "No, thank you," but he never spoke without being spoken to and his answers revealed nothing. After a few days, Gretti decided she would treat the trip as if she were voyaging alone, and nearly every hour of the day or night, that was how it felt.

Gretti especially savored the quiet as she slept in a bedroll far from any town or village. During wartime they'd camped in Godsbones, and there was never time alone. Gretti liked to be alone. She toyed with the idea that Amankha hadn't even sent a real message, that the queen had only sent Gretti on this trip as a mercy, knowing that she needed to be away from Scorpica for a while. That, she reflected, would be all right. The old man, though, she just couldn't make sense of.

Then, when she arrived at the house with the dogwoods out front, one mature, one young, the thin figure who emerged from the doorway looked somehow familiar. Gretti dismounted from the pony with the message in hand, her seat aching from the long miles on her mount, and wearily looked up.

When she recognized the woman standing there, she had no words.

Vishala dha Lulit smiled at her. "Gretti," she said. "Do you remember me?"

Gretti wanted to fling herself into the woman's arms. Someone who remembered Khara, someone from the old days before the Drought, before the war.

"Vishala," she breathed.

The woman's smile broadened. "Vish," she said, offering the informal name Gretti had never felt honored enough to call her, and then Gretti did leap into the other woman's embrace, feeling like she'd somehow come home.

"I was asked to bring you this message," said Gretti, then gestured to the man on the pony behind her. "And this visitor."

The hermit dismounted with a spryness Gretti hadn't seen from him at any point on their trip together. When he spoke, it was with the longest string of words that Gretti had heard from his lips. "I am called Elm. It's a pleasure to meet you, Vishala. The queen speaks very highly of you, and your dedication is peerless."

Gretti almost spun around in shock, but she mastered herself. Calmly, she said, "Kind of our queen to speak with you about Vish, when she didn't tell me that was who I was coming to meet."

Vish was the first to respond. She did so with a shrug and a cheerful, "Well, the queen does what she does," and Gretti didn't feel that left her with many options.

The hermit said, "I'll settle the ponies while you two talk. Would that be all right?" He looked to Vish and only Vish for a response.

Vish nodded. "Thank you. There's a stream beyond those trees. Refresh yourself as well."

While the old man was gone, the two women spoke at length in the yard. Gretti felt an odd undercurrent she couldn't put her finger on, but she had traveled a long way and was seeing one of her heroes, so she decided to let the sunshine wash over her and let her irritation slip away.

Vish's voice was husky, and when she spoke more than a few words at a time, her hand often drifted up to a scar on her throat. Gretti guessed that she'd been injured somehow in the years since they'd seen each other—by the look of her scar, not recently. Vish also kept the door behind her closed and didn't invite Gretti inside. There was something or someone in the house she didn't want Gretti to see. A lover? A treasure? Gretti didn't ask. It would be hostile to press too hard. And she was so grateful just to see the other woman again, to feel for a moment as she had more than a decade before, she didn't want to do anything to break the spell.

Vish didn't tell her everything, but she told her a few things she'd done. She'd taken Amankha to the Orphan Tree, as Gretti might know from Amankha herself, and ridden off to die afterward. But,

Vish admitted with a grin and a downward gesture, she hadn't died. She wandered until she found purpose with a small band of travelers; she only left them when she had to, when she broke a promise.

"Breaking a promise doesn't seem like you," said Gretti.

"Didn't mean to," Vish said. "But you know how it is. If you break a glass jar, it doesn't matter whether you meant to break it. It's still broken."

Gretti nodded.

Vish went on. "So I left that group, and traveled some more. Until the Paximites put out a call for the very best soldiers, and I thought I'd see what it was about. I ended up working on the King's Elite. Have you heard about them?"

Gretti was connecting the dots. "And that's where you found Amankha again."

Vish nodded soberly. "And after—after Paulus was killed, she was ready to murder Tamura on the spot, but I told her to wait and become a Scorpican first. To find an ally."

"She did," said Gretti. "I knew her right away."

"The spot on her back?"

Gretti nodded. "And she's where she should be, I think. She's a wise leader. Scorpica is better off for having her in charge."

"I knew she would be a good queen."

"Even a good queen needs good counsel. I'm sure she misses yours. Was the message asking you to come back?"

"No," said Vish. "But thank you for bringing it." By the shift in her tone, Gretti knew their conversation was almost over.

Gretti looked in the direction the old man had gone. "I'm not sure if I . . ."

Vish said, "He stays with me. Is that what you were wondering?"

Gretti had to admit, privately, that she was relieved. She would prefer her own company to the hermit's on the long return. Then there was only one question left to ask. "Is there a message to take back?"

"Yes. If you could wait . . ."

"Of course."

Gretti stood in the yard, turning her back to the door, and looked up at the midafternoon sky. The blue of the sky today was somewhat dimmed by gray, summer's heat beginning to wane, but the sun still warmed her cheeks as she smiled up. She thought she caught the barest sound of whispered conversation from behind the closed door. Instead of pressing closer to hear it, she stepped farther away, removing temptation.

The dogwoods had shed their leaves. She wished she could be here in spring to see them bud. Maybe she would be. Maybe Gretti would voyage back and forth, over and over, with messages between Queen Amankha and the woman who had once been her mother's most trusted councillor. That wouldn't be such a bad calling. It would make her feel like she had purpose. She missed that feeling.

Behind her, the door opened, and she heard Vish approach.

"For the queen," she said in that husky voice, pressing a packet into Gretti's hand.

Gretti took the packet and touched Vish on the shoulder, just once. "Thank you. I'll deliver it safely."

"Of course you will. And have you decided where to stop on your return?"

Gretti shrugged. "I've been riding until I tire. My bedroll has been enough."

"If you want to try something different," Vish suggested, with an odd bit of twinkle, "I think you'd enjoy Shifri. It's a trading post about three hours' ride north. Did you come by it on your way south?"

"No."

"Try it," she said. "Treat yourself to one night at an inn. There's one there, you'll know it by the sign, best food for leagues upon leagues. Sign of the Grape."

"Sign of the Grape," murmured Gretti. She tucked the packet for Amankha into her bag, mounted her pony, and headed off.

Hours later, she traveled the dusty roads of Shifri, thinking again of the look on Vish's face when she'd suggested the trading post. There was more here than just a delicious meal, Gretti was sure of it. She was indifferent to the idea of sleeping somewhere besides the ground, but she couldn't get that expression of Vish's out of her head. Back before Khara's death, when Vish had reigned as the queen's second-in-command, she'd done nothing by accident. So what Vish said, Gretti would do.

The inn itself, when she approached it, was clearly a quality establishment. The sign itself was freshly repainted, a small stable next door in perfect condition. Gretti was willing to bet most travelers in this part of the world were on foot, but she was glad she wasn't. She handed off her pony's reins to a trim young man and gave him instructions. Then she planted a quick kiss on the pony's nose before going inside.

The lower room was lined with tables and benches, just enough room between them to pass, and three out of four tables were full. Despite the crowd, the place was humming with soft conversation, no shouts or disruptions. A cozy fire roared at the far end of the room, the stones in front of it lined with cooking pots. She liked the place immediately.

A kitchen boy gestured her toward an empty table. "Meal or room? Both?"

"Meal, for now," she said. "Are there rooms?"

"Yes. Do you want one?"

"Don't know yet. How about the meal first?"

"Yes, *thena*," he said, and told her the price. Coins changed hands, he scurried off, and Gretti settled in to wait.

Nothing she saw looking around the Sign of the Grape contradicted her first impression. Women and men were comfortable here. If every inn were like this, thought Gretti, perhaps she'd use them more often. Then again, maybe she should stay wary. She'd been raised not to trust outsiders, and in a way, everyone here was an outsider. Or, thinking about it a different way, she was. But no one stared at her, despite her obviously Scorpican clothing. They went about their business. She'd go about hers.

The kitchen boy set a fragrant bowl in front of her, and it was all she could do not to fall on it. Rabbit, it smelled like, and piping hot besides. She hadn't realized how hungry she was. Just the smell made her want to ride all the way back to the house with the two dogwoods to thank Vish in person.

When she took her first sip of the rabbit stew, Gretti found a low moan escaping her throat. She couldn't remember the last time she'd tasted something so delicious.

"Nothing as wonderful as a satisfied patron," came a low voice near her ear.

She turned her head and looked at the speaker. He'd approached her, but not too closely, and stood by the table instead of seating himself next to her on the bench. His clothes were simple and flattering, a thin leather tunic cut into a V at the neck, lightly embellished with hand-stitching. A neatly trimmed beard emphasized the curve of his jaw, and his dark hair curled just over his ears and low on his forehead. His dark eyes sparkled.

"The cook should take the credit," Gretti answered.

"I'll tell her so," he said promptly. In a friendlier tone, he added, "But shouldn't the person who hired the cook get some credit as well?"

"I take it you hired the cook."

"I did. And everyone else who works here." He gestured around the room with obvious pride. There were two more kitchen boys in addition to the one she'd met, Gretti saw, and some kind of assistant or servant moving the cooking pots around by the fireplace. The main kitchen had to be elsewhere, but the fire here was also doing its work. This time, when she looked around, she caught one more sign of how carefully the place was cared for: the long wood tables were polished to a shine, nearly as smooth as glass, not the splintery things she remembered from long-ago visits to other inns.

His pride gave her a clue, and she asked the question even though she was almost certain of the answer. "Your inn?"

"My inn."

Gretti began to suspect it was not just the inn itself, or the rabbit stew, that Vish had chosen to recommend to her. She chose her next words accordingly. "You own it with your sister? Your wife?"

The man's smile was sly. "By myself alone."

Well, then. Whether Vish had intended this or not, Gretti had intentions of her own, and it was time to see if they aligned with reality. She tapped the table across from her. "A great achievement. Do you have time to sit with me?"

"I'll make the time." He sat, slinging a leg over the bench across from her, seating himself so they faced each other directly. He crossed his arms in front of his body on the table, leaned forward on his elbows. Despite the bustle to their left and right, they might as well have been alone in the room. His gaze was settled on her face. There was something a little overwhelming about having all his attention focused solely on her.

Gretti was nervous, suddenly. She couldn't tell whether his game attitude pleased or frightened her. It seemed almost too easy: find a man she was attracted to, make clear what she wanted. But what if she was mistaken? What if she was reading his signals all wrong? The young man she'd shared pleasures with at her first Sun Rites, that had truly been a lifetime ago. She could say she was out of the habit, but she'd never really been in it.

"You seem thoughtful," came the warm, low voice from across the table. "Have a lot on your mind?"

"More than I want to," she admitted.

The sly smile was on his face again, his tone confiding. "Lots of ways to occupy the mind."

"Just the mind?"

"No," he said, running a finger along the handle of the spoon she'd been using to eat. The rabbit stew was somehow gone already. Without the food, she didn't have an excuse to stay.

But before she could say so, he was speaking again. "Want a drink to wash that down?"

"What do you have on offer?"

"I have a lovely lily wine, very special."

She wasn't suspicious, but maybe she should be, and she pretended she was, to test both of them. "Is this how you make your money? Warm your patrons' bellies with good stew and then overcharge them for lily wine?"

"No charge," he said simply. She found it harder and harder to look away from his lips as he spoke. "This wine isn't for sale. Only for sharing."

"I'm curious to taste it."

"It's precious. I don't keep it down here. The bottle's in my room upstairs."

She could feel warmth rushing to her cheeks. This was the moment. "You stay at your own inn?"

"Tells you how proud I am of what I've built. Solid through and through."

"Show me the room, then. I'll judge."

He grinned. "I hope to please you."

She put her hands on either side of her empty bowl and pushed up from the table. He gestured toward a narrow set of stairs toward the back of the room, just beyond the fireplace. She preceded him up the stairs, but she could feel his eyes on her back all the way up, as surely as if he'd laid his hand on her. Heat was already building in her belly. She might only have the faintest memory of what it had been like to indulge in pleasures, but her body clearly remembered, eager to plunge back in.

At the end of the hall, he opened a door. Gretti didn't hesitate to step inside.

She couldn't see the room clearly and didn't want to. The faint guttering of a small lamp was all she saw, not even strong enough to illuminate the table upon which it stood. The door closed behind them. She knew looking away from the flame would let her eyes start to adjust to the darkness, but she kept her eyes fixed on the lamp anyway.

"I didn't lie to you. There really is lily wine," she heard him murmur behind her. "If that's what you want."

She would have nodded, but she knew it was too dark for him to see. So she spoke aloud, saying, "It isn't. I mean, I don't."

"Me neither," came his reply, closer now, moving from behind her to beside her. "But I wanted to offer. I never know. Some people take me at my word."

"You do this often?" she asked.

"Do you?"

"Does it matter?" she answered back.

When he spoke, she felt his finger on her arm, tracing her bicep the way he'd traced the handle of the spoon downstairs. Slow and deliberate. His voice was the same. "I saw you, I wanted you. You seemed—seem—to want me, too. I can't think of a single other thing in this world that matters right now, to be completely honest. So if you think of something, tell me."

She thought, but not too hard. He was right. Nothing else seemed to matter. Not the bustling room below, not the road ahead of her tomorrow, not even the rest of the room in which they stood.

"No," she murmured, turning her head, sensing how close he now stood. "Nothing."

None of it mattered. Only this man, and what they both wanted.

In the near darkness, she found him by touch. Soft lips, with the bristle-brush feeling of that unshaven spot under his lower lip, the clash of textures. They turned, wordless, searching. She knew from downstairs that his tunic had no lacing; she began to lift the hem, and they worked together, lifting it over his head and discarding it into the blackness. She heard him laugh, happily, softly.

She caught the back of his neck in her palm, bringing his face to hers, renewing the kiss. They both moved with greater hunger now. She slid her fingers up into his hair, curled them urgently into a fist. Her grip on his hair brought a low moan from his throat.

"Too much?" she asked.

"Not enough."

The way he said it set her further afire. The urgency overwhelmed her. She hated to pull herself back even long enough to discard her own tunic, but forced herself, and flung the cloth away. This time it was his hands that found her, large fingertips he dragged down her bare back. His fingertips were as rough as her own; he worked for his living, she could tell. She shivered with pleasure under his touch.

"I'd like to know your name," he said, "if you'd like to tell me."

"Gretti," she murmured into the skin of his throat. She felt him swallow hard as she ran her palms down the sides of his body and well below his waist. As long as it had been, she knew what came next. It wasn't hard to remember. She found the lacing at the front of his trousers, undid the tie with nimble fingers, and slid one hand inside.

"Ah, Gretti," he moaned back, a whisper against the dark.

"And your name?" she asked, though not sure he'd be able to speak at all, the way his breath was beginning to come in short, panting bursts.

"Garel," he said, breathing out the two short syllables, emphasis on the first. She could see well enough now in the dark to see his head thrown back, eyes closed. There was probably a bed in the room, but she didn't care to look around long enough to find it. Instead she put her other hand on Garel's waist to guide him and began stepping backward toward the nearest wall. He read her signals seamlessly, walking with her, matching step for step.

"Would you like me to call your name, Garel?" she asked, almost conversationally. Gretti had been many things over the past decade. A councillor, a warrior, a killer, more. Now, she was a flirt. Here in the dark she could let all those other selves fall away. Tonight, none of them mattered.

"Yes," he hissed softly, hot breath on her neck. "Please."

When she found the wall, Gretti pressed her back against it, planting her feet. She took Garel's hand and guided it between her legs. Even through the fabric of her leggings she could feel his delicious heat.

Then she whispered in his ear, "Well, then. Give me reason."

He did.

◆ CHAPTER 24 ◆

THE HEIR

Paxim

Stellari, Vish

Over the course of her life, Stellari had felt the full gamut of emotions, even if she had rarely let them show. When she saw the bodies of the toddler-queen and her mother curled in on each other in the same bed, motionless and lifeless, she felt her life's strongest, fiercest pang of regret.

She never should have let the mother stay with the queen, even for minutes, even with the schemers waiting downstairs. She thought they'd never get out of the palace, and they hadn't—but at the same time, they were no longer here.

If only she'd had the guards dispatch the intruding woman on sight. Shown no mercy whatsoever. If Stellari hadn't let the woman in, she wouldn't have had the chance to poison herself and her daughter rather than be parted again.

And now Stellari, who was used to having a wide array of choices, saw her options shrink down to only a handful, all unacceptable.

She couldn't raise the alarm. It would make her look a fool. And she couldn't let the truth out, that the toddler-queen had been killed on her watch—she'd be exiled, if she were lucky. The answer was simple. She needed another queen, preferably one that resembled the one she'd lost.

Her mind sprang into action, sharp and focused now, as if to make up for her failure. She turned to the only guard who had been inside the room as the others waited outside. "You. You will never tell anyone what you saw here today, is that clear? Or you'll be as dead as they are."

The woman swallowed and nodded, her eyes wide. She was a guard of some repute, even if Stellari couldn't remember her name, and she wouldn't want to see all her status vanish in a snap of someone's fingers. Stellari would have preferred it if no one else in the world knew what had happened here, but if one other person already knew, Stellari could live with that. It would take both of them to make sure no one else ever learned.

The guard said, her voice rough, "I couldn't stop her. It happened so fast. She had a vial with her, she gave the queen a drop to drink, and then she drank the rest—and then, All-Mother be blessed, it was awful, they . . ."

Stellari held up a hand. "Whatever you think happened, that's not what happened."

The guard swallowed hard. But Stellari could tell by the woman's eyes, she would clutch at whatever explanation the regent offered her. Any truth would be more palatable than what she'd witnessed.

"The queen is ill," she told the guard. "We are taking her to a healer. She will be fine. Understand?"

"Yes, Regent."

"This intruder—the poor deluded woman, she thought she was the queen's mother— took a poisoned draught and tried to put it to the queen's lips. The queen will be fine, but we are taking her to the best healer in Paxim to make sure there is no lasting damage."

"Yes. No lasting damage."

There would be no healer, of course, but no one would know that. The guard would drive the carriage. Stellari would ride inside with the young queen. And they would go directly, no stopping, to the house with the two dogwoods.

A girl would go in, a girl would come out. On this end, if the guard did her job, no one else needed to know, and in the wider world, no one would be the wiser. Well, except one person. Stellari told herself grimly that she would handle that person. It was really just a question of motivation.

◆

Vish usually would have heard a carriage pull up to the house, but she was on her knees rummaging around the trunk at the foot of the bed, searching for last year's heaviest cloak to shield her against the oncoming winter. Elm had gone to the market; Roksana was digging in the vegetable patch for the last of the pale, sweet carrots. So because she was on her knees with her shoulders around her ears, Vish heard nothing until the front door creaked open and then slammed shut again.

When she looked up through the open doorway between the bedroom and the front room, she saw two women standing inside her cottage. The first had her sword drawn. The second looked familiar, and it took Vish only a moment to place her: the regent of Paxim, who had visited memorably but briefly over a year before when her carriage had broken down outside.

It was the regent who spoke. "How old is the girl?"

Vish could have pretended not to know who or what she was talking about, but that would waste time. Instead she said, drawing herself up to standing, "Too young for strangers to ask after her."

"We're not strangers," the regent said, her mouth crooking up at one corner. "We're from the palace."

"That doesn't make you my friends, and if you're not friends, you're strangers."

The woman just said, "Bring her out so I can see her."

Vish wanted to reach for her swords. She should have been wearing them. She hadn't thought a threat would walk right into the house like this, giving her not even a minute to prepare. Perhaps she could keep the strangers talking, work her way around to her weapons, take it from there.

The regent saw Vish's eyes flick toward where the swords lay, and she motioned to the guard, who took two steps sideways and had her hands on Vish's swords before she could do a *mokhing* thing about it.

"This can be hard or it can be easy," the regent said. "Don't you prefer the latter?"

"Easy is not always right."

"True." The woman's eyes raked the small dwelling. Her thoroughness made Vish even more uneasy.

The guard broke in. "Stellari, I can see the girl. She's in the garden."

The regent nodded. "Let's get her."

Vish said, "I'm sure you understand I can't just let you take her. She's mine."

"Your daughter?" asked the regent.

"My responsibility."

The regent stepped forward. Vish saw that she, too, was armed, though the knife was in her boot, not her hand. The regent's eyes registered that Vish had spotted her weapon, and the woman smiled.

"I need her. I don't need you. Understand?"

Vish understood all too well.

She had just told these intruders that the easiest thing to do wasn't always the best. The choice that faced her now proved it. Sometimes the hardest thing to do was the right, perhaps only, choice.

Almost all her life, it seemed to Vish, she'd been watching over precious girls. She'd cared for Ama when Khara's fate came for her. She'd watched over Eminel in their days with the Rovers, especially after the death of Jehenit. Now she'd promised Ama to watch over Roksana. Even though Ama couldn't have imagined this particular threat to her daughter, Vish knew exactly what Ama would have wanted her to do.

"She'll go with you," said Vish, "if I come."

The regent leveled her gaze at Vish. Their eyes met. Vish saw grudging respect there, at least, and didn't care at the moment to dig deeper than that.

"She won't go with you otherwise," Vish went on, in a voice low enough not to reach the child's ears through the open window. "If you kill me, I'll be out of the way, but she'll have no one she trusts. You'll make it harder than it has to be."

The guard who had taken possession of Vish's swords grunted. The regent shot her a silencing look.

When she turned back to Vish, her voice was direct, but there was a gentleness in it. "How old is she?"

"Not yet two."

"Big for her age, then."

"I suppose."

"We should go," said the guard. "No time to waste."

Vish didn't want to ask the question. So she was relieved, along with a lot of other feelings, when the regent said, "All right. We'll take you both."

Vish took a step forward.

"Hold on," said the regent.

The regent whispered to the guard, who nodded, then completed a quick, efficient search of the cottage for weapons. She found several. All were added to the stack with the swords, which the guard loaded carefully into a lockbox on the back of the wagon. Everything else, they left behind.

As they stood in the doorway, the regent asked Vish, in a conversational tone, "What's your name?"

"I'm tired of coming up with names," Vish found herself saying. "You choose."

"What does the child call you?"

"Vee."

"See, was that so hard? Vee."

Vish nodded.

"We'll tell the girl she's queen. She'll be delighted."

"Don't tell her until we get to the palace," Vish said.

"Why?"

"She can't have too much change at once. She isn't used to it. Let me explain to her that she needs to ride with us, and that I will be with her the whole time, and more will be revealed later. I assure you, it's the best way."

"Well, if *you* assure me," said the regent dryly, but she did not refuse. She allowed Vish to talk quietly with Roksana, to wipe the dirt of the garden gently from her fingers and prepare her for travel. When Roksana shot a concerned glance in the regent's direction, the regent gave her a pleasant smile and a wave.

Then the four of them, a strange party, climbed into the carriage to travel to the palace, and Vish wondered if she would ever see the house with the dogwoods again.

◆

It seemed like a lifetime ago that Vish had walked across the mosaicked floors of the Paximite palace. Heliane had been queen, Paulus still lived, and Roksana hadn't even been born. Vish was torn between staring up at the beauty of the place and staring down at her feet to fight off how it made her feel.

The regent efficiently walked them to the queen's chambers, murmuring reassuring things in Roksana's direction as Vish trailed behind. Once the doors closed behind them, only the four of them there, the regent wheeled on Vish and pointed a threatening finger.

She said in a sharp voice, "You are one of the royal family's many cousins. If anyone asks who you are, that is what you will tell them. You understand?"

"Yes."

"And no weapons. You understand?"

"Yes."

"And you will not leave this room without my direct permission. You—"

"Regent," Vish said, cutting the woman off to make a point. "I understand. You may assume that everything you say to me, I understand. I am not a stupid woman."

"And neither am I," the regent snapped back. "I'm also not a woman who takes chances. I took a chance on you. Don't you ever give me cause to regret it."

Vish looked her straight in the eye and said, "I understand."

Then the regent turned to the guard who had accompanied them. Her voice was tense and direct. "None of this happened. You didn't see it."

"But we should discuss, perhaps—"

"I'll count to five," the regent said. "If you're still here on five, I'm not accountable."

The woman's face was dark with frustration, but she was gone by the time the regent got to three.

When it was just the three of them left in the room—Vish, the regent, and Roksana—the regent knelt in front of the girl. She spoke in a firm voice, facing the child, but Vish knew perfectly well that she, the other adult in the room, was actually the one being addressed.

"You are a fortunate girl, aren't you? Girls all across Paxim dream of being queens. And here you are, having that dream come true."

"How am I queen?" asked the toddler, her tiny brows knit in confusion.

"It's an interesting question," said the regent. Then she paused.

Vish understood instantly that she was meant to break in and make an attempt at an explanation that the child would understand and accept. She was the only one who knew the girl, after all. This was why she was here.

"Roksana," Vish began. "You haven't changed. Nothing has changed about you. You're exactly the same wonderful girl you've always been."

"Then why here? Not home?"

"You are at home," said Vish, and she saw the regent nodding along in approval. "Your new home. This is where you rightfully belong. There were some people who didn't want you to be queen, so we kept you secret. But the time for secrets is past. Now there's only truth. And the truth is this: you're the rightful queen of Paxim."

The girl took a long moment to think. Vish watched her closely. Then, her sweet young face bursting into a grin, the new queen of Paxim giggled.

"Queen!" she said.

The regent grinned back at the girl, ran a finger along her cheek in seeming tenderness. "You do need to do one thing. Play a game. And it might sound odd at first, but it's important, I promise. Can you do one thing?"

"I think?"

"You just need to answer to a different name. Lots of people change their names, you know, when something about their life changes."

"Really?"

"Oh, yes. I'm sure your guardian will agree with me. Wouldn't you?" She spoke to Vish without turning her head.

Even if it hadn't been in her best interest to tell the truth, Vish still would have agreed. "Yes. I've done that. Many others I know have too."

"Oh. All right."

"Not this time. As queen, you'll be known as Heliane the Second."

"Easy!"

Vish breathed a little easier, seeing the joy on the girl's face. Quite by accident the girl might have scotched the entire enterprise. They were walking on the dagger's edge, the two of them. They were useful now. Very useful, even, in Roksana's case. But not indispensable. Vish had been around powerful women enough to know that no one was truly essential. If an important person became unwieldy, there was always another way to get things done.

But Roksana was playing along perfectly, her wide eyes open and friendly, her manner utterly compliant. "Call me 'Eliane, I'll answer. Let's try."

"Heliane, would you like a crown?" asked the regent in a warm, friendly voice. "I have one just your size."

The girl-queen squealed, "Yes, please!"

The regent smiled and nodded, seemingly satisfied.

Mere hours later, Roksana had fully inhabited her new role, wearing sumptous clothes and a tiny crown, acting as if she had been there all along. She was presented in the throne room as a crowd gathered, Paximite senators and their husbands and wives, milling about and smiling.

Vish looked around. It made her want to laugh. All these women and men, bowing low to Roksana, honoring her as a child-queen. Seeing her as the heir to the throne of Paxim.

Which, of course, she was.

Vish was confident the regent had no idea what she'd actually done: brought the true heir to the throne to take the place of a girl who hadn't been the true heir at all. Vish didn't know what had happened to the previous child-queen and didn't want to know. She could only hope the regent hadn't been responsible. That sweet, laughing girl. Vish remembered her well from the year before. A woman who could kill a child was capable of anything. But for some reason she didn't think the regent had done that. Not because she wasn't capable, but because it wouldn't have served her purpose. The regent seemed like a woman who would never take an action without thinking about what effects it would have. A woman who never lost sight of her goal.

"Blessing on you!" Roksana was calling, waving to the woman and men nearby. "And you and you! Royal blessing!" Her smile was so big.

What would Ama think of all this? Vish wondered. But there was no way to get word to her. Not yet. Vish would have to come up with a strategy. Perhaps there was some way to communicate with Elm, who had no doubt come back to the empty cottage and wondered what had gone on. But for now, thought Vish, at least she was here. She would do everything in her power to keep the child safe.

Over the days and months to come, as she got used to the palace, Vish realized, she would have to sort the friends from the enemies.

But what was new about that? In a way, it seemed that was all she'd ever done.

PART IV

THE
GATE OF
HEROES

The All-Mother's Year 520

✦ CHAPTER 25 ✦

HEROES

The Underlands

Sessadon, Paulus, Semma

Sessadon seethed with anger as she worked her way back from the farthest reaches of the Underlands. Eresh wanted her help, yes, but also seemed bent on putting obstacles in her way. If the god truly wanted Sessadon to succeed, all She'd have to do was restore the sorcerer's magic, and all the gates would fly open in an instant. Sure, the rules of magic required both life force and sand for an incantation, but Eresh was a god, wasn't She? She could change the rules.

Unless Eresh wasn't as powerful as She claimed, which sent Sessadon's thoughts spiraling off in another direction entirely.

But she forced herself to think strategy as she picked her way through landscapes both familiar and impossible. As much as opening the Gate of Warriors hadn't turned out how she hoped—how dare that Scorpican shade dash through before her—it had been, basically, a success. A warrior had been key to opening the Gate of Warriors. So she had to admit, as she wandered her way through the vastness of the world of the dead, she already knew whose help she had to enlist to open the Gate of Heroes. He'd offered himself up to her as willingly as any Sun Rites sacrifice. She might as well take advantage.

All she had to do was find him, which felt like it took another eternity.

Time didn't pass here the way it did Above—or did it? Did it pass faster here, even? She hadn't thought about what things might look like Above once she got back there. Tamura was already dead, though not of old age. Would Eminel even still be living by the time Sessadon worked her way back Above? If she wasn't, that might take some of the fun out of revenge. But the passage of time was beyond her control, Sessadon realized. She had to focus on things that weren't.

Eventually she hit upon the idea that newly arrived shades were likely to cluster near the bridge, and since Paulus was curious about the stories of shades, perhaps he would be there. It seemed the right place to start.

As she'd hoped, the area was dense with shades, though she couldn't tell at a glance who might or might not be useful.

"Who are the heroes here?" she asked. "Step forward!"

Shades regarded her warily, some turning toward her, some turning away.

She tried again, attempting to add brightness and warmth to her voice, to be persuasive without sounding like she was trying to persuade. "I have need of a hero! For a mission. Please, who here was a hero Above? Do you wish to be a hero again?"

There was a long silence, and now ripples of different emotions ran through the crowd. A few cocked their heads with interest. She wanted to urge them forward but knew that sometimes the best thing to do was wait. She waited now, and pretended to be patient. Just as it had been Above, the appearance was more important than the reality.

Then the shade of Paulus stepped forward, unchanged from the last time she'd seen him, fine clothes and long curls and a sensitive air. Something commanding about him, even with his sad eyes, or perhaps because of them. "If you're looking for me, sorcerer, you could just say so."

Sessadon missed her magic in a general way down here, but right now she missed one specific incantation desperately. Alive, she would have been able to see inside Paulus's mind. The expression on his face was vaguely amused, satisfied, but there was something else there she couldn't read. She wished she had some idea what he was really thinking.

"You're not my only option," she told Paulus coolly.

"Your best one, though," he replied.

"Were you such a hero, in life?" she said. He'd died, and there was nothing inherently heroic in that, but nothing inherently shameful.

"I tried very hard to be," said Paulus, his air of lasting sadness still hanging on his shoulders like a cloak. "But that's not the only way I can help."

"You know the heroes," she said. "That's what you told me."

"And it's still true. So tell me what you think happens when we open the third gate. We rise, and then?"

"It isn't all life again for everyone. We can inhabit bodies of the recently dead in certain places."

He waved a hand, dismissive. "So there are conditions. There are always conditions, in stories like this."

"Stories like this?" she couldn't help but ask.

"All the great stories," he clarified. "Where the heroes fight for what's right. There are always conditions, qualifications, limitations. Those don't matter. We just need to stay within the lines."

"We will," she promised, not even being sure what the lines might be.

"But if it works?" he said, hope now shining in his eyes. "We can return to our loved ones Aboveground?"

She was tempted to just say yes, but was Eresh testing her? Watching her? The god might react badly if She found Sessadon had lied to shades to get their help. Certainly the god Herself would not stop short of trickery, but Sessadon knew enough about gods to know they set their own standards.

So she answered Paulus's question with a fair amount of honesty, without paying out enough rope to hang herself if caught out later. "Yes, we can return to them. Though I have to say, we will not do so in our own bodies, but the bodies of those who have died close to each queendom's most sacred place. Perhaps you've read a story like that, perhaps you haven't. But this is a story we are writing as we go along. I invite you to be this story's hero."

"You don't want it to be you?"

For once, she gave no thought to measuring out the exact right quantity of truth. She gave him the truth entire. "I'm not the hero," she told him.

He nodded, accepting.

She went on. "But I think you could be. I think you are. I believe that your help is what will make all the difference. If you're willing to try."

He beamed at that. Then he looked at her with such sincerity that if she'd had a heart, it might have broken a little. "So what happens? We just open the gate and go?"

"As far as I know," she said, again doing her best to tell the truth without sounding discouraging. The truth was that she knew nothing at all, but saying so wouldn't get him on her side, not in the least. She added another dash of truth for seasoning. "Once we pass the Voa, of course."

"I don't think you can just be a hero and the Voa will let you pass," he said, considering it. His thumb began stroking the sheath of the dagger he wore, seemingly absently. "I can't imagine it works that way."

"You can't?"

"I can imagine it," he said, a bit wryly, and she saw a glimpse of what he must have been like in life. Magnetic, appealing. "But I mean that I believe it will be harder. Because nothing worth having comes that easy."

"Who would know exactly how hard it might be? Do you have an idea?"

"Come," he said, and gestured for her to follow.

Sessadon trailed the shade of Paulus through amorphous territory, beyond the borders of what she'd visited into a new area, somewhere more shadowed, devoid of light or action. Not all areas of the Underlands were equally dead, she thought. This, wherever he was taking her, was one of the truly dead places.

At length the Underlands opened up in front of them, the dark easing into a slightly lighter horizon, though still shrouded, almost incomplete. As they moved forward she saw a quiet, shaded area underneath an enormous black-and-white tree. She'd never seen a tree like it: unsettling, with white bark on the trunk and branches, its vaguely triangular black leaves fluttering constantly in a nonexistent wind.

"The Tree of Unknowing," Paulus said. "And the pool underneath. I know someone who likes to come here."

When she concentrated, she could see a faint wisp, something white and a little bit gray, almost like a plume of smoke rising up near the water.

What are shades? she remembered asking someone, long ago.

And she remembered the long-ago answer. *A shade is a scrap of shadow wrapped around a soul.* This one seemed mostly shadow.

Then there was a woman between her and the shape. "What are you doing here?" said the shade of the woman.

"What are *you* doing here?" echoed Sessadon, because if someone took a combative tone with her, it was hard for her not to match it.

"I am Semma, first queen of the Scorpicae," said the woman. She had a generous mouth that made her face look sensual, but the rest of her was hard as a brick, and the weapon she wore on her hip was not for show. "I guard the Pool of Forgetting."

"Guard it from what?" asked Sessadon, genuinely unsure.

Then the warrior's face softened in confusion. "It's been so long. . . . I don't think I remember."

That made sense, thought Sessadon. Even if the woman had never taken a drink from the Pool of Forgetting, she'd been inhaling its vapor as long as she'd been here. If she truly was the first queen of Scorpica, that had been a very long time.

So Sessadon took a chance, and ventured, "Are you a hero?"

"Of course!" protested Semma. "Did I not say I was the first queen of Scorpica? Do you have any idea how hard it was to be the first one in charge of any queendom after the Great Peace? Do you know how exceptional a woman had to be in order to be chosen as one of the first queens?"

The words made Sessadon want to shove the queen directly into the Pool of Forgetting and drown her there, hold her under until she couldn't breathe . . . but of course the long-dead Semma was a shade, and what difference did breathing make anymore? Sessadon could not kill Semma. Her conscious mind knew it to a certainty. That did not stop her in any way, she thought ruefully, from wanting to.

"Semma, it's me," Paulus interrupted, his voice soothing, like a rider addressing an excitable horse.

The shade of the Scorpican queen turned toward him, her face still blank, but her brows lowering as if she was working hard, trying her very best to remember.

"Paulus," he supplied smoothly, with no judgment, friend to

friend. "I visit here sometimes, you probably recall. I come to see Oscuro. We are on a mission to fight the Voa and open the Gate of Heroes. Would you like to come with us? Since you are a hero yourself?"

Sessadon was astounded by how smoothly Paulus not only neutralized the potential opposition but invited cooperation, and she could do nothing but watch gratefully. This, she thought, was the benefit of bringing people closer. She couldn't have gotten this far alone. With the right people by her side, how much further could she go?

Semma nodded and said, her voice grave, "I could use a battle. It's been . . . a long time."

"Yes, you're right!" agreed Paulus, as if they were talking of days or weeks, not centuries, since the Scorpican queen had wielded her sword Above. "You must come with us. Please?"

And the queen was nodding again, even as Paulus was already steering their group back toward the wisp they'd originally spotted, the three of them moving in concert.

Then they were standing before the wisp, all steady and silent, waiting. The wisp flickered, its deep grays and blacks shading into whites and paler grays. The movement was too gentle to be called a roil, but the colors were in constant motion, slow as it might be. Sessadon had never seen another shade like this one, so evanescent, so detached from the form they'd had in life. Was it the Pool of Forgetting that had made it this way, or time alone, or something else entirely?

"This is one of the long-ago heroes of Paxim," Paulus said, a hint of his air of sadness returning. "His name was Oscuro. He was a king, the husband of Queen Theodora. He cultivated a palace garden, and when his wife sickened with a mysterious disease he saved her life with a precious plant. The stories never recorded his name, but when I began coming here, I found him."

"Why does he look like that?" asked Sessadon.

"Shades who've been here for centuries begin to fade. His memories and his connection to the earth are getting harder to maintain. And he . . . he's letting go. The form of a shade depends so much on their will to stay in that form, and if they don't have the will, the form dissolves. Oscuro has been considering drinking from the Pool of Forgetting, freeing himself from the memory of who he was on earth."

Sessadon felt she understood more, but not quite enough to make sense of this. "Why would he want to do that?"

"I don't want to talk about it here," said Paulus, his manner shifting, obviously uncomfortable.

"It's all right," said a low voice, a gravelly whisper, from the twist of smoke. "You have my permission, Kingling."

Paulus nodded his understanding. But he still winced as he said, "When shades come to the Underlands, they each make their choices about where in the vast Underlands they will linger . . . and, well, with whom. Theodora chose to spend eternity with her lover, not her husband."

"They left my name out of the books, but they left him out of the books entirely," the shade whispered.

"I need heroes," said Sessadon, putting it as plainly as she could. There might have been something more than self-interest in her plea, though she chose not to think about it too deeply. "Don't drink from the Pool of Forgetting just yet. Oscuro? Please?"

"Please?" echoed Paulus.

Semma said nothing, but she stood by without disagreeing, watching the twist of smoke with as much patience and interest as the rest of them.

Sessadon added, "You've got nothing to lose."

"You're an idiot," said Oscuro to Paulus, but with a note of fondness in his voice, becoming slightly more solid as he spoke.

Sessadon could make out the man's shade now, darkening around the edges, and his form moved toward the rest of them with a slow, steady gait.

Oscuro said to Paulus, wryly but not flippantly, "There's always more to lose."

◆

Oscuro, having endured in the Underlands for hundreds of years now, knew where the third gate to the world Above was located. He knew little of the third Voa, only that he had heard it might take different forms depending on who was perceiving it, but on the geography of the Gate of Heroes he was very clear.

"I even thought about giving it a go myself, some time ago," he said, his musical voice quiet and lovely. "I thought if I showed her I could be a hero . . . if she saw, she might . . . but anyway, I chose not to. Not then. But now? Let us see."

Sessadon found herself balking at following him in a way she had not with Paulus. Perhaps it was just the repetition, that she had never been a woman to trail after a man and now she found herself doing it twice in a short span of time. But privately she could see why Oscuro had not inspired his queen to fervent dedication—he moved like some kind of ground creature, low-bellied. She was in the middle of trying to decide whether he bore a closer resemblance to a lizard or a ferret, neither a particularly flattering image, when his footsteps slowed and then stopped.

They had arrived at the gate.

If she'd had breath, thought Sessadon, the Gate of Heroes would have taken it away. The gate was a huge bower of roses, a glorious, overflowing arch, as beautiful as anything any of them had seen in life. Sessadon estimated it was three times her height, but as they got nearer, she revised her estimate upward to four or five. And it was not just enormous, but beautiful.

The immense archway, its core material completely obscured by the flowers that grew over it, was an absolute riot of color. Vivid reds, pinks, and purples were flanked by the bright green of leaves and the darker, deeper green of thorns. The roses were all perfectly in bloom, not a scrap or note of brown on the edge of any petal, with an intense color she was not sure she'd ever seen before in a real flower Aboveground. She saw laurel, the hero's leaf, woven in with and mostly obscured by the roses, but she caught a bit of its scent wafting toward them. The roses, too, had an unmistakable smell, not unpleasant but commanding. If she had not been led here, thought Sessadon, perhaps she could have found it herself, if she'd only known it was a bower of roses she searched for.

The flowered arch of the Gate of Heroes soared high, leaving plenty of room to pass beneath, but their eyes were drawn over and over again to the flowers themselves, almost too lush to be believed, certainly too entrancing to be ignored.

"It's lovely," whispered Paulus.

"It is," agreed Oscuro, his voice still smoky and vague, though his form had grown more solid. There was something else in his voice that Sessadon couldn't identify. It sounded, she thought, like longing.

"Do you see what I see?" Oscuro went on, looking more solid by the moment. "Minari roses, ranunculus, freesia? Bay laurel, rosemary? And perhaps *klilia* there, at the edges, that white one with the star-shaped center. Is that *klilia*?"

"I don't know, Oscuro," Paulus replied. His voice was kind, but a bit lost. Sessadon guessed that he wanted to anchor Oscuro but didn't know how.

"I see everything I grew in my garden," Oscuro said, the shape of his hand rising to press to the shape of his cheek, this time sounding as if the words pained him, as if each of the thorns on the vine might pierce his tender heart. "Everything I grew, everything I lost."

"I never knew much about flowers," Paulus said, again kindly, but again without any particular hint of hope.

Sessadon broke in, her voice harsh, "I doubt the flowers are important." She worried she might do harm to Oscuro by interrupting his reverie, but she was more afraid she would lose him to his own memories and he would slip back into the form of a wisp of smoke. If he could stay solid, he might be valuable in the battle to come. A sharp poke was required to bring him back to the present moment, and she didn't shrink from delivering it. "Remember, the Voa is what matters. Whatever form the gate takes does not concern us. We must defeat the Voa, emerge victorious over it, or we will not open the gate."

"Are we sure that's what's required? Defeating the Voa?" asked Oscuro, the shape that should be his face still upturned toward the blooms, seeming to search the petals, stems, leaves one by one. She didn't know what he was searching for, and it didn't matter.

"What else could it be?" asked Sessadon, and beckoned them forward.

✦

In contrast with the clarity of the blooming roses and attendant greenery, the Voa itself, Paulus realized, was impossible to see. There was a kind of shadow figure, hunched low between the blooms, which he believed had to be the Voa, since nothing else here could be. And as they watched, it shifted, sometimes into a large, threatening shape, then one that was small and delicate.

"We can't defeat it if it won't take form," said Semma, her voice sharp. She seemed to have dedicated herself completely to the idea of defeating the Voa, which Paulus felt was a positive development. The more hands to help, the better, since none of them knew quite what to expect.

"We will defeat it," Sessadon said firmly, though it seemed to Paulus she had nothing to back up her confidence. Perhaps she'd decided they would defeat the Voa because they had to. If they'd been alone, he would have reminded her that a wish was not a plan.

The Voa continued to shift, from the furry shape of a bearlike creature with bared fangs, then growing pale and smaller like a mouflon with the white fangs melting into a round black snout, then the whole of it re-forming into something more humanoid, with legs and face and sword. Then its humanity was left behind as its bulk thickened into a tall cylinder like a tree shorn of its roots and branches, a wide, sterile trunk, bark falling off in diseased-looking patches.

There was something about the dying tree—not a tree, he realized, but it looked so much like a tree he couldn't think of it as anything else—that turned his stomach. What he wouldn't give to walk Above again, even if he couldn't get his own body back. To have that freedom, to breathe real air without that stinking note of rot he could never escape in the Underlands. For that, what wouldn't he do? Anything that might get him back to Ama was worth it.

"*Mokh* this," muttered Semma, impatient, but Sessadon held her back.

"Wait," said Sessadon, her form rigid, eyes watchful. "We need to know what we're fighting before we can fight it."

"Says you," Semma replied, but she stayed in place, watching with the rest of them, as the Voa continued to flicker and shift.

The trunk-like presence shifted, shimmered, cycling through a myriad of colors before seeming to settle on something not too unlike human skin. Silently, it continued to make less dramatic, subtler changes, shrinking into a form smaller than any of the shades who stood regarding it, getting smaller still.

When the presence resolved, saw Paulus, it had settled into the shape of a child.

At first he thought it was the Child who welcomed shades across the bridge from Above, but then he saw it was a girl. A girl with flashing eyes and wild shoulder-length plaits from which her curls insisted on escaping. The hair over her forehead was shaped into an unfashionable fringe she had cut herself when her mother wasn't looking, dangling down almost into those flashing eyes. She was partially dressed in the elegant purple of Paximite royalty, a child's tunic with elbow-length sleeves over undyed leggings.

Then there was no question. On the day she died, she'd stolen those leggings from one of the servants' children so she could sneak away and ride a horse she wasn't supposed to be riding. It was exactly what she'd been wearing the last time he'd seen her alive.

"Zofi." The name escaped Paulus's lips, not with any engagement from his mind whatsoever, simply a recognition that wouldn't be denied.

He had thought that the Voa was some sort of monster. But now, in front of him, he saw only his sister, as sweet and spirited as the day she'd died. She'd been taken from him so suddenly, alive and then dead. Now here she was again. Zofi, his sister, the only one he had ever known. Unmistakable.

"All-Mother's *muoni*," murmured the sorcerer, and if any of the shades facing the gate thought it unseemly to take the name of Eresh's mother in vain here in the Underlands, none of them spoke up to say so.

And if he thought he couldn't breathe upon the sight of his dead sister in her shade form under that remarkable bower of roses, Paulus wasn't at all prepared for how he would feel when her small, open face looked up at him and asked, in a tremulous voice, "Is that you, Paulus?"

He couldn't move. There was no way. He couldn't process what was happening, this gate, this Voa, the shape of his sister, who he had never encountered in all his wanderings through the world of the dead. Was it her? Was it not her? His feet had grown roots, locking him into the ground, no more able to move than a tree or the Bastion itself would have been.

Paulus mumbled, half to himself, "I don't know what to do."

Semma drew her sword grimly, the kiss of the blade against the sheath audible, a long, slow hiss they all heard as clear as day. "I do."

The Scorpican queen surged forward so quickly, her reflexes clearly as fast as in life, and what felt like Paulus's heart lurched in his chest. Despair rocked him—there was no way he could get there before her, no way—and then, somehow, he flew.

Before Paulus knew it, his arms were wrapped around the small form of his sister. His knees were on the ground, her little face pressed into his shoulder, the shelter of his arms encircling her small shoulders and head and back. He bent over her, his body a shield.

And even as he braced for the blow he was certain was coming, a part of him still savored the feel of her. Unbelievably, he could *feel* Zofi in his arms. When they'd been alive she had been the larger one, his body only the toddling, endlessly awkward frame of a three-year-old child still laden with baby fat. Hers had also been a child's body, but larger, with length in the limbs, a promise of a future that would one day leave childhood behind. Of course she had never grown to fulfill that promise. And here she was, still in the form of the sturdy six-year-old she'd been the day Philomel had thrown her, but without the broken neck, and here he was, a grown man, who but for the sleek sword of a Scorpican would have one day been king.

He was aware of time passing then. Next came awareness that though he had expected the sword to strike him, perhaps run him through, that had not yet come to pass. Not yet.

Instead he heard the fierce voice of the Scorpican—not the Scorpican who had killed him, but a far distant ancestor, centuries old if she was a day—telling him to stand aside.

"I don't want to hurt you," Semma said, her voice urgent and sincere enough that he believed her. "You can't save her. So all you can do is stand aside."

"No," Paulus said. He didn't know what would happen if Semma's sword sliced through him. Would he just melt away and take form elsewhere? Was there something deader than dead that, his shade pierced in the Underlands, he might become? His eyes were shut tight now, his head down as he hunched over his sister's much smaller form.

"Kingling!" Semma said, her voice half-strangled. "Let her go!"

"No," he said again, whispering the word down into his sister's hair. He expected the child in his arms to sob or cry, or to say anything at all, but she didn't. He could feel—again, it was impossible, what he felt—her intake of breath against his own chest, their hearts rapidly beating in a mismatched pattern, hers even faster than his, like a nervous bird's, like a patter of fast-falling rain.

Faintly he thought of the other two, of Sessadon the magician and Oscuro the man of the old tales, and worried that they might be preparing to take Semma's side. If all three of them descended on him, even if the other two weren't warriors, they would be able to overcome him. If the others each peeled an arm away from Zo's vulnerable form and Semma swung her mighty sword, the whole thing would be over. And then perhaps they would have defeated the Voa and opened the Gate of Heroes, but at what cost? He'd thought there was nothing in the world or beyond it that he wanted more than he wanted to see Ama again, but now, he wasn't so sure.

Paralyzed with indecision, all he could do was stay. He could hold Zofi, protect her. That was what he would do until one or both of them were run through.

But miraculously, that didn't happen. And instead of feeling the slice or swipe of the edge of a sharp blade, the next thing Paulus became aware of was an intensification of the scent of roses, which had already hung heavy in the air.

The bower of roses above his head seemed somehow to explode. Not with violence or force, but an impossible blooming in all directions, until his consciousness was somehow blanked out by the cascade of petals and stems and leaves and scent that swelled all around.

Then there was quiet. He no longer felt his sister's small, solid body in his arms. The scent of roses was gone, replaced by the smell of what? Cold stone?

And Paulus knew at once, but was not sure how he knew, that he had passed through the third gate between the Underlands and the world Above.

✦

Semma's sword was in her hand and she was ready to do what needed to be done, but in the moment when she blinked, everything changed.

There was no one to drive her sword through. No queenling, no kingling, not even a shadow under the arch of flowers. In that blink they were all gone.

Wait—was that movement? Yes. Legs, arms, a bent head trailing shoulder-length curls.

It was the kingling. His form passed under the bower, a blast of the rose scent ushering him along, and winked out as if it had never been.

Semma watched, stunned, as he vanished. She had misunderstood the gate. They all had, even Paulus, who she was sure had not protected the form of his sister out of understanding that protection, not destruction, would prove his mettle. Unwittingly, he had shown himself, and when he did, he'd shown himself to be a hero.

She opened her mouth to call after him, but—what would she say? And besides, he was gone.

Paulus had put someone else before himself, and now that Semma thought about it, everything snapped into place. Self-sacrifice was heroic. Slaying an enemy could be hero's work if it was the right enemy—the battlefield beyond would not otherwise have flowed with Scorpicae as far as the eye could see—but it was not always the goal. There were other courses of action, less clear. This enemy, or the being Semma had perceived as an enemy, had been only a little girl, without power or threat of her own. Someone to be protected, not vanquished. She could see it now.

Now that the test was over, and it seemed so clear what the test had been, Semma was almost ashamed of herself for having been so willing to slay a defenseless child. The only reason she didn't give in to complete despair was that she'd known cases when slaying the child would have been the right course of action. That she failed to see it in this case was a failure of judgment, not character.

And there was more uncertainty, because now that a hero had opened the gate, was he the only one who could pass through, or could other shades follow where he'd gone?

Semma had failed the test, clearly, and that concerned her. Perhaps if she tried to rush through she would be destroyed. She hung back, watching, telling herself it was not cowardice, but wisdom, to wait and watch when such an opportunity presented itself.

The other man, Oscuro, was nowhere to be seen. Had he followed Paulus's shade to the world Aboveground? He hadn't failed the test as clearly as Semma, but neither had he clearly passed it. He had also been a wisp of smoke not long ago, so in pushing toward the gate he might very well have torn himself into nothingness, not meaning to. She couldn't tell where he'd gone, only that he'd gone, which told her next to nothing.

Semma looked around for Sessadon, but then she heard a sound she couldn't quite place, and turned.

The flood of shades that surged toward her took her by surprise. She was surrounded, knocked aside, as they rushed not just past her, but through her, on their way to the newly opened gate.

The first dozen or so shades disappeared, their forms—she couldn't tell whether they were men or women, young or old, Scorpicae or Bastionites or figures from the time before the queendoms—moving from solidity to nothingness in an instant. They were there, surging, and then they were gone.

The second wave of shades, immediately behind them, slammed against an invisible barrier inside the flowery bower and fell, the next wave behind them piling up, form on form, shade on shade, until the gate itself was shrouded behind a mix of solid-looking bodies and hazy smoke.

Had a crush of humanity done this, the noise would have been horrific: screaming and crying, the sound of anguish rampant, the living bodies Below howling to be freed before they ceased living. But the sound here was more chaotic, everywhere and nowhere at once, impossible to contain or define. Semma rarely compared Above to Below—she'd been here long enough to forget—but the memory came rushing back now, clear and painful. Here, bodies were not such solid and fragile things. Here, there was no stink of blood and waste. There might be a feeling of life, but not life itself, not as they'd known it Above.

Semma turned in wonder and looked for the sorcerer, unsure if she'd gotten through in the first wave or lay smothered under the pile. It turned out that neither was true. Instead Semma saw the sorcerer not far away, standing and looking as Semma herself was doing, the face of her shade creased in a frown.

Before too long the shades had disentangled themselves, upper forms sliding away to make room for the lower forms to rise, until at last the flowery gate was seen again, no Voa to shroud it. The form of Zofi was no longer there—had she fled? Been freed? Taken a different shape? Semma didn't know. The guardian had vanished. What remained was the gate, which had been open but now, it seemed, was closed again.

Semma approached the sorcerer, who didn't turn toward her as she came nearer, all the sorcerer's attention focused on the arch of the gate. Its flowers looked perfect, undisturbed.

"It's not open," Semma said to the sorcerer, not knowing if what she said was true, testing for a response. She couldn't trust herself to guess what might happen next. She wasn't even quite sure what had already happened.

The sorcerer looked at her and shook her head, the corner of her mouth crooking into something not unlike a smile. "It's open," said Sessadon.

"Then why can't they get through?"

"No one else is dead," Sessadon said.

This made no sense to Semma. "Humans die all the time."

Sessadon said, "Not near the sacred places. It has to be near the sacred places."

"Why?"

"Because that was how things were built. You have to understand, the gates aren't supposed to work like this. They were designed to let only the worthy return. Instead of picking a lock, we're smashing locks. So not only the worthy are getting through. Once the gate's open, any shade can go."

"Except they're not going." Semma gestured.

"They will. Slowly. For each death in a sacred place Above, one shade rises from Below."

Semma asked the obvious question. "So what happens next?"

"Either we have to be patient, or we have to remove the next restriction. Allow shades to rise up, a life for a life, everywhere."

"Patience," sniffed Semma derisively. "Not generally the best option."

"Agreed."

"So what do we have to do to rise up all over the queendoms?" asked Semma.

Sessadon replied, the bit of smile disappearing as her mouth set in a grim line, "Open the next gate."

✦ CHAPTER 26 ✦

RISING

Across the Five Queendoms

Unlike the Drought of Girls, the rising of the shades through the third gate between worlds was not an egalitarian plague. It did not descend like a curtain and then lift like one, thoroughly applied and then completely removed. It wrought its devastation in pockets, bringing death and panic, joy and thrill and pain, unevenly distributed throughout the queendoms.

Nor was the rising of the shades an acknowledged plague with a name and a duration. For months afterward, most people didn't even believe it had ever happened. There were rumors, spreading like wildfire, of the dead returned; but for those not personally affected, the rumors were easy to ignore. One could walk right past a risen shade in the market and not recognize them for what they were. Most of the living were oblivious, and most of the dead stayed dead.

But there were exceptions, both among the dead and the living. Shades that managed, against all odds, to rise. Other shades whose destinies became clear when rising was denied them. Wrongdoers living Above whose misdeeds came back to haunt them—or more.

For some, the opening of the third gate was a greater disaster than the Drought of Girls had ever been.

✦ CHAPTER 27 ✦

THE TASTE OF WINE

Ursu, Paxim
Stellari

It was best to stay in the palace as much as possible, to make the point that she belonged there, but Stellari was careful to sleep in her own home at least once a week. Often she did so on the night before a Senate vote, since her home was closer than the palace to the Senate. The air turned a bit stale betweentimes, she found. She'd have to investigate whether the day servant who was supposed to be airing out the town house was actually doing so.

And as luxurious as the palace was, as much as she loved spending time there, being all alone felt like its own kind of luxury. Evander's mother had not in fact protested Stellari's rejection of him, perhaps understanding the futility of forcing together two wildcats. All that could go hang. There was nothing wrong with being alone, if one enjoyed one's own company.

Alone in her house, Stellari drank her wine. More than she should have, she knew, but there was no one there to tell her to stop. That was the other wonderful thing about being alone. No one to badger her with these silly rumors about shades rising from the dead, or talking about whether the position of regent should be put up for a vote, or staring at her out of narrowed eyes and asking what her plans were for the child-queen's education or her wardrobe or her name-day celebration.

Details and difficulties. Here, all of it melted away.

The deep red wine spread warmth within Stellari, and she savored its bitter edge. She remembered, what seemed like a lifetime ago, drinking the overly sweet gold wine Heliane favored. Heliane was gone now. No one could ever make Stellari drink that wine again. She would, now and forever, do as she liked.

Unobserved, the regent drank down the rest of the goblet in one long gulp. She filled it back up to the top, then set the bottle back in the cabinet. She loved how the wine left a thin film on the inside of the bluish glass. Even when the wine was gone, the glass was changed.

Hmm. She liked that line. Maybe she could use it in a speech.

"Senators!" she shouted into the empty air around her. "We are still changed by the Drought of Girls, changed forever! Like the goblet from which we drink wine . . ."

Not quite right. Too complex.

"We are like glass," she said. "We are strong, we resist, but we can still be stained by what we carry."

No, that wasn't right either. She should probably stop drinking soon, if she wanted to show up at the Senate tomorrow without a headache. Even the best wine could leave a mark, if one drank too much.

This time she merely sipped, and touched her tongue to her lips to moisten them with the wine's flavor. She remembered the taste of this same wine on other lips, when Rahul had been here. She knew he wasn't coming back. She didn't want him back, she told herself. The Rahul she missed had been gone long before he left.

Another sip of wine, and another.

"We are like goblets, not glass, but stone," she said. "Or silver. Silver? Opaque. No one knows what we carry inside."

A voice from the darkness said, "Your analogies are getting worse, not better."

She blinked slowly, wondering whose voice she'd conjured up. There was something familiar about the cadence, but not the tone. Alone in the dark, imagining things. What would others think of the mighty regent, if they saw her now?

"Interesting. I thought you'd run," said the voice, and that was when Stellari realized she hadn't conjured it. This voice wasn't in her imagination.

She wasn't alone after all.

Still careful, still controlled, Stellari kept her grip on the goblet, and slowly turned her neck to scan the room. There, in the doorway, a shadow.

"I don't run," she said. It seemed the only thing to say.

"At a distance," the voice said, "it's hard to tell a brave woman from a fool."

"Show yourself," Stellari said, more sternly.

The stranger stepped forward. A woman in a dark cloak, hood thrown back and pooled loosely on her shoulders. She was too clean to be a beggar. Her hair was stark white, her hands empty. Stellari was fairly certain she'd never seen the woman before in her life.

"Ah, Stellari," the voice said chidingly, lingering on each syllable of her name. "You always did like your wine."

"You address me like a familiar." Stellari kept her voice cool. The hand holding the goblet of wine didn't tremble. "Yet you are a stranger, an invader in my house. I will ask you once, politely, to leave."

The woman seemed unbothered. It was her utter calm, more than anything else, that disturbed Stellari. There was no desperation or furtiveness to her. She stood as if she, not Stellari, belonged in this room.

Stellari sat down on her most comfortable chaise, extending the hand with the goblet to dangle free, pretending nonchalance. If this stranger—this invader of the regent's peace—could show no emotion, Stellari could match her note for note.

"You can't guess who I am, then?" The voice had a mocking edge now.

Stellari felt disoriented. She should know, she told herself. She felt off-balance. Sitting hadn't helped steady her. A stranger was in her home and she was the one who felt wrong? She struggled to catch up. Too much wine, for certain.

Closer to the lamp now, the woman emerged from the shadows. Stellari looked hard at her face even while she tried to look like she didn't care. Nothing familiar about the curve of the cheek, the shape of the hairline, the set of her shoulders. This was a face Stellari didn't know.

But then, when she looked closely, she thought she could see the expression of another face somehow overlaid on these features. Someone who had always watched, listened, attuned herself to others around her. Someone who had been a diplomat first and foremost because she was born for it.

As she watched, the woman laughed bitterly and ran her hands through her white, white hair. It was the hair that pushed Stellari's understanding into realization.

Hair white as snow, crowned to show her power.

"You killed me," said Heliane, her voice steady, dry. "I'm here to return the favor."

A chill ran through her, but Stellari had not risen this high by giving in to weakness. She thought about taking another sip of the wine, but instead continued to let the goblet dangle.

Stellari said matter-of-factly, "You can't be here. You're dead."

"The gate opened," said Heliane, "and I made sure to be ready to come through when it did. I had a very good reason to come back, you know. Someone I wanted to see."

"But you're—not you."

Heliane looked down at her body as if it were an unfamiliar suit of clothing. "The body is someone else's, true. But you know who I am, don't you? I'd be insulted if you didn't. I'd like to think killing me mattered enough for you to remember."

Stellari said, "I didn't kill you, Heliane. What would make you think so?"

"Oh, you're disappointing me," said the body Heliane was inhabiting. "After all we've been through. To lie so boldly. But I suppose that's how you got where you are."

"I never laid a hand on you."

"You got away with it because no one but Inbar knew. But did you know poor Inbar is in the Underlands now? Our shades found each other. She was still distraught, told me she couldn't believe the charms you'd given her hadn't kept me safe. I understood right away what you'd done. And I knew you had to pay." Her tone was cool and even, unemotional, as if she were simply reciting a list. Stellari didn't like it one bit.

Very well, then. Stellari could be calm too. Matching her tone to Heliane's, Stellari said, "You won't kill me."

With a meaningful look at the wine, Heliane replied, "I already did."

Stellari's eyelids were getting heavy. Or were they? Was she imagining it, based on what the intruder had said?

Yes, there had been a bitterness to the wine, but she liked her wine bitter. She hadn't noticed it tasting any different than usual. Maybe this version of Heliane was bluffing. Or maybe it wasn't Heliane at all, just someone who wanted Stellari to think she was Heliane, another enemy with plans of her own. This was the downside to thinking about every dimension of every possible plan, thought Stellari. It made you see that in every situation there were nearly infinite possibilities. The trick was in choosing the right one.

"You can't be here," Stellari said. The dead stayed dead. If there was anything she could be certain of, it was that.

"You heard the rumors," Heliane said, taking another step toward Stellari, setting her feet on the edge of the white rug. "There was never a rumor in all of Paxim you didn't think was worth hearing. Dead bodies coming back to life. Near the sacred places."

"Just rumors," scoffed Stellari, but an odd warmth was spreading outward from her throat, making her light-headed. She fell back on the chaise.

The woman who claimed to be Heliane said, "No, not this time."

If the wine was indeed poisoned, Stellari wondered if it would hurt. Some poisons did. Some poisons killed by suffocation, others with seizures, others with great racking pain. But some were just like going to sleep. If she'd been poisoned, thought Stellari, she hoped it was one of the sleep-like ones.

She hadn't done so many bad things, really. She was a good person. She just knew what she wanted and would do anything to get it. She had risen from nothing and earned her power. Heliane was the only person she'd actually killed, wasn't she? And not even with her own hands. Stellari should have killed more, maybe. If she were going to die for her wrongs anyway, she should have committed more wrongs.

Stellari's lips were numbing now, her words coming more slowly. "This isn't you."

"Not my body," agreed Heliane, running a hand through her white hair. "But my shade. So now, my hands. My will. My choice."

She could get up and check the bottle, thought Stellari. She'd poured from it, how many times tonight? It was over there in the cabinet. If she looked, she would see. Perhaps the bottle would smell of bitter almonds, or show signs of tampering. That way she might know whether this person—this shade in another person's body, how was that even possible?—was telling the truth.

Only standing up felt like too much work, just now. Everything felt heavy. The goblet, in particular. Stellari had been pretending to dangle it, but now it was all she could do to clutch it and keep it from falling. As she breathed shallowly, closing her eyes, she focused on her fingers. But their strength was ebbing. Before long, she couldn't hold on to the goblet anymore. It fell.

Red wine spilled like blood. But unlike blood, as it dried, it remained red.

Stellari would have been furious to see the ruined rug, an indelible red stain against pristine white, had her eyes ever opened again.

✦ CHAPTER 28 ✦

GONE

The Holy City, Sestia
Olivi

In the morning, it was Yegen who brought Olivi the news. It was highly unusual for a servant to wake her; she generally rose early, and this time when the knock on her door came, the sun had not yet risen.

Yegen was one of the youngest servants in the Edifice, probably two or three years younger than Olivi, and slight as a reed. She always enjoyed his company. Not because he was one of the most beautiful, which he was, but because he was quick to smile.

Yegen wasn't smiling when he woke Olivi. There was a look in his eyes she'd never seen there. All at once she realized why she liked him; he reminded her a little of Timion. She rarely thought of Timion anymore, she realized, swimming up from sleep. It was as if that whole nightmare had happened to someone else.

The flickering torch was the first thing she saw. Her eyes adjusted just enough to see the slight figure who held it, and as he notched it into the holder just inside the door, that was when she saw the resemblance.

She didn't have the chance to speak before Yegen let out a long, fraught sigh.

"I'm so sorry, I'm so sorry," he said, bowing toward the ground, and at first Olivi thought he was apologizing for waking her unexpectedly.

"It's all right," she said.

He blurted, "No, it isn't."

She held her tongue for a moment, waiting to see what he would say. Perhaps she was misreading the situation. If he was apologizing for something else, she didn't know what it could be.

"Her door was open," he said. "We went in."

"What?"

"She wasn't there."

He had to be talking about Concordia. "Surely she's been gone from her room without explanation before?"

"No, never."

She was completely awake now. "Gone out for a walk? Risen in the dark to seek comfort in the *lacrum*?"

"We've looked everywhere."

"Surely not the entire city," she said gently.

"Everywhere in the Edifice. Someone thought they saw her heading toward the tomb, but no one here has the secret of entering it; that's knowledge only entrusted to the High Xara."

"So if the High Xara is missing, the only one who could find her is the High Xara?"

Yegen looked down at his sandals. Olivi realized her tone had been too curt, too sarcastic. She hadn't meant it that way. She was terrified.

More gently, she asked Yegen, "Why did you wake me? Why not one of the Daras?"

He said, "I hoped you would know what to do."

"I know the first thing to do," she said with a confidence she didn't feel. "The first thing to do is pray."

So, for the first time, Olivi was bold enough to go, without Concordia's permission, to the *lacrum*. Yegen trailed her all the way there. The door stood closed, unguarded.

"Stand guard by the door," she told him.

"If someone asks who's inside, should I lie?"

She thought about this, then said, "Do what the Holy One moves you to do."

The young servant's brow creased in concern. "The Holy One doesn't know who I am. It isn't Her will that moves me. I only ever do what Xaras and Daras tell me."

And she, realized Olivi, was neither a Xara nor a Dara. There had never been any definition of what she was to Concordia, and it seemed that now she was entirely on her own.

Olivi tried to think of what a Xara would do. Not necessarily Concordia, but a Xara who held to their ideals. She looked Yegen up and down, reflecting, and said, "Don't lie. It's better not to."

"Thank you." He didn't point out that he didn't need to obey her. He took up his position next to the door and stared off into the distance while she slipped through the doorway and felt the shock of the cold marble under her feet. The door snicked shut behind her.

And then Olivi, a young woman with no particular place, whose only ally had mysteriously vanished, took a look around the holiest place in her nation. She didn't feel like crying. She didn't feel particularly like anything, she realized. She didn't want to ride a wave of emotion. She just wanted answers.

When Olivi had prayed to the Holy One before, Concordia had so often been beside her, she'd generally done so only in her head. With Concordia gone—for now, or forever?—she spoke aloud.

"Blessed Sestia," she said. "Give me guidance. Your priest is missing. I remain. And I don't know what to do."

Not missing, she heard the god's voice say. Whatever else was going on, She had not deserted Olivi. Now, as much as she had thought herself beyond emotion in the moment, she felt a wave of relief.

"Not missing?" she asked the god.

I know where she is.

Olivi felt an almost irresistible urge to giggle. Of course the god knew.

"And will she return? Should I wait for her?"

No.

"What should I do?" she asked the god. She hated the note of desperation in her voice, but there was no use in trying to hide it from the god anyway, she supposed. The Holy One knew and saw all. Only She knew what had happened to the High Xara, and She knew what Olivi needed to do next. Olivi would do whatever it was, without question. She only needed to know.

But the god's response was not a command. *What do you want to do?* asked the voice of the Holy One.

"Want? Me?"

Yes.

What an odd question. Especially for a god to ask. Olivi had not thought much about what she actually wanted, at least not since she'd been packed into a wagon with Timion and brought here to the Edifice to be sacrificed. She had spent plenty of time thinking and wondering about the god's plans, and Concordia's plans, but not her own plans. She closed her eyes and felt the cool marble underneath her bare feet. She thought of how she had been living. She thought of what she wanted.

"Holy One," said Olivi, "I want my mother."

So do I. There was a note in the god's voice that Olivi had never heard before, a note like fond reminiscence. A tenderness. *Her name was Veritas, when she was a Xara.*

Olivi knew Norah had come to the Edifice, but after the one time they'd caught a glimpse of each other, Concordia had forbidden the two to visit. Olivi had obeyed without question. She hadn't known why her mother had come. But hopefully she was still in the Edifice.

And now it made so much sense. Why the god had brought Olivi here, and now, her mother as well. Olivi didn't know why the High Xara Concordia had disappeared, and perhaps it didn't matter. She would have her mother back. The Holy One wanted it so.

Tears already pricking at the corners of her eyes, chest feeling both hollow and full with the surprise of it, Olivi said on a breath, "Your will be done."

◆

When the young servant Yegen came to tell Norah she was needed in the *lacrum*, Norah thought there must be some mistake. If Concordia had need of her, she might have her old friend fetched, but the *lacrum*? The holiest of places? That struck her as odd. Still, she went without complaint.

But nothing could have prepared her for the sight that greeted her in the *lacrum*, once Yegen had closed the door behind her: not Concordia at all, but her daughter, Olivi, with arms wide open.

Norah rushed forward into her daughter's embrace.

Once they had laughed and cried themselves into a state of acceptance, Olivi cupped her mother's cheek. "The god has told me a great deal. We have work to do."

Norah said, "But where is the High Xara?"

"Gone. And not coming back, according to the Holy One. So we must find a path forward in her absence."

"We?"

"Primarily, you. You will be the High Xara. As you always should have been."

And Olivi told her mother everything she'd learned from the

voice of the Holy One: that Concordia had, perhaps not with evil intent but certainly knowing she was doing wrong, deprived Norah of the life she should have had.

"Holy One," Norah asked aloud, "are you certain? That I am worthy?"

The god's voice came to both of them. *Yes.*

Norah wasn't sure what she should feel. Anger, perhaps, at having been denied the place she should have had all these years. Wonder, at entering the holiest space in all the queendom. Grief, knowing that the woman who had once been her closest friend had not been who she thought she was. Joy, at the god's desire to restore everything Norah had once lost.

She confessed to her daughter, "I don't know how I feel about this news."

Olivi pressed her hands to her mother's and said, "This is a moment. You will have power for so much longer than right now. Take your time."

And the wisdom, the patience, in her daughter's voice made Norah want to cry all over again.

She told Olivi, "You sounded like a Xara just then."

Olivi shook her head. "Xaras are just people. I don't think the last High Xara was good at remembering that."

"Did you know I named you for her? As a child, her given name was Olivi."

"I never knew. She never said."

Norah—or was she Veritas once more?—subsided again into silence. She knew she could let herself be consumed with anger at her old friend for depriving her of those years of rule. In just the same way she could have been angry with Xelander for leading her astray, tempting her to abandon her Xara principles. But she had made that choice with a clear head, and she would not regret the daughter who had grown from the indulgence, no matter what else she had or had not done. The only thing she had cause to regret was doubting the Holy One in the time after Olivi was taken. Those years when she had turned her back on her god and deprived herself of the Holy One's reassuring voice. Now she knew her daughter heard that voice, too.

And now, here they both were. This was right. This was happening. And as Norah thought about it, she realized that all those other years—the years she had worked and made friends and raised her daughter and stared up at the blue sky over green hills—those years had worth too. The person she would be as High Xara, queen of the nation, was who she had always been. Wiser and stronger for every year she'd spent on the earth, no matter where she'd spent it.

Olivi squeezed her hand again. "It will take some time to understand all this. But now, we need to prepare."

"Prepare?"

The girl's voice was firm and calm as she said, "The robes first. And I'll need to prepare the ash and the saffron; I refreshed Concordia's streak once a season when the color began to fade, so I think I have everything I need to do yours. Before you appear to the Daras, we'll make sure you're the High Xara already."

Norah was hit with a sharp memory. Herself, on her knees, as Concordia cut the saffron streak from her hair before forcing her into exile. Then, another memory: Xelander watching, covering his own guilt with imperiousness, the worst hypocrite of them all.

Hush, came the Holy One's voice in her head. *He is gone. She made sure of it before she went.*

Norah breathed out. There was truly nothing to keep her from taking her rightful place at the head of the nation.

"Yes," she said to Olivi. "Let's start now."

Once they had done what they needed to, once the Holy One had told them what came next, they walked hand in hand to meet the assembled Daras. Most of them were unfamiliar, but Norah spotted a few familiar faces in the crowd, Daras who had served here even before the Drought had begun. She picked one to begin with.

"Dara Justicia," she said, walking forward and extending a hand toward a broad-shouldered woman with an arrow-shaped birthmark beneath her right eye. "It's good to see you again."

The Dara paused, and Norah could practically see her mind working. Her thoughts and wishes, her fears, all of it counterbalanced by the wisdom of the moment: Speak, or keep her own counsel?

In the end, Dara Justicia said, "It's good to see you, too. What would you have us call you?"

At that, the new High Xara laughed. "Call me what I always should have been. The High Xara Veritas."

Then one of the younger Daras, one Veritas didn't know, spoke. "And the girl who accompanies you? Neither Xara nor Dara? What should we call her?"

Veritas raised her chin. She settled her arm around her daughter's shoulders. She remembered the way that Concordia had offered her only a sliver of what she was due, beribboned and bound with conditions on every side. It was no way to live.

The High Xara Veritas said to the Dara, "This is Olivi. She is my daughter. And the god loves her the same as She loves me. As She loves all of us. I will not turn away from earthly love in any of its forms."

"The god might have something to say about that," sniped the young Dara.

"And if She does," responded Veritas, practically glowing with righteous joy, "She can, and will, say it to me."

The Daras whispered among themselves, and Dara Justicia pulled at the sleeve of the younger Dara. Veritas couldn't hear what she said, but the tone was one of caution.

The younger Dara pulled her sleeve out of Justicia's grasp. "How do we know the god speaks to you? What proof is there?"

"Belief doesn't require proof," explained Veritas. "Belief is belief. If you don't have faith, you're free to leave. The god only wants those here who are loyal to Her."

"But how do we know you're loyal? We don't know you, we don't know what you've done."

Olivi was the one who broke in then, clearly nervous about speaking, but chin high and voice strong. "You never knew Concordia either, if you think you did."

That didn't seem to satisfy the Dara. So Veritas added, "Again, if you don't agree with me taking the position of High Xara, I invite you to go serve the god in some other way. But She wants me here, and I will accept nothing less than what She wants for me."

"You think She wants you to take over, not having served?"

"I served. Here and elsewhere."

The older Dara said to the younger, "You may not realize that the Xara Veritas served here in the Edifice, before the Drought."

"Why did you leave?"

The truth would serve. "Concordia sent me away."

The young Dara was starting to put two and two together. "Because of your daughter? Because you violated the holy precept of chastity?"

Veritas wanted to laugh, but didn't. "The god doesn't want our chastity. The god wants us to serve how we wish to serve. Pleasures are not something that Xaras and Daras need to deny themselves. In fact, if you knew the truth, many of the Xaras of the past who claimed chastity were practicing no such thing. The sin was never in the doing. The sin was in the discovery. And in my communion with the god, I will say, She doesn't judge us for any of it. She made pleasures for our enjoyment. What sin is there in enjoying Her gifts?"

The young Dara grumbled in outrage, looking to her right and left, hoping to enlist others to her cause. "Next thing, you'll be saying that the god doesn't want the Sun Rites either. Since you know so much about what She wants."

"She wants the Sun Rites," said Veritas, but didn't say out loud what she was thinking, *But maybe not the sacrifice.* There would be time for that. Best not to create more controversy than necessary on her very first day.

Olivi said, "Today has brought a great deal of change. Now that we have some certainty on how to go forward, perhaps it is time to rest and pray."

"I am still uncertain!" shouted the young Dara.

"Is she the only one?" asked Veritas. Looking from face to face, she did see some uncertainty, though most of the older Daras seemed disinclined to draw attention to themselves. They only wanted to go along, to get along. They were getting what they wanted out of being Daras. Fussing about queens seemed like too much trouble. All except for this young firebrand.

"And before you offer some kind of sign," scoffed the young Dara, "you couldn't give any sign that would convince me. Such things are easily faked. I want the god's honest truth."

Veritas and Olivi looked at each other. What could make this girl happy? Was there any point in trying?

The god's voice in Veritas's head said, *Take her hands. Tell her that I want her to stay for five days. If she wishes to go after that, I will bless her journey.*

Veritas did as the god said.

"Very well," said the young Dara. "Five days."

After five days of observing the High Xara Veritas, how she worshipped the god, how she tended carefully to the needs of everyone in the Edifice, how deeply she cared about the future of every last person in the queendom, the young Dara never mentioned leaving again.

✦ CHAPTER 29 ✦

IN THE NIGHT

The fourth month of the All-Mother's Year 520

Scorpica

Azur

Azur heard the ruckus from her bedroll, but she hesitated before rising. Madazur slept next to her. The girl roused so easily. Azur couldn't count the number of times since her return to Scorpica that she had opened her eyes before the sun and wanted to rise, but was too afraid to wake the girl. Instead she lay there waiting, watching the edges of the tent begin, slowly, to glow.

After a year in the Bastion, she savored both the visible sunrise and the warm little body against her. Those days had gone quickly. These would too.

But tonight she hadn't woken up on her own. She'd been awakened by sound, a sound out of place. And the noises in the night only got louder, more alarming. A shout of anger. A protest. A chorus of whispers. Then, what sounded very much like a small animal's cry. More anger, questioning.

Then, from out there in the dark, the First Mother heard someone call her own name.

"Azur!" The voice was sharp, high. It didn't repeat.

That tore it. She had to get up, even if she awakened Madazur. The worst that would happen if she woke the child was a wasted, restless night; the worst that would happen if she ignored danger was that someone might die. She eased herself away from the girl breath by breath, only moving on the exhale, and got her feet under her as quickly as she could.

Azur had no idea what to expect out there. She grabbed her dagger, more versatile and closer than her sword, and stood. She paused only to consider sandals or warmer clothes, weighed time against need, and declared herself ready.

Azur opened the tent flap a bare minimum and slipped out into the night.

There was no sun in the sky, and she was disoriented from sleep, so she had no idea whether it was closer to sunset or sunrise. She only knew that the flames of torches danced in the darkness, showing warriors on the move.

The ruckus came from the perimeter. As First Mother, Azur could have chosen to sleep closer to the center of the camp, but she preferred privacy, and she wanted a tent to herself with her daughter now that they were reunited. She rarely asked for special treatment, but this, she cherished.

Nights like tonight, it came in handy. The guards could probably handle any kind of incursion—was that what this was?—but Azur also wanted to be of use if she could. Not to kill anyone, unless it was absolutely necessary, but to feel the thrill of adrenaline in her veins. That was the only thing she missed about the war.

"Azur!" came the voice again. This time, Azur thought she could place it.

But no, it couldn't be her. That voice was a Bastion voice. Here they were in the dark of a Scorpican midnight. Ravian didn't belong here.

Then Azur saw the shape of a woman on the perimeter, guards

facing her with their weapons up. Azur could see the warriors' backs better than she could see the intruder. The woman's upheld palms were the most visible part of her. Most of her was swaddled in a heavy cloak. While she watched, the woman used one of her hands to lower the hood of her cloak, and Azur's breath caught in her throat. The woman did look an awful lot like Ravian.

Still. Even if Ravian had come, for whatever reason, Azur told herself, she wouldn't be alone. There was no way Ravian would have left her daughter behind.

But that cloak. It was heavy wool, thicker than needed for a spring night like this. And knowing Ravian's body, having observed it closely while teaching the woman her sword skills, Azur knew her outline well. Such a slim body didn't need such a bulky cloak. Azur thought about the sound she had heard earlier. Everything clicked into place.

She rushed the last remaining steps, crashed through the line of guards. From close up, she could see that the woman was indeed the Bastionite, as odd as that seemed. There was the face she remembered, flames flickering on Ravian's worried expression.

Azur said, "Wait! I know her."

"Hold," said Zalma, sounding annoyed.

Ravian seemed to sag with relief, and Azur ran forward, holding her arms out in case she needed to catch Ravian and the young daughter she'd hidden under her cloak. But at a look from Ravian, she slowed, then stopped without closing the distance.

Ravian pulled herself upright until she stood steady on her feet. Then Azur noticed that the woman's leg was bleeding. "What is this?"

The Bastionite, calm but with a tense voice that Azur understood meant suppressed pain, said, "I didn't announce myself fast enough. I was in the camp before I knew I'd found it. I should have waited for morning."

"You should have," agreed Azur.

"My soldiers did nothing wrong," came Zalma's voice. "She intruded where she doesn't belong. She's lucky we didn't kill her. It would have been justified."

Azur turned, taking a moment to better understand. The guard to Zalma's right, an older woman named Guish, stood with an empty bow pointing at the ground. Zalma had said *lucky we didn't kill her*, not *lucky we didn't shoot her*. They were all lucky, Azur supposed, that Guish's aim wasn't as good as some others. She had only grazed the target.

For Ravian's sake, Azur couldn't escalate the situation. So she said, in a calm tone, "We're not arguing that right now. This woman is a friend of mine from the Bastion."

"Oh, a 'friend'?" Zalma's voice was thick with innuendo.

Three years before, Zalma would have been completely justified in assuming that any relationship Azur had was purely sexual. Now, however, Azur found herself offended. Heat flared to her cheeks, though she was sure no one could see it in the darkness.

"Yes," Azur said firmly, "a friend. I do have them, you know, unlike you."

Zalma bristled, drawing herself up to her full height, though it was not impressive. "I won't argue with you in front of a stranger, First Mother. But you best keep a civil tongue in your head."

"Or what?" asked a voice from the darkness, and that voice was familiar enough that neither Azur nor Zalma had to think twice about who it belonged to.

"Queen," said Zalma, inclining her head as Amankha approached.

The queen of the Scorpicae was dressed in a simple nightshift identical to Azur's own. She joined the group of warriors and surveyed the assembled faces. Azur could practically read Amankha's mind as she noted each of the visible signs.

The presence of Azur. The spent bow. The bleeding stranger. The vestiges of anger on Zalma's face. Even, Azur saw, Ravian's outsize cloak.

Her voice measured, the queen said to Azur, "You can explain, I hope?"

Zalma said, "This intruder—"

Amankha held up a hand. "I asked Azur," she said.

"Ravian was one of my students in the Bastion," said Azur to the queen, noticing belatedly that there was more desperation in her voice than there should have been. She needed to indicate that this woman was important without betraying just how important she was to her. Azur hadn't even really realized how much she wanted to see Ravian again until she was standing right here. But now? It suddenly seemed essential that she be here in Ravian's company as long as she could.

Azur took a long breath and began again. "Ravian was my best student. Guish shot her and drew blood. Before we take any other action, we should dress the wound."

Amankha seemed to consider this, then turned to Ravian, who still stood on her own two feet, though unsteadily. "And what do you say to this, intruder?"

Ravian bowed her head to the queen, a protective hand pressing her daughter against her chest under the cloak. "The wound can wait. I want to tell you why I'm here."

The queen shrugged. "Don't tell me you're going to tell me. Just speak."

"I left the Bastion behind," said Ravian. "I'm never going back. This is where I belong."

Zalma let out a loud noise of disapproval, but the queen didn't turn. Her eyes were on Ravian.

"When Azur came to us . . . I learned how to fight. I picked up a weapon for the first time. Under her tutelage, I saw. I saw a better future for myself, and I came here to embrace it. I want to be a warrior," said Ravian, tears in her eyes. She pulled the front of her cloak aside to show the young daughter who rested against her torso in a sling. "And I want my daughter to be a warrior too."

Amankha looked back and forth from the stranger to Azur, her face expressionless.

Azur's heart throbbed in her chest. She refused to look at any of the other assembled warriors, knowing what they thought was irrelevant. Amankha would not be swayed by others' opinions. To her queen, Azur said simply, "Please."

Queen Amankha walked toward the stranger. They all held their breath.

Then the queen extended her right arm, letting it hang in the air, and reached out for Ravian's right arm with her other hand. The other woman's eyes were worried, watchful, but she let the queen pull her arm forward.

The queen wrapped Ravian's hand around her own, showing her how to fit her grip to the shape of the queen's forearm, so their positions mirrored each other, equal.

"This is how we seal a pact," said the queen.

"So sealed," said Ravian, holding both the queen's arm and her gaze.

Amankha went on, her tone almost conversational. "Here, we use our mother's names as part of our own. Do you know your mother's name?"

Ravian answered, "I was told she was called Favil."

"Queen!" interrupted Zalma. "Should we not test her?"

"I won't go back," the woman said, her eyes on the queen alone. "This is where I belong. If you refuse me, my daughter and I will find another queendom. But nowhere else will ever be home."

Zalma said, "You can go anywhere but here. So many other queendoms to choose from. Pick one."

The queen's expression was unreadable. But she turned to Zalma, not Ravian, eyes glittering in the torchlight.

Amankha said to the smith, "You're asking because the previous queen required tests, correct?"

"Yes. You know she did," Zalma scoffed. "You had to pass them yourself, didn't you? Since you weren't a Scorpican?"

"I was always a Scorpican," said Amankha, proud, determined.

Zalma was undeterred. "Except when you weren't. For years. When the woman who killed your mother reigned by right. Where did you hide, after you ran away?"

"Enough of this," the queen said sharply. "I do remember the tests for new warriors, and I understand why they were used. During the war, Tamura feared spies. She wanted to ensure that women joining our nation were doing so for the right reasons. It was a necessary choice for the time."

"But Tamura—"

"I think you know by now, Zalma dha Fionen," said Amankha, in a voice that drifted from amusement to anger. "I am not Tamura."

Azur realized she had been holding her breath. But at those words from Amankha, she exhaled.

Ravian's gaze met the queen's. The child in her sling gave a sleepy grumble.

"We hear your choice and honor it," said the queen. She raised her chin and spoke her next words, addressed to the woman and child in front of her, but clearly intended for all listening ears.

"Then, welcome to the nation of Scorpica as our newest warriors," said the queen, and tightened their forearm grasp. "Welcome, Ravian dha Favil."

Ravian teetered a little on her feet, but smiled, grateful.

Then the queen gave a tiny nod downward. "And your daughter's name?"

"Diti."

"Then welcome, Diti dha Ravian. May the Scorpion smile on you."

✦ CHAPTER 30 ✦

RETURNED

The fifth month of the All-Mother's Year 521

In the Bastion

Amankha, Paulus

It was a positive sign that visits between the Scorpican and Bastionite queens were now a formal matter, thought Amankha, yet she missed those earlier days now. She would have rather ridden alone through the gates to see Hikmet, to talk with her, even wander through the market without a purpose. But everything had such meaning, she couldn't afford not to think about every detail.

Exchanging teachers had been a successful gambit, and it was time for the next stage. To ask Hikmet, while she was still queen, to take on a Scorpican Queensguard. It would be a bold step, but logical: if Scorpicae could be trusted as Queensguards, eventually they could take on other assignments again, and they could look forward to a future that regained some of the glory of their past.

So Amankha was surrounded by a Queensguard of five fellow Scorpicae as they all moved through the northern gate from the grassy ground of their homeland to the ringing stone of the Bastion. Amankha felt pressed on all sides, but she couldn't afford to show any hint of weakness. She simply pretended the rattle of swords against the ceremonial amber-plate armor of her companions was music to her Scorpican ears. All six of them held their heads high as they proceeded to the meeting place.

Amankha had planned her proposal carefully. During her years in Paxim with Paulus, watching Heliane do her work, she'd learned so much without even knowing she was learning. She knew now that if you wanted to persuade someone to do what you wanted, you needed to put things in their terms, tell them exactly how they would benefit. People preferred to act in their own self-interest. You just had to arrange things so that their interests and your interests aligned. She'd witnessed Heliane do it on every scale from global to intimate; she'd experienced it herself firsthand in a more subtle, insidious way when Heliane had given her a tea to drink and lied to her about its purpose.

Amankha physically shook herself to brush away the memories. That had been another time in her life. She would have gone back to the earlier one in a heartbeat, but that wasn't an option, and she owed much to many people in this one. She needed to make good.

Her Queensguard left her at the door of the audience chamber, only the two queens face-to-face.

Amankha noticed that Hikmet, too, was treating these visits more formally. Her scarlet cloak as bright as freshly spilled blood. Amankha knew that red was the color of honor in the Bastion, with no one but the Board of Scholars allowed to wear it. She couldn't stop thinking about her days in the Bastion, but she needed to set those memories aside, she realized. She was here as a queen of Scorpica.

The negotiation itself went as well as it possibly could. She spoke to Queen Hikmet of logic and mutual benefit. No emotions, no favors, no wheedling. Simply laying out the case. With most people, logic and reason were less useful than emotional appeals, but not in this case. Queens of the Bastion were, above all else, reasonable.

Amankha made her case to the red-cloaked, somber-faced queen, and when she finished, she clasped her own hands together to show she was done, a Bastionite affectation. Queen Hikmet was not the one who would make the final decision; all queens of the Bastion ruled by consensus with the help of their entire board. So Amankha knew she would not have an answer immediately, but she laid out her case in such a way that she knew Queen Hikmet would be able make the case her own. That was the most she could hope for, really.

After she and Queen Hikmet sealed their agreement, Amankha stepped back, but then she paused, not ready to leave. Memories of her days in the Bastion surged forward again. She breathed in the scent of cool stone, thinking of the long halls and high walls that had surrounded her every day of her life for years.

The red-cloaked queen of the Bastion watched her, no particular emotion on her face, neither impatient nor indulgent. Indulgence was not the way of the Bastion.

Amankha felt the moment stretch out. She let it stretch, and she caught the Bastionite queen's eye, then let the corner of her mouth turn up in a rueful smile. At length she ventured, "I suppose I should reclaim my Queensguard and move on."

Queen Hikmet said, "Are you sure you want to?"

Seizing the opening, Amankha said softly to the other queen, "Want has nothing to do with it, does it?"

Hikmet's sudden smile was disproportionately large on her small face, jarringly bright, and a laugh bubbled up in her throat. The mirth transformed her. Amankha felt her own smile growing in response.

"Only we queens know," Hikmet said, shaking her head a bit ruefully. She plucked at the edge of the red cloak. "I won't be a queen much longer, but I'm already tired of it. Two years is more than enough."

"And when you're queen no longer, you can go back to making more decisions about how to live your own life?"

"Yes and no." The diminutive scholar shrugged. "I'll still be on the board. I'll still be one of the people who need to contribute to the consensus. I'll still have eyes watching me, and tongues wagging over what I do, and all sorts of people with all sorts of opinions about whether my contribution to governance has been right or wrong. But the day after my rule ends, am I going to slip the board and swim naked in the Salt Maw? Yes, I am."

Amankha found herself chuckling. "Sounds splendid. If chilly."

"Depends on the season. I suppose you don't get to look forward to the day when you're no longer queen."

"No," Amankha responded, feeling her solemnity returning. "It's different for me."

"Everything is."

"Yes."

Hikmet ran her hand over her tightly pinned cap of hair and said, her voice light and conversational, "Would you like a break, then?"

Amankha eyed her, almost suspicious, and responded, "What kind of a break did you have in mind?"

"Your Queensguard stands outside the door, waiting," Hikmet said, pointing to the door where Amankha had come in. Amankha's eyes flew to it automatically. The door was heavy, thick, forbidding.

"But as it happens," Hikmet continued, "that's not the only door." She pointed toward the other end of the room.

The stone wall she'd indicated looked flat and featureless, but Amankha knew from growing up in the Bastion's nurseries that many walls here were not what they seemed. Whoever had built the Bastion had done so with more tricks and technologies than modern minds could grasp.

Careful not to let her curiosity show too clearly in her voice, Amankha said, "Are you offering me . . . a tunnel?"

"Something else. A kind of invention. They don't use it in the nurseries, so it wouldn't be familiar to you. But as a fellow queen, I can share this one thing. I think it's all right if you know just one of our small secrets."

Hikmet laid her palm flat on the wall. A section of stone slid aside to reveal a small chamber with a pulley system inside it, ropes and metal wheels and other complicated-looking machinery Amankha didn't know all the names for. Indicating it, the Bastionite queen said, "We call this an ascender."

"Ah."

Still with a light, merry touch to her voice, Hikmet asked, "Would you like to go down or up?"

"Surprise me," said Amankha.

"I would if I could," said Queen Hikmet, that wide grin dominating her small face once again. "But once you're inside, you make the decision. Pull here and you'll go down. Pull here and you'll go up. You can do both if you want. I'll order a meal for both of us sent to this room and tell everyone the negotiations are continuing. You can stay on this side of the door for hours and travel all throughout this network of tunnels and up to the turret, and your Queensguard will be none the wiser."

It sounded wonderful, and Amankha didn't distrust the Bastionite queen, but she didn't want to be foolhardy at someone else's expense. "You're not worried you'll get caught? If they insist on storming in here and find me gone, they may attack first and ask questions later."

"I'm not so helpless as all that, Queen Amankha," said Hikmet, handing her a long gray cloak with a hood. "I may be a reluctant queen, a bored queen, a temporary queen, but I assure you I am still a queen. My orders will be followed."

For the first time in a while, Amankha let herself want something. No one would be harmed and she could have precious time to herself. She could step back into her life soon enough; just for now, she would step out of it. If she wanted to, she could lose herself in the deep tunnels where she and Paulus had once met as children. In this cloak she would look like no one of importance. Then there was no reason to delay any further.

"Thank you, Hikmet," said Amankha, and stepped into the ascender, then slid the stone panel shut behind her. She reached out to the wheel that the queen had told her would send her down into the earth, and she pulled. The stone room lurched and shuddered. She heard a deep, low grinding noise. Then she began to descend.

Someone not raised in the Bastion's tunnels might have been nervous, but Amankha felt no fear. Whoever had built the Bastion, ever so long ago, had built it to last. She could take a great gulp of air even inside the small stone room as it ground its way down toward the center of the earth, and she knew that once she reached the tunnels, she'd be able to breathe there, too. Whether it was engineering or magic or a combination of the two, she knew the Bastion would cradle and care for her and anyone else who walked its halls. In its impassive, eternal way, it always had.

When Amankha slid open the panel again, deep underground, she was grateful for the glowing light near the door. Clearly enchanted lights had been left here, more permanent than torches, but so precious she was sure they couldn't be used very widely. There were two options for which way to go: down a long, narrow hall or into a large room. She chose the room.

She'd seen large rooms deep in the underground of the Bastion, but never like this one. A huge door stood open, but she could see its thickness, and the immense room beyond. It was like a large bunker. Had Queen Hikmet wanted her to see that this was here? She must have, or at least not been opposed to the possibility. *Down or up, the choice is yours.* Hikmet was no fool.

Same as any other child raised in the Bastion, Amankha had heard the rumors of an underground bunker. No one she knew had ever seen it, but they all swore it existed deep in the bowels of the fortress, a secret room that could keep an unknown number of people safe for months, perhaps years. This looked like the place. Vast and open in the center, it shunted off at the edges into smaller rooms, in which shelves were lined with stored food, giving off the reassuring smells of dried fruit and jerked meat, jugs of wine wafting out just the faintest sweet-sour note.

Then, from one of the small rooms on the right, she heard a young-sounding man's voice ask softly, "Madrik?"

Amankha whirled, hand on her sword, ready to draw. A sharp chill ran from her heart to her fingertips, cutting through her. She'd been a fool to trust the Bastionite queen, letting herself be sent into the Bastion's deepest tunnels without her Queensguard.

She drew.

Her eyes hadn't fully adjusted to the darkness, and though she was certain the young man's voice had come from nearby, she saw no one who could have spoken. Blade held out in front of her, she swung her body carefully to the right, her eyes sweeping the darkness, ready to strike at any moment.

"Ah. You're not her," the same voice said, but weakly, and though Amankha kept her sword up, she felt a soft wave of relief. The young man wasn't attacking. If the Bastionite queen had sent Amankha into an ambush, it would have been clear by now. Assassins attacked without warning. They didn't lurk. They didn't whisper.

"I'm not her, I'm sorry," Amankha answered, and then she saw something shift just at the edges of her sight. A blur of something pale among the stacks of supplies. She drew closer to where she'd seen the movement, one catlike step at a time. Forcing a conversational tone, she asked, "Who are you?"

"Nobody, now," came the answer.

When she finally drew close enough to see the man, Amankha stifled a gasp.

A knife gleamed from the darkness, but this man was no assassin. The pale fabric she'd seen was his chiton, pinned at the shoulders with wheel-shaped closures, its light green nettlecloth marking him as a Midwife. Only from the chest up was it pale. He'd slit his wrists with long vertical cuts, and his hands lay limply in his lap along with the dropped knife, blood dying the lower half of his garments dark.

"We used to meet here," he said, his voice growing softer. But now, Amankha was close enough to hear. "I sent a note for her to come if she still wanted me. But she didn't."

"That's no reason to—" Amankha caught herself. She'd never understood, even in her darkest days after the loss of Paulus, why a person would rather be dead than alive. But she could tell at a glance that urging this young man to live wouldn't make a whit of difference. It was already too late. He'd already succeeded.

She wanted to reach for his hands to comfort him, but there was so much blood.

So instead she knelt in front of him, set her sword down, and placed her hands on his knees. "I'm sorry. I'll stay with you as long as you need me to. So you're not alone."

At that his eyes opened wider, but not with gratitude. "*Mokh* your platitudes. We all die alone."

The burst of anger seemed to drain what was left of his strength, and Amankha was unsure what to do next. So she stayed, her hands on the dying man's knees, her own knees stiffening on the cold floor. There was something holy about the quiet all around them, two bodies bending close in the darkness, a kind of carved-out peace.

Amankha stayed there with the foolish young man, whether or not he wished it, as his breath grew shallower and shallower and then stilled.

There was no anger in him then, she saw, not anymore. No spirit. No life.

Her knees aching, Amankha rose and retrieved her sword, tucking it back into its sheath. She was thinking of what she would tell the Bastionite queen—she would have to tell her, of course—when she heard the last noise she expected.

One deep breath.

She leapt back from the body, her hand not leaving the pommel of the sword she'd just finished sheathing, and looked down in disbelief. She almost would have let herself believe that he'd been alive the whole time, she'd just missed it, except that in the dim light she also saw his wrists healing themselves, the thick dark lines sealing and disappearing until both forearms lay smooth and untouched from wrist to elbow.

Then his eyes opened.

She took another few steps back, both sure and unsure of what she was seeing. It was magic, certainly, but what kind? Had the man's spirit returned to his body, or was there another explanation? She kept her hand on her sword, but didn't draw it. She could be ready without being rash.

Then she heard a whisper from a corner and she tensed. It was hard to tell what direction a sound came from in all these warrens, deep in stone.

She neared the glowing light by the ascender again, placing her back against the wall to defend against danger from any direction. But all she could see now was the body of the dead man—or the man she'd thought was dead—rising on unsteady feet, reaching out to balance himself against the thick wall nearby. Had she not seen his fatal wound heal itself, she would not have known what he was. Having seen it, she could not forget. The bloody knife clattered, falling as he rose.

"What are you?" she asked.

He seemed to consider the question. His eyes were hungry, catching glimmers of light and reflecting them back to her, his face slack with something she couldn't quite identify in the half-light—shock? Want?

She tried again. "Who are you?"

The man tilted his head, staring at her, and then his eyes went wide.

She opened her mouth to say her name, but before she could, he beat her to it. In a dry voice, firmer than she would have expected, he said, "Ama?"

"How can you—" she began, and then thought better of it. She didn't confirm or deny her identity. Instead she said, "And who are you?"

"I want to tell you, but I don't think you'll believe me," he said, and something about the way he spoke made her breath hitch. Even though the voice wasn't the same, the body wasn't the same, there were no similarities that would call her lost lover to mind, she still knew.

Quietly, with wonder, she asked, "Paulus?"

✦

He'd awakened in a body, wrists afire with pain that swarmed up and through the entire body as if a sun burned inside him, but only for a moment. After that initial burst of pain he could feel the wounds that had killed the body knitting, healing. Suddenly the pain was only a memory.

Then he'd managed to stand, struggling to master this new body's limbs. He remembered how mobile he'd been as a shade, how unlimited. In contrast, this was constricting, almost suffocating. But a body was what he'd wanted, wasn't it? He'd agreed to work with Sessadon to come back Aboveground exactly like this. He'd managed to open the Gate of Heroes by sheltering the Voa in his sister's form, willing to sacrifice everything to protect her. She hadn't really been Zo, he saw that now, but he'd believed in the moment that she was. And thank goodness, too. That had been the test. He'd passed.

And now, unbelievably, he stood here not only in a body, but a body whose eyes looked at Ama, the person he loved most in the world.

He didn't immediately recognize the place where they stood, but he could guess. Surrounded by stone, they must be in the Bastion, where they'd once met as children. Some god or another must be on his side.

But he didn't have time to savor his victory. He could tell by the look on Ama's face that she wasn't sure what to think. How he had loved that look in life, the expression she made when she was considering something, making a decision. Now it worried him. She could be moments away from either fleeing the scene entirely or drawing that sword at her hip to stab this new body right through the heart. Paulus didn't know for sure what would happen to his soul if the new body died, but he could guess. That shade who'd gone Aboveground had sunk right back down Below when her second body had been killed. He had to assume the same would happen to him. To die at Ama's hands would be the cruelest turn of events he could imagine.

So Paulus, in the body of a stranger, put up his hands in surrender. "Yes. It's me. Ama, I can't—I can't believe it."

"Neither can I," she said, and he worried he detected a faint note of derision in the sound.

"Do you not believe it's me? Because it is. You can ask me anything in the world and I'll answer it, here and now. It's me, Ama. It's Paulus. I swear."

She tilted her head and looked at him, and now he saw the intense longing in her dark eyes, another expression he had loved so much in life.

Paulus said, "I shouldn't have gone. I went because it would have been a good story. For the books, you know? Like Alev and Vela. Like Roksana riding Golagal to her daughter's side before she died. I saw myself—I wanted to be a hero."

"You were always a hero to me," said Ama, her face crumpling, and then her arms were around him, and he felt the fresh sensation of how the eyes of his new body stung when he cried.

After a while he gathered his breath to talk, but he didn't want to let go of her, not for a moment. Instead, he lifted his head from her shoulder and whispered with his new mouth into her ear.

"I was a fool," he said.

"You were brave," she said, "and also foolish."

"I'm so sorry. If I could take it back, I would. I left you with nothing."

She shifted, pressing her mouth against his neck, and he felt the beginning of a smile against his skin. The sensation was unbearably powerful. That was what a body was good for, he realized. So limiting but so full of possibility.

"Actually," said Ama, "you did leave me with something. Something that became a someone."

"What?"

Quietly, Ama said, "Her name is Roksana."

Paulus understood immediately and the eyes of his borrowed body overflowed with tears, his borrowed hands gripping her waist tightly, a cry in his throat.

"If I'd stayed," he said, feeling broken, torn apart. "If I'd stayed . . . I would have met her. We would have . . . we could have . . ."

She kissed his new mouth then for the first time, a soft but insistent kiss, her lips held against his until he quieted.

Then she said, "What's done is done. But she's perfect, Paulus. You'll meet her someday, and you'll see."

"I have no doubt she's perfect. She's yours."

"Yours, too."

Paulus said, trying to add lightness to it, "I was hardly perfect."

"Neither of us was. Or are." She shook her head. "But together, we made something better."

"Where is she? Is she with my mother?"

"Oh, Paulus," she said, her face falling. He knew what she was going to say before she said it. "Your mother no longer lives. I'm sorry."

"I didn't see her," he said. "In the Underlands. But they are vast. I didn't see Zo either, until . . ."

"Until?"

He wanted to explain everything, about the gates and Sessadon and his journey here, but he was suddenly aware they might not have all the time in the world. "Never mind that now. Are we in the Bastion? Why?"

She said, "I came for a diplomatic mission, and the queen let me come down here to clear my head. You . . . well, wait! Does this mean the third gate is open?"

"You know about the gates?"

"My grandmother Ellimi," she said. "She came through the second gate. She said only the recently dead in Godsbones could be taken over by a rising shade, but if the third gate was open . . ."

"Yes. The most sacred place in each queendom. So I guess this is the Bastion's."

"But we don't have to stay here," said Ama, grasping his hands. "I can take you to . . ." but then she trailed off.

"Take me where?"

"Paulus," she said, "so much has changed since I lost you." She didn't know whether he knew how long it had been. More than two years now.

"Tell me what's happened."

It was hard to even choose where to begin. She did the best she could. "I'm not Ama anymore, not exactly. I'm Amankha dha Khara, queen of Scorpica."

He let go of her and dropped to his knees, partly to give himself time to process the news, and partly because he simply felt weak.

From above him her voice came, gentle and teasing. "You know we don't do that in Scorpica, right?"

"Men don't do anything in Scorpica," he blurted. Then he grew more serious. "Ama . . . I mean, I guess, Queen Amankha . . . I wouldn't be welcome in Scorpica."

"No, you wouldn't," she agreed.

"In the name of Panic," he sighed. "Why do I have a man's body?"

They stared at each other for a long moment. She was the first to break the gaze, looking at the stone walls around them, the bunker, the blood on the floor.

"Come," she said, holding out her hands. "I can't take you to Scorpica, but there's one place I can take you."

He put his hands in hers and she pulled him to his feet. Then she led him to a stone wall. At first it looked like all the others, but when she pressed her palm flat against it, the wall opened up. Inside was a kind of hanging box, large enough for two people to stand in.

"What is that?" he asked.

"Do you trust me?"

He squeezed her hand with his borrowed one. "Always."

✦

When the ascender door opened on the upper parapet above the queen's quarters, Amankha showed Paulus the sky. Wind whipped her borrowed cloak as she led him, in his new body, across the high stones.

"It's strange," she said. "Touching you. Talking to you. When it's . . . not your face."

"But it's me."

"But it's you." She'd doubted him at first, in those initial moments, but the doubt was gone. Her stunned pleasure at finding him was already threatened by the fear of losing him again. Trying to push aside that feeling, she said, "I have a million questions I want to ask."

"I'm happy to answer a million and one," he said.

The wind felt cold on her skin, chapping her cheeks. She looked out over the landscape. The sky was overcast. She felt a baseless regret. Paulus, having risen from the dark of the Underlands to walk the earth once more, should have been welcomed with sunshine. "My love, I'm sorry. We don't have long."

His brows knit.

"The queen gave me time to hide here, but we can't stay. You can't come to Scorpica with me. So where do you go? Home to Paxim?"

"I don't know if I can," he said. His manner was grim, more practical than he'd been in his first life. "Even when I had my mother's support and momentum behind me, I had enemies. Now—well, now, it's impossible. No one will believe this is me. I'm helpless."

"Never helpless," she said, and at a loss for anything better to do, kissed him. The response felt inadequate, but so did every other.

Paulus drew back from the kiss, a bit rueful. "Not helpless, then. Let us say limited. In this body I can neither take my rightful place as ruler of Paxim nor join you as your companion in Scorpica."

"If you only had a different body," sighed Amankha.

It was Paulus's turn to stare out over the breathtaking view. His profile was so different than the one she remembered: a larger nose, lower cheekbones, a rounder jaw. But there was something about these far-gazing eyes that pulled at her heartstrings, achingly familiar. Yes. In his first life, Paulus had always had his eyes on the horizon.

Paulus said, "I could."

She'd only expressed regret, not meant it as a suggestion, but now she had to consider the possibility. Yes, as far as they knew, he could rise again in a different body. But first, he'd have to die again.

"Ama. If I died, I could—what if I could?"

"Can you choose a body?" she said. "Is that how it works?"

"I didn't this time," he admitted. "But it was the first time I'd done it. And we were just opening the gate. Now the gate is standing open. If I had time to consider . . ."

"Ellimi said it's the holiest places in each of the queendoms. So if you could even choose the place and not the body—"

He interrupted, picking up the thought. "If I choose to rise in Scorpica, I'll rise in a woman's body. Where's the holiest place in Scorpica?"

She frowned. "We don't really have temples, or—wait." She snapped her fingers. The sound was inaudible against the high wind. "The Scorpion's Pass. I bet that's it. She's our holiest figure and it's named for her, and there's even an altar there."

"Do women die there very often?"

"Not often. So maybe—maybe that won't work. Maybe you should just stay."

He turned away from the view and his eyes were liquid, regretful. "But we've already agreed I can't stay."

"Maybe we just haven't thought of the answer yet. You could stay here in the Bastion, and I could visit. . . ."

He shook his borrowed head. "I don't belong here. Remember, I've lived here before. The Bastion isn't great at finding places for people they think don't belong."

"You could work in the nurseries, or—"

"Ama." He grabbed her shoulders. "We could settle for that, yes. A sliver of a life. But would it make either of us happy? Don't you want more?"

"I want you," she said, more nakedly honest than she felt she'd ever been during Paulus's first life, holding nothing back from him. "That's all that matters."

"Then I'll try. I'll go back to the Underlands. I'll find a way to come back in a woman's body. I can do it, Ama. I can figure it out. There's just one question."

"There are a lot of questions," she answered, meaning it as a light rejoinder, but it came out much sadder than she'd intended.

"Only one question I want to ask you. Can I ask?"

"Yes."

"If I came back as a woman. The same person on the inside that you love, that loves you, but different on the outside. More different than this." He indicated his current body. "A woman, Ama."

Her answer was swift, instant. "I love you, Paulus. Not your body."

"I remember you were very fond of my body."

"I was," she said, letting herself smile, though the smile didn't stay long on her face. "But that one's gone now, isn't it? Are you trying to talk me out of this plan?"

He shook his head, resolved. "I want whatever plan makes it possible for us to be together. I know a woman's body doesn't mean total freedom, but it means a lot more freedom than I have now. More possibilities. So the only reason not to do it would be if you wouldn't want . . . if you felt . . ."

Even over the wind, Amankha heard Paulus's breath, fast and shallow, as he waited for her answer.

When she came to her decision, Amankha met his gaze with her own and reached out to cradle his chin.

"Paulus," she told him, "I promise to love you for you, whatever happens. Come back woman or man or neither or both. Just come back to me and I'm yours forever. Is that what you want to hear?"

His eyes were warm and hopeful, his voice trembling with emotion. "Only if it's true."

"It's true." She kissed him once, said the word again, "True," then a kiss like punctuation, and then she alternated kisses with repetitions of the word as if repetition could prove how deeply she felt, how much she needed him to believe her. *True. True. True.*

Words could not express the feeling of Paulus's kiss from lips that were not Paulus's. She could have kissed him forever, but she knew it wouldn't matter. A few more minutes wouldn't change anything. They would be parted again. They'd agreed there was no other way. And even though she saw the wisdom of it, she dreaded the next step.

"I will return," said Paulus.

"But when?"

"That's something we can't know," said Paulus. "But know it will happen. And know I love you."

"Know I love you," said Amankha, and kissed him again until she was gasping for breath.

Then he took a step back. "Look at me," he said, smiling.

She fixed the unfamiliar face with the familiar smile in her mind.

"Close your eyes."

He was still smiling when her eyes shut tight. Then she heard him step back once more, two steps, three, and then there were no more footfalls. He had left her with that smile, she was sure, to make her last sight of him in this life a good one.

On some level, he was probably thinking of what a story it would make one day. *And the kingling Paulus, in his second body, fell from the greatest height in the Five Queendoms, and he went down smiling.*

The fall was so long she doubted if the sound of the landing body would even reach her. The parapet was so high, the rocks so far below. But just in case, she covered her ears firmly with both hands, hunching down on the stone. She had not been there to witness his first death. Neither would she witness his second.

When Paulus came to her again, she told herself, in whatever third body he chose, that one would be for keeps.

✦ CHAPTER 31 ✦

ROVERS

Daybreak Palace and Ursu, Paxim

Eminel, Fasiq

Ingini was the tallest, most striking member of Eminel's Queens-guard, her posture rigid and her chin always high. While Eminel wasn't particularly fond of her, she did enjoy how clearly Ingini's voice rang out when she had something to announce. Ingini loved announcing.

Tired of feeling besieged, Eminel had begun to receive visitors in the throne room less frequently, setting aside time once a week for her courtiers to approach her. This way, she could see many people in a short time, then no one at all for the next six days. It seemed a fair bargain. Eminel always assigned Ingini to attend her on these days, allowing the woman to use her announcing voice, which made every visit feel like an occasion.

Today, as evening approached, the steady stream of supplicants had slowed to a trickle. As Ingini stepped outside the double doors to admit the next visitor, Eminel was briefly alone in the throne room, stretching and bracing herself. At least she could be alone again tomorrow.

Then Ingini entered, an unreadable expression on her face. She pulled the doors shut firmly behind her with both hands. This in itself was odd; Eminel felt a wave of tension sweep through her. Unbidden, her right hand drifted up to stroke the curves of the snake necklace. Its blue glass was smooth under her fingertips.

"Queen Eminel," Ingini said now, her head high and her voice as clear as a gong, though they were the only two people present. "A group of visitors wishes to enter your presence."

Most supplicants came alone, though it wasn't unusual to have groups of two or three from the same matriclan approach. But Ingini always announced the name of at least one visitor. And there was something in the way Ingini said the plural, *visitors*, that made Eminel even warier.

"Very well," Eminel said. "Tell me more. What kind of visitors?"

Uncharacteristically, Ingini faltered, seeming unsure. She glanced behind her, then looked to the queen again. Her voice was only a shadow of its usual imperious shout when she said, "Assorted."

And Eminel knew. She stood from her throne, her long bone-colored robe brushing the tops of her bare feet, then the ground. She could almost feel the tears springing to her eyes already. "Did they say whether they're Paximites? Is there a giant? Maybe a pair of twins?"

"Twins," confirmed Ingini. Still a bit uncertain, she said, "Will you receive them here?"

Eminel didn't hesitate. "Yes. Immediately."

Ingini's voice was again a powerful, clear shout, as she said, "Come!"

The wide doors swung open. Three figures crossed the threshold, two of the same height, the third a bit shorter. Their faces were not exactly as Eminel had remembered them—how could they be, after so many years?—but they were still so familiar, so dear, that her first impulse was to run down the few stairs of her raised platform and wrap all three of them in her arms.

But she held herself back, knowing Ingini would share what she saw, not wanting to give any indication of just how much she treasured these people. Along with her mother, Jehenit, they had once raised her. No one here knew that, and she wasn't about to tell. Eminel, Well of All-Magic, Master of Sand, and Destroyer of Fear, hadn't made it this far showing weakness.

"Welcome, visitors, to Daybreak Palace," Eminel said formally. "Ingini, you may leave us now."

The Queensguard's main weapons were invisible and magical in nature, but they also carried swords, mostly for show. Ingini rested her hand on the pommel of hers as she said, "Are you sure, Queen?"

"Yes." Eminel focused on Ingini, to make sure she understood. She was tempted to add a magical nudge of emphasis, but it was unnecessary. Ingini would not disobey. "You may wait outside."

"Yes, Queen."

Then the tall Arcan backed out of the doors, which swung closed behind her, and at last, Eminel was alone with the Rovers she'd sought.

Eminel almost laughed when she turned her attention back to the small motley group. The twins gave an instant impression of greater maturity, their jaws stronger, their movements more confident and smooth. For all that, their eyes were round as full moons, taking in the splendor around them. They were clearly impressed. The lines on Hermei's face had deepened—he apparently still refused to use his illusion magic—and his expression was harder to read.

The thief was first to speak, tilting his face up at Eminel, scrutinizing her. "Well. You've come up in the world, young one."

"Not so young anymore."

"Not so old, either," he answered back. "And as tall as me now."

"Hard to tell how tall anyone is from this far away," Eminel said, and gave in to her urge to descend the stairs, though she forced herself to go slowly. She could tell what Hermei was thinking then, even without magic; his eyes were guarded as he watched her approach, as if considering stepping back.

But he stood his ground, and she returned his caution with caution, stopping before she reached him. She let her arms dangle at her sides. She had to be careful to appear nonthreatening. When last they met she was a child, and he was the one who had told her she had powers; but now her powers, and the seat they had won her, were obvious to all.

Once she stood close, facing him, she saw he was right. They were the same height, almost exactly. "So different than we were, and yet the same," she said, with gentle wonder.

"Not the same if you're a queen now," said one of the twins.

"Didn't know for sure we knew a queen," the other muttered. "We guessed maybe? Didn't know how many Eminels there might be on this side of the border."

"I'm glad you came," Eminel said. "I wasn't sure you would."

Hermei nodded, his eyes still guarded. "The Seeker explained. She said you wanted us. And it wasn't like we were doing anything so exciting, so we took a vote and decided, why not?"

"A vote!" exclaimed Eminel on a laugh. "When I was with you, she never would've stood for that kind of nonsense. Would've grumbled about how you weren't braid-crowns and all that."

No one responded, so she added gently, "How things have changed."

"So many things," one of the twins echoed.

The time had come. She had noticed, of course, that Fasiq wasn't with them, but had hoped they would explain. But she couldn't let the question hang over them any longer. She had to ask. "Fasiq? She's not . . ."

Hermei was the first to understand what she was asking. "Not dead," he said quietly.

Eminel's shoulders sagged in relief. As long as it had been since she'd seen the giant, she couldn't imagine a world where Fasiq wasn't at least swashbuckling around somewhere, stirring up trouble. Silvering her scar, boasting about her lovers, making sure her reputation as a bandit for the ages was alive and well. Legends like Fasiq didn't die.

One of the twins said, "Well. As far as we know. It's been . . . how long?"

"Half a year, maybe a year?" said his brother.

Hermei shook his head. "Not so long."

The first twin frowned. "A year at least. That market? Wineberries were in season. You know they don't last."

"Ah." Hermei looked down, plucked at a silver ring Eminel didn't recognize. "Well, you may be right about the wineberries."

Eminel had held her tongue as long as she could, but the tension was unbearable. "So you're not all traveling together still? What happened?"

"Well," Hermei said, looking reluctant. "It wasn't a bad parting, as these things go. No falling-out, nothing like that. But she . . ."

One twin, Luben, interrupted. Eminel remembered now how to tell them apart, dredging up the trick from her deepest memories. She checked to see which side they wore their daggers on. Luben, the one she'd danced with all those years ago in Hayk, was left-handed. His brother, Elechus, was not. "The three of us here, we wanted to go farther afield. Try our luck in Sestia a bit, where things were quieter. And she said no. She won't leave Paxim. Not for any reason. She swore."

"Swore on what?"

"The Bandit God, I imagine," Luben said.

"I mean . . . swore why, exactly?"

Elechus said, "Swore she wouldn't set foot outside Paxim until she found her again."

"Her?" asked Eminel, but as soon as the word left her mouth, she realized she knew. "You mean Fasiq's looking for the Shade?"

"Her," confirmed Hermei.

Eminel had nothing to say. If the giant had made up her mind not to leave the queendom where she'd last seen the love of her life, no one was going to change that. Not even Arca's queen.

"We wanted to see you," Hermei said. "But if you don't want us without her . . ."

"I do," she replied, a little too loudly. "Stay for a while. I have something to ask."

Hermei and the twins looked at each other. Luben said, "Of course we'll stay awhile."

"We happen to have some free time just now," Elechus added.

Eminel said, "You too, Hermei? You'll stay?"

Hermei nodded once, solemnly. Eminel's heart soared.

She found them the right accommodations, not too ornate, and had food sent to their rooms in case they didn't want to mingle with magicians. She visited them often, but left them time to themselves as well. She held back from using magic in their presence, reaching back to the innocence of the days before she'd known her power. The twins told escalating stories of their Sestian adventures, culminating in a scene of each running across the hills with live sheep slung over their shoulders, reducing Eminel to helpless tears. Hermei was slower to warm, his eyes regarding her carefully, until she taught him to play *whishnuk*. Then he finally seemed to relax.

After one turning of the moon, once they were all comfortable, Eminel found her moment. She had deliberated endlessly and finally decided to simply ask for what she wanted. No artifice, no manipulation, no magic. Just a simple request to her longtime friends. She asked. them to stay on for a time, to join her Queensguard. Smiling, they accepted.

And if it wasn't quite how it had been back in the days they'd traveled together as bandits—especially without the charismatic giant Fasiq to tell them all what to do—it was the happiest Eminel could remember being in years.

Only having Beyda back would make her happier, and the last time they'd spoken, the scribe had told Eminel that she still needed more time. Beyda asked Eminel to wait in readiness. That was exactly what the queen of Arca would do. Now Eminel had found the people who, if she needed them to, would go to the ends of the earth to get Beyda back.

Until then, she would wait. Even if she hated waiting.

◆

As best she remembered it, Fasiq had gone entire years, possibly decades, without doubting herself. All those years as a bandit, she'd never wavered. Skating the edges of the law had been the right choice. She'd occasionally trusted the wrong people, or fallen in love with the wrong people, yes, and sometimes those two groups were even the same, but she'd always managed to fix her mistakes and move on. Mistakes weren't the same as regrets. Neither was the same as self-doubt. She would have sworn to the Bandit God that she hadn't doubted herself since she'd been a mere child, if ever.

Still. There were, these days, she had to admit, moments. Ever since she'd sworn—standing at the altar of a temple of the Bandit God back in Hayk before that town's name had come to mean something entirely different—never to leave Paxim until she found the Shade again.

She knew by then that the Shade wasn't from Paxim, of course, though her lover had never said the words aloud. The Shade had never declared herself Scorpican. They'd whispered countless words to each other, Fasiq in her brassy, buckwheat-honey voice and the

Shade in her harsh rasp, but the Shade had never actually said those particular words aloud. She hadn't needed to.

But Fasiq knew that the Shade would never return to Scorpica, though she didn't know exactly how she knew. Whatever had made the woman leave the warrior nation and discard her name, it had to have been serious. A woman like that wouldn't be easily swayed. So when the Shade disappeared from Hayk at the same time Eminel was taken from the Bandit God's temple, leaving behind a dead magician and an open door in the wreckage, Fasiq swore to find her.

She hadn't thought it would take this long. Eight years, now. But Fasiq's god had served her well in so many ways, she wasn't about to abandon the search just because it had gone on longer than she expected.

Fasiq missed the Rovers, of course she did. But bandits needed to move, and move freely. When things heated up, they needed the option to seek quieter pastures, possibly literally, over the border in Sestia. For her part, she needed to settle down for a bit in the capital. So she'd sent them on their way.

Ursu was the most important city in Paxim. Fasiq had avoided it for years. But it was the last major place she hadn't looked for the Shade, and her search was more important than anything else. She started at the city's temple of the Bandit God and worked her way outward from there.

Now months had passed, and the money was running short. Fasiq would either need to leave the city to get some funds from her stash, or find something approaching legal employment. She didn't like the former and she had no experience with the latter. So she was making decisions on the fly. Today her decision was to spend one of her last coppers on a bag of bruised oranges and peel them as slowly as she could while watching people walk in and out of the market.

She was down to her third-to-last orange and feeling slightly sick to her stomach when a woman approached her.

"You're very large," said the woman.

Fasiq restrained herself from rolling her eyes, and relished the surge of pride she felt from managing to do that in the face of such irritation. She only said, "Yes."

The woman was clearly well-off, wearing a blue robe, her hair intricately braided. Fasiq suspected that she might in fact be a senator. Regular women, even with money, didn't generally go in for hairstyles this complex. Still, best not to make assumptions. She waited to hear what the woman had to say.

Directly, firmly, the woman asked, "Are you in need of employment?"

"I suppose that depends," Fasiq said carefully.

"On?"

"What sort of employment you're offering." If it was legitimate, Fasiq owed the Bandit God an immense sacrifice. If it wasn't, well, that was all right too. Legitimacy was optional. Given her background, illegitimacy might be even better.

"Of course," said the Paximite woman, her chin pointing down. Fasiq thought perhaps she was looking at the giant's feet, inspecting her sandals. For what reason, Fasiq couldn't fathom. The woman—senator, maybe, but maybe not—went on. "I wouldn't expect you to accept my offer before you know what that offer entails. Shall we discuss it in private?"

"All respect," Fasiq said, looking down at the neat part dividing the woman's intricately braided hair, "I don't go anywhere in private with people I don't know. And I don't know you. But I'm happy to discuss your offer here."

The other woman lifted her chin and looked Fasiq directly in the face. Her eyes were intelligent, her attitude just shy of confrontational. She hadn't been looking down out of fear, that much seemed obvious now. If anything, her gaze was a little too unflinching.

Fasiq refused to be the one to look away.

The other woman apparently came to a decision. The expression on her face softened, though there was still an intensity there. "A compromise," she offered.

"I'm listening."

"Let us walk and talk. Out to the aqueduct, if you agree? Not much company there in this weather, but public enough."

It was a smart compromise, but Fasiq just had to test her a bit more before she agreed. "And if I don't like what I hear, I can pick you up and toss you in."

The Paximite woman in the blue robe passed the test with flying colors. Not a jot of fear showed on her face; she didn't even flinch.

"Perfect," she replied. "That's just the type of thing I might be interested in hiring you for."

Fasiq grinned. "Lead on."

✦ CHAPTER 32 ✦

A Weapon

Adaj and Daybreak Palace, Arca
Aster, Eminel

When the day came, Aster wasn't ready, but Aster wasn't sure they would ever be ready. Rahul woke them with no warning in what felt like the middle of the night.

"Get up," he said. "It's time."

"Time for what?"

"We're traveling. To see the queen."

Aster stretched, pretending to come awake slowly, though the sudden shock had brought them to full alertness despite the odd hour. "Just to see her?"

"You know what I mean," Rahul said, his voice a growl. He seemed to be holding himself back from speaking too loudly, though there was certainly no one around to hear. "This is the day."

Aster dipped gently into Rahul's mind, just a bit, and the thought sat there, ripe for the plucking: *We're going to kill her.*

When Aster didn't respond to what he'd said, Rahul prodded, saying, "I've got your pack ready. You don't need to do anything else.

Just get dressed and come outside. We'll walk to Odimisk to join the cart along its route."

They felt a kind of excitement. Even though what was about to happen was awful, Aster realized with a sick feeling. This assassination attempt was doomed to fail, and afterward, Rahul and Aster would not likely survive. At least they'd left behind those relentless months of testing Aster's powers over and over, and after those, the months of hiding the truth of what they'd discovered they could do. Something new, even if terrible, was happening.

For all that, the wagon ride was still miserable, Rahul making Aster repeat the plan over and over, talking through every last detail. Aster didn't see how the plan could possibly work. They wondered if Rahul had once been brilliant, as powerful as he thought himself, though he sounded completely mad from Aster's vantage. Did he really think killing the queen would make him king? Even if they succeeded, which they wouldn't?

He seemed to think the queen was just a puppet, a weak figurehead who ruled mostly by luck and misplaced trust. Aster knew nothing of the queen, but they'd seen their mother, Stellari, in action for years. Aster knew that women in charge didn't get or stay that way without intelligence and relentlessness. As baffling and distant as Stellari had been, Aster knew she'd worked hard for her power. There was something to admire in that. All told, though, neither Stellari nor Rahul made a great role model. Aster would have to make their own way.

If they survived to do so.

At the end of the long cart ride, the first sight of Daybreak Palace took Aster's breath away.

They'd never seen anything like it. From far away, they first saw the sandstone cliff with its golden hue, as if the desert itself had risen up into a flat wave and frozen there forever. As the wagon got closer and closer to the palace, the stunning details came clear. The shad-

owed entryway. The uprising spires. Something so sharp and danger-
ous about it all, sending a deep chill through Aster's blood, but also in
some way unutterably beautiful.

Then they were inside.

✦

When Ingini announced, "Yulia, from Chorine," Eminel's first thought
was to send her away. A minor courtier, an unimportant matriclan.
Still, supplication days were meant for any courtiers, so she decided
to hear the woman out.

She was surprised, though, when the woman didn't enter alone. Instead, an unfamiliar child trailed her, wearing unremarkable clothes.
Yulia's eyes flicked up and down, and when they settled on Eminel's face
for a moment, she saw that the courtier's gaze was intelligent, piercing.
The child's eyes were fixed to the floor.

"Yulia," Eminel said. "I didn't realize you'd bring a friend."

"Pardon my intrusion," Yulia said.

There was something wrong with Yulia's voice. That was the first
sign. She looked exactly like Eminel remembered her, but she didn't
sound like herself. She wasn't unusually awkward; if anything, she
sounded too confident. Too comfortable. What in Velja's name was
going on?

"No pardon is needed," Eminel said graciously. "Unless that's
what you're here to ask for."

"Not exactly, honored Queen."

"Something like a pardon? Or some other request?"

As she watched Yulia wring her hands together, Eminel racked
her brain for facts about the woman. She was nearly a cipher. The
only thing Eminel really remembered about her was that she was one
of the few whose husband had been around for more than a decade.
When the previous queen, Mirri, had discovered a conspiracy among

the courtiers' husbands, she'd killed the guilty, one after another, smiting the men's heads from their shoulders with blasts of fierce magic. Apparently Yulia's husband hadn't been part of the conspiracy. Or at least Queen Mirri hadn't known he was, which wasn't the same thing.

Yulia had opened her mouth to answer but had not yet spoken when a loud voice called from behind them all.

"Queen!" came a call from the doorway, Ingini's voice ringing out again, a sudden interruption.

Eminel said to her Queensguard, feigning patience, "As you can see, I have just begun a discussion with the last visitors you brought me. Why interrupt?"

The guard was chagrined, but charged ahead. "Sobek insists on speaking with you."

"Sobek!" exclaimed Eminel. "Can't it wait?"

"She says it can't. Please. An emergency, she says."

At this interruption, Yulia's face creased. The expression was gone a moment later, but Eminel had caught it before it disappeared. Something about the suggestion of Sobek made Yulia uncomfortable. Or was it the idea of any interruption at all? She knew the best way to find out. She gestured to Ingini to let Sobek in.

Sobek looked as she always did, matronly and comforting. Eminel quickly shielded her mind against Sobek's magic, knowing that without protection, Sobek's persuasive powers would quickly cause Eminel to agree to anything Sobek said. Eminel had made that mistake years ago, but never since.

"Sobek!" she greeted the intruding courtier with showy pleasure. "Please, explain what you have to say that absolutely cannot wait."

Sobek looked past Eminel's shoulder to the others in the room: Yulia and the shy youngster, who still had not made a sound. She said only two words. "The child."

"What about the child?" asked Eminel, but just as quickly, she knew.

There was only one kind of child Sobek had ever been interested in. The kind that queens had sent Seekers for years and years to find. The kind Sobek had brought back to Daybreak Palace and trained, sent into trials to test their limits, let die when it suited the queen before Eminel. Drained of their power, until Eminel put a stop to it.

Sobek only ever cared about all-magic girls. If Sobek cared about this child, Eminel could draw only one conclusion.

"Child," Eminel said, using her most queenly voice, the imperious one that no one could disobey. "What is your name?"

The child looked utterly shocked to be noticed. In that oddly confident voice, Yulia interrupted before the child could speak. "She isn't important."

"Everyone is important to someone," said Eminel, chastising Yulia. The woman's confidence had become irritating. Eminel only found confidence attractive when it appeared side by side with humility. With this courtier, that was clearly not the case. Again, Eminel got the sense something was very wrong. "Child, I'll ask you again, what is your name?"

The child's eyes went to her companion, whose brow lowered, her message clear. The child ignored the message. "I'm called Aster."

"Aster, a lovely name," said Eminel. "Aster, could you come here, please?"

"She stays with me," interrupted Yulia.

Eminel reached gently into the child's mind. *You don't have to stay with her if you don't want to.*

The child didn't look surprised or upset to have her mind touched. And in half a moment, Eminel heard an answering voice, polite and clear, inside her own mind. *Thank you. I'm afraid of what he'll do if I come to you.*

He?

He's only pretending to be Yulia. His name is Rahul.

Eminel had heard that name. There'd been a persistent rumor, in the years since she'd taken power, that a man named Rahul was working to find a way to claim magic for all men. Whether or not this was the Rahul in question, it seemed clear he was up to no good.

Gently, the queen asked Aster, *Has he hurt you?*

No, came the answer. *But he wants to hurt you.*

Eminel felt a cold shiver down her spine. Her instinct had been right. This Yulia was not the real Yulia, and this man was clearly untrustworthy. Now the only question was whether the child was telling the truth. Well, that was easy enough to find out.

Sobek interrupted, "Queen Eminel. It's important that—"

Eminel hushed her. "I understand. I need to finish this audience first. Have patience."

Without releasing the veil that protected her mind from Sobek's charm—it wouldn't do to succumb to the other courtier's mind-control power in the middle of assessing this threat—Eminel quickly cast an enchantment for seeing through illusion. And just as the child said, the face and body that Eminel had perceived as Yulia belonged to a man with low brows and intense eyes, his body tense with coiled energy.

"So, Yulia," Queen Eminel said to the imposter, "let us turn our attention back to the purpose of this audience. You have not said, so I will ask. Tell me why you are here."

"Honored Queen Eminel, I want you to bless me," the man said, in that voice imperfectly Yulia's, attempting now to give it a note of respect and warmth. "I want to kneel at your feet and have you lay hands on my head. I have a sickness that needs healing. Please. Only you can help me."

Eminel asked the child, *Should I do it? What does he plan?*

Once you're not paying attention to me, he wants me to grab your life force and not let go. To hold you still. That's all he asked me to do. The child's words came into Eminel's mind smoothly, softly. Power behind them, shimmering.

Ah. I can figure out the rest from there, thank you.

To the man disguised as Yulia, Eminel said, "Come."

He came.

"Kneel."

He knelt.

Eminel placed her hands on Rahul's head. Just as the child had predicted, he gave a quick signal. But instead of the child attempting to hold her still, Eminel used her power to hold the man still. He didn't stand a chance.

She stripped him of his power, peeling the illusion off like the skin of an orange, until anyone in the room could see a man kneeling there instead of the courtier Yulia. Sobek gasped aloud.

"Guards," called Eminel in a voice loud enough to bring the rest of the Queensguard running to stand behind Ingini. Casually, she continued, "Please come take this man away. Hold him in chains downstairs. And perhaps we will send him to the Fingernail. I will consider his fate."

Eminel knew that if Rahul could talk, he would be screaming, but her hold on him was complete. She nodded to the Queensguard, and two stepped up to take him by the arms, pulling him backward so only his heels dragged across the ground. In moments, they were gone. Seeing him hauled away by the Queensguard felt almost cruel. He was so overmatched. Still, she had no regrets about the decision.

She turned her mind to a more important question: What would happen to the child?

"Aster," she said, "come sit with me."

With a calm that surprised Eminel, Aster walked to the chair that a servant pulled out, and took a seat. Aster was smaller than Eminel by two handspans, and looked to be about seven years younger, maybe eight. Born right in the middle of the Drought, then. Aster's confidence, Eminel decided, was the kind she liked. Not outsize, not outrageous, just simply there.

The queen said, "Thank you for telling me."

"His plan wasn't going to work. I would've been a fool not to."

"I preferred to think you told me because it was the right thing to do and you didn't want to see me die," Eminel said dryly, "but if you only confessed because it was a bad plan, so be it."

"That too," said Aster, one corner of their mouth just beginning to turn up. They sobered again quickly. "About not wanting to see you die. I couldn't have followed through, helping to kill you. You did nothing to deserve it."

"Others may disagree," Eminel said dryly. "But thank you. Whatever your reasons, you did the right thing. Now we just need to decide what to do with you."

"You don't need to do anything with me," the child hastened to say. "I can . . . just go."

"Can you? Go where?"

There was no immediate answer. Eminel took this as a sign that she had probably been right. If this man had been the only influential adult in the child's life, the child was going to need a guardian. And if the child were all-magic, the choice of guardian mattered very much.

"You're how old? Ten years?"

The child nodded solemnly.

"And he called you she. Twice."

"He did." There was no particular emotion in the matter-of-fact response. This in itself spoke volumes.

Eminel chose her next words carefully. She neither wanted to scare the child nor reveal to her court the enormity of what was at stake.

Casually, Eminel said to Sobek, "Could you leave us, please?"

Sobek protested, "But if she—"

"No," said Eminel. "Thank you for your service. You have my gratitude. I will take it from here."

She could feel Sobek's power prodding at her mind. That was clumsy, but apparently the woman was desperate. But Eminel was plenty powerful enough to resist.

The queen used only her words when she said to the courtier, "Sobek. No. Leave now."

Once the courtier was gone and only the queen and child remained, Eminel sat on the floor near the child's chair. It was largely impossible for a queen not to be intimidating—this was still her palace, her throne room, her snake necklace—but she would do what she could.

Eminel said in a quiet voice, "Aster, that would make you a girl born during the Drought of Girls. The only one I've ever heard of, someone no one knew existed. It's . . . unusual."

"Not just a girl," muttered Aster.

She wasn't sure what the child meant by that, so she simply repeated the words, turning them into a gentle question. "Not just a girl?"

"I feel . . . I mean . . ." The child seemed more unsure now, but pressed on. In a firmer voice, Aster said, "I'm . . . both."

Now Eminel understood. It was clear enough. "You're both male and female. Two-fold."

The child nodded. "In Paxim they called people like me two-fold. In Arca . . . it sounds like they don't have people like me here."

Eminel leaned forward. "People like you are everywhere. I mean, in that sense. In another sense, there's no one exactly like you anywhere in the world."

A soft noise escaped Aster. Eminel wasn't sure whether it was surprise or relief, or perhaps a little of both. She stayed on the ground, looking up, and asked, "The man who brought you here. He sired you?"

"He said so," answered Aster dismissively.

"Well, one never knows, I suppose. You do resemble him, though, around the eyes. I just wondered what his relationship was to you."

"I had two parents," said Aster. "But we left my mother back in Paxim."

"Does she know where you are?"

Something in the child's face darkened, just a little. Not anger. Something more subtle and complex. "I doubt it. And I doubt she cares."

"If you want, we can find a way to contact her."

"No, thank you," said Aster firmly.

Eminel seemed a little surprised at that, but continued on. "I must admit, I'm a bit confused. I've never heard even a rumor of a girl born during the Drought. Why didn't anyone know about you?"

"He disguised me. As a boy. All those years we lived in Paxim. We came to Arca several years ago."

Eminel was still not quite sure she understood. "Disguised you? Like with clothes?"

"With magic."

"Oh." Now things were starting to come clear. "So he had strong illusion magic, more than men usually have."

"Yes, I suppose so."

"And he brought you to Arca why?"

"To discover my gifts. And once he discovered them, to use them for his ends."

"To kill me," Eminel said.

"Yes."

"But, Velja be praised, he didn't succeed."

"No."

Eminel's voice was as gentle as she could make it. "So what do we do now?"

The child met her gaze with sad eyes and responded, "I have no idea."

Eminel came up to her knees and took the child's hands. "Well. We don't need to make any major decisions today. You can stay with us a while. While we both think about the right next step to take."

The child nodded wordlessly.

She could have left it there, Eminel knew, but there was just too much. No one needed to know just yet, but this child's world had been blown apart. Protecting Aster had to be the priority. Yet—if the child had all-magic, like Sobek said, then they might also need to be protected from themselves.

"One more thing," Eminel said. "Your magic."

"Yes."

"What else can you do? Hold life force, read and speak into minds, anything else?"

"Yes." Aster looked down, obviously uncomfortable.

"Yes, and?" prodded Eminel. "Other mind magic, or other things entirely? Fire, water, air?"

"Yes," Aster said again. "All of that."

"All-magic."

"Yes."

"Do you know what that means?"

The child's eyes got even sadder. "That I could be powerful."

"You could."

"But I don't want to be powerful. I prayed to Velja that I wouldn't have magic, and She gave me this power instead."

"Yes," said Eminel dryly. "That sounds like something She would do."

Aster stared down at their hands, their small and nimble fingers, as if contemplating their power. "Rahul only wanted to use me as a weapon. That's why I didn't want the magic. I just wanted to be left alone. But I never will now, will I?"

"I don't know," Eminel said. She wouldn't dress it up. She believed in the truth, and she remembered what had happened to her as a child, how her power had been hidden from her and denied. How she and her mother had never really had the chance to know each other because one of them was too busy keeping secrets.

Aster said in a smaller voice, "But sometimes, I've started to like it. The power. How it feels. I just worry about losing control. Like my power has me and not the other way around."

Eminel remembered her earliest days with Sessadon, that same fear mixed with longing. How easily she could have gotten drunk on power and forgotten her humanity, as her mentor had.

"You can learn control," Eminel told the child. "You just need someone to learn from."

Aster looked at her.

Eminel found herself overwhelmed by an unexpected burst of joy. She almost blurted out, *I can teach you*, but decided she needed to hold herself back just a bit, for now.

"We'll talk soon, Aster," she told the child, settling back on her heels.

Aster nodded.

Eminel already knew, though, what she would do. As clearly as if Velja were still speaking to her in words, she knew the god's will.

This child needed guidance. Their path to each other had been winding, but they were matched now, each in need of the other.

Could any hand but Velja's have steered them?

✦ CHAPTER 33 ✦

DELIVERED

Spring, the All-Mother's Year 520
Scorpica
Gretti, Amankha

Three seasons after she visited the Sign of the Grape, Gretti's hair had grown almost all the way to her shoulders, and she loved the feel of it brushing her skin. It was a shame, she thought, that she'd have to be shorn again after giving birth. But that was the way in Scorpica. To wear one's hair long while the child grew, and then once she or he was born, either share a warrior with the rest of the nation, or give an extraneous child away.

Gretti mostly hunted alone these days. She wanted to spend time with Amankha, but she also knew that she was an unwelcome reminder of the days before. Of wartime. As much as she had protested, she was still the architect of the war. She had still been there when it happened. Amankha hadn't. So when the queen made diplomatic journeys to the Bastion, for example, Gretti had chosen not to accompany her. Gretti's counsel could and did go with Amankha, but not her physical form.

And how her physical form had changed these past few months. Had it been like this the first time, all those years ago? She barely remembered that first pregnancy, her body swelling and changing and then returning as if there had never been a child at all. But this time, she noticed every change, and she savored each one. Even her eyelashes changed, growing thick. Some warriors had difficult pregnancies, vomiting and suffering, but Gretti felt blessed by the changes in her. The only thing that made her pause was to remember that at the end of it, all this work might be for nothing. She might grow a child within her for three seasons, scream and howl in pain as birth overtook her, then have nothing more to remember the child than a single kiss on the head before surrendering him to some other queendom forever.

It was hot for hunting, and among the many changes in Gretti's heavier, pregnant body was a near-constant feeling of being overheated. Sweat ran in tracks everywhere—between her shoulder blades, down her temples, in the small of her back. It wasn't entirely an unpleasant feeling. She was out in the wild exerting herself. She was working hard. Her body was making life in the background while she was doing exactly what she chose to do. There was nothing to be sad about, if she kept her focus on the present moment.

She heard a crash in the underbrush, and immediately all her senses were on high alert. It sounded large—a boar, perhaps? No one had brought in a boar yet this season; it was a bit early for them, but this might be a rogue. There was a small stream in the direction the sound had come from. A perfect place to catch an animal unaware.

Gretti's feet made no sound as she neared.

Through the brush she could see almost nothing, just a pale blur of movement. Then the movement halted. Was the animal still there, next to the water? Faint sounds, a kind of mewling, perhaps. She couldn't pin down what kind of animal it might be. A boar would likely be louder, a darker presence, but whatever was there blended into the rushing water of the stream. Still, even though the sound was faint, it gave her something to aim for.

Just as she was about to release her arrow, in the same moment she let fly, she heard an arrow whistle past her own ear. Her fingers spasmed in surprise, her arrow going wide.

"Scorpion's tits!" shouted a voice from the direction she'd aimed.

First, Gretti flung herself to the ground, making sure that if another arrow came at the same angle, she wouldn't be there to meet it. She landed hard on her stomach and cursed her own foolishness. She'd moved by instinct. Apparently her instinct had forgotten about her swollen belly. She'd heard from other women that the body automatically protected the child-to-be, but hers didn't. There was no pain, not yet, but a twist of worry worked its way down her throat and into her belly as she took the measure of her situation.

Then she looked up to see who had spoken. The smear of movement hung in her vision off to the left.

"Gretti," said a voice from that exact direction, and the twist of worry wrung tighter. Not an animal, then. Her blood ran cold.

Struggling, Gretti moved up to her knees, then peered through the brush between them. She couldn't see who spoke, but the voice was familiar, when she thought long enough to try to place it. Hesitantly, she said, "Azur?"

"No harm meant," came the other woman's voice, tight somehow.

There was no satisfaction in guessing right. When Gretti stood, what she saw made her sicker than she would have imagined.

At the edge of the stream hunched the small form of Madazur, trailing her dainty fingers through the moving water. Hers was the shape Gretti had seen, the shape at which Gretti had aimed. The arrow was nowhere to be seen, but Gretti couldn't have missed her by much.

Behind the girl, her body mostly obscured by a large rock, stood her mother, Azur.

Gretti closed the space between them in long strides, outraged. "What in the Underlands are you doing here?"

Azur's eyes narrowed, but her face was flushed, and Gretti knew instantly that the First Mother was more afraid than outraged. "We go where we like! She wanted to follow the stream, so we . . ."

"*She* wanted? She's a child! You're not! You should have known better!" To prevent hunting accidents, only one party at a time was allowed to hunt in certain sections of the woods; today, this section had been Gretti's. To find other Scorpicae here was a grave misstep, no matter who they were.

"Well," Azur said, her voice locked tight, "you have certainly taught me a lesson."

"Thank the Scorpion things are as they are." That was as close as Gretti could come to saying what had almost happened. She couldn't imagine what would have come to pass if she'd accidentally slain the precious child. Her heart fluttered in her chest, unsteady.

"Thank the Scorpion," echoed Azur.

Gretti had trouble catching her breath, which she chalked up to shock, until the pain came.

The pain wasn't a stab or a squeeze, but some other kind of slithering feeling, a rolling wave that seemed to spread in all directions at once.

Her face must have shown the pain, because Azur said, "Are you all right?"

Gretti shot her a look, but didn't answer with words. Mostly, she wasn't sure what the answer should be. She was all right for the moment, yes, but she had a sinking feeling she was about to be much, much worse off, with absolutely nothing she could do about it.

Gretti told the First Mother, "We should go back to camp."

"We should."

Neither moved, until Gretti realized that Azur didn't seem to know which direction to walk in. That was what had happened, then, why the First Mother had stumbled into something else's hunting ground; following her daughter, she'd gotten lost. Of course she wouldn't admit her error. The polite thing to do would be not to call attention to it.

"Lost your way, then?" Gretti said to Azur.

There was a long moment when the First Mother ignored what Gretti had said, staring back at the boulder she'd been hiding behind as if it were the most fascinating thing she'd ever seen.

Then the next pain came, and Gretti fell to her knees. The sinking feeling returned, swamped her. Unlike Azur, she knew exactly where they were, and she knew it was a full hour's walk back to camp at regular speed. She also knew enough about childbirth to know that walking made the child come faster. She might make it, Scorpion willing. But she might not.

Azur's brow creased in worry. She took a step toward Gretti but didn't touch her. Then she glanced back toward her daughter, still hunched on the bank of the stream, singing a tuneless song. Azur said quietly, under her breath, "Is it time?"

"It may be."

"Have you—did you—before?"

"Such a long time ago," Gretti said, feeling her chest tighten. "I don't even remember what it was like."

"No matter. It's not just different for everyone; it's different for the same woman each time. Or so I've been told. I can help get you back to camp. Let's go."

For a moment, it seemed possible. Gretti took a fifth step, a sixth, before she felt a pain scurry like a lizard from one hip to the other. The very idea of walking became ridiculous. To the First Mother, she said calmly, "You go. I'm not going to make it."

"I'm no midwife," said Azur. "I'll go, send someone back to . . ."

"No, stay!" shouted Gretti. She hadn't meant to shout.

Azur gave her an appraising stare, one Gretti squirmed under. It made her want to try. But pushing through was foolish. They'd only make it partway. At least here they had soft moss, and water. It wasn't the worst place to welcome a new warrior, if that was what was going to happen today.

Her thoughts diving to a melancholy place, Gretti thought that if she were going to release her own life instead of welcoming a new one, this wasn't such a bad place to do that, either. The late afternoon light slanted in through gaps in the leafy trees. It was such a Scorpican place, she thought. A thousand times in the deep red sands of Godsbones, she'd pictured the homeland she'd longed for. She had imagined something exactly like this. And now either she would die here, or welcome her child here, or both.

"How much do you remember? From bearing her?" asked Gretti.

Azur looked panicked. She glanced over at Madazur again, then took a deep breath. "I don't think it matters. I think you do what your body wants to do."

"You can leave me alone if you want. If you think there's nothing you can do to help. You can take your daughter home, instead."

Azur shook her head, no hesitation. "I will remain. If you need anything at all, I can at least be better than no one."

"Promise?" said Gretti through a slanted smile. It was morbid humor, but there was no other humor she could muster at the moment. She had gotten herself into a terrible situation. She'd almost killed this woman's child, and now she'd put herself completely at the First Mother's mercy. Did the First Mother even have mercy? That hadn't been her reputation, back in the Godsbones days.

But people could change, Gretti told herself. Azur had been nothing but diligent since returning to Scorpica. She had served on assignment in the Bastion, just as Amankha had asked. She had been an attentive, seemingly loving mother to Madazur. As Azur had proposed, having her here would be better than no one at all, with labor coming on like a hard-charging boar.

But labor came and went, sometimes with pains close together, sometimes with waits so long between that Gretti was tempted to get up and try again for the camp. As the sun was setting, she said to Azur, "You were right. We should have gone. I'm sorry. You can still go."

Azur looked up at the dimming sky and shook her head. "No. I'll stay."

She insisted Gretti move farther upstream, where a bend formed a bit of natural shelter, and busied Madazur pulling handfuls of moss to build Gretti something like a bed to lie on. Gretti hunched and rose, bent and straightened, leaned and crouched, but she was afraid that if she lay down, she might never rise again. So she smiled at the girl, thanked her, but stayed far away from the growing heap of moss.

More hours passed. They lit torches against the dark. The girl slept. From time to time, the pains woke Gretti. Every time she cried out in pain and opened her eyes, she saw Azur hunching beside her.

"You should sleep," she told the First Mother.

"*You* should," was Azur's only answer.

How long did it go on? Gretti had no idea. She only knew that when the pains started coming close together without pause, the sky had not yet lightened. Madazur was still sleeping. Azur was still wide awake.

When the child arrived at last, once Gretti's sob of pain subsided, there was silence.

Azur said nothing. The baby didn't seem to be making any noise. Gretti didn't want to ask, she didn't want to know, but she heard her voice asking breathlessly, "The baby?"

Tenderly the First Mother turned the baby's face toward the new mother, and Gretti saw in the torchlight that the child's chest was rising and falling. Then and only then, after Gretti felt the rush of relief that she'd given birth to a living child, the baby gave its first thin cry.

"Thank the Scorpion," said Gretti.

"No thanks for me?" answered Azur, but her voice was light, playful.

Gretti, voice thin with both emotion and exhaustion, said, "I'm glad you were here."

Azur said nothing to respond to that, and busied herself with an action Gretti couldn't quite follow. Gretti forced her head up a little so she could see. Azur was wrapping the child in some kind of fabric, protecting its tender new body from the night air's chill.

Then Azur said, "Perhaps you may not want to thank me. Since I don't want any of the blame."

"I—why not?"

Azur's voice had gone cool, but her hands were still gentle as she laid the red-faced baby on Gretti's chest. The fabric covered the baby from foot to shoulders, only the head, slicked with wet black hair, standing out. "I'm sorry. Not a warrior."

Gretti looked down at her child. Her son.

She thought she would feel disappointment, but nothing like that came to her. She was grateful. She was exhausted. But she was not disappointed, and she was not sorry.

Azur said, "If you don't want to hold him, I can take him."

It felt nearly impossible to raise her hand, but at the same time, Gretti knew the movement was essential. She curled her palm protectively over the tiny back. "No."

No more disagreement from Azur. For a long moment Gretti kept her exhausted eyes on the sky. Still black, still lightless except for half a moon and a scattering of far-off stars. Wisps of cloud blocked the rest. They'd have to return to camp, somehow. Or Azur could go and send someone back for her, but Gretti didn't want to be carried like an invalid. She would rest until she could walk under her own power. She would reenter the camp on her own two feet.

It seemed unbelievable, how things had just changed. As if the sky itself had canted sideways. She'd had no idea when she'd left the camp to hunt that she'd come back with a son in her arms. But she knew how things went. The strange circumstances were entirely beside the point. Whenever and wherever they were born, boys had no place in Scorpica.

"The baby!" piped a delighted, high voice. Little Madazur had awoken, and here she was, eyes shining like polished coins in the darkness.

"Yes," said her mother. "The baby was born."

It seemed so inadequate to Gretti, that one word, *born*, so short and simple for a process that was anything but.

Madazur hummed a tune under her breath. Gretti recognized it instantly. She picked it up and sang, in a hush, to her son.

When the warrior has brought in the victory
Climbed the road home so rocky and steep
When a girl helps a girl helps a girl
Peace be upon the land, and sleep.

"Girl?" asked Madazur.

"Not a girl," her mother answered.

The child said, "Baby," and began humming the tune again. Then she asked, "What's his name?"

Gretti didn't know what to say. She'd sung the song without thinking of the line about *girl helps a girl*. It was the only lullaby she knew. And now Madazur was asking a question for which there was no answer that Gretti could give, according to tradition.

"Boys in Scorpica don't usually get names," Azur told her daughter, patience in her voice. "They don't stay. They go to live in other queendoms."

Gretti thought the child would ask why, but she didn't. She seemed to accept her mother's explanation as all there was to say.

Instead she pointed and said, "What's that?"

The new mother followed where the child's finger pointed. It was the cord that tied mother to child. Gretti hadn't been thinking about the fact that the two of them were still linked. The moment she'd realized she had a son, she should have been thinking about how quickly she'd be giving him away. But it hadn't occurred to her. They were still linked, still almost one. And she couldn't get Madazur's question out of her head now. What was his name? What should she call him? It felt urgent that she decide.

But then Azur, unaware of the turmoil inside the new mother's head, spoke to Gretti instead of answering her daughter's question. "I don't have a birthing blade. But I have this." She unsheathed her dagger and showed it to Gretti. With a sick lurch, Gretti recognized it. It was a bone-handled dagger, one Gretti had last seen in the hand of Tamura dha Mada and would never forget.

The blade had been Mada's, first. Tamura had brought it with her when she returned from the Fingernail, the day she Challenged Khara for the queendom and won. Tamura had not dealt the fatal blow with the dagger—she had killed Khara with the edge of a shield, brutally, finally—but it had been hers, and seeing it now put a feeling in Gretti's chest like burning.

"Are you listening?" said Azur in a tone that made Gretti realize she had been repeating herself.

Gretti forced herself to say, "Yes."

"Then let me sever the cord. It needs to be done."

"No," bit out Gretti.

"It does."

Gretti said, "But not by you. Give me the blade."

Confusion creased Azur's brow, but as Gretti met her gaze steadily, it cleared.

"I'll set it here for you," said Azur, and laid it near Gretti's hand. Some warriors claimed that handing someone a blade severed the friendship between those two warriors; Azur and Gretti didn't exactly have a friendship to sever, but Gretti appreciated that Azur respected the tradition.

"You're more Scorpican than most warriors born here," said Gretti. She was a little dizzy from the strain of the birth. She'd meant to think it, not say it.

"Thank you," Azur answered. "I'm honored."

Gretti picked up the blade.

Azur backed up three steps and gathered her child into her lap. Not to protect her from Gretti, not for any other reason the new mother could see. Madazur turned and nuzzled against her mother's shoulder; Azur's hand went up to cup the back of the girl's head.

"You love your child," Gretti said.

Azur looked up, startled. "Of course I do."

"Did you, at first?"

The two stared at each other, the scent of blood in the air. The first light of dawn began to warm the sky. Gretti's son, still bound to her, squirmed on her chest. The toddler's eyes were bright.

Gretti said, "Never mind. Forget I asked."

Azur gave her a firm nod, their eyes meeting. It was a complex, silent response. Not an answer, but an acknowledgment. Gretti had accurately seen, back then, an ambivalence in the First Mother. Gretti wondered what Azur saw, looking at her now. But it wasn't something she wanted to discuss. The night had been long. The day to come would be longer. And after that, there was more life to live, for both of them. And if Gretti made the choice she wanted to make, their lives were about to diverge.

Azur said, "Are you sure you won't accept help?"

"I've accepted plenty already."

"I suppose you did. I don't know if you're glad I was here, but . . . I am."

The new mother pushed herself up to a sitting position. The day was coming on fast now, the sky turning pale near the horizon, though she still needed the torchlight to do her work. She dipped her hands in the cup of water that Madazur had brought her from the stream. She would have to get closer to the stream to wash her whole self and the baby soon enough, but for now, she only needed her hands clean. Once they were, she shook them dry and picked up the bone-handled dagger. She used it to cut two strings of equal length from the end of her tunic lacing. She tied the first one at the boy's navel, the other farther up the cord. A wave of weakness crashed over her, but she fought it off. She would do this herself.

Scorpican warriors had no sons. If they gave birth to boys, the boys might become Paximites, or Bastionites, or Sestians, or Arcans. But they were never men of Scorpica. There was no such thing.

She laid the boy, squalling with a thin cry, across her thighs. "Still," she said, and as if he understood, he quieted. His eyes were open, unfocused, staring into the early morning gray. Gretti realized she was cold now and shivered. She hadn't noticed the temperature for hours. But she was coming back to herself now. She let herself shiver once more, then steadied her hands.

Gretti could feel Azur watching her. Her mind raced. She shook off another shiver and began to cut through the cord. Even as sharp as the blade was, the cord was tough, and it took a while to yield. Blood spilled between them. They had been one. Now they would be two. And because one of them could never be a Scorpican, thought Gretti, perhaps neither of them should be.

The blade broke through.

When the two ends of the severed cord fell away, Gretti realized a much greater severing had taken place. Not her from her son, but her from her homeland.

She could be a Scorpican warrior or she could be this boy's

mother. *Veld*, she decided to call him. An old word that meant forest. He'd been born in the forest, would belong to this place forever in some way. But he would never lay eyes on this patch of Scorpican forest again. And neither would she.

It was clearer than anything in her life had ever been. She had to choose between the two. She made her choice.

◆

When Amankha returned from her latest trip to the Bastion, the camp felt unsettled. Even in the short time it took her to ride into the camp, release her pony into the paddock, and walk between the tents for a few short minutes, she felt it. Then she took a moment to decide to ask someone about it, and who to ask. It would be absurd for the queen to simply guess at things.

So she found Azur, who was cleaning weapons at the smith's tents, and asked her without preamble, "What is going on?"

"One of your warriors is gone. I'm sorry."

Her face was so grave that Amankha couldn't help asking. Better to know than not know. "Dead?"

"No," Azur said, glancing over her shoulder. Zalma, the smith, had heard them speaking and began to draw near. Amankha saw Azur tense. She thought they had been allies once, but the tension between the two was thick and obvious. It had been surprising to find Azur this close to the smith in the first place, but Amankha supposed the chance to touch so many weapons had drawn her, even if she wouldn't be able to use them in the way she had once preferred.

Zalma said, "Are you telling her about the traitor?"

"Traitor?" asked Amankha, now even more curious—and worried— than she had been.

"Everyone has her opinion," said Azur, which Amankha thought might have been the most diplomatic thing she'd ever heard the First

Mother say. What it sounded like she was really saying, to the queen, was that Azur did not agree with Zalma.

Zalma spat in the dirt. "Your councillor. Don't know why you trusted her. She turned on the previous queen, now she's turned on you."

There was only one councillor Amankha could think of who Zalma would have described that way. She looked to Azur for an explanation.

Azur, her face sober, said, "Gretti gave birth while you were gone. To a boy. Rather than give him up, she left."

Had she been alone, Amankha would have responded with sadness, but as it was, she saw the need to keep her reaction to herself. "Thank you for telling me. I would have looked for her. Do we know where she went?"

Zalma said, "Who cares? Buried in a Sestian pile of sheep shit, for all we know."

Again, Amankha looked to Azur.

The First Mother said, "We don't know, no. She didn't say. Only that she was leaving, and she was sorry she couldn't stay long enough for you to return. She regrets no longer being able to stand by your side."

"I regret it too," said Amankha. She would mourn privately, but she could at least acknowledge the loss, whoever was looking on.

Zalma said, "I regret I didn't get to swing my hammer straight into her face."

"*Zalma,*" responded the queen, her tone a growl. She didn't look at the smith, but her hand rested on the hilt of her sword.

The smith shrugged. "Warriors who desert get what's coming."

"She served Scorpica for decades. She earned her rest." She raised her eyes to glare at Zalma.

The smith looked unrepentant. "True warriors never rest. She's a traitor. You won't hear me ever say different. And there's plenty who agree with me."

"Your opinion has been heard," said Amankha. "Now I need to speak with my council."

Zalma, who had not been asked to join the council, got the message. Shooting a cold look at Azur, she turned and stalked off.

Once the two of them were alone again, Azur said quietly, "Do you want me to call the council?"

"Yes, but for midday," said Amankha. "I need some time."

Azur said, "As you wish, my queen."

"And thank you. For the news."

Azur nodded. Then, looking around to make sure no one was watching, she passed a small folded note into Amankha's hand.

Carefully, Amankha opened it. Gretti had drawn the two dogwoods, one high and broad, the other young and narrow. She suppressed a smile. Elm still guarded the cottage and carried messages back and forth from Vish; Gretti knew it was a safe place. Had Amankha been here when Gretti decided to leave, she would have urged Gretti to go there with her son. Vish and Roksana were in the palace now, a strange turn of events, but it sounded like Roksana was still safe, and that was the only important thing. Now Gretti would have the cottage, and if Amankha needed to get her a message, she would know how. The long leagues from here to there were an obstacle, but not a barrier.

Relieved, Amankha was turning to go to her tent when Azur spoke a soft, single word that Amankha didn't quite catch.

"What was that?" the queen asked.

"Veld," said Azur, soft enough that only the two of them could hear. "That's Gretti's son's name. Veld. He was born strong. I was there. She'll be a good mother."

Amankha stepped closer to Azur and put her hand on the First

Mother's elbow. Her tone was tighter this time, more emotional, as she said again, "Thank you."

Azur nodded wordlessly.

Then Amankha went to her tent and lowered the flap behind her. She was happy for Gretti, proud of her, but sad for herself. She would mourn the loss of her councillor and friend. Amankha might never have become queen of Scorpica if not for Gretti. She owed her so much, and now that Gretti had left Scorpica, Amankha would never be able to repay her.

It wasn't until Amankha sat by herself in her tent, the evening shadows clustering around her, that she let herself really think about what it had taken for Gretti to leave her queendom. The older woman had never hinted at intending to leave if she bore a son. Amankha wondered if she had intended it all along or if she'd made the choice only after seeing her son's face.

As she lay down alone, Amankha couldn't help but think of how her own child had felt in her arms, in those first moments after birth. That faint wail, growing louder; those dark brown eyes, opening. She had been determined in her decision from the beginning, and it sounded like Gretti had been too, but they had made such different decisions.

There were so many paths a mother could choose, so many different ways to demonstrate her love, thought Amankha. It wasn't as simple as always holding a child close. What was the most important thing? Safety? Family? Honor? She could never have seen herself making the choice that Gretti had. Her mother's choice too had been so different from her own.

There were so many ways to be a mother. Had she chosen the right one?

PART V

THE

GATE OF

MONSTERS

The All-Mother's Year 521

✦ CHAPTER 34 ✦

MONSTERS

The Underlands

Eresh, Sessadon

In her centuries ruling the Underlands, Eresh had seen fools come and go—hundreds of them, thousands, hundreds of thousands—but it was hard to recall a dead woman as dogged as the sorcerer Sessadon.

Eresh knew, of course, that the Arcan's arrogance was legendary. But for all her arrogance, Sessadon did have tremendous power and savvy, and not just related to her magic. When Sessadon came to Eresh and proposed this idea of opening gates, the god had seen no risk in it. Let the ambitious, foolhardy Arcan try. If the sorcerer opened the gates, wonderful; if she failed, she would do no harm.

What Eresh had not counted on was Her own reaction. That partway along the journey of watching the sorcerer attempt to open the gates, the god had started to hope

Sessadon would succeed. She wouldn't break Her agreement with Her sisters to smooth the shade's way—but She watched, and wondered, and when the second and third gates opened, She knew.

Even though Her years here were endless, She could feel them passing with a keen new awareness as the sorcerer went on her quest. The god wanted those gates open, all five of them, because as foolish as Sessadon had been, when she'd put her proposal to the god, the sorcerer had also been entirely right.

It was unfair that Eresh ruled only this confined space, this land of the ineffective dead, while Her sisters could come and go as they pleased. It did Her no good to own dead souls, no matter how numerous, when Her sisters claimed all those Above. All those people living and fighting, seeking pleasures, singing and striving, making heroes of themselves. By the time humans became shades, the vast majority had already done the most interesting things they would ever do. All that was left was shapeless wandering, without stakes, without urgency. Only people Above changed history's course.

Eresh could recall a few exceptions, a handful of shades who managed to succeed in the Underlands in some way they'd never managed Aboveground. A century ago, one of the Sestian sacrifices, slain after ten-and-four years Above, somehow managed to gestate and birth a shade child, nurturing her on shade milk, watching her shade form grow. Two centuries before that, a pangender shade who'd always loved the high mountains that surrounded the Bastion had actually managed to transform the landscape of the Underlands themselves, creating a mountain where no mountain had been, halfway between the bone bridge and the Tree of Unknowing. But nearly every shade, whether they were women or men or neither or both, could pass centuries in the Underlands without strife.

And after all this time, all these years of sameness and limits and what was starting to feel a lot like captivity, Eresh had begun to think a little strife might be necessary.

The sisters hadn't created the gates, just like they hadn't created the Bastion; there were things in this world that defied even the understanding of gods. Privately, Eresh thought—for She'd had centuries to consider—that their mother had created the gates before She vanished. For what purpose, Eresh had no idea, and the All-Mother had not created the Voas who protected the gates. But for as long as Eresh could remember, even when the Underlands were still mid-creation as the three sisters carved up the world, the gates themselves had always been here.

Still, it had been at least a century since Eresh had bothered inspecting the fourth gate for Herself, so after She cast Sessadon to the farthest corner of the Underlands to test her mettle, She went.

The fourth gate was as unlike the others as they had been from each other. Not an arch of flowers, like the second gate, nor shaped stone, like the third. This one was a cave. A hole. Anyone who wished to pass through it needed to descend, which shouldn't seem like a challenge in a world that was already far below anywhere any living person had ever been, but Eresh still saw how it might give a cautious shade pause.

Sessadon was not a cautious shade, thought Eresh, but she would still be daunted by the fourth gate. There was certainly a chance she wouldn't succeed.

But Eresh couldn't help hoping she would.

◆

As she searched all over the Underlands for the fourth gate, Sessadon could feel disruption rippling through the entire land of the dead. It spread like ink in water, swirling and spreading until it was every-where. If she'd had a body, she would have shivered with the plea-sure of it; as it was, she savored every time she sensed that one more shade knew what she'd done, even if they didn't know she was the one who'd done it. She was making her mark. If she'd failed to do so in the way she wanted Above, she could at least revel in changing the Underlands, arguably something far fewer people had done. And of course, if she succeeded fully, the world Above would be forever changed as well. She delighted in that as much as she'd ever delighted in anything.

There were not nearly enough deaths Above to satisfy the need Below, of course, so there were hundreds, perhaps even thousands, of shades milling about near the open Gate of Heroes. Sessadon stayed attentive to the rumors of what was happening there. On occasion she even visited, and once saw a group of five shades in the form of girls in identical robes, who held hands and rushed the gate together. Improbably, when they passed under the gate they disappeared in unison. Five lives Above had become shades; five shades Below had the chance to live again. It was beautiful, in its way, thought Sessadon. She had never shown Velja proper veneration Above, she thought, but now, she realized that true power and joy, more than anything else in the world Above or Under, lay in sowing chaos.

Seeing the crush of shades waiting, some with hope and some without, at the third gate, Sessadon felt even more excited about opening the fourth gate. So many clamored to return Aboveground now. There were others, of course, who wouldn't bother, believing that existence in the Underlands, such as it was, was a better bargain. After all, everything Above was temporary.

All sorts of things could happen to a body. It was a bag of fragile guts barely encased in a thin outer layer, all of it decaying from the moment it was created, and it was a wonder any living body lasted as long as it did. If one had the choice, why not remain a shade, unfettered? But there were still those with ties Above who longed to reclaim bodily forms, even if they were unfamiliar forms in potentially unfamiliar lands. If Sessadon wanted to continue making her mark, she'd need to capitalize on that without shame or question.

And she wouldn't be able to do it alone. She resented Ellimi for rushing to inhabit a body during the opening of the second gate, but Sessadon never could have fought the second Voa without her; similarly, she recognized she would not have opened the third gate without Paulus. It was his willingness to sacrifice anything and everything for the form he perceived as his sister, Zofi, that had opened the third gate. Sessadon would never have done that on her own. Sacrifice was not in her nature.

She would find the fourth gate, and then she would decide whose help she needed to open it. There was no sense in choosing a partner for an unknown task.

The fourth gate was a cave, endlessly deep, terrifyingly deep. Less a cave than a chasm. And seated at its mouth was a Voa that looked like a man, skin bluish and waxen as if he'd been frozen solid, the look on his face an incongruous, unsettling half smile.

"My name is Volos," said the Voa in a rumbling, deep voice. "What do you seek?"

Sessadon said, "I wish to open the gate."

"You are not the first to try. But if you succeed," said Volos, "shades will live again."

"How?" she couldn't help asking.

Then Sessadon heard the very last thing she expected: a third voice.

"Because of me," the voice said. It sounded like a woman's, high in pitch, and very tired. It came from the darkness behind Volos, where no light reached.

Even as long as she'd been here, as much as she'd seen, it was hard for Sessadon to remember the world Below always offered more for her to attempt to understand.

On instinct, Sessadon asked gently, "And who are you?"

"I had a name once," mused the woman's voice. "I don't remember it anymore."

Sessadon wasn't sure how to respond to that, but she didn't have to. The lower voice of Volos spoke next.

"Unah was her name. She lived in the time before the queendoms, but she worshipped Velja, and she had powerful magic," the Voa rumbled. "Her talent was to double herself."

"Double yourself?" Sessadon asked, aiming her question in the direction of where she'd last heard the dead woman's voice.

"Yes." The voice still had an exhausted quality to it, but she spoke more loudly this time. "I was a magician and a warrior. Our leader wanted to be peaceful, but I was arrogant. I wanted to take over a neighboring tribe's territory. So I attacked."

Sessadon had never heard the story. She wondered why not. Then something occurred to her. "You said *you* attacked? Just you?"

"I made myself all the bodies I needed," said the woman's voice, a new pain in it. "Made myself into two, then four. Eight. Sixteen. When I was an army, I attacked."

Sessadon found herself leaning forward. If only she'd thought of this power when she was alive. She wondered if she could have done it. She had the feeling of her fingers itching, wanting to try.

Unah said, "And I defeated every member of the neighboring tribe. No matter how many of me they killed, I made more. They slaughtered me over and over, yet I stood. In the end, every woman, man, and child of their village was dead, and one of me remained standing."

"So you won."

"I returned to my tribe," said Unah. "And they were all dead."

"Spies? Another force? Who killed them?"

The disembodied voice said, quietly, "I did."

Sessadon would have asked how, but she knew the woman would tell her. Unah's story clearly burned in her. She wouldn't stop until it was all out.

SESTIA ✦ 421

"Every time I made a double of myself, I drew on them for life force. Every time I made a life, I took a life."

"But you could have—"

"I know," said Unah. "If I'd only thought of it, I could have focused my energy, drawn the life force from my enemies instead of my friends. But I was foolhardy. Blustered ahead. Kept the plan to myself because I didn't want anyone to tell me not to do it. And I killed everyone I ever loved. The neighboring tribe was dead, but so was mine. If I'd only been happy with what I had."

"I'm so sorry," murmured Sessadon.

As if she hadn't heard, the woman's voice went on. "I prayed to Velja and begged her to kill me. I wanted so badly to die. But instead of killing me, she changed my magic. I didn't realize at the time. I thought she'd only refused me."

Sessadon looked at the Voa to see his reaction to this heartbreaking story. His head was tilted, a fond look on his face, as he listened to the woman's voice from the darkness. Even without a body, Sessadon felt a shiver.

"Until I stabbed myself in the heart, and as that body died, I made myself a new one to inhabit, and the new me kept living. But in a different shape every time. A different being. I was a woman, a child, a person of no gender, a man, a woman again. Different every time. I died dozens of times. Hundreds. The queendoms were born and still I lived. Whether I found the strength to kill myself or simply waited for my current body to die, it didn't matter. The magic wouldn't let me go."

Sessadon was aghast. How could a person's sanity survive such torture? She supposed the answer was that, most likely, it hadn't.

"And it might have gone on like that forever," said the Voa's low rumble, "but I was lonely."

There was a soft sigh in the darkness, rich with an emotion Sessadon couldn't identify.

Volos said, "I'd been alone so long, ever since I was stationed at the fourth gate. I begged Eresh to find me a companion. She and Velja decided that Unah would be my perfect companion, because she would be always with me, and if she wanted to make us a whole sea of companions, she could."

This time the woman's voice said nothing.

Sessadon said, "So if the fourth gate opens, you make the bodies. Any shade can have the body they wore in life, because you can make it for them."

The woman's voice murmured "Yes," with no joy or pleasure in it.

Sessadon felt a small satisfaction at knowing Eresh could indeed allow magic Below when She wanted, but it dissipated quickly. Whether the god could bend Her own rules didn't matter if She wouldn't bend them for Sessadon's benefit.

The Voa said, "All you have to do is open the gate."

"And how do I do that?" Sessadon asked.

Volos's laughter was an unpleasant rumble, like the earth shaking, with a pinched edge. "My job is to guard it against people like you. I will stay here happily with Unah until time itself draws to a close. Why would I tell you?"

Sessadon thought about this. In life and death alike, she had offered people what they wanted, motivated them to do what she wanted for their own purposes. But this Voa—he had everything he wanted. She had no way to motivate him, nor did she have a way to defeat him.

So she walked away thinking, instead, about Unah. Because if there was one thing Sessadon had been good at doing Above, it was death, and all Unah had ever wanted since her terrible, tragic mistake had been to die.

Now that Sessadon knew where the gate was, she could find her way back to it. So she let herself walk away, thinking, racking her brain for an answer on how to proceed. This gate could not be approached quite like any of the others.

The sorcerer found herself walking toward somewhere she wasn't sure she wanted to go, but her feet led her toward the familiar: the Tree of Unknowing.

As she approached the tree, and had she been breathing still, she would have taken in a sharp breath. The white tree with its black leaves was stunning, wholly unnatural yet so right-seeming, reflecting in the perfect, waveless pool beneath.

The next thing she noticed was the sound. It started as something like a gasp but quickly became shrill.

And it was coming from the shade of a young man who she'd never expected to see here again: the onetime kingling Paulus.

The shade of Paulus shouted and wept, his voice ranging from high to low. He seemed to be addressing the tree itself, but as Sessadon cautiously approached, she spotted a faint shade that she had not, at first, seen. A man leaning against the trunk of the tree.

The shade of a man, she realized, who must be Oscuro.

"Paulus?" she said.

He looked over his shoulder at her and seemed to register her briefly before turning back.

"Oscuro!" he shouted, confirming her suspicion about the other shade's identity. "Oscuro, it's me!"

The faint outline of the other man's face looked straight at Paulus without a trace of recognition or emotion.

Finally, Paulus spoke over his shoulder to Sessadon, saying, "He did it."

She didn't immediately understand. "Did what?"

"He drank from the Pool of Forgetting," Paulus said. "He no longer remembers."

"Remembers what?"

"Anything."

And even as they watched, the outline of the shade that had once been the man Oscuro faded even more, softening at the edges, disappearing.

"Paulus?" she ventured. "How are you here?"

The shade of the young man turned to her, and although he bore a strong resemblance to the shade who had opened the Gate of Heroes, he'd also changed. There was tension and intensity in his face, sadness in his eyes, but above all, an air of resignation that changed his whole aspect. He looked like he'd aged years since she saw him last. Which she supposed was possible, given that shades could change their appearances. What she needed to know was what had made him feel this way.

"I wanted to talk to him. To tell him. Who else would I tell?"

"But Paulus," she said again, choosing her words carefully. "What happened? I thought you went Above."

"I did," he said grimly.

"And you were killed so soon?"

"No, I was not killed."

"Then how are you back?"

"I killed *myself*," he spat. "I intended to. I rose in one body, but I was greedy, and I wanted a different one. And now . . ."

"Now what?"

He turned his back on the barely there shade of Oscuro entirely, closing his eyes against any sight, but facing Sessadon once more. "I tried to go through the gate again. And it wouldn't let me."

"Are you sure there just weren't any bodies? That's happened in the past."

"The shade before me went. The shade behind me went. What do you think? Do you think the fault was in the gate, or in me?"

Sessadon understood then. "So you can rise once . . . but not again."

"Not again," agreed Paulus, opening his eyes, his voice full of infinite sadness.

"I don't suppose you want to help me open the Gate of Monsters?"

"I don't want to help anyone do anything. If I could, I'd take a knife to the throat of the god Herself."

Sessadon couldn't help but peer around them, sure the god would hear. An idea had sprung into her head, though, and she couldn't shake it. In a flash she decided it was worth exploring, testing. To the shade of Paulus, she said, "You can't mean that."

"Oh, I can. And I suspect you agree with me. If there were a way, wouldn't you want to destroy the god? And take all this"—he gestured to the Underlands—"for yourself? I'm sure you're at least as capable."

Privately, Sessadon agreed with him. She couldn't say it out loud for fear the god would hear her, but she certainly didn't disagree.

The shade of Paulus frowned at her silence. He said, "Don't you think you would rule the Underlands better than She does?"

"No one else," said Sessadon carefully, "would be the same."

He nodded at her, catching on.

"I have to open the Gate of Monsters," she said.

"You do."

"So you'll help me?"

Paulus said, "I will."

Both of them knew it wasn't just the gate they were talking about.

It was perfect, she realized. She had enjoyed the power of changing the face of the Underlands even without her magic. Especially if she could trick the god into restoring her magic, now that she knew it was possible, she could do so much more. She could rule.

Paulus said, his air serious, "It's either that or drink from the pool myself."

"Don't do that," she said, surprising herself with her own vehemence.

He turned his head toward her curiously.

"I haven't had an ally in so long," she said. "I would hate to lose you before we've even had a chance to begin."

Then, from behind Paulus, came a whisper. Sessadon could see nothing at the base of the tree where the shade of Oscuro had been, but she heard his final word as clear as anything.

"Goodbye," the whisper said.

The effect on Paulus was instantaneous. He threw himself toward the tree and placed his palms on the ground where the trunk vanished. A sob wrenched itself from him and he pressed his face between his palms, crying into the ground, his pain roaring through his prostrate form.

Sessadon stepped back quietly. She knew he wasn't only crying over Oscuro. To make the choice he'd made, to give up his second chance at existence Above without knowing that the sacrifice couldn't be undone? She couldn't imagine the regret he must feel.

She got no joy from watching him suffer, but she didn't mind the thought that he had now become more desperate than ever. It could only benefit her purpose.

Paulus had been a good-hearted man while he'd been living. But even a good-hearted man could be pushed to his limit. And Paulus's trials had clearly taken him to the very edge. He was only the barest margin away from crumbling.

Once a man was broken, there was no telling what he might do.

Sessadon was counting on it.

✦ CHAPTER 35 ✦

ALL-MAGIC

Daybreak Palace, Arca

Aster

When the queen summoned Aster to her chamber, Aster was unquestionably afraid to go, but they also knew they could not refuse.

And they dreaded what would happen when they arrived in the queen's presence. Even if it hadn't been their idea, and even if it hadn't come to pass, Aster had come to Daybreak Palace to kill Queen Eminel. Could that be so easily forgiven?

True, on the day it happened, the queen had seemed kind. But after Aster was out of her presence, they had plenty of time to worry about their future. Every decision, every action, had consequences. If there was to be punishment, they would accept it. The only question was what form that punishment would take.

So they dragged their feet while they followed the servant down the long, dug-out halls of Daybreak Palace. They distracted themselves with how glorious the palace was. The Arcan dwellings where Aster had lived had always been humble in the extreme. It was hard to believe that the same methods could make something so magnificent. You could call these tunnels or hallways, but either way, their ceilings soared high above Aster's head, and the feeling of lightness here was remarkable, considering how far underground they must be by now. Aster had never been underground in the Bastion but wondered if the stone there could accomplish such a feat. Then again, with magic, anything was possible.

"Here," said the servant, and stopped. Aster barely missed stumbling right into the servant's back.

They stood next to a pair of high double doors, flanked on either side by sword-wearing women in long cloaks. The Queensguard, Aster realized. The swords were for show. If the stories were true, any of these women could disembowel them with a glance. And after looking at them for only moments, Aster believed the stories.

The servant knocked on the door and called, "Queen, your guest."

Guest? What a euphemism.

"Enter," came a voice, and when the servant swung the double doors wide open, Aster saw no choice but to walk right in.

The queen stood there waiting, alone, in chambers less elegant than Aster would have expected. The room was luxurious, of course, but also spare. Aster examined the walls, the floor, the furniture. They delayed as long as they could by looking at every single thing in the room besides the person who had summoned them.

"Hello, Aster," said Queen Eminel, her voice soft. "Thank you for coming."

And so, finally, uneasily, Aster looked at the queen. She looked fearsome, her bone-white clothes, the blue snake necklace gleaming at her neck, her quartz hand an eternal reminder that she was like no other woman. She'd been friendly to Aster, but might that change? Could she be trusted?

Eminel said, "Aster, I asked you here because I'd like to see what you can do."

"Oh."

The queen cocked her head as if surprised. When she spoke again, her voice was softer yet. "I see. You don't seem excited about that. I promise it won't be a trial. And if you're not in the mood for it today, we'll wait. Let's sit and have some honeyed goat's milk first. Have you had honeyed milk?"

Aster shook their head.

Eminel gestured to the low-backed couch, the nearest piece of furniture to both of them. It was covered in a thick gray fabric that looked as soft as fur. Aster sat. Eminel herself lifted a tray from a table near the door and set it on a low hassock in front of Aster. Immediately a sweet smell rose up from a small pitcher wrapped in a thick towel to keep it warm.

Eminel poured a creamy liquid into one cup, then the other. She sat on the couch next to Aster, but not too close. She raised her own cup and took a sip from it, then raised an eyebrow.

Aster took a tentative first sip and had to swallow a gasp of delight. The sweetness of the warm milk was startling, but not cloying, simply perfect. It was the most delicious thing they'd ever tasted in their life.

"You like it?"

Aster nodded enthusiastically.

Eminel grinned. Something about her expression made her look young as a child. "You know what's even better? Having date buns with it. Can we?"

"Yes, please."

Eminel rang for the buns, then turned back to Aster and refilled their cup with the fragrant milk, sending up another waft of sweet steam. "While we wait, let's talk about all-magic, just talk. Is that all right?"

Aster nodded. Talking about magic didn't seem nearly as daunting as attempting to do it. Surely the queen was intentionally trying to put them at ease.

"I discovered my magic by accident," said Eminel, looking down into her cup. Her demeanor became less enthusiastic, more thoughtful. "It was terrifying. The first time I was aware of it, it burst out of me. I had no control. And I hurt someone."

"Someone close to you?" Aster asked quietly.

"Physically close," Eminel responded, with an unreadable expression. Her quartz fingertips tapped the edge of the tray, then withdrew. "I hurt more than one person, actually. Some of them deserved it."

She paused, appearing to come to a decision, and started again. "But I don't want to focus on that. Any power can be used either for good or bad. And either way, control is essential. So if I'm going to teach you, that's the most important thing for us to start with. Control."

"You want to teach me?"

"I do," said Eminel, "if you want to be taught. I don't know if you know anything about how all-magic girls were treated in the past."

The queen paused, and Aster realized she was waiting for a response. Aster gave her the truth. "No. I don't know much. Only what Rahul told me."

"Someday I want to hear what he told you. But not right now. All right?"

"All right."

A soft knock sounded at the door. Eminel called, "Enter."

A simply dressed woman, likely another servant, entered with a tray similar to the one that held the milk.

"Over here," Eminel said, gesturing. The servant set down the tray, and Aster smelled the familiar, yeasty warmth of freshly baked bread alongside another sweet note, different from the milk but just as intriguing.

The queen said, "Thank you," and the servant departed.

Eminel immediately picked up a bun and tore it in half, then half again. She dipped a piece in her milk, waited a moment, then popped it into her mouth. She closed her eyes and hummed her enjoyment.

Aster followed suit. Tearing, dipping, waiting, tasting. After a long moment of savoring, they said, "You're right. Even better."

"I don't want to linger on this," said Eminel, her voice somewhat apologetic, "so I'll only say that the previous queen's treatment of all-magic girls was appalling. We don't follow those ways anymore. I don't intend to test your limits, or the limits of any other all-magic users we might find. But I do want to make sure that you—or, again, anyone with all-magic—learn how to control it, so they don't pose a danger."

"A danger to themselves, or others?"

"Either. Both." The queen fell silent, tearing what remained of her date bun into smaller and smaller pieces. She lay one on her tongue, closed her eyes, and appeared to lose herself in savoring it.

"Are they always girls?"

"As far as I know," said Eminel, "but I don't know everything. So there may have been people like you, two-fold people, similarly talented."

"How am I here?" asked Aster.

Eminel seemed to choose her words carefully. "How do you mean that? Here in Daybreak Palace?"

"No." Aster, too, had to carefully select which words to use. "No girls were born, right? For years? And yet, I'm here."

"You are. And my understanding is that Rahul used his magic to make you appear to be a boy. Just a boy."

"Yes."

"And even your mother didn't know."

Aster felt an unaccustomed pang. Had Stellari known the truth, would things have unfolded differently? They answered, "No, she didn't."

"We don't know how people would have perceived you without magic. And to me, it doesn't seem to matter. What people perceive isn't the same as the truth, anyway. Does that make sense?"

Aster nodded, then took a sip of milk.

The queen said, "I have a theory, if you'd like to hear it."

"I would."

Eminel said, "The sorcerer Sessadon, you know who that is? You've heard of her?"

Rahul had never spoken the woman's name directly to Aster, but they'd heard the circle of men talking about her, during those meetings back in Odimisk. "She caused the Drought of Girls. With a spell."

"Yes. And she was a very powerful sorcerer, but that kind of magic, that takes a huge amount of work and energy. It's possible that at some point, in the years of the Drought, the spell might have slipped. For months or days or even just a moment. And if the spell wasn't in effect . . ."

Aster understood her perfectly. "That could have been when I was born."

"That's what I'm thinking. But again, we have no way of knowing for sure. And in every way that matters, that's not important."

"Why not?"

"You are who you are. Whatever the explanation, if there even is one, that's fact. Who you are is someone very special," said Eminel, and smiled. She reached out and covered Aster's hand with her own.

Aster wondered if the queen even realized that the hand she'd reached out with was the quartz one. But if Aster closed their eyes, they wouldn't have known that the hand was quartz. It felt just as warm and soothing as flesh.

Aster said, "I don't know what to say to that."

Eminel's smile was patient. "You don't have to say anything."

Aster wanted so very, very badly to believe her.

The milk was gone, and only one bun remained. Aster wouldn't be the one to take the last bite when there was a queen in the room. So now Aster had nothing to do with their hands. They felt tense, knowing that the time had probably come for Eminel to ask harder questions. To test their magic and see it firsthand. Aster didn't want to do that, not today. They just wanted to sit here with the queen, not being judged or tested. They just wanted to be.

The moment was long. Aster was afraid to speak, worried anything they said would be wrong.

When the queen finally spoke, her voice was cheerful, but a bit tentative. She asked, "Can you stay a little longer, Aster? I want to teach you to play a game."

Aster tried to push the dread away. Maybe they were assuming too much. "With magic?"

"No, no," said the queen, still smiling. "It's not like that. No magic. Just strategy. Can I show you?"

"Of course."

Eminel got up and walked over to a shelf at the far side of the room. When she returned, she bore a box in both hands that she set down on the hassock in front of Aster. But this time, instead of sitting next to them, she sat down on a stool on the opposite side. She could still reach across and grab the last of the buns, which she did. Then she flicked a latch on the side of the box and it opened up into a game board, pocked with holes at regular intervals and lined on both sides with deep grooves that held stone pegs in all colors of the rainbow.

"It's called *whishnuk*," said Eminel, "and I bet you'll be great at it."

The pieces and the board both gleamed, polished to a high shine. The squares of the board were made of pale, smooth types of stone, the pegs from something brighter, more precious. Aster didn't know the names for most of those stones, but they recognized the deep green of jade, the bright blue of lapis. They dared to sneak a glance at the queen's face. She too was looking down at the bright colors of the pegs, focusing on their beauty.

Carefully, tentatively, Aster gathered their power. They pictured the *psama*, which was tucked underneath their tunic, warmed by their skin. They reached out as softly as they could and touched the mind of the queen. It was a little like sticking a hand into a rushing river, the current threatening to pull one's whole self in. But Aster centered themselves, reaching just a bit deeper for enough power to stand firm. And before long, she understood what the queen wanted.

I wish Beyda were here, but I can't just wait for her, the queen was thinking. *I need someone like her. Someone who doesn't judge me or use me or think I'm using them. Maybe this is where a friendship like that begins.*

The queen of Arca, Aster realized, was lonely. What she needed, what she was asking for without words, was companionship. Someone to be there with her. Not a rival, not a lover, not even a trainee. The queen was looking for a friend.

And she didn't even know that that was also exactly what Aster needed too.

Effortlessly, Aster released their magic, letting the enchantment subside until they could no longer hear the queen's thoughts. They reached out toward the *whishnuk* board and plucked out the nearest peg, a deep green piece of polished jade. It felt cool and solid in their fingers.

Aster said to the queen, "Show me."

✦ CHAPTER 36 ✦

VOTE

The Senate floor, Ursu, Paxim

Fasiq, Vish

Her first day as bailiff on the floor of the Paximite Senate, Fasiq had never been so uncomfortable.

It seemed incredible that no one at all was looking at her. She'd spent what felt like nearly every day of her life being stared at no matter what she did. Today, here she stood like an awkward, outsize vulture in a flock of delicate bee-eaters, yet not a single person seemed to even glance her way? *Civilization,* she thought with a snort.

At least she had entertainment. The senators were a fascinating bunch to watch. All with their hair in braids, all wearing blue robes, and yet the variation represented here was infinite. Quiet women in pale blue, sharp-faced women in dark blue, watchful women in sky blue, nervous women in river blue. These were the most powerful women in the nation that Fasiq had spent much of her life robbing. And they were so preoccupied with their own activities that they ignored her in their midst.

Was it gratitude that kept her from picking their pockets? Or was she just unprepared? Without Hermei or the twins by her side, filching goods from people's pockets was a lot harder. She missed her gang. But she'd sworn to stay here in Paxim until she found the woman they'd known as the Shade—the woman she'd loved—and she had no intention of breaking that promise. She'd sworn it to the Bandit God, and that god was the only thing she loved besides the Shade and money.

Fasiq's own robe was a simple, undyed cloth, but it still felt luxurious. The name of the woman who hired her had turned out to be Juni, and Juni was the consul, the head of the entire Paximite Senate. She wasn't just one of these powerful women; she was the most powerful of them all. If Fasiq could be convinced to throw in her lot with a stranger, she could do a lot worse than the one who'd found her.

On the day they met, Fasiq had passed the night under Juni's own roof, eaten the woman's food, slept on a cot provided for her in a quiet room. She felt she was getting one over on the senator. Then again, she thought, she didn't know exactly how far she'd have to go to earn what she was getting. When Juni explained that a guard for her household was needed, and that all Fasiq needed to do was stand there and look terrifying, Fasiq answered, "Finally, the job I was made for!"

In response, Juni had stepped closer to Fasiq and put one hand gently on the giant's forearm. Then the consul earnestly replied, "I'm sure you could do anything you put your mind to." It made Fasiq uncomfortable, frankly. Earnest was not a mode she operated in.

After a few months as a guard, Fasiq got the sense she was being saved for something. That being a guard wasn't the end of Juni's plans for her. When she mentioned it to Juni, the consul laughed. "I should have known you'd guess. You'll be bailiff for the Senate one of these days. I'll let you know when the time comes."

The time had, indeed, come. Now the senators were clucking and fussing and shouting again, and Juni looked at Fasiq pointedly.

Five times, each louder than the last, Fasiq banged the heel of her pike against the stone beneath her feet. By the fifth bang, everyone around her had gone quiet. Now everyone was looking at her after all. They looked scared. Which, thought Fasiq, was exactly why Juni had picked her out of a crowd all those months ago. Perhaps they were both getting the best of this bargain. Not every deal had a bad end.

"Let us continue," Juni said. "I have been proud to serve as the interim regent until the time for an election came, but we are here today to choose a new regent. For good."

More shouting, but one voice rose above the rest. It came from a woman in a robe as blue as a robin's egg, her hair not quite as magnificent as some of the others, her arms crossed over her chest in a clearly contentious pose. "But what are the qualifications? The constraints? This body has never chosen a regent before. There's never been a need."

Juni replied, no patience in her voice, "And All-Mother willing, there will never be a need again, but today, there is. So we vote."

The same senator began to object again, her tone plaintive, but others shouted her down. She tried again, raising both arms high, but again the other senators hissed and booed until she stopped trying to shout over them.

If this continued, Fasiq wondered whether she'd be called upon to escort the senator out of the chamber. She would obviously do whatever her boss required. Fasiq looked to the consul, but Juni was looking away. Her gaze was steadily passing over the crowd, looking at each senator in turn, clearly evaluating each.

Eventually, once it became clear no one was willing to listen to her, the woman in robin's-egg blue chose to sulk. She even turned her back on the rest of the senators and crossed her arms like a toddler in a snit. Even in silence her face was comically expressive; once Fasiq started looking around the room, she realized that the senators' faces were telling entire stories, their expressions worthy of a theater, as if every last one were an actor on the stage.

A flurry of activity began, different senators making their voices heard, shouting names along with phrases or sentences with just enough unfamiliar words that Fasiq couldn't get the gist. Several were shouting what sounded like their own names, or others, and asking to be counted, and occasionally Juni would acknowledge someone by repeating a few words and adding the word "recognized," and the hubbub would die down for just a moment, then five or six senators would hurl more names or words into the silence.

Other than that occasional recognition, there was no particular rhythm to the conversation that Fasiq could identify. There must have been rules, because every once in a while, someone would shout that some particular rule had been violated. This led to another hubbub about "Rules!" and "I object!" and "Noncompliant!" and then the song started all over again.

Within minutes several nominees' names had been put forward, and whispers were being passed around like currency. Fasiq simply watched. There was nothing else to be done. She'd been hired to stand in this room and here she would stand. Even if she didn't have honor, not exactly, she had a line she wouldn't cross. She only cheated people she knew for sure she would never see again.

Then the giant realized Juni was staring straight at her, with her head cocked to the side. Fasiq returned her gaze, trying to understand if she was being asked to do something. If she was, she couldn't figure it out. Juni's gaze slid away, and Fasiq breathed easy for a moment, until she realized that another senator had been staring at Juni, then transferred her gaze directly to Fasiq.

This one was tall, though not nearly as tall as Fasiq, and as solid as a temple pillar. Round-cheeked and snub-nosed, her face had a natural sweetness that Fasiq could immediately tell she had spent most of her adult life trying to downplay. Her robe was more austere than most. Her braid-crown was parted into two swirls, almost like horns rising toward the back of her head.

"Phinesh of Nigelus asking to be counted," shouted the tall one. Her eyes were still on Fasiq's, but she wasn't addressing her, and it was like a gong going off in Fasiq's head. Why was this woman staring at her? Had she done something wrong?

"Phinesh of Nigelus recognized," Juni said, her voice ringing out above the others.

"I nominate . . . what was your name?"

Fasiq looked around to see who the senator was talking to. No one seemed to be responding. The senator had to clear her throat and incline her head pointedly before Fasiq realized why no one else had given the senator an answer.

The senator was talking to her. Fasiq.

It was hard not to stammer, but the giant managed. She made her voice as loud as she could, and she could be very loud when she wanted. "Fasiq is my name, *thena*."

"Excellent!" said the senator, as if Fasiq had provided the right answer to an important question. "And you are a born-and-bred Paximite, aren't you, Fasiq?"

Fasiq couldn't imagine why she was being asked the question, but responding with her default flippancy probably wouldn't reflect well on Juni. She didn't want to embarrass her employer. So she might as well be truthful and direct. Again, she made sure she was loud enough to be heard. "I am."

With clear satisfaction, the senator called out over the heads of the others in a loud voice, "Then she is eligible to serve as regent! I, Phinesh of Nigelus, nominate Fasiq, the Senate bailiff, for the honor."

The sound that followed was like nothing Fasiq had ever heard. But, she realized, she'd never heard the ocean, so perhaps this was what that sounded like. Like a storm or a rush of water, like voices raised in disbelief and approval and tense laughter, like a rumble under the earth, like all those things at once. The Senate chamber was in an uproar. And for once, Fasiq hadn't done a thing to cause a ruckus. But somehow this was still because of her.

Where was Juni? The consul's face would tell her how to respond. But in that moment, Fasiq couldn't find her in the crowd. She'd have to do what came naturally.

So the giant raised her chin and tilted her head to make sure her silvered scar caught the light, shot a cocky grin over the heads of the disbelieving senators, and said, "Who, me? What an honor."

"Unprecedented!" shouted a senator with a crown piled so high it looked like she might be risking her neck.

"Genius!" shouted another right back at her.

"A travesty!" The shouts began to fly fast and thick in every direction. "Shocking!" "A breath of fresh air!" "Let's put it to a vote!" "I'm with the stranger!"

She couldn't decide whether to egg them on, step back in false modesty, or fall to her knees laughing. In the end she did none of these things. She simply put her hand over her heart, let her smile fade into a more serious expression, and bowed her head toward the gathering. She hoped this gesture looked like humble acceptance.

There was a very good chance this gaggle of rich women was about to change her life. There was nothing she could do to stop it. Best, then, to look as if she didn't mind.

A banging sound came from the front of the room, stone on stone. "Order!" someone shouted.

The din increased, then faded slightly, then faded a bit more.

The woman at the front, clearly a person of some power, shouted to be heard above the continuing hubbub. "Senator Marageda of Nordur seconds the nomination of the Senate bailiff, the woman called Fasiq! Fasiq of . . . ?" She trailed off and looked in Fasiq's direction.

"I claim no home other than Paxim," responded Fasiq. She was fairly pleased with that answer.

"Fasiq of Paxim!" called Senator Marageda. "She has been nominated. Are there any further contenders?"

After that Fasiq lost track of the names shouted and who shouted them. Each name was greeted both with cheers of hearty approval and hisses of derision. She could see where all this was headed. She thought she liked it. What an interesting life this was.

The bang of stone on stone came again, and it was the woman at the front whose voice rang out above all the rest.

"Five nominations. Five candidates. Let each who has nominated someone speak for her choice."

That was when the speeches started to get boring. Fasiq let her eyes rest on each speaker but could not have repeated a word any of the first four said. She was watching, not listening. She looked at each speaker as they began to make their case, but moments later, she would turn her attention to the audience, watching to see how these words were received. And she could see on the faces of these senators that they could not support the first candidate, or the second, or the third, or the fourth. They were all fellow senators. And no fellow senator could be trusted.

"You have heard these women make their case," said the fifth speaker, round-faced Senator Phinesh, and that was when Fasiq began to receive information through her ears again. Mostly it was because she knew Phinesh was about to start talking about the giant herself, and there could be no more fascinating topic.

Her voice direct, Phinesh said, "I will make my case simply. Juni has ruled wisely, but she is ineligible to continue to serve in two positions, and she has chosen to remain consul. The previous regent, whose name you all know, was a powerful senator who bullied and bribed her way there. Today we have a chance to rectify that mistake, not repeat it. I love my fellow senators, but I don't trust them with the highest office in the land alongside the queen. Why do we have both a Senate and a monarch? Because each wields a different kind of power. When one person wields both types of power, you concentrate too much potential for wrongdoing in one person's hands."

"Hear, hear," called Fasiq almost absently, then realized her outburst had caused people to turn in her direction. She fought the urge to stare anxiously at the floor. Instead she raised her chin again, light flickering off her silvered scar like a wink. In her fiercest bandit days she'd always treated herself as a legend. Today, under these very different circumstances, she'd draw on that confidence again. She knew instinctively that these women only respected confidence. Humility would smell like blood.

Phinesh didn't look Fasiq's way, but the giant still had the sense that her unexpected supporter approved. The murmurs of the Senate softened, and when Phinesh went on, her voice was even stronger. "We can only trust someone truly independent. And this woman is beholden to none of us. Afraid of nothing and no one."

Fasiq stood there looking unafraid. What else was called for?

"While an unconventional choice, I truly believe she is the only right choice," Phinesh said triumphantly. "Your votes will send a clear message that we of the Senate do not play politics with people's lives!" She thumped her chest with a fist. "We believe that the young queen must be protected at all costs. We choose a physically strong person to be her constant companion. We choose a levelheaded, wise woman to guide the child. We choose a free thinker, with no loyalties, no influences, no family affiliations. We choose Fasiq of Paxim."

It was all Fasiq could do not to fling her hands in the air and cheer for herself, but she knew the occasion required solemnity. She stayed silent this time.

"Outrageous!" shouted a voice from the crowd.

Senator Marageda, the other one who had spoken up for Fasiq, suddenly whistled through her teeth. The sound was so sharp it felt like a spike to the skull, thought the giant. Others must have agreed, because the silence that descended on the Senate chamber was astoundingly complete. Even when she'd walked in before the session had started, thought Fasiq, the ambient noise had been worse than this. She reveled in the relative comfort.

"Who questions the choice?" asked Marageda.

"I do!" called another voice. Fasiq hoped it was the woman who everyone had ignored at the beginning, but it turned out to be a clearly senior member of the group, a woman of medium height whose complex braids were shot through with silver.

"The consul recognizes Robai of Spring Hill," said Juni.

Senator Robai crossed her arms over her chest, fixed Fasiq with a look, and said, "I hear many assertions. With few facts to back them up."

No one else seemed to respond to this, so Fasiq took it upon herself to answer. "I can provide all the facts you might want. You have questions? Ask away."

Robai didn't hesitate. "Why were you nominated? And seconded? You play the part of surprised innocent well, but it all seems a little too pat—did you plot today's action with these senators in advance?"

"If you knew me, *thena*," Fasiq said dryly, "you'd know I never think that far ahead."

It was the wrong thing to say, and she knew it, but only after the words had already escaped her lips.

The senator cocked an eyebrow. Fasiq had always been jealous of women who could do that.

Not hurrying, as if she'd planned to say this all along, Fasiq added, "But I realize you don't know me. Which is why you're asking questions that you have every right to ask."

"Yes," Robai said coolly. "I'm aware I have the right to ask them."

In Fasiq's experience, people loved being told they were right, but apparently that wasn't enough for this one. She wanted to look around to see how the other senators were taking this, but didn't dare. She kept her attention on Senator Robai and tried to look humble, though she didn't have much practice.

"Please, *thena*," she said, lowering her eyelashes. "I'm eager to satisfy your curiosity, and that of your fellow senators."

"Very well. Is it true that you have no family affiliations?"

She answered without hesitation. "Absolutely."

"Really? No one anywhere in the world who could call you sister, daughter, mother?"

"Not a one," said Fasiq. The people who'd meant the most to her in the world were those she'd chosen, back in her bandit days, not anyone with a blood tie. "I was an only child orphaned young, and when no one claims you, you have no choice but to make your own way."

Several senators murmured and nodded in approval, which Robai seemed not to like. Her next question was just as sharp as the first. "No loyalties at all?"

"Only to the law," fibbed Fasiq, "and the All-Mother."

"No influences, as one of your supporters claimed?"

"Who's had the chance to try to influence me? The consul hired me as bailiff, and she is the only one of you I've ever seen before today. Do any of the rest of you know me? Raise your hand if you've ever seen my face." She raised her hand to demonstrate, but no other hands rose to join.

"Enough of this!" called out Senator Marageda. Everyone else fell silent. Probably, reflected Fasiq, because they didn't want to hear that painfully sharp whistle of hers again.

Marageda went on, "We have each spoken for our choice, myself included. It is time to move to a vote. Rules state that during the counting of the votes, further outbursts will not only result in the offender's ejection from the chamber, but will negate their vote. Does anyone believe the rules don't apply to her?"

Fasiq added a glower to underline her supporter's words. She held loosely to the pike, as if it were a prop and not a weapon. Perhaps, she reflected, it was. She had the distinct feeling this whole thing had been stage-managed by someone, though she wasn't sure who.

As the proceeding went forward, though she tried to pay attention, Fasiq found she couldn't follow the counting of the votes. She was pretty sure she wasn't meant to. Women like this kept their rituals arcane to make sure not too many of their secrets got out.

So it was a genuine surprise when the consul—who the giant realized belatedly had said nothing during the entire nomination and voting process unless directly called on—cleared her throat and announced, "I recognize the new, duly elected regent, Fasiq of Paxim."

Fasiq wanted to say something clever, but all that came out was "Oh."

The senators applauded and it was another sound like thunder, like the ocean, like diving into the rapids of a river swifter than Fasiq had ever seen.

She kept her questions to herself. There would be time to ask them. Now, she could only stand in wonder.

"Next order of business," called Juni. Her voice was carefully level, but Fasiq thought she caught an undercurrent of joy in it. "The Senate has need of a new bailiff. With no objections, I will begin the search immediately and have one in place by our next session."

Palms flew, slapping thighs, and Juni said, "Motion passes. Thank you, senators."

The rest of the session was mercifully brief. Fasiq was able to keep her composure the entire time. Once the official close of business was called, she carefully avoided looking at any particular lawmaker, and instead proceeded out the same door where she'd come in. She left the pike where it had been handed to her, in a sort of cloakroom, but kept on the robe, since she wasn't wearing anything underneath. That done, she proceeded out into the street, heading for Juni's dwelling.

She made sure she was well away from the Senate, with none of the senators in sight, before she let herself laugh and laugh and laugh.

✦

Juni had told Vish to expect a guest that evening, but she hadn't given any indication of who it might be or when they'd be coming.

It was one of the things Vish liked least about life in the palace: she was never in control. But at least she was here with Roksana, making sure the girl was safe in body and spirit, and in a way, that was better. There were times Vish remembered having more control, yet feeling entirely helpless.

She'd let Ama know through messages that her daughter was still being cared for, though they hadn't been able to arrange a meeting since the consul had stolen them from their home. When the regent Stellari died, Vish thought about revealing the entire charade, but decided they were actually safer where they were. The old regent's scheme had actually landed Roksana, known as Heliane the Second to the outside world, in the place she ultimately belonged; Stellari couldn't have known what a kindness she was doing, Vish knew, because kindness had not been her business. Vish hoped the Scorpican queen trusted her enough to know that everything would be fine.

Roksana was the last girl she'd take care of, Vish decided. After this, she'd live for herself.

Though what would that even look like? She had loved once, but those days were over, and that person was gone. If she could have one wish . . . but she couldn't, wouldn't. There was no point in even imagining that path.

Vish heard a knock on the outer door and an exchange of voices, and she was instantly alert. Even with the Queensguard outside her chambers she never felt comfortable, insisting on wearing her swords after Stellari was no longer there to forbid it. Vish had never liked Stellari, but she didn't rejoice in the woman's death. She wasn't that kind of person. Still, she'd felt better once she could arm herself again.

The newer regent, Juni, had been kind, if distant. She'd given Vish little direction, only warning her that a new regent was soon to be appointed. Vish had wanted to ask her if there was any way of making sure the new person was kind and just. Instead, she'd said nothing.

Vish heard members of the Queensguard standing down, murmuring greetings. It had to be Juni who had knocked on the outer door. She was the only one they respected and trusted enough to welcome so warmly.

". . . promised to introduce her to the new regent as soon as was reasonable," Juni was saying to someone, maybe the Queensguard, maybe another visitor who hadn't yet spoken.

Vish was disappointed. She had hoped, somehow, that she might be appointed as regent, even though she was powerless here. She wasn't even a Paximite. So this must be the "guest" who she'd be meeting: a new regent, the one who would manage affairs on behalf of the young queen until she reached maturity. A stranger who would have complete power over Roksana and her future. Vish braced herself. She'd have to be careful not to let her trepidation show. She didn't want to start off on the wrong foot with such a powerful woman. It could make all the difference.

The voices came closer. Vish felt her heart hammering in her chest and tried to will it to slow down.

The new voice, warm like buckwheat honey, was chuckling as the two conversed just outside the inner door. "You couldn't have known, when you asked me to be bailiff . . ."

Juni replied with a laugh, "Couldn't I?"

After a polite knock and a brief pause, someone swung open the inner door without waiting for a response. Two women came into the room, the first, shorter one holding the door open for the second, taller one. The shorter one wore a blue robe, the taller—so much taller—a plainer garment that was the least remarkable thing about her. So very much else about her was remarkable: her impressive stature, her booming laugh, and the silver scar that bisected her familiar face. Vish couldn't help the sob of recognition that leapt up in her throat.

The first visitor, of course, was Juni. The second—somehow!—was Fasiq.

The moment of recognition surged through Vish's blood like lightning. She had never felt anything in her life so deeply.

Fasiq. Her love. Right in front of her, alive, almost close enough to touch.

The consul was bringing Fasiq closer, gesturing at Vish as she spoke in a merry, animated tone, apparently oblivious to the current running through the air.

"These, of course, are the queen's chambers, where you are welcome, though you must always announce yourself to the Queensguard before you enter. There must be rules, even for a regent. And this is the queen's closest companion and protector," Juni said, gesturing in Vish's direction. "We call her Vee."

Fasiq's eyes bored into Vish's as she murmured quietly, "I used to call her the Shade."

The look on the giant's broad face, a kind of dazed pleasure, told Vish everything she needed to know.

Juni, for her part, was shocked speechless. Her eyes flicked between the two women, up to Fasiq's face, down to Vish's, up to Fasiq's again. Vish had never known the consul to lose her words, but apparently, this was enough.

Vish said to Juni, her tone casual, "We knew each other."

The consul was still looking back and forth between them. "I had no idea."

"How could you?" said the giant. "But I've been looking for her for years."

"You have?" said Vish. The words were stuck in her throat, grinding their way out, her voice almost as husky as it had been when the injury to her throat had been fresh.

"Oh, Vish," Fasiq said, looking at her as if no one else existed, her brown eyes fathomless. "Of course I have."

"Begging your pardon," Juni interrupted in a strangely chipper voice. "I need your permission for something."

Fasiq and Vish both shook themselves, coming back to awareness. The giant spoke first. "Which one of us?"

"Both, I think," said Juni. "One of you as the queen's protector. The other as her regent."

"Go on," Vish and Fasiq said in unison, then both laughed in unison at the echo.

Juni smiled warmly. "I would like to take the queen to the kitchens for a treat. There's no need for either of you to accompany us, unless you want to. But I think I've proven you can trust me. Have I?"

Vish nodded. "You have."

Juni said to the toddler-queen, "Would you like a honey cake?"

The child nodded her head with enthusiasm. Juni put out her hand for the two to walk side by side. Her little brow furrowed in concentration, she walked to Juni and put her hand in the consul's hand.

Juni gave a satisfied smile. She looked up at the giant and the warrior, both seemingly frozen in place. "I'll keep her in my charge. We'll have a treat and then I'll ready her for sleep. We'll enter through the regent's chambers to the queen's bedroom. So we won't come through this way. Is that all right?"

A sly smile spread across Fasiq's scarred face. The twist of her mouth put an ache in Vish's heart, the best kind of ache.

"Goodbye for now, then," said the consul, and the tiny queen flapped a hand in cheerful farewell, and both of the remaining women watched them walk out of the room until the inner door closed behind them.

Then, for the first time in nearly a decade, they were together and alone.

Fasiq bestowed a grin on her, crooked and endearing, so pure it pierced straight to Vish's heart all over again.

"You were looking for me," Vish said softly, a statement.

The smile didn't leave Fasiq's face. Gently, she spoke as she drew nearer and nearer, closing the space between them. "They say, when you've lost something, it's always in the last place you look."

Tears shone in Vish's upturned eyes. "Fasiq," she said softly, a warm hint of something inexpressible in her voice.

The giant held up a finger for silence. Fasiq shook her head, and even in the shake of her head, there was love.

"It's always in the last place you look," said the giant, "because when you find what you were looking for, you know what happens? You stop looking."

Then they were in each other's arms, the giant cradling the back of Vish's head in her immense palm, Vish laying her cheek against Fasiq's chest. Both sighed as if they'd finally come home.

✦ CHAPTER 37 ✦

PACT

The Underlands

Sessadon

After she gave him time to grieve his friend Oscuro, Sessadon let Paulus wander, following him at a distance. He didn't seem to notice her tracking him, or if he knew, he didn't seem to care. At first he seemed to wander aimlessly. After a while, she realized he was heading in the direction of the battlefield beyond. He sat himself down to watch the warriors spar. She watched him in silence for a while, until she decided that the time was right to approach him.

In a gentle, conversational tone, the sorcerer said to the shade of the dead kingling, "Do they remind you of her?"

"No," he said, and grief was in his voice. "No one's like her. I only thought that if she died . . . well, maybe she might come here? Because she was raised in the Bastion and served in the Paximite army, but she was born a warrior?"

"She might," agreed Sessadon, to placate him.

"But she isn't here. Which makes me happy. She should live. But I won't . . . I can't . . . I'll never see her again up there. No matter how many gates you open."

"About that."

He sighed. "You want my help, don't you."

"I do. Think of the joy you experienced, even though it was fleeting. You saw her again. Spoke with her. Touched her?"

He nodded, swallowed hard.

"And if we open the fourth gate, do you know how many shades will get to do that? Thousands."

"If we open the fifth gate, do you know what happens?" he said.

Sessadon paused. She hadn't even thought that far ahead, frankly.

"There's no division between the worlds anymore. No dead, no living. Some of the stories say that means the end of the world. So I need you to promise that if we open the fourth gate together, you won't open the fifth."

Sessadon reached out a hand. "So promised." She didn't feel bad about lying to him. Once the gate was open, he wouldn't be able to close it. She wasn't even sure who could.

"Tell me about the Voa of the fourth gate."

She told him about Volos, deep-voiced and frozen and content, and Unah, his unfortunate companion.

"And Unah's magic works here? When yours doesn't?"

Sessadon frowned. "Eresh told me it wasn't possible. Clearly, it is."

"You're right, she must be lying. Or—maybe they're close enough to the world Above to get life force from there?"

Excitement surged within her. Perhaps she wouldn't even need the god to give her magic back. If she had all the abilities here she'd had Above? She would show the god how powerful she really could be.

"Let us go, then," he said. "To the fourth gate."

When they neared the black cave, she thought she saw him hesitate.

"It's daunting, I know," she said. "But this is the only way."

"I have a plan."

"You ready to share that plan with me?"

"I am." And he produced a small bottle, brown glass, and sloshed it so she could hear that it contained liquid.

"What's that?"

"A potion."

"Magic?"

"Closest thing to it, down here," he said. "Oscuro gave it to me before he . . ." And he trailed off.

"You were a good friend to him."

Paulus shook his head as if to clear it. "Anyway. In the legends, the secret of the fourth gate is that you need to go down. That's why it's a cave. You go down, not up."

"But that's impossible. We're already in the Underlands. So up is the only way."

Paulus raised the bottle. "With this, we can do one impossible thing."

"You're not making any sense."

There was excitement in his voice when he said, "I know. But we're not bound by sense here. Are we?"

"We're bound by something."

"The Underlands has its own laws. And the fourth gate, the cave, has laws of its own too. Which is where this enchantment comes in."

If the potion could help him do one impossible thing, thought Sessadon, he should have used it to go Above again. But perhaps its effects were limited to the Underlands. Or if he hadn't thought about using it to return Above despite the rules of the gates, she wasn't about to tell him.

"It helps us go down. Lower. Even though we shouldn't be able to. But that's the secret of the cave. You have to go down to go up. To get past Volos."

Sessadon said, "I don't think it's going to work."

"Only one way to find out," said Paulus, and raised the bottle to his lips.

The sorcerer saw him swallow once, the knot of his throat bobbing. Then he tipped the bottle upright again and held it out toward her. "Your turn."

She scrutinized him, but he looked unchanged, and there was no reason for him to try to trick her at this point. They were in this together, whatever this was.

Sessadon raised the bottle to her lips and drained it dry.

The first thing she noticed was that the liquid felt cool in her throat, even though she had no throat, and she marveled at it. The Underlands was an endlessly mystifying, endlessly interesting world. She was fighting hard to leave it, but at the same time it fascinated her. Some part of her, she realized, would miss it when she went.

Then the cool, easy feeling in her throat changed into something entirely different.

"Paulus?" she asked. "Take this?"

She held the empty bottle out toward him, but before he could reach for it, it dropped from her hand. It didn't seem to shatter on the ground. There was no sound, at least. When things had broken Above, she remembered, they made a sound.

Did it hurt? Was that what she was feeling? No. It wasn't pain, it was something else. A wrongness. Sessadon blinked, or felt like she blinked. She looked at Paulus's form, the shade she'd come to know, but his edges had become undefined. When she tried to perceive him more clearly, putting all her attention on him, that only seemed to blur his edges more, until he was barely a cloud or a wisp.

She had the sense of having made some kind of mistake. She asked again, "Paulus?"

"Yes?"

Then she realized she couldn't remember what she'd wanted to ask him. She plucked at her sleeve, which like Paulus was becoming less defined, and she worried her fingers would follow suit.

"Paulus," she said this time, not a question. It was urgent that he tell her what she needed to know. But she couldn't form the words to ask.

In a steady voice, Paulus said, "I lied to you."

"What?" But she understood quickly. The potion. It wasn't what he said it was.

Stammering, the sorcerer asked, "W—wha—what was in that bottle?"

"Water from the Pool of Forgetting," said Paulus, with confidence. "So you'll forget. All of it. Your plots and plans. Your own name. Every bit. And it serves you right."

"You drank it too," she said, her head swimming.

"Yes," he said in a soft voice. "But that's the difference between us. I *want* to forget."

Her final moment of clarity came far too late. Paulus had never wanted to destroy Eresh. That was a ruse. He had only wanted to destroy her. Sessadon.

And he'd done it.

The face on the sorcerer's shade had lowered brows, an expression of intense anger, for only a moment. Then the expression began to smooth. The clutched fists relaxed, fingers dangling; the tension in the body released. As the memories leaked away, spreading out into nothingness, the form that had been the sorcerer stumbled.

Then she turned her face to the horizon, staring at the shape of the fourth gate, the cave's open mouth like a creature yawning, and thought, *What is that? I've never seen anything like it.*

◆ CHAPTER 38 ◆

MOTHER AND DAUGHTER

The Holy City, Sestia

Olivi

As much as Olivi had learned alongside Concordia, it was nothing compared to what she learned once her mother became High Xara. It was strange how the place was the same, nearly everything was the same, but the addition of one person and subtraction of one person changed the entire world.

Her mother taught her every one of the arcane rules of being a Xara, even the ones that contradicted each other, and when Olivi said, "That doesn't make any sense," Veritas said, "Yes, that's absolutely correct."

"But why are there so many contradictions?"

"The god is perfect," the High Xara answered. "But all Her thoughts and rules and guidelines are interpreted by people. And people are not perfect. None of us. Not you and not me, and certainly no one who came before."

"So what are we supposed to do about that?"

"Our best. That's all any of us can do. Our best."

Veritas asked the Daras to suggest new rules of their own, and she set a plan for reviewing the rules that were already in place. It would take time, probably years, to completely review all the guidelines, but that was all right; she could make her life a project, and happily live out her days working toward that goal. What else was her life for, but to serve the god? The best thing she could do was remake the Edifice and its inhabitants to do a better job in Her service. Concordia had done a great deal of damage. It hadn't all been her fault—she'd served in the toughest years of crisis that Sestia had ever seen—but now that those years were behind them, it was time to heal. Veritas was ready to give everything for healing, and the fact that her daughter was there to work alongside her meant that she now had everything she wanted.

Olivi seemed content. She was a quiet, watchful young woman, and Veritas was happy to see that her experience didn't seem to have scarred her. Veritas preferred not to think about how close she'd come to losing her daughter, or the years they'd spent apart. Things had taken time to come to fruition. There was no sense in wishing they'd been different—they could so easily have been so much worse.

When Veritas had spent enough time with her daughter to get to know her again, to be sure of her confidence, she made one more decision. The month before the Sun Rites, her mother mixed a strong-smelling combination of ash and vinegar and bleached the color from a section of hair along Olivi's hairline, then dyed it with saffron.

Olivi knew exactly what it meant, but she was still surprised when her mother said the words. "You'll be a Xara alongside me."

Olivi's eyes were wide. "Can we do that? I'm sure it's never been done before."

"No, it hasn't. Which isn't a good enough reason."

Olivi nodded.

"Concordia . . ." Veritas struggled with how to say what her predecessor had done. "She did what she felt she had to do, I'm sure. But because of what she did, there are no Xaras where there should be Xaras. So the least I can do is start to correct that."

"And next year, when there are five-year-olds, we can choose a class of Xaras-to-be. That's the way it's done, right?"

"It has been, yes," said Veritas, thinking of how scared she'd been when she was taken from everything she'd ever known, even though it was an honor, even though she believed it was what the god wanted.

"We'll ask Her what She wants," said Olivi. "I suppose She'll tell us."

Veritas slung her arm around her daughter's shoulders and pulled her close. The weight of her, the feeling of her heartbeat, it was the most comforting thing she could imagine. To be together after so long apart. To realize that those years of the Drought were behind them, and better, fuller years lay ahead.

"And the rites?" asked Olivi. "Will we follow the traditions at the Sun Rites?"

The truth was that Veritas wasn't sure. She planned to talk to the god about what She really wanted, whether a change was possible, in how the ceremony unfolded. Whatever happened, she would make her peace with it. The world was a place beyond imagining.

"The Rites won't be quite like they've ever been before," said the High Xara Veritas to her daughter, "because they'll be ours."

✦ CHAPTER 39 ✦

REUNIONS

Arca
Aster, Eminel

Once Aster had been at the Arcan court for a year, it felt like they'd been there an eternity. They couldn't believe they'd ever been afraid of the queen. It was hard to believe, too, that they'd ever been afraid of their own magic, which now burned in them like a soft, banked fire, providing just the right amount of light and warmth.

The queen was hardly the most nurturing of taskmasters—she certainly put Aster through their paces—but she never made the mistakes that Rahul had made. When she pushed, it was only to help Aster see that they were capable of more. To send a physical object a bit farther, to make a flame burn a moment longer. And every time Aster succeeded, they felt like the queen relished the success as much as Aster did.

There was no announcement of who Aster was or why they were at court, but everyone seemed to understand quickly that they were special to the queen—if not her adopted child, then at least a close relation. They stayed in the rooms designated for the queen's matriclan. And they were tutored in non-magical precepts along with boys their age, which led to the other amazing thing Aster had trouble believing: they now had half a dozen people in the world they considered friends.

Aster became friends, also, with Eminel's friends the Rovers—in fact, they formed a sort of bridge between the Arcans and the strangers. The twins played a kind of ball game with rotten fruit, using leavings from the kitchen to keep their sword skills honed; noticing Aster's interest, the twin named Luben offered to teach them the sword. Once the other boys saw, they clamored to be allowed to join. Luben gladly took them all on as students. After a session it was not uncommon for swords, walls, and students alike to be splattered with shreds of beet greens and apple pulp.

Whenever Aster paused to remember the lonely years they'd had growing up in Paxim, they still felt a hollowness lingering in their belly. But they knew it didn't have to last. All they had to do was turn their face toward Eminel and gather magic in their hands, or laugh at Luben swinging at an oncoming hail of overripe figs, and that hollow space inside filled with warmth and certainty.

Aster tried not to think too much about the future. They knew that no girls with all-magic had been born during the Drought of Girls, and as of yet, none of the very young girls born after the Drought had shown all-magic powers. Accordingly, there were no women under twenty years of age who were eligible to become queen. And Eminel showed no signs of wanting to give up the snake necklace. The matriclans were always clamoring for favors and improved positions, but none of them had an all-magic girl to put forward for queenship, so they knew the limits of their power. Eminel had never said anything about Aster taking on the rule of Arca if something happened to her, but that wasn't Eminel's way. She didn't spend time talking about things that might or might not happen. She focused on the present. Aster tried to do the same, because Eminel did. And Aster couldn't think of any better way to live than to be just like Queen Eminel.

✦

When it was time to go to the rites, Eminel couldn't stop thinking about how she'd traveled there the last time, five years and a lifetime ago. In that ornate carriage, with Sessadon on one seat and the dead body of the previous queen on the other, riveted and terrified, afraid at any moment that Sessadon might see through Eminel's magic and cut her life short. That hadn't happened, but the mere idea of riding in that carriage again made her a little sick to her stomach. There had to be a better way.

"I'm nervous about it," she confessed to Aster over their latest game of *whishnuk*. Eminel regularly beat Aster but refused to play anything but her best, not wanting to teach the younger magician the wrong lesson. Their relationship was mentor and mentee, yes, a little bit like parent and child, but Eminel resisted keeping herself too high above Aster. She remembered how her own mother had over-protected her—out of love, yes, but still—and wanted to give Aster every chance to grow up a different way.

"You don't want to ride in that carriage?"

"No."

Aster looked her in the eye and spoke as if what they said was the only possible logical answer. "So don't."

Eminel thought about it. Of course Aster was right. She was the queen. No one could make her do something she didn't want to do, including this. She mused on the possibilities. "Something less . . . royal. Plainer."

"Certainly. Or, not a carriage at all." Aster shrugged, then laughed. "Think bigger! You're a queen, after all."

"Sometimes it feels like power makes you less free, not more."

Aster rolled their eyes. "Talk to someone who's actually power-less and you might change your mind. Anyway. Here's a thought. When's the happiest you've ever been, traveling?"

An image flashed to mind instantly. "Riding on a pony across Paxim, toward Sestia, after the battle of Hayk. By myself. Because I loved being alone."

"Well." Aster considered. "You can't go alone."

"Can't I?"

"At least, you shouldn't. Not least because I don't want to go by myself, and I don't want to stay here."

Eminel smiled at this, then looked thoughtful. "I could ride with a caravan, I think, as long as I wasn't enclosed. If I could just see the road ahead of me. But you're right, I can't go completely alone."

"Was there another time you were happy traveling?"

Her heart hurt just thinking about it, but again, she answered without pause. "In a wagon with the Rovers."

"Wait, when did you travel with the Rovers?"

She'd forgotten that the young magician only knew Hermei and the twins as members of her Queensguard. There was so much no one else knew. "When I was young."

"Well, have you considered asking them if you could ride in their wagon?"

Eminel focused her attention on the game again long enough to take another one of their *whishnuk* pegs. Then she said, "Aster, you're brilliant."

"Just not great at this game," said Aster, nodding at the pile of pegs next to the queen.

"This game isn't the only game. And certainly not the most important one. Shall we ring for some honeyed goat's milk?"

With an impish smile, Aster touched the *psama* under their tunic and used their mind to pull the bellpull nearest the door. The bell sounded out loud and clear.

"Show-off," said Eminel, beaming.

◆

The Rovers agreed quickly, and though several other carriages and wagons had to go with them to bring the rest of the queen of Arca's entourage, Eminel found that she was able to recapture some of the magic of traveling with only the Rovers. Once upon a time, she remembered, the previous queen of Arca had set up rings of tents with herself at the center. Eminel's camp was different, spread out along a line, each group setting up camp next to their conveyance.

In the evenings, her small band sat around its own fireside, the rest of the court at a distance. The twins slept under the wagon, flanking Aster. Eminel found she couldn't sleep in the wagon as she once had. But she liked sleeping by the fire on all but the most inclement nights. She only wished the giant were here with them. She could have sent a Seeker to look for Fasiq, but what good would that have done? She wasn't willing to compel the giant to leave the nation she'd sworn she wouldn't leave. Occasionally she was tempted to send a Seeker anyway, just to know where Fasiq was and that she was well, but for now Eminel was fine with not knowing. There were mysteries in life. That was as it should be.

The journey itself existed out of time, beautiful and temporary, and Eminel was almost sad when they arrived at their destination. She had to acknowledge the rest of the court then, women from every matriclan arrayed carefully around her to confirm their high status as they entered the walled Holy City. Once at the Edifice, they were escorted inside and shown where they would rest, thick mattresses arrayed to sleep any number of people in any number of rooms, each queendom's residents in their own separate section.

It wasn't until their third day there that Eminel and her group met any envoys from other nations. The Scorpicae hadn't arrived yet. When she met the Bastionites, she quickly scanned a few minds for a glimpse of Beyda's whereabouts in vain, and the meeting was otherwise uneventful. But she was unprepared for the surprise of the group from Paxim.

The temple-palace of the Sestians was a maze of unbroken whiteness, easy to get lost in. Their guide had indicated that the Arcans should wait and then disappeared around a corner, so they were all shuffling their feet and glancing at each other, waiting more or less patiently. Eminel smiled at Aster to set the young one at ease; she could see Aster's nervousness written all over their face. Aster had been from Paxim once, after all. She wondered if they missed anything about it.

Eminel was still caught up in her thoughts when their guide reappeared, obviously discomfited, and said, "Move aside, queen coming through," and Eminel was about to spit *I* am *a queen, you know*, when she found herself face-to-face—or, really, face to mid-chest—with an elegantly dressed Fasiq. The giant was carrying a young girl on her hip, also dressed in finery, and Eminel was struck absolutely dumb from the shock of it.

"Well, what in the name of the Underlands are you doing here?" said Fasiq, and grinned merrily. Eminel supposed she was older, but there was nothing about her that seemed changed from the last time they'd seen each other: the silver scar, the sharp gaze, the vaguely delighted air.

"It—I—I'm the queen of Arca, Fasiq," Eminel stammered, gesturing to the blue snake necklace that rested heavy on her neck. It felt warm and comforting now.

Fasiq laughed. "I know you are! Where do you think I've been, under a rock?"

"I haven't got any idea where you've been."

"Fair point, Queen Eminel. Oof, that sounds so odd, but congratulations. Have you met Heli?" She bounced the girl on her hip.

"You're supposed to say 'Queen Heliane the Second,' Fasiq," corrected the child haughtily, but there was a grin on her face that matched the giant's.

"Oh, yes! Your Royalness! How could I forget!"

The young queen of Paxim, secure in her perch on Fasiq's hip, rolled her eyes toward Eminel. "The regent keeps forgetting. I don't know how."

"Regent!" said Eminel. "What a turn of events."

Fasiq shrugged. "I could say the same." And she gestured to the three Rovers flanking Eminel, who beamed back at her, though no one made a move to touch each other. Their eyes were glued to the child on Fasiq's hip.

The tiny queen said, "Fasiq, let's go. It's boring here."

Fasiq looked meaningfully at Eminel. "Would you come with us for a cup of tea? It doesn't have to be a whole diplomatic mission, I hope. We were just headed back to our rooms. Someone got a little confused about the schedule."

She looked over at the guide, who seemed to wither visibly under the giant's pointed glare.

"No harm done," said Eminel quickly, to put the envoy at ease. "A cup of tea would be lovely."

They all kept themselves in check long enough to make it through a few more blank white hallways, into the rooms assigned to the Paximite delegation, and then Fasiq issued a few more commands. In moments the tea was ready, the queen was playing quietly in the corner with what Eminel instantly recognized as a *whishnuk* board, and most of the Paximite Queensguard had moved outside the doors, leaving only one inside the room.

Then Eminel let a long-held sob escape her throat and flung herself into the giant's arms. They were all laughing and talking at once. The Paximite queen looked alarmed at the noise; Aster moved from behind Eminel to soothe the girl, introduce themselves, and sit down on the other side of the *whishnuk* board.

Hermei said, "It's good to see you again, Fasiq."

"How'd you all end up together? Don't tell me coincidence, because I don't believe in those."

"She invited us, and we responded," Hermei said. His expression betrayed nothing, but Eminel could hear the emotion in his voice; he was overwhelmed.

Fasiq put on a mock pout, crossing her enormous arms. "Why didn't I get an invitation? Honestly, Eminel, didn't I teach you any manners?"

Eminel said, "No, you absolutely didn't."

The giant's scarred face broke out in another grin. "She speaks true!"

Eminel said, "I would've been so happy to see you. But the Rovers told me about your promise. You swore you wouldn't leave Paxim until you found her. The Shade."

Fasiq said, "And I kept that promise."

The remaining member of the Paximite Queensguard, her long, cream-colored cloak swirling, said in a husky whisper, "Eminel."

Tears were on Eminel's face again even as she turned; she hadn't looked closely at the guard, but now that she did, she instantly recognized the familiar, thin face of the Shade. Now she was stunned nearly speechless. "You two . . . and you . . ."

The Shade smiled. "Eminel. It's so good to see you."

There were more hugs, more exclamations; Elechus was the first to hug the Shade, but his brother threw himself into the same embrace a moment later. They hugged her until she made a muffled grunt of annoyance. Then the adults hugged in different combinations, making more noises, flinging themselves about.

For her part, ignoring all the hubbub, little Heliane the Second listened closely as Aster explained what an interesting game *whishnuk* could be. The two of them kept their heads down, examining each peg in turn, while the adults made fools of themselves, blubbering and carrying on.

Eventually, they settled down to talk, and Eminel accepted a cup of the straw-yellow tea that the Sestians seemed to enjoy so much. It wasn't honeyed goat's milk, but it would have to do.

She looked around and savored the moment. Everyone she cared about in the world, everyone but Beyda, in one place. She would have to be content with nearly everything she wanted. Most people didn't get that much. Sometimes, happiness was a choice.

✦ CHAPTER 40 ✦

RITES

Midsummer, the All-Mother's Year 521, the night before the Sun Rites
The Holy City, Sestia
Amankha

As it happened, Queen Amankha of the Scorpicae very nearly missed the first and last Sun Rites of her reign.

She had chosen her entourage with care, and it was no particular warrior's fault, what happened along the way. She left behind two warriors intentionally: Azur, because she trusted her, and Zalma, because she didn't. Beyond that, the choices quickly fell into place.

Because there were no Scorpicae of ten-and-five years of age in the entire queendom to serve as bladebearer for the Sun Rites, Queen Amankha had to make do. She had to choose between selecting a girl under five years of age—there were dozens of those now, including Madazur, but they all seemed too precious to drag to the far side of the world—or over twenty. In the end she bestowed the honor on the smith's apprentice, a nut-brown young woman, shy and small, who they all called Wren. Wren was older than Amankha herself but seemed younger, and any attempt to ally herself with the smith's apprentice might counteract the influence of the smith, so Amankha felt secure in her choice.

Wren rode at the center of the column with Amankha herself, protected by warriors all around. Nikhit and Ibis, two warriors who'd served out the war at the Scorpion's Pass and were more than happy to return to the main camps of Scorpica when their assignment terms ended, rode in the lead. An archer named Khamash brought up the rear alone, vigilant in the extreme; the nursing baby she wore in a sling, a warrior of three months whose name she chose not to reveal, impaired neither her watchfulness nor, when called upon, her aim.

The first of the minor calamities struck not long after they exited the Bastion's southern gate into the flat plains of Paxim. The road was largely smooth but not perfectly so, and Ibis's pony caught a hind leg in a gopher hole, nearly throwing her rider and acquiring an unshakable limp. After a conference, Nikhit and Ibis rode back to the Bastion and handed off the pony to someone who could get it back to Scorpica to heal; thereafter they rode double on Nikhit's pony, which they were both perfectly content to do. But the caravan lost half a day with the distraction.

From there, the mishaps gained speed like a boulder rolling downhill. Wren was struck by a sudden fever and couldn't keep down either food or water for more than a day; it was only when Amankha ordered the caravan halted that the bladebearer confessed she'd tasted a tempting purplish berry that grew near their last water source. If she'd asked any of the more experienced warriors before she tried it, they would have told her the wineberry was a powerful emetic, useful in its way, but the opposite of nourishing. Amankha didn't punish her, figuring the illness was punishment enough, but again, a little more time was lost.

A forced detour around a trading post where high spring floods had washed out a bridge. An extra day of hunting to replace food lost when someone forgot to secure their stores and the camp was raided in the night by something furry and plump that could have been either an unusually small bear or an unusually large raccoon. Half a day here, a day there, as they crossed Paxim in the direction of Sestia. A trip that should have taken a month at most stretched on an extra week, then longer.

Queen Amankha did her best to remain patient. She wanted to break away from the caravan, to ride ahead, to get to the Holy City faster to see the people who mattered most to her in the world. But as queen, she couldn't. If she drove her heels into her pony's side and took off at a clip, the rest of her warriors would simply follow. And forget sneaking away. These were some of the best trackers in her queendom, and likely the other four as well. She couldn't move faster than her fellow warriors could. With one thing and another, the days bled away.

By the time they could finally glimpse the white temple-palace of the Holy City in the distance, Amankha was exhausted and resigned. And if her calculations were correct, they'd arrived only the day before the rites were to begin. At least it was early morning. The pink light of dawn touching the gleaming white surfaces of the temple-palace took the queen's breath away. Had there been more time, she would have paused to watch, but there wasn't.

Even before they got to the city, a messenger rode out to meet them. She didn't waste time asking if they were Scorpicae—the answer was obvious—but announced herself with good cheer. "Greetings! I am Olivi, a Xara of Sestia, and I welcome you in the name of the High Xara Veritas."

"Veritas?" asked Ibis before Amankha could say anything. "I thought Concordia was the High Xara here."

"She was," said the young woman simply. "Now Veritas reigns.

And she asked me to come out to meet you, and to show you to the cherry grove. Queen Amankha?"

Amankha followed her.

Introductions sent Amankha's head spinning. Her bladebearer, Wren, accompanied her everywhere except into the grove of cherry trees.

"Only queens," intoned the High Xara. Amankha knew why this was. Before the Sun Rites of the All-Mother's Year 511, Tamura had invaded the sacred space with her Queensguard. The current queen of Scorpica was not the same queen of those rites, nor was the High Xara—none were, in fact—but their nations remembered. It was not wrong to take care.

Before they parted, it felt urgent for Amankha to say to the blade-bearer, "I remember my mother saying the cherries were the most delicious she'd ever tasted. I always wondered if they were as good as she said. When I got older, I wondered if maybe it was only the fact that she rarely got to taste them that made them special."

Wren bobbed her head. "And now you get to decide for yourself. And I want you to tell me, after."

"I will," Amankha promised. Then the moment came where she had to walk forward alone.

The grove was beautiful, dappled with sunlight. As lovely as any-where in Scorpica or Paxim or the Bastion that Amankha had ever seen. If she'd been truly alone there or if she'd been surrounded by friends, she knew she would have felt its peace. But to walk in with-out her guard, still exhausted from travel, she felt naked.

She saw familiar faces and unfamiliar ones. The bowl of cher-ries placed before her overflowed with plump, shiny fruit, just as her mother had described to her all those years ago. When she bit into her first one, she thought, *Just as good as she said*, and cried.

There was one face at the table, both familiar and unfamiliar, that held Amankha's gaze. Three years old with plump, round cheeks and dark hair in two neat plaits, mostly contained but with curls threatening to spring free. Her face was charming, her hands grubby, and Amankha felt an outpouring of love roll through her with such force it threatened to knock her to the ground.

The girl known as Heliane the Second to all the world, but to her mother as Roksana, sat in the lap of a massive giant with a silver scar across her face. This, realized Amankha, must be the new regent of Paxim. The giant fed the tiny queen cherries cut in half. Every time the girl took a bite, she giggled. Amankha's arms ached to hold her, but she didn't reach out. The tears might not just have been about the taste of the cherries.

Once the cherries were eaten, and everyone's fingers were stained red with their luscious juice, the queens slowly began to leave the grove. The new queen of the Bastion, the one who had succeeded Hikmet, left before Amankha could even greet her; the Arcan queen Eminel left next, with a sober, polite nod in Amankha's direction. The High Xara, a compact, friendly-looking woman of perhaps forty or forty-five years, waited in the grove with her hands lightly clasped, clearly waiting to be the last to leave.

So it wasn't hard for Amankha to fall into step next to the regent of Paxim, the stranger who carried Amankha's precious daughter in her arms. And as they left the grove and were rejoined by their Queensguards, Amankha caught sight of a familiar face among the guards of the Paximite queen. It was Vish. Still too thin, still with a drawn face and that wound at her throat, but there she was. The woman she'd always be able to depend on. The woman who had kept Roksana safe, just as she'd promised.

The giant, still toting the small queen of Paxim on her hip, said to her guards, "I will take the queen for a walk. We'll have just one guard with us. Vee?"

As the members of the Paximite Queensguard moved off, except for Vish, Amankha turned to her bladebearer. "Wren, please let the others know I'll be back after a short walk. I need to stretch my legs after the long journey. Can you do that?"

Wren nodded soberly and hastened off in the direction of the temple-palace.

Vish, the giant, and Amankha fell into a slow, steady rhythm. The path through the woods here was level. When it narrowed, the giant moved ahead, murmuring to the girl she carried, leaving Vish and Amankha to walk next to each other.

That was when Vish looked at Amankha and asked, "How *are* you?" with such intensity it hurt.

"Well enough," Amankha replied. "I wish we had more time."

Vish's eyes flicked back to make sure the others had gone, then returned to Amankha. "Make use of what we have," she said.

"Thank you."

Then the tiny queen, looking back at Amankha over the giant's shoulder, piped up, "Who are you?"

Amankha wanted to tell her the truth so badly, but instead, she looked to Vish. She forced herself to ask the question she did not want the wrong answer to. "Does she call you mama?"

"No," said Vish. "She calls me *dashla*, as she should."

"*Dashla*?"

"You would say *tishi*," Vish clarified quietly, her eyes hooded.

Of course, thought Amankha, of course. Her daughter wouldn't have been taught the Scorpican term of endearment, not being raised as the rightful queen of Paxim. Amankha herself felt she would never fit in no matter where she went; she'd doomed her child to the same life, she supposed. She wished there were another way. She was tempted, just for a wild moment, to grab the girl and whisk her back to Scorpica, to make that queendom a home for both of them. But

Roksana was only half Scorpican, and the other half of her heritage was the most important to Amankha. She was owed the queendom of Paxim. Her mother would not endanger that.

"*Dashla* Vee," said the girl, pointing, a tentative smile playing across her small features. Amankha hadn't seen her daughter since five days after her birth, and the way her face had grown and changed in these past three years took her breath away. Amankha saw Paulus in the bow of Roksana's lips, the curve of her ear, the warmth of her gaze. Suddenly it felt like an enormous fist was squeezing Amankha's heart.

Then the girl said, "And *dashla* Fasiq," pointing to the giant.

"I can be an auntie," said the giant in a warm voice, obviously delighted by the child. "I'm already a regent. And, I think, a horse."

"Are you a *dashla*?" the child asked Amankha.

Amankha had thought long and hard about what to say to her daughter. Instead of answering her question, she said, "I came to tell you stories, young one. Do you like stories?"

"Yes!" The child's face was eager.

"Let's sit under a tree."

Fasiq set the girl down gently. Without hesitation, the tiny queen took Amankha by the hand and led her to the tree she'd chosen. They sat down together. Amankha tried to stop staring at the girl, but Roksana didn't seem to mind.

"Start your stories now," said the girl, with the certainty of the very young, and seemed ready to listen.

Amankha thought about how to begin. She was keenly aware how little time they had, though she already knew that even hours, days, weeks would not be enough. So she began with what she thought was most important. "Do you know any stories of the kingling?"

"King-ling?" asked the child, the word obviously unfamiliar.

Amankha wanted to wrap her arms around the child and hold

her forever. She wanted to spill every secret to her, to claim the girl as her own. But children, even well-trained children, were known to share secrets. And if she didn't want Roksana to tell, Roksana could not know.

Instead Amankha took a deep breath. "Paulus was the kingling of Paxim, your country, son of the great Queen Heliane the First."

The girl cocked her head. "Your country?"

"No. I live in Scorpica. Far north of here, past the Bastion."

"Why you here?"

"I'm just traveling through," said Amankha quietly, and again came that feeling of squeezing in her chest. "Do you want to hear the kingling's story?"

"Yes, please."

And so Amankha told her daughter about Paulus, the most powerful kingling of Paxim, the man who would have been king. How he began as a boy with a family and lost each one of them in turn. How he sought solace in books and old stories, disappearing into words. How much comfort and joy he found there. How his mother protected and nurtured him, and when Heliane had cause to worry for his safety, how she'd found him a bodyguard who never left his side. How he triumphed in a skirmish against a group of disguised warriors, how brave he was, how proud. And then how he rode out against a strong enemy and, despite his talents and bravery, was vanquished, and voyaged to the Underlands, as we all eventually must.

The story was long, and though the girl had begun by watching Amankha with cautious eyes, she had settled herself against the tree and looked sleepier and sleepier. By the time Amankha finished the story, adding that although only Scorpicae believe in the battlefield beyond, if it were ever possible for a man of Paxim to go to that part of the Underlands, Paulus surely would, Roksana's eyes had long since closed.

Amankha wished she could have held the girl on her lap as she fell asleep. She would have liked to stroke her daughter's hair, to feel the damp cheek on her thigh, to bear the child's weight, if only for a short time. But she wished a lot of things that she knew weren't possible. And because the child wasn't resting on her, there was nothing to hold Amankha down when it was time for her to rise and leave.

Quietly, Amankha said, "Thank you," first to Fasiq, then to Vish.

Vish gave a gesture so small and furtive Amankha almost didn't see it. And maybe she didn't see exactly what Vish did. But she knew what it looked like. That finger pulling back as if tugging on a bowstring, the twist of the wrist and the hand gliding upward.

Good hunting.

✦

At the end of the day, as Amankha readied herself to sleep in the common quarters granted to the Scorpicae for use during their stay in Sestia, the soft mattress where she lay down reminded her of another bed long ago. One she'd almost forgotten, or made herself forget. Nothing like the Bastion's standard-issue bunks, nor the bedrolls she'd used both as a Scorpican and as a Paximite warrior. She had only slept on a thick mattress this luxurious a handful of times in her life. She remembered each one with the clarity of a cloudless blue sky. Her fifteenth year, so precious. Every time, Paulus had been there beside her.

She missed Paulus. She would always miss Paulus. But until he returned from the Underlands, if he ever returned, she would content herself knowing she had done her best for their daughter.

Amankha lay swaddled in the thick warmth of the Sestian bed and remembered that fleeting time, those happy days and nights with Paulus, before she'd lost him. Perhaps someday she would find someone else to love. But it still felt like a betrayal, so she would not go seeking pleasures as she knew the other warriors would. Tonight, awaiting tomorrow's rites, she would only settle into this bed that reminded her so much of her love, her kingling, and pretend she felt his arms around her.

It would be the last time, she decided.

Not her last time to think of Paulus—she would never stop thinking of him—but she would never again return to this building and sleep in this bed or one like it. In five years, she wouldn't come back to the Holy City as the queen of Scorpica. This time would be the only time.

Amankha had made the right choice to rule Scorpica as its queen, she decided; she didn't regret that. She'd taken the queendom from power-hungry, desperate Tamura, who would have destroyed it. Amankha could be proud of that. She had taken some steps toward winning back the confidence of the other queendoms, though there was a long road ahead. She wouldn't be able to stay to see the work done, but she'd begun the work, and she knew who could continue it after her.

Amankha had made the choice, after Paulus was killed and Roksana born, to become the queen of Scorpica. To challenge Tamura and defeat her or die trying. Then she had chosen to rule. To help the nation where she'd been born, strengthen its warriors, chart a course forward. But none of these choices were forever. She had chosen which woman to be, for that time: a queen. In the next year or two, she would choose to take her position as another sort of woman: Roksana's mother. Wherever she needed to be, whoever she needed to be, in order to make that happen, that was who she would become.

Any story could have a happy ending depending on where you decided to end it.

So instead of shying away from the bed, she climbed into it, and immediately felt a rush of emotion as her body sank into its softness.

The bed was not much wider than her body, much narrower than the bed she'd shared with Paulus had been, but that had been a bed for a kingling. The beds for the Scorpican delegation were all the same size, big enough. The bed wanted to swallow her; she wanted to let it.

The warmth of the room, the softness of the bed, the buzz of the other warriors in the chamber, it all made a soothing song. Despite the exhaustion they must have felt from the journey, of the dozen women of her entourage, none but her had yet lain down. They had stripped off their traveling garb and washed themselves with the basins provided, then dressed again, in fresher clothing. She had already guessed why by the time she heard them whispering about where they would take their pleasures.

"I heard," one whispered, "men gather at the bend of the river."

"You can't just listen to any old rumor," another warrior chastised.

"I heard it from Azur," replied the first one.

"Well, then."

Amankha smiled. Azur had willingly foregone the chance to come to the rites when her queen asked it of her; the old Azur would never have done so. Amankha hadn't been in Scorpica during the years Azur was taking her place as a warrior, but the woman's exploits were absolutely legendary. Stories were told about Azur's first visit to the Sun Rites in a tone of hushed awe. Their queen knew as well as anyone that if there were something to be known about pleasures, Azur was the one to know it.

But Azur was not the woman she had been when she was young, not anymore. None of them were.

As Amankha lay on the bed, the lamps in the room were extinguished one by one, until only a single light remained, just to the side of the door. The buzz of the excited warriors thinned out by ones and twos as the Scorpicae departed for their unknown destinations. There were a dozen warriors present and then there were ten; ten became eight, eight became five, until the last two whispering warriors departed together, leaving only Amankha in the chamber.

She rose long enough to shuck her traveling garb and dress in the simple shift provided by their hosts. She splashed herself with water from the basin nearest her bed. When the door to the hallway opened, she thought it might be a servant—one of those breathtakingly beautiful men the Sestians seemed to grow in abundance—come to check the lamp or bring fresh water for the night.

But the person who came in through the door was no servant. Her feet were bare and silent. Amankha's heart swelled, because she had been all over the known world and she'd never known any woman to walk that quietly who wasn't a Scorpican.

Her heart swelled further when she noted the woman's slight limp and thin frame.

The woman lowered her hood. "Ama," she said.

"Vish," the queen answered.

"Just a quick visit?" asked Amankha.

"As much time as I dare."

"Which is how much?"

"I suppose, not much at all. I don't dare as much as I once did."

"You don't need to," said Amankha. "Even a moment is enough."

The older warrior leaned in and kissed Amankha in the middle of her forehead, a soft benediction.

"Your mother would be proud," she whispered.

Overcome with emotion, Amankha had no words. She could only swallow hard and nod her thanks.

Then Vish was gone as quickly and silently as she'd come.

Alone, Amankha sat on her overstuffed mattress, preparing to sleep. Morning would bring the rites. She could already see it all unfolding in her mind's eye. Once she took the sacred blade from Wren, she would bear the blade ahead of her as she walked out among her fellow queens. Before her, the Bastionite queen, bearing the book in which the next chapter of the queendoms' future would be written. After her, the Arcan queen Eminel, her flesh hand and quartz hand demurely linked in front of her, waiting for her god to speak. Amankha felt a kinship with all of them, but especially Eminel— a woman her own age, who knew what it was like to be the youngest girl for leagues on end, a curiosity, and then to run a country, all those subjects depending entirely on her. Leading them would be the new High Xara, her compact body striding forward with the confidence her god had vested in her, ready to do what was necessary to keep the peace.

And there would be Amankha's daughter, her sunny, small face turned forward, riding on the shoulders of a giant. No one would look at the little queen and see the Scorpican in her, but they didn't need to. She was a young queen of Paxim now. She was where she deserved to be.

Stretching and yawning, the queen of Scorpica listened to the night around her, hearing only her own breath in the silence. The last lamp near the door guttered out, full darkness falling. The darkness didn't scare Amankha; when her sister warriors returned, treading on soft feet after their adventures, they would bring enough light to see by. And if they didn't? Day would dawn soon enough. In the meantime, she would rest. Tomorrow would bring the Sun Rites. She would need her strength. They all would.

Amankha dha Khara lay down in the jet-black dark and slept.

✦ END OF BOOK THREE ✦

Acknowledgments

When I got the wild idea that someone should write a matriarchal, feminist *Game of Thrones*—and then the even wilder idea that the someone in question should be me—I had no idea how many people would throw themselves so enthusiastically into bringing that idea to life. I am, to put it simply, incredibly lucky.

Writing can be a solitary pursuit, but publishing is a collaborative one. I'm grateful to everyone who has played a role in building the world of the Five Queendoms, and I apologize to those whose names aren't included below. The fault is one of poor memory, not ingratitude.

As with *Scorpica* and *Arca*, I'm thrilled to thank Holly Root, Alyssa Maltese, and the rest of the team at Root Literary for their energy, warmth, and expertise. At Saga, thanks to Joe Monti for shepherding this one to the finish line and to Caroline Tew for managing schedules and details with patience and persistence. Thanks to Savannah Breckenridge, Ritika Karnik, Ella Latham, Karintha Parker, Olivia Perrault, and Sarah Wright for your invaluable efforts in making this book sing at every stage of the process.

And huge, huge thanks to three more people who've contributed to all three books in fantastic ways: Victo Ngai, for knocking my socks off yet again with striking cover art (just look at those textures!); Shiromi Arserio, for narrating all three books more elegantly than I could have imagined; and Valerie Shea, queen of copy editors, for again flagging approximately a thousand mistakes in my draft (timelines! blocking! lore!) with a friendly, gracious "Reconcile?"

Then there's you. Thank you. Thank you to readers and audiobook listeners for joining me in this wild made-up world. Thank you to booksellers and librarians who put these books in the hands of readers who've been craving them. Thank you to the reviewers, reporters, and podcasters who help get the word out about books you love—an art all its own. Thank you to my amazing fellow authors for your support everywhere from the Instagram grid to Comic Con panels to the bowling alleys of Boston. Let's keep doing this as long as we possibly can.